Praise for National Bestselling and Award-Winning Author

JODI THOMAS

"Ms. Thomas's nam̄ ... ... 's
fav̄ ... ...

"Jodi Thomas ... tender you breathless!"
—*Romantic Times*

"Jodi Thomas's writing is exquisite and often
lyrical . . . a very talented writer."
—*Inside Romance*

THE TEXAN AND THE LADY
**The unexpected romance of a lovely young
Harvey Girl and the danger-loving lawman
who stole her heart . . .**

"The woman who made Texans tender . . . Jodi Thomas
shows us hard-living men with grit and guts, and the
determined young women who soften their hearts."
—PAMELA MORSI,
Bestselling author of *Something Shady* and *Wild Oats*

PRAIRIE SONG
**Her most sweeping novel of love and glory in the
heart of Texas . . . and of Maggie and Grayson—
whose passion held a power and
fury all its own . . .**

"A thoroughly entertaining romance."
—*Gothic Journal*

THE TENDER TEXAN
Winner of the Romance Writers of America Best Historical Series Romance Award of 1991

"Excellent . . . Have the tissues ready; this tender story will tug at your heart. Memorable reading."
—*Rendezvous*

"This marvelous, sensitive, emotional romance is destined to be cherished by readers . . . a spellbinding love story . . . filled with the special magic that makes a book a treasure."
—*Romantic Times*

TO TAME A TEXAN'S HEART
Half the folks in America loved reading the gunslinging tales of Granite Westwind. But nobody knew the real story behind the legend: Granite Westwind was a woman . . .

"Earthy, vibrant, funny and poignant, *To Tame a Texan's Heart* is Jodi Thomas at her best . . . a wonderful, colorful love story."
—*Romantic Times*

And now her latest novel . . .

FOREVER IN TEXAS
Sanford Colston thought he had women figured out—then he met Hannah . . .

Forever In Texas

Jodi Thomas

JOVE BOOKS, NEW YORK

FOREVER IN TEXAS

A Jove Book / published by arrangement with
the author

PRINTING HISTORY
Jove edition / September 1995

ISBN: 0-515-11710-2

A JOVE BOOK®
Jove Books are published by The Berkley Publishing Group,
200 Madison Avenue, New York, New York 10016.
JOVE and the "J" design are trademarks
belonging to Jove Publications, Inc.

PRINTED IN THE UNITED STATES OF AMERICA

10 9 8 7 6 5 4 3 2 1

Dedicated to the People of Old Saints Roost
and to Their Descendants in Clarendon

A special thank you to
Connee McAnear
Susan Nelson
Sanford Thompson
for all their help and advice.

Prologue ✦

HANNAH RANDELL WIPED the mixture of rain and tears from her eyes and stared across the darkness at the depot's platform twenty yards away. The northbound out of Dallas was being delayed for some reason.

Two men in wet-darkened yellow slickers stood guard at each end of the walkway leading to the train. Hannah's only hope of living another day was to catch the train, and these two hired guns from the Harwell ranch made that hope slimmer by the minute. Only a ghost could pass them unnoticed. Absently, she opened the carpetbag at her side and stroked the warm fur of her cat, resting within. The old calico was the only living thing who would miss her when Hannah died.

A lone man, draped in a huge greatcoat and wide-brimmed Stetson, jumped from one of the passenger cars and moved in fluid steps away from the train. Lightning flashes made him disappear and reappear every few seconds as he drew closer to Hannah.

"You'd best stay with the others, mister!" the conductor yelled from the shelter of the train steps. "We'll be pulling out soon as we get a wire saying the tracks are clear up north."

The tall, lean shadow didn't slow his pace. "Blow the whistle twice when you're ready. I'll hear it!" he shouted back into the rain. "I've had all the people I can stomach for one night."

The conductor waved, as if to say "good riddance," and melted into the interior of the car while the stranger took the platform steps two at a time. He crossed the street with his hat down against the rain and entered the hotel door only inches from where Hannah stood hidden between buildings.

She glanced at the Harwell men guarding the steps; they'd barely noticed the man. An idea washed through her mind, helping her forget the cold. She lifted the soaked hem of her skirt with one hand and her mother's worn carpetbag with the other. Trudging into the muddy alley toward the hotel's back door, she whispered, "I think I've got a plan, Sneeze."

Though the cat didn't answer, the words of Hannah's mother from years ago echoed in the young woman's mind. *Survive. Do whatever you have to do, but survive.*

Hannah wondered if that might include killing a man before this storm ended.

Chapter 1 ❖

Midnight
Dallas, Texas

SANFORD COLSTON STEPPED off the train and turned his collar up against the icy rain. There was no sense getting angry about the delay. It couldn't be helped. But he was tired of waiting with the others in the crowded passenger car. He needed space and silence, even if he had to brave the storm to get it.

Two men stood on the platform in the rain, as though watching for something or someone. Sanford could see rifles beneath their slickers and wondered what kind of trouble would come riding in on a night like this. It might be snowing farther north, but the freezing downpour in Dallas was enough to keep the devil indoors tonight.

Raising the brim of his hat just enough to see the outline of an old hotel across the street, he headed in long strides toward it, needing desperately to be alone. Being trapped in a car with drunks, loud salesmen, chattery old women, and babies continually crying had proven to be too disagreeable an ending to an already horrible day.

Silence was what he needed, Ford thought. It was what he'd always needed. Ford's father had once told him to stay apart from people, that he'd be better off alone. Though Ford was his only son, his father had preferred to see him only when necessary. So, since childhood, loneliness was Ford's only traveling companion. People had a way of reminding him of his father's advice.

The aging desk clerk didn't even look up as he exchanged a room key for the cash Ford laid on the counter. "Second door to the left of the stairs," the clerk said with a coloring of Irish in his tone. "Ye're too late for even coffee from the kitchen, but ye've got the floor to yeself tonight. Rain's drowned out all me profit."

Without saying a word, Ford climbed the stairs. He'd never spent much time in towns the size of Dallas, but he guessed they were pretty much the same everywhere—quiet, except for Saturday nights and elections. His sister, Gavrila, however, had warned him Dallas and Fort Worth would be full of wickedness. Though he placed little concern in her usual overreaction, as a precaution he'd worn his Colts.

The hallway smelled of mildew, and the lock on his door didn't work. Not that it mattered, since he was the only one on the floor, yet Ford liked order. Without sparking a light, he removed his gun belt and hung it on the iron bedpost. Guessing the sheets would be less than clean, he took off his coat and stretched his long frame out atop the covers. Since he'd been able to afford it, he'd bought the best quality clothing available from mail-order catalogs, but even these clothes would be wrinkled by morning.

The room was as dark as his mood. He'd failed! The

whole town of Saints Roost was depending on him. The council had made it seem so simple. Since Sanford Colston was the only member of the school board who didn't have a family to care for, he'd been elected to make the trip to Dallas in the middle of one of the worst winters Texans had ever experienced. All Ford had to do was hire a new schoolteacher.

Lightning flashed outside and thunder rattled the thin panes of his room's only window. Ford closed his eyes, not caring about the storm. "Just as you predicted, Gavrila," he whispered, remembering his sister's parting words. "I had as much luck finding a teacher as I've had finding a wife."

He could understand why no woman would want to be married to him. Even Gavrila couldn't stand to be around him for long. *You're not ugly, exactly,* his sister said once as a child, trying to be kind. *God just gave you features that don't quite match. Your nose is too big and your chin too square. You've eyes so dark they seem to look right through a person.*

Even if a girl could get used to you, she'd still not want to have your children. Sanford, just the way you stand, so still and all, makes chills spread up my spine. And you never say anything. Father always wondered that you learned to talk at all, always hiding out like it wasn't in your nature to be around people.

Ford let the memories flow in the darkness of this cheap room, as if the walls could no longer hold them out like his foot-thick bricks could at home. He'd been taller than anyone his age in school, yet so thin he didn't have a chance in a fight. When everyone else would stand around talking, Ford would only watch. Even later, when he was grown and had a ranch of his own, he couldn't think of more than a few words to say to anyone. Most people were like his sister, who talked at him and never to him.

Until he was twenty, his bones looked like they threatened to break the skin. Folks called him "spider," and "willow," and "skeleton." They laughed at his huge hands and feet, as though they'd paid money to see a freak. When he didn't respond, they'd look at him with a sadness about them.

Finally, Ford matured. His body filled out with muscles from hard work, and his hands and feet seemed to fit his tall frame. His face, however, never adjusted with age. An aunt had summed it up last July by saying "handsome" was a handle Sanford Colston would never have to worry about having tacked to his back.

Staring up at the water-spotted ceiling during lightning flashes, Ford decided that though he didn't mind the loneliness, he resented the cruelty he'd suffered in school. He thought serving on the school board might help, but what good could he do if he couldn't even find a teacher?

Slowly, his mind searched through every applicant's file he'd studied. Only two had met the qualifications necessary and were willing to take over in the middle of a school year. Before he could interview one, however, she decided to marry, and the other had refused to go to the Texas panhandle. He wished he could have bent the rules and hired one of the remaining applicants, but the school board was adamant in their requirements . . . eight years of schooling and one year of higher education, plus un-married, highly principled, well groomed, and of course, Methodist, since Saints Roost was a Methodist town. By the time a woman collected all those qualities, she was either planning a wedding or too set in her ways to travel.

When the door rattled during a sudden roll of thunder, he didn't bother to look around. The muffled sound of a cat meowing whispered through the blackness. A slight breeze cooled his cheek as the haunting rustle of a gun clearing leather drifted to him.

Moving with swiftness, Ford reached toward the bed-post. Too late. One weapon was missing from its holster. His boots hit the floor with a thud as he stared into the blackness, almost tasting danger in the thick air. The skin stretched tight across his knuckles as Ford once more heard the cry of an angry cat trapped somewhere in the night.

"Don't move, mister, or I'll shoot!" a woman ordered. Her voice was high with panic.

Sanford started to stand, but froze at the distinct sound of the hammer being pulled back on a revolver. Again the muffled scratching, fighting sound of a cat echoed Ford's own frustration.

"Who are you?" His voice sounded harsh even to him-self. "What do you want? I've little money, if you've come to rob me."

His eyes focused enough to see her outline. She was tall, very tall for a woman. He could smell sweat, and mud . . . and blood. He could just make out her form be-fore him, her carpetbag in one hand and his gun in the other. The tingle of her bracelets chimed in the thick air as her hand shook slightly with the weight of the gun.

"I don't want your money," she answered sharply. "Take off your clothes!"

"What!" He'd never heard such a ridiculous demand in his life. "I most certainly will not!"

"Look, mister, I don't want to have to kill you, but I will if need be."

"But you'd hang."

"I'll be dead before morning anyway if you don't give me those clothes. Now, you can take them off, or I'll remove them from your corpse."

"You'd kill me for my clothes?" Ford realized he sounded like a child. The woman was dangerous, maybe even insane. What other kind of person would sneak into a man's room, point a gun at him, then demand he disrobe?

"Don't push me, mister, or I swear I'll make you coffin heavy. Now stop asking questions and start stripping."

Ford pulled off his vest and began unbuttoning his shirt. "I've clean clothes in my bag. You're welcome to them."

"No!" she shouted above the storm. "I need what you had on when you left the train."

After pulling out his shirttail, he unbuckled his belt. Curiosity far outweighed fear in his mind as he continued. He'd lived his life in what dime novels called "the Wild West" and never been robbed. Now he had a real live villain before him.

"Hurry up!" she snapped. "I have to be long gone by

sunup. Put your clothes on the bed and back up into the corner."

"Do you want my drawers, too?" His thumb pushed into the waistband of his underwear.

"No!" she answered. "And you should wear an undershirt in this weather. You'll catch your death."

"A mothering robber—how unusual." Ford tried hard to see her face.

"Hurry up!" she answered. "Back up."

He did as ordered, thinking if he lived through this adventure, he'd finally have something to tell around the cracker barrel at the general store.

Moving into the far corner of the room, he folded his powerful arms over his bare chest and watched her outline. She carefully placed his gun only an inch from her reach as she started removing her own clothes.

"Make a move toward me, mister, and I swear I'll shoot. Don't get any ideas about jumping for the gun. You may be fast, but you wouldn't want to bet your life on it."

Ford smiled. He must be mad. He was almost enjoying this. No one back home would ever believe such a thing could happen to him. Not to Sanford Colston, the man everyone seemed to speak to only long enough to be polite.

"Mind my asking, why me?" He watched her in the blinks of lightning as she pulled off her skirt. The material hit the floor in a wet plop.

"You were the only one getting off the train."

Light flashed again as she pulled her shirt over her hand. Ford sucked in a quick breath as he saw her body clearly for a second. She was beautiful. Tall and willowy with full breasts pushing up from a plain camisole. Ebony hair tumbled past rounded hips.

Her beauty washed over him with a sudden flash of fire. "You're lovely," he whispered.

She grabbed his shirt from the bed and pulled it on. "Well, take a good look, mister, 'cause you'll never be seeing me again. If you're smart, you'll forget you saw me now. Anyone who knows me dies."

"I don't think I'll ever forget seeing you," he answered honestly.

Pulling on his pants, she laughed. "You sound like you've never seen a woman undress. I didn't get a good look at you back there on the street, but I didn't think you were a boy." His belt circled her waist twice. "What are you, some kind of priest . . . or virgin?"

Ford's hard jaw turned to granite. "I'm not a priest." He wasn't about to discuss his personal life with the thief stealing his clothes. She'd hardly be interested in how few single girls there were in his town compared to the endless number of men.

At twenty-five, everyone assumed a man had been with several women, even a man like Sanford. He had never admitted or denied anything about his knowledge of women. But this robber in the shadows had asked a question no one else had ever dared. He watched as she picked up his gun and moved toward him.

"Lie on the bed, facedown, with your hands behind you," she ordered in a voice that shook with fear.

He moved slowly, knowing he could fight for the gun when she started to tie his hands. But to do so, he'd have to frighten her more, or maybe even hurt her. "Is this how every guest of the hotel is greeted? Are you the desk clerk's woman?"

She pulled his wrist behind him with her free hand. "I'm nobody's woman, mister. Nobody's."

The cold imprint of the revolver pressed into the center of his back as she tied his hands with a rope she'd been using as her belt. "Thanks for cooperating. I really didn't want to shoot you."

He twisted slightly so he could see her shadow. "Would you have?"

"All my life I've been doing what I had to. I reckon I'd kill you if need be. You're about my last hope. Before I saw you get off that train I had nowhere to turn." Something about the darkness made it easy to be honest. "Just once I wish someone would . . ." She didn't finish.

Ford knew how she felt. He'd felt that way every time a woman turned him down for something as harmless as a Sunday walk. "I hope someday someone will do whatever it is you wish for," he whispered as he watched her open her bag and pull a huge calico cat from the folds.

"You brought your cat on a robbery!" Ford couldn't hide his smile.

"I had nowhere else to leave him." The woman removed several metal bracelets from her wrists and dropped them into the bag, then fought the calico to get him back inside.

"Maybe you should think a little harder about this life of crime you're in. I have no love for cats, and I've never known a bandit, but I don't think they usually travel with pets."

"You'd love Sneeze if you got to know him better," she defended the cat as she locked the animal back into the bag. "Which you won't, since I'll never see you again."

"I wish you luck, Miss Nobody's Woman," he mumbled as he watched her braid her hair and twist it into his hat. Anyone who could love a cat couldn't be all that bad.

She knelt by the bed, only a few inches from his face. Her ribs rested lightly against his shoulder. "Thanks, mister." Her hand touched his back. She spread her fingers wide as she moved across his muscles to the gun.

"You're no boy," she added, turning her hand over, allowing her knuckles to brush against the warmth of his flesh. "These muscles came from years of hard work, I'd guess."

Ford closed his eyes, memorizing the way a woman's touch felt on his bare skin. Her fingers were light, almost caressing, as though she were stealing this feel of him while she had the opportunity.

"I have to gag you." She pulled away slowly, replacing his weapon in the holster on the bedpost.

"I won't yell out." Ford hated the thought of having a rag shoved into his mouth. "If you'll forget the gag, I'll give you till first light."

Her words brushed his face as she moved near again with silent swiftness. "But why?"

He didn't answer. She was so close, he could feel the warmth of her even through his thick cotton shirt, which she now wore.

"Why should you help me?" She moved slightly, until

the warm cotton touched his arm. "Why should I trust you?"

"Because," he said, his words raw with honesty, "I've never lied." He had no answer to give her to the first question. Reason told him to go to the sheriff as soon as she left, but he knew he wouldn't.

Lightly, she brushed the hair from his brow. "I think I believe you. I wish I could see your face. You're quite a gentleman, mister. Maybe the first one I've ever met."

"I'm glad you can't see my face," he responded. "You might understand why I live a priest's life." He felt her breathe as the shirt she wore pressed against his side.

"If you stay quiet till dawn, I'll always remember you as the handsome man I kissed one night while I robbed him."

"Kissed?" Even as he said the word, she lowered her lips to his. At first the touch was light, almost timid. As though he were a breed apart from all she'd ever known and she had to touch him once before she left. But when his mouth parted in welcome, she moved closer, cupping the sides of his face with her hands.

A storm spread through Ford's body. All his senses seemed magnified at once. He felt the warmth of her fingers against his day's growth of beard. The softness of her breast pushed against his arm. She tasted sweeter than honey and brown sugar, with a flavor of wildness he'd never known. He treasured the taste of her like a connoisseur must value priceless wine.

As if she'd longed to be kissed with such tenderness, she responded willingly, moving her fingers into the thickness of his hair, pressing her mouth harder against his. She might steal his clothes, but not his kiss. That he gave willingly.

Her head lowered beside his and her body leaned across his shoulder. His strained muscles tightened even more with the feel of her softness washing over him as their kiss deepened.

When he strained suddenly against the ties binding his hands, she moved away with a sigh of regret. There was no need for words; they both knew he struggled not to free himself, but to be able to hold her.

Silently, she slipped into his huge coat.

He wanted to yell "don't go!", but a man doesn't call back a thief. As she buttoned the coat, he saw her outline against the window. Dressed in his clothes, her silhouette became his in the shadowy light.

"Good-bye, stranger," she whispered as she moved toward the door with her carpetbag in one hand. "And as my Gypsy mother used to say, 'may the angels bless your days and the fairies enchant your dreams.'"

"Good-bye, Nobody's Woman."

In a blink, she disappeared into the night.

Ford lay still for a long time, then slowly twisted his hands until the binding loosened. He sat up in bed and stared out at the rain.

I've been bewitched, he thought, still feeling the pressure of her lips on his mouth, the touch of her fingers over his back. Part of him wanted to look for her, another part wished she'd been a dream, for he had no room for a woman like her in his life.

Dawn crept into the room in watery shades of blue. Though the hotel was every bit as dirty as he'd thought it might be, Ford barely noticed. His mind was focused on the memory of a figure he'd seen only in shadow.

She was the embodiment of every vice he'd fought all his life: dishonest, criminal, wild. But he couldn't push her image from his mind. He'd fought hard to never do anything wrong, and now with his silence he'd helped a robber escape.

Lifting her discarded clothes into the light, he saw the patches and mending on thread-thin cloth. A beggar's rags. But there was nothing poor about the woman he'd seen in the night. She'd been rich with life, richer maybe than he'd ever be.

A tap sounded on his door, rattling Ford from his thoughts.

"Train's leaving!" the desk clerk's voice yelled, as if in a hurry to be rid of the hotel's only guest.

Ford reached for his hand-tooled leather bag. He'd been so hypnotized, he hadn't even heard the whistle. In only a few minutes he was dressed and running for the station. He was at the platform before he remembered his ticket was in the breast pocket of his coat.

Hurriedly, he rummaged in his bag for enough money to buy another ticket and jumped aboard the last passenger car as the train pulled away. Now he hardly noticed the crowds, the smells, the voices, for his thoughts were filled with a beautiful thief he'd never see again.

❖ *Chapter 2*

ICY RAIN PINGED on the top of the passenger cars and melted down the windows, distorting the view of a weak sunrise. Passengers, too tired to even pretend to sleep, grumbled and wiggled on benches they'd once thought of as comfortable. The train whistle sounded in one long, determined blow.

Hannah squared her shoulders and kept her hat low as the conductor punched her ticket. She was relieved when he made no attempt at conversation and simply moved to the next passenger. The screams of a crying baby in the seat behind Hannah drowned out Sneeze's meows from the carpetbag.

This just might work, Hannah thought as she slid her hand into the bag to calm her cat. He was a great deal of trouble and increased her chances of getting caught, but she couldn't leave him behind. Sneeze was all she owned, besides the carpetbag and her mother's thin gold bracelets, which had been hand tooled by a Gypsy grandfather.

As the cars jerked into action, a piece of bread rolled against Hannah's boot. She glanced around. Several

lunch boxes, probably bought through the windows of
the train at the last stop, now cluttered the car's floor. A
graying bite of meat hung out like a tongue from the
half-eaten roll at her feet. Hannah hesitantly reached toward the bread, noticing how dirty her hands were, with
their broken nails and scratches marked in dried blood.
She pulled the meat from the bread and lowered it into
the bag for Sneeze. For a long moment she looked at the
roll, trying to remember when she'd eaten last.

Slowly, she lowered the bread back to the floor, shoving
it with her boot in the direction of the other trash. The mice
would eat tonight, but she'd not finish another's meal.

Sneeze relaxed as he ate the meat without any such
scruples. Hannah tried to plan her next move, but she
couldn't keep her thoughts off the man she'd left tied up in
the hotel room. He'd been calm when she'd robbed him.
Now, wrapped in his clothes, she could smell the warm,
clean scent of him. The stranger could spare the garments,
she figured, and judging from their quality, he must have
plenty of money. But she disliked thinking about him
heading north without a hat or heavy coat. He'd been a
gentleman. He hadn't sworn or threatened her when she'd
robbed him.

The stranger had been soft-spoken. A type she'd
known little of in her life. Until she and her mother settled in Fort Worth, they hadn't stayed anywhere long
enough to get to know anyone.

Her mother said it was because they had Gypsy blood
and were therefore wandering souls. But Hannah knew it
was more because her mother worried about Hannah's
father coming after them. Dana Randell told Hannah

she'd bundled her up when Hannah was only a month old and escaped from a man who'd refused to marry her and threatened their lives if anyone ever found out about Hannah being his child.

When Hannah was eight, Dana decided Fort Worth would be as far as they'd run. She found a job cooking in a little café/saloon, where most of the men were rough drifters just looking for a cheap meal and a few drinks before moving on. An old confederate officer named Hickory Wilson owned the place on the outskirts of Fort Worth. He was good enough to give them a room in the back and wages, and unlike some of the men Dana Randell tried to work for, he asked nothing more from his employee. Dana died of a fever when Hannah was twelve; Hickory hardly seemed to notice when the child took over her mother's chores. Most of the time he asked only to be left alone with his bottle, his memories, and his wounds.

No matter how much Hannah scrubbed the café area, it always smelled as the train did now—of spoiling food and unwashed bodies. She thought of trying one of the other cars, but guessed they'd be just as dirty and crowded.

Hannah suddenly wished she were back at the café, that she'd never met Jude Davis . . . that the killing had never happened. But there was no going back. Ever. Her life was forever changed. Even to the point of committing a crime tonight, something Hannah had never done before. But Jude Davis had been the one evil Hickory Wilson's old shotgun couldn't protect her from. Because of him, she'd have to leave Texas as soon as possible and never return.

She felt bad about robbing the stranger, but it was the only way she'd been able to step on the train without detection. Hannah had merely inconvenienced the man, while his clothing might save her life. She'd seen the yellow slickers on the gunmen and knew her time had run out.

Snuggling deep into the coat, she realized all her life she'd watched her mother look around corners and step into the shadows when anyone unknown walked near. Now she would do the same thing. Her mother had feared Hannah's father might find them, but Hannah's hunters were nameless gunmen Jude had told her worked for the Harwell ranch. He'd said they would make him a great deal of money fast, but all they did was kill him, and Hannah didn't even know why.

Two weeks ago, she'd accepted Jude Davis's proposal, thinking her life would be peaceful if she married. He had a spread east of Fort Worth and needed a wife to help with the place. Hannah needed somewhere to belong. But each night of their engagement, he'd proven himself less kind and more demanding. The night before they were to marry, he'd hurt her with his roughness. When she'd tried to call off the wedding, he'd laughed and slapped her hard as a promise of what was to come.

She'd cried most of the night, knowing she had no one to protect her against Jude. Hickory Wilson had ignored Hannah's screams, and she guessed he wouldn't stop Jude from taking her even if she was fighting. She had

no money, no horse, no one to help her, but the bruises
told her she couldn't marry Jude Davis.

She'd planned to walk away at dawn with nothing but
her mother's old bag and her cat. But when she'd
crossed the café, Jude and Hickory were at the bar,
drinking and congratulating one another on something
they'd done. When Jude saw her, it took him a moment
to realize what she planned. He knocked her halfway
across the room with his first blow.

Her screams were drowned out by three men storming
the saloon. They wore new canvas slickers unlike any
she'd ever seen and carried huge rifles beneath the folds.
They fired off several rounds while yelling questions at
Jude and Hickory. She rolled beneath a table as they circled the two men and laughingly demanded answers
from the corpses.

While the bullets flew, no one noticed Hannah. She
wrapped her arms around her knees and hid her head as
though she could disappear completely. The gunfire
echoed off the walls and filled the room with smoke.

Hannah moaned above the train's rattle as she remembered the sight of Jude tumbling to the floor in a splatter-
ing of his own blood.

"You say something?" an old soldier beside her asked.
He still wore his twenty-year-old confederate hat as
though the war had just ended. "I don't hear too good.
Been riding these trains too long, I reckon."

"No." Hannah made her voice low. "I didn't say anything."

The old fellow nodded, then turned to the two
cowhands next to him and began a long rendition of what

this country had been like just after the war. The story was too polished not to have been told many times.

Hannah drifted into sleep remembering the way the stranger's lips had tasted when she'd kissed them. She'd been foolish to kiss him, but there was something so good about the man. A kind of goodness she'd never been near. What had he said . . . that he never lied?

Her dreams came slowly, like dark-winged creatures drifting on a silent cloud of nightmares. Dreams of being alone, of fighting battles where winning awarded only momentary safety and losing brought pain too great for tears. Memories of growing through her teens with no one to help celebrate each year's passing.

The winter sun was long past noon when Hannah reopened her eyes, but the aging reb was still talking. Now his tale was of the buffalo wars fought hard across the top parts of Texas.

As the train signaled a stop ahead, the man turned from historian to tour guide. "You fellows don't want to stop in that little settlement up by the caprock. Folks call the place Saints Roost, 'cause most of the town feels they've come to bring religion to the lawless West. Ain't no drinking, gambling, or anything else fun going on in that place. Heard tell even the railroad isn't planning to go near there."

Though the train was slowing, the old man continued, "See that fellow waiting with a wagon? I'd bet ya two bits he's come to pick up one of them upstanding saints. I've seen him before. Hauls supplies mostly, but meets the train regularly to save folks the cost of the stage. Even talked to a man from Saints Roost a few days ago who made the trip down to Dallas same time as I did. Colston was his name, as I recall. He was hoping to find a schoolteacher, but I don't reckon he's had any luck. No woman in her right mind would want to get stuck in a little nowhere town like that with nothing but Bible-thumping Methodists to talk to."

As the train heaved to a stop, Hannah watched a lone man jump from the steps of the car in front of them. He carried a finely tooled leather bag, but had no hat or coat to guard against the thin mist of snow that whirled in the air.

She couldn't pull her gaze from him. Taller than most men, with powerful muscles beneath his cotton shirt and plain wool pants, he moved like a wild animal, sleek and purposeful. He had to be the man she'd kissed in the hotel, for even now the memory of the way his back had felt warmed her palm. His face was deeply tanned and set hard against the weather, with sharp angles that looked as if they'd been carved out of a wood that wouldn't give to rounding easily.

"That's the fellow I was telling y'all about. The one looking for a schoolteacher for Saints Roost," the old soldier beside her told his companions. "I knew he'd be heading back alone, probably with that teacher contract still in his pocket."

Hannah felt the folds of a single page of paper in the breast pocket of her stolen coat. It had been behind the ticket she'd found, but she hadn't taken the time to read the paper.

With only a moment's hesitation, she jumped from her seat, grabbed her bag, and ran. Hannah could see the tiny window of escape she'd been hoping for opening, and the only thing that stood in her way was one man. If she could be brave enough to try the impossible, maybe she'd be safe.

"Afternoon, Smith," Ford said as he tossed his bag into the covered wagon and unstrapped his gun belt for a more comfortable ride home. "Good of you to meet the train. I'd hate waiting another day for the stage."

Smith was a little man with reddish hair and cheeks so full they seemed to saddlebag his face. "Welcome home, Brother Colston." Smith wiped his nose with the back of his first finger. "I hope your trip proved fruitful."

Before Ford could answer, a woman stepped to his side and linked her hand through his arm. "I'm sorry I was late, Mr. Colston." She'd removed the hat, and her hair hung in one long braid down her back.

Her hesitation at pronouncing his name was so slight Ford knew Smith wouldn't have noticed. The wind lost all chill as Ford realized the woman beside him was wearing his clothes. Her hair was liquid midnight, her eyes dark blue.

She continued without giving him a chance to find his voice. "I had to talk with the conductor about having my trunk shipped." She looked at Smith and smiled shyly. "Mr. Colston was kind enough to lend me his coat when mine was soaked in mud."

She looked so embarrassed Ford almost felt sorry for her. Her clothes had been soaked in mud, but he doubted that had much to do with why she'd robbed him.

Handing Sanford Colston his own hat and her bag, she climbed onto the bench beside Smith. "And to make matters worse, my trunk was accidentally put on the southbound train this morning, so I have nothing to change into. If Mr. Colston hadn't been with me, I don't know what I'd have done."

Smith smiled at her, taking in every word she said as gospel.

Staring at the ragged carpetbag, Ford could feel the cat twisting inside, trying to fight his way out. Maybe the lady was still playing games, but her pet seemed ready to call it quits. Carefully, he placed her bag behind the bench and opened the latch a few inches so the animal could breathe.

"Oh, I'm so sorry, Mr. Smith." She glanced at Ford still standing beside the wagon. He swore he saw her wink before adding, "Mr. Colston didn't have a chance to introduce me." She held out her hand to Smith. "I'm Hannah R—"

Ford again noticed a hesitation so slight it wouldn't even measure up to a pause.

"—Wright. I'm the new schoolteacher. Got the contract tucked away in my pocket."

Smith bit off his right glove and took her fingers in his large, dirt-encrusted hand, as if he'd been bestowed a great privilege. "Just call me Smith, Miss Wright. Folks called me that for so long I've forgotten if it's my first or last name. It's a mighty great honor I have to be taking you to Saints Roost."

Never, never in Sanford's life had anything like this happened! He forced himself to breathe. He couldn't let this woman, this thief, just step in and lie about being the new teacher . . . but what should he say? For once, Smith looked sober. He might remember some of the story. Usually when Smith ventured to the depot, he drank all he could while waiting for the train, and whoever arrived would find him dead drunk atop the supplies in the back of the covered wagon.

Judging from the way Smith stared at the woman, Ford didn't want to even guess which one of them the redheaded farmer would believe if Ford tried to tell his side of the story. Plus, it was starting to snow heavily, and they couldn't very well stand here and argue.

Ford glanced at the carpetbag, hoping the cat might bolt and then she'd have to follow. But no such luck. The carpetbag didn't even twitch.

Reluctantly, Ford climbed onto the seat beside Hannah, feeling like a fool forced to act in a play for which he'd never seen a script. Not that Smith was behaving like himself, either. Without warning, the little man pulled out a quilt he'd never shared with anyone and offered it to Hannah. He even apologized for the weather, as if he would've personally tried for a better day if he'd known she was coming.

She thanked him sweetly and insisted on spreading the quilt over all three of their laps.

Smith slapped the horses into action without even commenting on why the woman wore pants. Even though she was dressed in a wool coat down to her ankles, Smith seemed to have realized she was a lady. His speech slowed, as though he were choosing every word carefully.

Running a huge hand through his damp hair, Ford paused only a moment before silently offering her the hat. After all, it seemed to go with the coat, and if he was going to get snowed on, the little that missed his head wouldn't make much difference.

She accepted his offer, her fingers brushing the side of his hand during the exchange. The woman took his breath away with the slight touch, and he wondered how long it would be before all common sense failed him.

Suddenly deciding he couldn't allow this charade to continue any longer, Ford cleared his throat. Did this bandit think she could just jump in a wagon and claim to be the teacher he'd been sent to Dallas to find? Last night had been something that involved only him, but fooling an entire community was quite different and he wouldn't allow it.

Just as Ford opened his mouth to tell Smith they'd better stop by the sheriff's office, Hannah's hand found his beneath the blanket. She held on tightly with trembling fingers as she asked Smith how long it would take them to get to Saints Roost.

Ford couldn't remain indifferent. Though her voice was soft and conversational, her grip was a cry for help that touched his soul. Slowly, gently, he closed his massive hand around hers and stilled her icy fingers with his warmth. This lovely woman was in trouble and she'd reached out to him for help—something no one had ever done. What harm could a few hours' protection do?

Hannah felt his hand wrap around hers and knew he'd remain silent. She'd found his weakness: he was a good man. He couldn't turn away from someone in need, no matter how wrong her actions. Her heart almost wished she'd be around long enough to understand him, but her mind knew she was somehow putting him in danger by asking for only a few more hours. The men who killed Jude seemed determined not to stop until they killed her also. She'd seen someone following her dozens of times since she'd left Fort Worth, but she'd somehow always managed to stay ahead of them.

With each mile the storm grew worse, but Ford barely noticed the cold. At some point, he'd placed his arm around Hannah's back to help brace her, and she'd cuddled against him. Smith was forced to concentrate on the driving while Ford held Hannah. The road was poor traveling on dry days, in snow it became treacherous.

Finally, after endless hours, Smith pulled up the reins. "I better get off here, Brother Colston, as we pass my place. I'd planned on taking you all the way in and returning with the horses after I unloaded, but I think I'll pick up the rig later if you'll just leave it in the barn. My bones need warming and the missus will be looking for me."

Ford nodded. The snow had gotten so bad that he could hardly see the dugout Smith and his pack of six lived in. No wonder Smith and his family always looked like moles. Their home was more burrow than house.

Taking the reins, Ford yelled above the wind, "Get inside and warm up!"

"Good-bye, Smith." Hannah waved. "Thanks for picking me up."

Smith smiled at her. The red stalks of his hair sticking out from beneath his hat were white with ice, but his smile was warm. "Mighty glad to have you here, Miss

Hannah. It's an honor, it is, to have a fine lady like you to teach our children."

Slapping the horses, Ford moved forward. He wanted to shout back that the farmer wouldn't be seeing Hannah again because she'd be on the first train leaving after the storm. But he held his tongue, thinking of what he'd say to her as soon as they were out of the weather and face-to-face. In some unbalanced way he felt responsible.

If he'd stopped the robbery, she wouldn't have lied to Smith. It didn't reason out, but somehow he owed her at least a chance.

Hannah spread the blanket over them and kept her head low. The snow fell in huge patches now, blocking all scenery. They moved in silence through a blur of white.

Several minutes later, Ford directed the team beneath an iron archway that joined with a circle C brand at center. He urged the horses up a short lane that led to a house with a barn in back.

"I'll take care of the horses!" he yelled above the wind. "You wait inside."

He climbed down from the wagon and swung her over the snow-packed steps and onto the porch. She was lighter than he'd thought she'd be. "Start a fire if one's not already going," he ordered as he handed her the wiggling carpetbag.

Hannah didn't say a word. She'd felt the power of his grip on her waist and, for the first time, feared what he might do when they were alone.

She'd been nothing but a nuisance. Hickory Wilson used to say that Hannah was a blue-eyed Gypsy and born to trouble. She guessed Mr. Colston would probably agree with Hickory fully.

Opening the unlocked door, she stepped inside and glanced from corner to corner as she'd seen her mother do a thousand times. The house smelled of fresh pine and lemon oil. Finely laced doilies sat atop polished tables and needlepoint seemed everywhere from rugs to pictures.

For a long minute, Hannah remained stone still. She was almost afraid to venture into a room so perfect. A tall clock chimed against one wall, and a fine china tea service reflected the last light of day from a small bay window.

Slowly, Hannah removed the overcoat and hung it beside another jacket in the hallway. She placed the hat on a peg of polished brass and removed her shoes before walking to the fireplace. Her socks were damp but she didn't dare track anything into the house.

When she opened Sneeze's prison, he looked up at her as if she were bothering him and made no effort to climb out of the warm carpetbag. Hannah carefully placed the bag near the hearth.

Though the room was bitter cold, fresh logs were already stacked in a fireplace that had been swept clean of past ashes. Polished mantel, spotless glass, shining hardwood floors—everything was in place, as if no one lived in this dwelling, but merely inspected it from time to time.

Hannah had only seen houses like this through windows as her mother and she walked some summer evenings years ago. There was an order to everything, a beauty she'd never be able to afford. She remembered thinking when Jude asked her to marry him that she'd take the last of her wages and buy a checkered tablecloth and maybe curtains. Gingham would look pretty shabby in this room of lace and china.

As she struck the match, she heard him come in from somewhere in the back. If she leaned away from the fireplace she could see both the back and front doors. She fought the urge to yell "Don't track in snow!" and then felt like a fool. Just because she'd never been inside a house so neat didn't mean he was foreign to it.

She glanced over her shoulder at each piece of furniture, all stately, finely carved, almost delicate. This wasn't his house! She'd bet on it. He was a big man, and this was a woman's house. Either he'd allowed his wife to decorate it, or he'd brought her to someone else's home.

"You get the fire going?" he asked as he moved into the room. "I filled a kettle with water and thought we'd have tea while we try to figure out this mess."

She'd expected him to yell at her, call her names and threaten to beat her for all the trouble she'd caused him. But the man simply knelt and hung a small teapot on a hook over the logs.

His shirt was wet from the snow, and his hair hung damp across his forehead. Absently, she moved closer and ran her hand across the width of his shoulders, as though she could dust the damp away. If ever God made a man to be touched it was this one, she thought as she whispered, "You'd better get into dry clothes."

Strong muscles tightened, but he didn't move. There

was a silence about this man, almost as if he'd spent his life completely alone.

The fire was fully ablaze when he turned toward her. He didn't look as though he'd ever been cold. His winter blue eyes watched her and she felt the sense of being really noticed by someone.

"I'll watch the tea while you change," she added, more to slice the silence than offer help.

Slowly he raised his gaze to her face, then glanced back at the garments she wore. "The only spare clothing I travel with is being used at the moment."

"But can't you go upstairs? Isn't this your house?"

He straightened to his full height. "Well, yes and no. Yes, I own the house. It was my father's before he and my stepmother died, and no, I don't live here. My sister does. She'd planned to rent the spare bedroom out to the new schoolteacher."

"Your sister?" Hannah glanced around as if they'd somehow overlooked her in the shadows.

Ford chuckled, a quick stilted sound that comes to men who have laughed little. "No, you didn't miss her. She's small, but never silent enough to be skipped. If you met her, you'd understand why I live several miles out of town."

"Does she mother you?" Hannah could only imagine how much a man like him might hate being mothered.

"No one's ever mothered me." His words were simply said, without emotion. "Gavrila sees herself as the center of the universe, and since my birth a year after hers, I have no doubt she's viewed me as a disturbance in her otherwise perfect world."

Hannah laughed. "I'd love to meet her. I could just introduce myself as the robber her brother brought home to live with her."

Ford didn't laugh. "I'm sure she's at a friend's house, waiting for the storm to let up. She's never been one to stay home in daylight, or be far from her own fire after dark. Which," he hesitated, "doesn't give us much time to talk, because believe me, you can miss the honor of meeting her. So we'd better think of something to do with you fast."

Hannah stiffened. Here it comes, she thought, the yelling, the anger. She doubted this Mr. Colston could think of any names she hadn't already been called for years by Hickory Wilson. He'd been a fair employer, but fond of complaining and criticism.

Ford watched her closely. She had a quiet kind of beauty that would glow if cherished or wither if unnoticed. Pain rippled in her eyes from a wound deep within. He guessed she'd suffered dearly, despite her loveliness. He remembered how hollow her voice had sounded when she'd told him that she was nobody's woman.

Somehow he'd thought only the homely suffered. It always seemed that way with him and his sister, Gavrila.

He'd been barely out of the cradle when he'd realized that the rules that applied to him didn't fit his year-older sibling. She'd been excused of any crime after only smiling, and he'd been whipped while his father swore to make a gentleman of Ford if he had to beat it into him. And Ford had learned. He'd learned to step back and not expect anything of anyone.

Suddenly realizing he'd been staring at Hannah, Ford looked away and moved toward the kitchen. "I'll get the cups." He couldn't raise his voice or his hand to this lovely creature, no matter what she'd done.

Hannah watched him go, her muscles shaking from bracing for the blow that never came. He's up to something, she thought. No man is so calm. I've robbed him and forced him to aid in a crime. He's only hesitating while he plots his revenge. Maybe he's planning to kill me? No. He'd have done that on the road and buried the body.

Perhaps he's going to attack me and have his way? Hannah had to smile. Not likely, she decided. In truth, she'd been the one advancing on him. His nearness brought her unexpected pleasure. Each time they'd touched it had been her doing.

Maybe he's going to blackmail me? For what? she thought. Even the clothes on her back already belonged to him.

She was still arguing with herself about how he planned to punish her when he came back into the room. He carried a tray with cups and a tin of biscuits on it. He'd wrapped a towel around his neck to catch the water from his hair.

"Mind if we sit by the fire? I haven't felt like I could fit in a chair in this house since my stepmother redecorated when I was fifteen." He knelt in front of the hearth and placed the tray on a stool. "If you're agreeable, I thought we could have our tea in peace before we decide how I'm going to get you back to the depot. This may not be the sort of town you're used to. Folks round here don't take kindly to robbers dropping by to teach their children."

"How would you know what kind of town I'm from?" Hannah felt as if her Gypsy heritage was somehow showing, like a petticoat an inch longer than a skirt. What did he think she usually did, go from town to town robbing?

"I don't know anything about you," he admitted.

Hannah wasn't about to sit down with a stranger and tell him her life story. Not the real one, anyway. The less he knew, the safer he'd be.

"There's nothing to tell. My name is Hannah and my cat is Sneeze. I have no family and no home."

He studied the firelight as it danced across her wild blue eyes. There was more to tell, he guessed, far more.

Chapter 3 ❖

SLOWLY, HANNAH LOWERED herself into the Victorian glider beside where he sat cross-legged on the floor. The dainty chair moved silently back and forth with her weight, while her tired body relaxed against the down-filled softness of the cushions. Watching this man called Colston carefully, she tried to make her muscles relax.

His huge hands handled the cups with care as he poured tea and placed a hard biscuit on each saucer.

"May I have an extra biscuit?" she asked, knowing the question was probably impolite.

He handed her the tin box with MARYLAND'S BEST printed in blue on all four sides. She'd seen boxes like this before, set high on the general store shelf, out of reach and out of the price range of most folks.

Hannah wiped her hands on the cotton shirt she wore and tried take one cookie with the proper amount of slowness. Hunger made her task impossible. She had three biscuits in her mouth when she looked up into his eyes.

"When we warm up a little," he began, trying hard to make his statement casual, "I could cook you up some eggs. Breakfast is about the only meal I can cook that's worth eating."

Warmth spread across her cheeks. "Thank you, but the tea is fine." Silently, she tried to calculate how many more biscuits she could eat before he'd comment.

He glanced away as though he'd read her mind and didn't want her to think he was noticing.

"Where are you from, Hannah Wright—if that truly is your name?" His voice was low, almost conversational.

"Originally, New Orleans," she answered between bites. "My father and mother are dead." So far she'd told the truth. At least as much as she knew. Chances were her father was dead by now. According to what her mother told her, he wished they were. "You married, Mr. Colston? If that really is your name?"

Ford glanced at her and smiled, a wide grin that made his face soften slightly.

"My name's Sanford, but I can't remember ever being called that by anyone but my sister, Gavrila. Everyone else calls me Ford. I've lived all my adult life near this settlement. My dad was one of the first Methodists to buy land here. But I never lived in town. I've been on my own since I was fifteen. Made enough money hauling buffalo bones to Wichita Falls to buy my own spread."

"But why here?"

"My dad preached in half the towns in Tennessee. When he remarried, I think he wanted to start a new life, and Saints Roost sounded grand. I followed but lived on my own. My stepmother used to say I looked like I was half-wild, and she didn't like being around me much."

"You haven't answered my question." Hannah liked the openness about this man. He talked as though there were nothing in his life he wouldn't tell even a stranger, for he had nothing to hide.

"No, I'm not married. Even if I wanted to be, which I don't, it wouldn't be easy finding a woman who wants to live way out here."

He glanced away from her, into the fire, then quickly changed the subject. "How about you? Are you married?"

"No," she answered, remembering Jude Davis's proposal. He'd been a regular at the café on weekends, but he'd never really said much to anyone except Hickory until the night he asked her to marry him. When she'd said yes, he'd commented to everyone that a wife was cheaper than hiring a cook. She'd been hurt, but decided she'd have her own house and her own kitchen. That was enough to ask for in life. It was more than her mother had ever had.

Cramming two more cookies into her mouth, she added, "I don't plan to ever settle down in one place long enough to watch the seasons change. I'm getting out of Texas as soon as I can." The memory of the last evening she and Jude had together crossed her thoughts. He'd been in the café earlier that last night, hardly saying a word to her even when she'd patted him on the shoulder. But when she'd walked out the back door toward her room, he'd been waiting in the shadows. Without warning he'd grabbed a fistful of her hair and twisted until she felt the roots give. *You'd better remember something tomorrow after we're married,* she remembered him saying. *Never touch me in public, but in private you'd best be willing to do anything I say.*

Hannah forced the memory aside. Jude was dead now; there was no use still being afraid of him. "I'll never marry," she said with determination. "Never!"

"That's understandable in your line of work," Ford answered as he stretched long, powerful legs in front of him before once more crossing them.

Hannah tried to figure out if he was joking or serious. She'd have to tell him far too much if she tried to explain why she had stolen his clothes—so much that it might put his life in danger. Hannah knew there were too many questions she couldn't answer, even if she had someone to tell her story to. She'd seen a murder, but had no idea what had caused Harwell's men to be so angry at Jude and Hickory. Even if she stayed alive long enough to testify, it would just be her word against theirs.

"I'll take you back to the train as soon as the weather clears." He drained his cup in one swallow. "In proper clothes, you should be able to travel out of Texas and maybe start a life without crime somewhere else."

"What's the hitch?" Except for her mother, no one had ever helped her without wanting something in return. "Why aren't you turning me in? You're a preacher's son. Isn't there some scripture about not stealing?"

Ford slung his wet hair out of his eyes. "No catch. And I'm a preacher's son, not a preacher. You can mail me back the money as soon as you're on your feet." He couldn't answer her second question. There was no arguing that the right thing to do was to turn her over to the authorities. He was probably the hundredth person she'd robbed or stolen from. But he wanted no part of locking her away.

Hannah suddenly felt she owed this man a great deal. Not because he could have turned her in at the depot and didn't, but because he treated her like she was something more than trash. Occasionally she'd seen a man treat a woman like she was delicate and treasured, but no one had ever acted that way toward Hannah.

Lifting the towel from his shoulders, she ordered, "Take off your shirt."

With one eyebrow raised slightly, he studied her cautiously. "Not again?"

Hannah couldn't stop the laughter. "No." She giggled. "If you'll take off that wet shirt, we could let it dry close to the fire, and I could towel your hair."

He hesitated.

"Come on, Ford Colston. It's not as if I haven't seen you bare to the waist before."

Suddenly both eyebrows went up as he stared at her with bottomless blue-gray eyes before unbuttoning his shirt. She couldn't read his thoughts, but she guessed he was thinking about last night . . . about the way she'd robbed him and how she'd kissed him afterward.

Hannah tried to ease the tension. "I'll let you ask all the questions you like while I keep you from catching your death." She knew she sounded like an overprotective mother, but didn't care. She wanted to be near him again and this was the only way she could think of doing so. "Only consider the possibility I robbed you for no reason at all. It was just something I had to do, like some folks have to steal a bite from the candy counter at the mercantile."

He draped his shirt over the empty chair facing the rocker she sat in and resumed his place on the floor in front of the fire. The golden light danced off his shoulders, reminding her of a statue rather than a flesh-and-blood man.

Kneeling behind him, she covered his hair with the towel.

Ford leaned his head back and sighed as she continued to rub the warm cloth against his thick brown hair. "Why'd you tell Smith you were the schoolteacher? You could be in Indian territory by now if you'd stayed with the train. Or even into Kansas City."

Hannah thought of saying she was out of money and the ticket only went to that stop, but she knew that wasn't the answer. "I liked the sound of a place called Saints Roost. It sounded like heaven."

"It's not," he whispered from beneath the towel. "The rules are hard and fast here, with no tolerance for even a hint of anything improper. Sometimes I think half the town is made up of preachers, or retired preachers eager to pass on their prelearned sermons."

"Then why do you stay?" She'd stopped rubbing and pulled the towel to his shoulders. Absently, she moved her hands into his hair and straightened the mahogany mass with her fingers.

"It's as good a place as any for a man like me," he answered, turning toward her but not meeting her gaze.

"A man like you?" She could see a loneliness in his eyes. Hannah had met all kinds of men in her life, but had no idea what he was talking about. To her, a man who owned more than one house was surely a rich man, and as a preacher's son, he must be respected.

"Never mind." He pulled away from her, mentally more than physically. "Answer me one more question—and I want the truth, for I'll only ask it once. Whichever way you answer I'll still help you make that train in a few hours."

"All right." Her fingers stopped moving through his hair, but she didn't lean away.

"Did you kill anyone or commit some other horrible crime?"

"You mean besides robbing you?"

He twisted slightly to look at her more closely. "Yes, besides robbing me."

She started to say never, then paused. Finally, he faced her directly, waiting so still she wasn't sure he breathed. Looking into his worried eyes, Hannah answered, "No."

The memories came—all she'd been thinking about was the sting of Jude's slap when Harwell's men stormed the café. Gunfire seemed to explode from all directions. Jude's body hitting the floor, his finger still pulling the trigger of his Patterson. Hickory Wilson shouting as if the gunfire were only children making too much racket in his place. The next rounds were aimed at him but she didn't see him fall. She tried to disappear, pull away from the pain and noise. And then she was running.

Everything from the past week came crushing down on Hannah at once. She'd hidden behind the potato bins on the porch of the café for hours. When finally everything was quiet, she'd crawled out and run through the

alley toward Sheriff Andrews's office. Two of the gunmen who'd done the killing were sitting on the sheriff's
bench just outside the jail. Her only place of refuge vanished when she recognized the killers in their new yellow slickers. She could still hear the ringing in her ears
of gunfire and smell the stench of death around her. The
feeling that someone was following her still made the
hair on the back of her neck stand on end.

With no one to help her, she left Fort Worth and
headed toward Dallas, staying well off the road for
safety. But when she'd finally reached Dallas, the hired
guns had been there watching the train. Somehow they'd
tracked her, and without money or friends it would only
be a matter of time before she too was dead. And she
didn't even know why. But she'd heard patches of conversations at the café and knew that once Harwell paid
his men for a job, they didn't go back until it was done
and all the ends cleaned up. Killing a witness was no
more than a loose end to these men.

Slowly, Hannah moved closer to Sanford, lightly
pressing her cheek against his back. He was all the good
in the world she could see. His parents had lived in a
house with teacups and lace doilies, while her mother
had died without even owning a dress that wasn't worn
and patched. He wore fine wool clothing and polished
Colts. She had nothing. Nothing. He treated her with
kindness, when a week ago Jude had tried to prove she
was nobody—even on the eve of their wedding.

When Ford felt the tears on his shoulder, he could no
longer remain stone. He turned, pulling Hannah into his
arms with gentle strength, feeling her silent cry as

though she were screaming. She wept softly against his heart as he rocked her in his lap. The sleepless night they'd both had weakened reason, and they clung to one another.

Gently, his hands brushed away the tears. "I believe you," he whispered against her hair. "Hannah, you don't have to tell me anything. I'll help you. Whatever trouble you're in, there must be a way out."

Clinging to him, she felt once more the warmth of being near him. She didn't care if he believed her or not, because she knew as soon as the snow stopped he'd send her away. All that mattered right now was that he held her, and she didn't feel so alone.

The tears drained all energy from her body, and she cradled against him. He lightly stroked her cheeks with the back of his hand, reassuring Hannah that he meant her no harm.

"Another question," he whispered. "Why'd you kiss me last night?"

His fingers touched the corner of her lips as he spoke.

Hannah smiled. "I liked the way you felt. You feel so strong and warm." She opened her eyes and looked up into the shadows of his face. "I wanted to see how a man like you kissed."

He stiffened. "A man like me?"

Spreading her fingers across his throat, she added, "A man who can be kind and caring even while he's being robbed."

Tight muscles relaxed slightly beneath her touch, but the veins at his throat still pounded blood wildly. "And how did I kiss?" He closed his eyes, wishing he could take back the impulsive question.

Hannah straightened until her body was parallel with his and her lips were only an inch from his mouth. "You kissed as if everything were all new and fresh. Like you'd never been kissed before. As if I'd never been kissed and you were afraid of startling me away."

He waited only a breath away for her to move closer, and she found the realization that it was her decision intoxicating. His hands were moving over her shoulders, touching her but not holding her.

"Ford?" she whispered, liking the sound of his name.

"Yes," he answered tightly, forcing himself to maintain control.

"I'd like to give back that kiss I took from you last night."

Lightly, she leaned her breasts against his chest and touched her lips to his.

All control snapped in him as he drew her near. He'd never thought a woman would come to him so willingly. The knowledge that she'd be gone soon encouraged him to allow this insanity between them to continue before reason forced him to pull away.

Running her hands over his bare shoulders, Hannah felt Ford shudder with pleasure, and the kiss deepened to something she'd never before experienced. He wasn't advancing as if to conquer or use her, he was giving. She'd been grabbed and kissed by a few of the cowhands, sometimes as a joke, sometimes in the hope she'd respond. But Hannah had always fought against their dirty hands and foul-tasting mouths, wanting none of what they offered.

"We shouldn't be doing this," Ford whispered, even as his lips ignored his warning.

"I need to say good-bye," she answered as his mouth brushed her cheek. He belonged in another world than hers, a world of schools and churches and rules.

"Good-bye," he whispered against her ear. "Someday we may meet again. Maybe we'll be properly introduced, and I'll ask you to go out walking with me after church."

Hannah giggled as his words tickled her ear and his fantasy warmed her heart. "And I'll say yes, Mr. Colston. I can think of no finer man I'd like to go walking with."

Ford's hold tightened slightly. "After several strolls and a few dinners with family, I'll ask if I might kiss you."

"And if I say yes?" Hannah whispered, loving the dream he painted.

Huge hands framed her face. "Then I'll kiss you very politely." He lightly touched his mouth to hers.

He'd expected her to pull away, but Hannah leaned against him and parted her lips to his kiss.

This time he kissed her fully and completely. He needed to believe that he could care for someone and that, miraculously, a woman could care for him. She was only a dream, passing him on one snowy day, but he knew he'd remember her touch for a lifetime.

Neither of them heard the front door opening or felt the wind blowing snow into the entry.

Reality didn't pull him from heaven until Ford heard his sister scream his name.

They scrambled to their feet like children caught. Ford stepped protectively in front of Hannah as several men, including the town's minister, rushed into the room to see what tiny, fragile Gavrila found so upsetting.

Ford's features hardened to granite as his sister collapsed in one of her chairs, wailing about the family being ruined. The Reverend Carhart raised a pointed finger toward Ford, as though sentencing him to hell with one stroke.

"Cover yourself, Sanford!" Gavrila cried and looked away from her brother, disgust etched on her face. "Isn't it horrible enough that we have to find you sinning without having to look upon you uncovered?"

Ford grabbed his still damp shirt and tried to think of where to start. "I can explain," he began, wondering if he really could.

Smith pushed from behind the crowd. He looked almost sorry for the young couple. "I told them the schoolteacher was here. I thought they'd want to meet her as soon as possible."

"The schoolteacher!" Gavrila whined. "He's dishonored a schoolteacher! Heaven save us all."

Hannah found her voice. "He has done nothing of the sort." She had no idea who these people were, and from the way they were acting, she wasn't sure she ever wanted to know them.

Gavrila waved her handkerchief in front of her, filtering the scene before her. "Be honest, girl. We know you wouldn't be in his arms if Sanford hadn't forced you."

The petite woman held her head up, determined to accept the family horror with honor. "We all know by looking at my brother the kind of man he is."

Hannah didn't know whether to be angry at whatever they were accusing Ford of being or feel sorry for him for having an insane sister. "And what kind of man is he?" she asked, remembering how she and Ford had said the same thing to one another earlier.

All the other men seemed to take a step backward, as though afraid they'd be asked to answer her question. Gavrila had center stage all to herself.

She waved her lace banner once more and looked directly at Hannah. "He's the kind of man no nice, halfway pleasant looking woman would ever let kiss her."

"Are you saying I'm not nice or pretty?" Hannah questioned.

"Oh, no, dear," Gavrila reassured. "You're as lovely as Smith told us you were. A bit tall perhaps, but we all have some cross to bear. And you'd have to be respectable or you'd never have been recommended by the agency for an interview to teach."

"Then you're saying Ford was kissing me against my will?"

Gavrila looked at the minister for help, but the man could have been a pillar of salt for all the assistance he gave.

"Was he?" Gavrila looked truly puzzled.

Ford moved to speak, but Hannah cut him off. "No," she answered. "He most certainly was not."

Gavrila was speechless for the first time in her life. She closed her water blue eyes and leaned back with her hands folded over her heart. "Bury me now in an unmarked grave. I'm ready to go, Lord, and I want no one knowing I'm one of the Colstons after this."

The reverend moved forward slowly, dismissing Gavrila's death cry. "Miss Wright, if what you say is true, I see only one way to avoid a scandal."

Gavrila began shaking her head, as though it were suddenly loose and she couldn't control the vibrations. "A scandal is something we've never had in Saints Roost, or in the Colston family. I shake to ever guess what my dear dead father would say if he was here to see his son today."

The leader of the community looked at Ford with the seriousness of a judge. "Brother Colston, was this woman kissing you against your will?"

"No." Ford wished he could be angry or mad or even sorry. In truth, he wished they'd all disappear so he could hold Hannah again.

"Then bring me my Bible; we're going to have a wedding right here, right now."

"But . . ." both Hannah and Ford said at once. No one seemed to hear them.

The reverend dusted the snow from his shoulder, no longer in a hurry now that he'd decided on a plan of action. "We'll give you a few minutes to ask her proper, Brother Colston, but no matter what you say we're having a wedding before sundown. Looking at you both, I see you're adults and should both know what your behavior would lead to."

"What?" Hannah whispered, wondering if any of

these insane people even knew what year it was. This wasn't the Dark Ages.

"Marriage, miss, marriage." Carhart nodded and all the men silently seconded him. "That's what what you were doing just now leads to."

Ford glanced at the others. Three men were already taking off their coats and rolling up their sleeves. He knew they'd gladly beat him to a pulp, then hold him up for the ceremony if need be. After all, it was their duty as members of the church to help backsliders back to the right path. This was a respectable town like no other in Texas. A man didn't sit by the fire nearly naked, kissing a woman, unless he wore a band of gold on his left hand.

Closing his eyes, Ford swore beneath his breath as he never had aloud. If Hannah had only said he'd forced her, at least she would have been free.

The preacher and his followers moved to the windows, discussing the weather, allowing Ford and Hannah a few moments alone.

"Don't worry," Ford whispered. "If I have to fight every man in this room, including Reverend Carhart, you won't have to marry me."

Hannah felt so sorry for him. He should be mad at her for getting them into this mess, but instead he acted like the horror of the matter would lie in a marriage to him.

Silently, she slipped her hand into his. "A woman would be honored to be your wife, Ford, but I have to move on. I never plan to belong to any man, and the last place I'll stay is in Texas."

He nodded, but his eyes told her he knew the truth no

matter what she said. He somehow believed his sister's philosophy, that no woman would marry him willingly.

"You can't fight these men. What would you do next? Box everyone in town. This is your home. You can't stand and fight, and you can't run. I know what it's like not to have a place to call home."

"There's no other way."

"Yes, there is." She could feel her hand tremble inside his strong grip. "You could marry me."

"What?" He looked as if the men had already delivered a blow. She was suggesting they go through with it. His father would be thrown out of heaven for swearing if he looked down now and saw his son thinking of marrying a thief. And his stepmother would go through her dying screams all over again to think that any woman was having to marry her stepson.

Hannah hurried before she lost her courage. "We could marry, just for a few days, and pretend to be husband and wife to all the town. Next week when everything calms down, I could disappear." She didn't want to admit how selfish she was being, but hiding out in Saints Roost would give her time to think of where to go next. And with his last name, she'd be harder to track.

Ford smiled, but no humor touched his eyes. "They'd think I killed you and hang me by a fortnight if you disappeared."

"Then I'll stay a month, but no longer. And I'd need your word that we'll be married in name only. Since neither of us ever plans to marry anyway, this ceremony will mean nothing. By early spring we can go our separate ways."

He was standing so still, she wasn't sure he understood. "Look. I need a place to hide and you're as close as I've come to trusting anyone. You need a way out of this mess. My guess is that sister of yours gives you a hard time about not marrying. Well, now you can stop her nagging for good. We'll marry, then I'll just disappear one night, and you can dig a grave and visit it weekly just like you were a loving husband."

She could tell Ford wasn't good at thinking up stories, but that had been her main way of surviving during her endless hours of work. "All right, we can tell folks I'm sick and you can take me to Dallas or somewhere to a doctor. In a few weeks you could come back with an empty coffin and bury me. Then folks would feel real sorry and you'd be a widower."

"I don't tell lies," he whispered, but his words didn't hold the determination they had only hours before.

"You wouldn't have to. Just pretend it is too painful to talk about me, and no one would ever ask."

Ford frowned. "Mind if I get the wedding over with before I go to the funeral?" Both were looking to be about as much fun at the moment. "If I agree to this farce of a marriage, I want all the cards on the table right now. It would be worth a great deal to live in peace without everyone looking at me as if I should be pitied for never finding a woman to step out with me. A wife for even a short time might stop all the gossips."

Leaning close, he had to ask, "You'd promise to do no robbing while you're in Saints Roost?"

His words stung like a slap. She'd forgotten he saw

her as a thief. Pulling her hand away from his, she nodded.

"What else do you want?" he asked. "I seek to be fair with you about this."

Before she had time to think, she answered, "On the night I disappear, I'll take something you value and you must swear you won't try to follow me to get it back. I won't take too much, but I'll need a little help getting settled." If he was to believe her a thief, she might as well continue the occupation. Whatever she took might help her survive somewhere else.

Ford could think of nothing he valued more than his land, and she could hardly get it in her carpetbag. He'd let her take the money he kept in his desk at the ranch. He was planning to give her most of it anyway. "Agreed. But don't bother saying good-bye. We got in enough trouble saying it this time."

Hannah offered her hand in a shake.

"A cat!" Gavrila screamed as Sneeze climbed out of Hannah's bag and stretched. "I hate cats!" All the men jumped, causing Sneeze to dart behind a chair.

For several minutes everyone except Gavrila scrambled around trying to catch the calico. When Hannah finally held her cat, the poor animal was in full claw-drawn panic.

Gavrila cried over and over again about how she hated animals, proving to Hannah that any woman who could not see the goodness in Ford or like cats must be crazy.

Ford directed Hannah to the kitchen. "One thing I should tell you about my sister. She has only two levels of volume, hysterical and preachy."

"And I should tell you," Hannah said as she petted her cat slowly with loving strokes while Ford poured milk. "Sneeze is part of the deal. Where I go, he goes."

"Fair enough." Ford offered his arm. "Shall we go get married now, Mrs. Colston?"

Hannah took his arm, feeling as if she were stepping into another world, if only for a month. "Until the bargain's end, Mr. Colston."

"Until the end," he agreed, thinking that for one month at least Hannah would be "somebody's woman." As far as others would know, she'd be his.

Chapter 4

"DEARLY BELOVED . . ." REVEREND Carhart's voice rose throughout the little sitting room.

Ford could feel Hannah's fingers trembling against his palm. His muscles tightened with the now familiar longing to help her. In many ways she reminded him of a wild creature caught in a trap. Only this time, he realized he was the trap.

The preacher's words drifted around Ford, but he wasn't listening. He was thinking about how selfish he'd been to agree to the marriage. The temporary bond might help her out with a place to stay, but for him it would mean peace for the rest of his life from all the harsh comments folks made behind his back. In a month she'd be on her way and he'd be a respectable widower. The gossips would have little to talk about. When he didn't go calling on any women, they'd think it was because of the memory of his wife.

He wanted to tell Hannah, *I'll be good to you this month. I promise. I'll see that you have proper clothes and enough food. I'll make sure no one hurts you.* But all he said was, "I do," when the minister looked at him.

She might be a thief, but no one in town knew that. He'd treat Hannah so good that even Allison Donley would wonder why she hadn't allowed him to court her. Just as everyone saw only the ugly in him, they were about to see only the beauty in Hannah.

"You may kiss your bride, Ford," Carhart said with a chuckle, "just as you were doing when we came in."

Ford moved slowly toward her, but she didn't respond. Hannah was staring at him with a look on her face that said she'd just signed her own death warrant. If he'd thought she was scared before, it was nothing compared to now.

He lightly brushed her cheek with his lips and whispered, "It won't be so bad being married to me. I'll never hurt you and you only have to be around me in public. I'll stay out of your way the rest of the time; I swear."

Hannah wanted to answer that he already had hurt her by seeing her only as a thief, but she had to make this charade work for the next month. Ford was her only hope of being able to hide. She cupped the back of his neck with her hand and whispered, "What should I do?"

Ford's warm laughter brushed against her cheek. "Would it be too much trouble to act like you're happy about the marriage?"

Without warning, Hannah circled her arms around his neck and hugged him. For a moment, Ford didn't know how to react. He'd never felt a woman press against the full length of him. When he wrapped his arms around her, he knew they must look happy to the others, but he could feel the stiffness in her embrace. Any warmth he felt from her body next to his was cooled by the knowledge that she was forcing herself to hug him. But he had to make it believable.

He lifted her off the ground with his hug and swung her around the room, sending delicate furniture tumbling. Gavrila screamed, Reverend Carhart laughed, and several of the other men let out hoots. But Ford buried his face in her hair and crushed her to him, loving the feel of a woman in his arms, if only as a charade.

When he finally set her on her feet, they were both flushed and laughing. He stared into her eyes, wondering if she'd enjoyed being in his arms a fraction as much as he had liked holding her.

"Well," Carhart said as he slapped Ford on the back, "it appears I did the right thing hitching you two up. I wasn't sure either of you took to the wedding idea, but it's plain you're in love and you'll take to marriage. I wish you many children, Brother Colston."

Before Ford could think of anything to say, Gavrila forced her way into the circle of well-wishers. "Don't be ridiculous, Reverend. How could they be in love? They couldn't have known one another but for a matter of hours."

The reverend patted Gavrila on the shoulder as though she were a child. "It's not a matter of time with love. I knew I loved my wife the moment I set eyes on her; unfortunately, she hated Texas just as quickly." He motioned for the other men to follow as he moved toward the door. "We'd best be getting back to our homes."

Gavrila followed the men to the entry and closed the front door behind them. She then walked back into the room with her shoulders squared, as if ready for yet another battle. "I suppose you'll be staying here for the night, and I'll have to cook you both supper and make out the spare room. Lord knows it's too bad outside to go find Molly to help me."

"No," Ford answered quietly. "I think I'll take Hannah home with me tonight. Before we were married she could have stayed with you, but now she's my wife. As always, I'll sleep at Canyon's Rim tonight, and she'll be with me."

Gavrila let out a frustrated sigh. "But the night's cold and this is, after all, your house."

Ford lifted his coat and held it open for Hannah, smiling at his sister as if he could read her mind. "Don't worry, Gavrila, this will still be your place. I've never spent a night under this roof and I don't plan to now. If we saddle up instead of taking the carriage, we can be home in half an hour."

Hannah didn't say a word. She'd gladly ride hours in the snow to be out of this house. Everything about it seemed perfect, but it didn't welcome her. Her mother used to tell her stories about how sometimes houses have souls of their own. Hannah didn't know if she believed such a thing, but she could feel the coldness in the room that no fireplace could warm.

Ford put on the extra jacket she'd seen hanging in the hallway and crammed his hat low. "While I saddle the horses, see if you can't find my wife a wool scarf for her hair, Gavrila."

Bristling, his sister followed his order in jerky movements.

He nodded to Hannah and disappeared toward the barn.

Hannah watched him go, wondering what she could say to the little woman before her.

Her worry proved pointless, for Gavrila never stopped talking from the time Ford closed the door until they heard his footsteps returning. After very little sleep in days, Hannah didn't try to remember a word. She had a feeling it would all be repeated. Her new sister-in-law had the irritating habit of starting every sentence with "I." "I think, I believe, I feel, I probably shouldn't say anything about this, but."

When she heard the horses, Hannah walked out on the porch and raised her arms to Ford, thankful to be leaving the house and the woman. As he'd done before, he lifted her over the steps.

"Can you ride?" he whispered.

"A little," she answered.

"Then the bay is yours. He's gentle." Ford boosted her onto the saddle as if she didn't weigh more than a doll. "Lucky you have on trousers, for I have no sidesaddle."

Hannah felt his gloved hand slide along her calf to her boot and insure her foot was solid in the stirrup. The action was quick, almost impersonal, but his touch affected her as it had before, warming her insides.

"Don't forget this thing." Gavrila tossed the bag from the doorway. When the old carpetbag hit the mound of snow just off the porch, all three heard both her gold bracelets clang and Sneeze meow. "I never liked cats," Gavrila protested. "Funny little creatures you can't really own or control."

Ford lifted the bag to Hannah. "I'd guess they're not too fond of you either, dear sister."

He tied one end of a lead rope to the bay's bridle and looped the other end over his saddle horn. "Hang on, darlin'!" Ford yelled as he mounted his horse. "We'll be home soon." Hannah noticed Ford's words were directed more toward his sister, who stood with the door open only enough to watch, than to her.

They rode in the moonlight across virgin snow. The wind whirled around them, building two-foot drifts that looked like tiny mountain ranges over the endless flatness of the great plains. The lights of other homes twinkled across the night, growing farther and farther apart as they rode north.

The wind seemed to whisper to her, and Hannah smiled, remembering how her mother always told her the wind wanted to dance with her and that was why it pulled at her clothes and whirled around her. She wished the wind were a being and could blow away all tracks she might have left so she'd be safe in Texas a little longer.

Ford didn't say a word or even turn around as he picked their path. Hannah wondered if he was regretting not trying to fight his way out of getting married. She knew she was not the kind of woman he would have chosen to marry—even for a month. If he knew more about her, he'd be even less interested in having her as a wife. Her mother had been a Gypsy who lived with a man she loved but never married. When people almost found out they'd had a child, Hannah's father began to hate her mother and threatened to make sure no one ever learned of her or the baby. So Hannah's mother had taken a boat one night from New Orleans to Texas, always fearing Hannah's father might find them. Hannah was raised in ranch kitchens from place to place, never calling anywhere home. She knew nothing of being a lady. She'd never even been in a church, and her little schooling had been at the kitchen table with used books her mother would borrow. How could she ever be a wife to a man like Ford, even for a month?

Hannah looked up from her thoughts as the land suddenly opened up into a wide canyon, stretching deep into the earth and running for miles as far as she could see in both directions. The winter moon reflected off the snow, making the night seem bright with light. The view was unbelievable, like something you see in a painting but know never exists in the world. Sometime, thousands of years ago, the land must have cracked, splitting a wide rip into the earth, layered in colors of rocks spreading like gaudy bands from a Spanish skirt.

"I built my house on the edge of the canyon, just below the rim," Ford said as he carefully led them down a path marked on both sides by a fence made from twisted mesquite branches. "The cliffs offer some protection, plus I never tire of the view."

"It's beautiful!" Hannah couldn't find more eloquent words to tell him. She wanted to see such a place in daylight. She found it hard to believe that such flat, monotonous land could suddenly give birth to such beauty. Somehow, he'd found a place where the canyon widened before continuing. He'd built his house in the small spread of land just below the canyon's rim so that from a distance a rider wouldn't even realize it was there. The space was wide enough for the house, a barn, several smaller buildings, and a pasture banked on one side by the canyon and on the other by a rock wall.

Thick adobe framed the front of the home with a chimney that had been built of area rock. The back of the house appeared to be shoved into the canyon wall, as though the place had grown naturally out of the rock.

Hannah jumped off her horse without waiting for Ford. She wanted to see what a place like this one would look like inside. Sometimes, when she and her mother had traveled, they'd seen houses built like this one, but never so wide.

"I'll light the lantern," Ford said as he dismounted and pulled down one of many lanterns hanging from hooks along the front of the house. "The place isn't locked. You make yourself at home, and I'll take care of the horses."

He handed Hannah the light and moved away. She could hear him taking a deep breath as though he hadn't been able to breathe deeply until now. He was home.

For a long moment she stood at the doorway, afraid of what she might find inside. She'd heard many of the people on the frontier lived little better than animals. Was this a house or a cave? Carefully, she set the carpet-bag down and released the latch.

Opening the solid door, she raised the light ahead of her. Sneeze jumped from the bag and bolted over the threshold before she could stop him. Hannah took a step to follow. The room seemed to stand at attention in warm colors of dark orange and brown.

Hannah moved onward.

The light from her lantern filled the dark space, revealing beautiful handmade furniture. Heavy, durable furniture. A couch long enough to sleep on stood in front of a fireplace, and a massive rocker was turned toward the dawn windows. Richly colored rugs covered pinewood floors and hung on the walls like huge paintings. This was Ford's house.

She smiled. If rooms had souls, this one must surely be kind. Moving to a long table stacked with books and papers, Hannah lit another lamp, then another beside the fireplace. She wanted to see everything. Sneeze followed her from corner to corner, until he spotted a blanket that had been tossed over one end of the couch. There the cat found his bed and curled up, no longer interested in exploring.

"How do you like my house?" Ford asked from the doorway. He carried an armful of wood in one hand and his bag in the other. "I built the walls a foot thick to keep the place warm in the winter and cool in the summer. Most of the furniture I fashioned myself, and I buy the rugs from an old woman over near Tascosa who makes them."

"It's clean," Hannah answered, realizing that he'd never know how wonderful that was to her. She could smell the aroma of fresh pine and polishing oil and newly washed cotton.

"Thanks." Ford knelt and started the fire. "I have one of the ranch hands' wives come in once a week to do laundry and sweep up, but I like order so there is usually little for her to do."

"I like order, too, when I can find it." Hannah wondered when there had ever been order in her life. Even the room she'd always shared with her mother had been cluttered with their few possessions. After her mother died, the room had been only a place to sleep when she was too tired to work anymore. "Or maybe I only dream of order."

Ford stood. He dusted off his pants and looked to be at a loss for something else to say. For a long minute they just stared at one another, feeling like two mutes at choir rehearsal.

When he suddenly moved, he noticed she jumped back a step. Ford lifted his hands, palms up. How could she think that he was about to hit her? Ford wasn't sure he wanted to know the answer. "I thought I'd show you the rest of the house. The rooms are big, but there're not many. A kitchen is on the left, with a little dining area where I usually take my breakfast so I can watch the dawn." He moved to the right. "I built two bedrooms on this side of the main room, with a connecting dressing and bathing area." He pointed to two doors along the same wall. "There's an old Franklin stove in the dressing area to heat water so you don't have to haul from the kitchen when you want a bath."

Hannah followed him through the first bedroom door.

"When I built the place three years ago, I guess I thought I'd be having company sometimes. You're my first overnight guest. I haven't had much need for this room."

She looked around the large room, which was furnished in the same heavy, hardwood, handmade way as the living area. She admired a four-poster bed, a plain square armoire, and two tables on either side of the bed.

They walked through a small space between the bedrooms that he'd called the dressing area. It held a tin bathtub and the stove, plus a mirror and shaving stand. Wood was stacked neatly in one corner, and the room's only shelf held a row of towels. Beneath the shelf, Hannah noticed a chamber pot and an extra washbasin.

Ford held open the door, passing through to the other bedroom. "This is my bedroom, but I thought you should take it. There's a fireplace in one corner that will keep you warm, and I can put a lock on the door closing off the dressing area from the other bedroom so you'll have your privacy, just like I promised. The sheets should be clean and you'll get the morning sun."

"But . . ."

"I can wash up in the kitchen so the dressing area is yours." He looked nervous. "And I'll let you know when I need a bath."

"No, you keep your room. I can have the other." She couldn't believe he was giving her the best of the two when the least was more than she'd ever had.

He shook his head slowly, as though he'd hear no more argument. "I'd feel better if you had the bedroom with a fireplace."

Hannah agreed with a nod and a whispered "thank you."

He went to his armoire and cleared out the first two drawers before it dawned on him that she would have nothing to put in the empty space. Slow down, he reminded himself. Why was it every time he was around a woman even near his own age he thought he had to do everything in double time? He seemed to assume that if he didn't hurry she'd be gone before he ever had a second chance.

Taking a deep breath, he handed her one of his nightshirts. "Why don't I allow you time for a warm bath while I cook us up something?" He dug in the back of his bottom drawer and pulled out a wool robe Gavrila had given him for Christmas last year. "You're welcome to whatever else I have that you need," he mumbled as he handed her the clothes.

Hesitantly, Hannah reached for the clothing. Twenty-four hours ago she'd taken what she needed at gunpoint, and now he was giving it to her. "Thank you," she managed, then smiled. "I'm glad I didn't have to take these off your dead body."

He caught the direction of her thoughts and laughed. "So am I."

Without another word he was gone, leaving her time to look around his room while she waited for the water to boil. She could find nothing in the room that she thought valuable enough to take when she left. Everything was clean, orderly, nice, but not of any great value. What *was* priceless in this house she could never pack away in her carpetbag. It was peace.

An hour later she tiptoed on bare feet from the bedroom. Her hair hung long and damp past her waist, but she felt warm in Ford's nightshirt and long robe. The tub had been the first bath she'd had in over a week, and

Hannah was sure she'd scrubbed off several pounds of dirt.

When she entered the kitchen, she'd expected to find it like the rest of the house, neat and orderly. But it looked like a chuck wagon that had rolled over several times. Pots were everywhere, along with supplies stacked on top of more supplies.

Ford looked up from a cutting board where he'd been slicing thick pieces of bread. "Sorry about the mess. While I was gone, my men brought in the rest of the winter supplies for both me and the bunkhouse. It must have started snowing before they had time to put anything up."

Hannah moved around the cutting board and looked at the little table by the window. It was set for two. Her plate was covered with at least half a dozen scrambled eggs and enough bacon to feed several men. Ford's plate was piled even higher.

"I made coffee, but you might prefer milk. Fellows say I make the worst coffee in the state." He pulled out her chair as he spoke.

Awkwardly, Hannah moved into the chair. No one had ever performed such a simple politeness for her, yet Ford acted as though it not only was proper, but an expected kindness.

"I think I'll try the milk."

"One milk." He pulled a jug from the cool box and poured her a big glass. Then he set the freshly sliced bread on the table and joined her.

Hannah could never remember being so hungry. She

forced herself to take the first few bites slowly, complimenting him on his cooking before she continued.

Ford smiled with pride. "I had to learn to cook some of the basics or I'd have starved to death the first few years out here. Now I can afford to buy most everything I need, like bread and butter, but at first I had to make do with what I knew—which was just enough to keep me from starving."

"Didn't you eat with your family?" Hannah asked as she reached for her milk.

"My father invited me a few times after he married. Even said his new wife was a wonderful cook. But being invited and being welcomed are two different things. I always told them I needed to get back to work, and they never seemed to mind my not coming."

Hannah could see the hurt in his eyes. He might look to be a strong, fully grown man, but there was still a little boy somewhere beneath all the muscles. "But why?"

Ford shrugged. "It wasn't my stepmother's fault. My father only had room in his heart for one child, and Gavrila was his darling from the minute she was born. Even when I was growing up, he usually had me doing chores until dark, and I always had to take my supper alone on the porch." His smile didn't reach his eyes. "That's probably why I always eat in the back of the kitchen now. It's homey."

He shoved his plate closer to the center of the table and leaned his chair back as he sipped his coffee. "Funny thing was, when my father and his wife died in a stagecoach accident down by El Paso, his will left everything to me."

"Maybe he loved you?"

Ford shook his head. "Maybe he figured I'd feel responsible for Gavrila. He knew if he left it all to me, I'd take care of her for the rest of her life, and that'll cost far more than the inheritance he left."

Standing, Ford stared out at his sleeping land. "I can't believe I'm rattling on like this. I must be starved for company. Sorry."

Hannah covered her second piece of bread with cream gravy. "I understand. For some reason it's easier to give a stranger the overall view of your life than it is to talk to people you're around all the time. I've noticed that on trips. Most folks you sit beside can hardly wait to tell you their life story before the next stop."

Ford didn't speak for a long time. He just looked out at the night and thought about all he'd like to tell her. At the same time he wished she knew nothing about him, as she had last night in the hotel. He almost wished they could forever be two strangers who crossed in the darkness. "But we're not strangers," he said aloud. "If this farce is to work, there are things you have to know. Things a man would naturally tell his new wife."

"All right," she answered. "Tell me just who Ford Colston is."

"That's no easy order." He knew he had to be complete and direct or he could cause her problems in a few days when folks started meeting her. "I own both the house in town and this ranch. We run a few hundred head of cattle, and I started breeding Appaloosas two years ago. I serve on the school board, which you know, and am in church every Sunday. Other than that I keep pretty much to my own company."

"Ever been in love or engaged to be married? If there is some unhappy woman in town tonight because you spoiled her plans, I'd like to know now."

"No," Ford laughed. "I wish I could say there was. All the young ladies in this settlement have managed to stay clear of me. With men outnumbering women so greatly, I'm not even on anyone's dance card. If I were, Gavrila would convince them I'm wild and ungentlemanly enough to be erased quickly. How about you, Mrs. Colston?"

Hannah stared down at her empty plate. He was so honest, it was hard to lie to him. Maybe she could keep it simple and try the truth. "I was engaged once, for a week."

"What happened?" Ford poured himself more coffee.

"He died the morning of our wedding."

"I'm sorry," Ford whispered, wishing she'd look up at him. He reached to touch her arm, and when she pulled away he saw a cut just above her wrist.

Hannah wanted to scream that she wasn't sorry. Not after the way Jude had handled her the night before he died. She would have killed him herself by nightfall if Jude had been able to carry out his threat of making her marry him.

Remembering how she'd once thought Jude to be a good choice for a husband, Hannah couldn't help but think that maybe Ford might turn on her also. She forced herself to straighten, pulling her nerves together. "We need to talk about other things," she said. "Of rules."

Ford could feel her mood chill as drastically as though someone had opened the back door and the temperature in the room had dropped ten degrees in a second's time. "Of rules," he repeated as he stood and pulled a medicine box down from the shelf.

"I'd like a lock on both doors . . . the one to my bedroom and the one to the dressing area . . . before I go to bed."

"It's not necessary, but agreed." Ford held his palm up and waited for her to extend her arm. He was more interested in treating the cut than in any rules she might list.

"And I'd like your word that you'll not touch me in private." Hannah allowed him to doctor the wound she'd gotten while moving through an alley in the rain the night they'd met. She'd been so frightened and hungry that the cuts had seemed unimportant.

"Agreed." Ford could feel himself walling up as he always did with people. He needed to put space between them before she hurt him. "And in public?" His face was stone but his hands caring as he wrapped a clean bandage around her wrist.

"I think, to look like we are newlyweds, we should be as close as possible when in public. I don't want anyone wondering about us or asking questions." There was a safeness about touching him in public, but she wasn't sure what would happen if they touched any other time. She'd turn Jude's rules around completely, always touching in public, never in private. "Also, you can call me 'darling.' It sounds believable enough. No one has ever called me that."

Ford tried to keep surprise from showing on his face.

He wasn't sure why she'd wanted the endearment. Maybe in a month's time he'd know this woman a little better. He'd called her that earlier just to irritate his sister, and Hannah not only hadn't minded, she'd asked that he repeat it.

"Well, darlin', I'd better get those bolts on your doors so you can go to bed. I don't know about you, but it has been two days since I've had any sleep."

He didn't bother putting on his coat as he walked out the back door and crossed to the barn for the toolbox. He needed to think, and for some reason, he needed to feel the cold.

By the time he'd finished with the locks, Hannah was sound asleep on the couch. Ford watched her for a while, wondering what to do. If he left her there, she wouldn't feel safe, for she wouldn't be behind her bolts. If he carried her to bed, there might be hell to pay in the morning.

Finally he decided he was too tired to just wait around until she woke up and walked to bed on her own. Gently he lifted her and carried her to the bedroom that had been his since he'd built the house. He pulled the covers back with one hand and placed her, robe and all, between clean sheets. Then he lit the corner fireplace, locked the bedroom door from the inside, and passed through the dressing area to the other bedroom.

Despite the late hour, sleep didn't come easy. Ford couldn't get the memory of the way Hannah had looked sleeping in his bed from his mind. He remembered the feel of her in his arms after the wedding and the way she'd jumped when he'd moved too fast toward her once. Finally, he realized one fact—that even if *he* wanted her to be a true wife, which he didn't, she'd never come to *his* bed. A public wife for a month was all he'd ever have.

He felt as though he'd only just closed his eyes in sleep when someone jumped on him in full running force and began shaking him with all their might. Just as he forced one eye open to daylight, his dreams were shattered completely by Hannah's screams.

Chapter 5 ❖

"FORD! WAKE UP! Bandits are trying to break in the house!"

He shook his head, forcing sleep away. Hannah was above him, her hair flowing wildly around her as she tried to pull his shoulder up, not realizing her weight on his chest was the principle reason he wasn't moving.

"Wake up before we die!"

Gently he closed his hands around her waist and placed her far enough away from him so he could sit up in bed. He rubbed his eyes and tried to make his mind focus. It seemed only a moment since he'd fallen asleep. The light from this canyon-side bedroom was never direct, but judging from the amount filtering through the curtains, it must be long after sunrise. "We may need to talk about how you wake me each morning, darlin'. There must be a compromise somewhere between a whisper and a full attack."

"No! This is no joke." Hannah shoved him hard. "There's a mob outside trying to break in!"

In the three years he'd been here he'd never seen a soul, except for his two hired hands, who rode in from their own places, and sometimes one of their women to help him with the cleaning. He'd given them the weekend off. Perhaps it was a herd of cattle, but not people. People would simply open the door, not break in. Ford hadn't locked his door since he'd built the house. There was no need. No one had ever dropped by.

"I . . ."

A rumbling, stampeding sound rattled from the front of the house. The thick walls took the booming blows in steadfast stillness, but the air inside seemed to whirl with a thundering noise.

Hannah jumped from his bed, shoving her hair back and pushing up the sleeves of the nightshirt she wore. "See, I told you we're being attacked." Her fists were balled, ready to fight. "Get out of bed!"

Ford jerked on his pants as he hopped from the room. He hurried through the dressing area they shared and into his own bedroom, where she'd slept.

Hannah followed, running like a child at the parade's tail who wanted to see the front. "What are you going to do?"

Ford didn't answer as he pulled a pair of rifles and a box of shells from the space above his wardrobe.

"Do you think it's Indians? Or maybe cattle rustlers?" Hannah began to pace as he loaded the first gun. The clamor outside sounded like fifty children banging on pots all at once. "Are you planning to shoot to kill or just wound them?"

Ford leaned both guns on his bare shoulder and unlocked her bedroom door as he headed to the main room.

"Ford! What are you going to do?" Hannah screamed.

Looking at her for the first time since he'd heard the racket, anger sparked in his eyes. Not at her, or at whoever was making all the uproar outside, but at himself for not thinking of her and how scared she must be. In the morning light, dressed in only his nightshirt, her wild hair alive with movement around her, she'd never looked more beautiful, or more terrified.

"I'm sorry," he whispered, wishing he had time to comfort her. "Don't worry. I don't know if I'll shoot, but I'll do whatever I have to in order to protect my home. No one's going to hurt you without killing me first. Do you understand, Hannah? I promise."

She nodded.

He'd meant the words as comfort, but she didn't look reassured. Fear still danced in her eyes.

Sneeze circled Hannah's legs, seemingly unaware of all the noise beyond the walls. Hannah picked him up and held him tightly, too frightened to even ask questions now.

"Stand back," Ford ordered as he crossed to the window.

After one quick glance, he set the guns down and took a step toward her. "Hannah, it's . . ."

The door exploded open. Bodies flowed in like a human river. Sneeze jumped from her arms for safety beneath the table. Hannah bolted toward Ford. The room filled with people of all sizes and ages, everyone talking at once.

Ford pulled her under his arm, feeling her tremble.

Carhart's voice boomed above the rest. "We've come

to give you a shivaree, Brother Colston! Then we'll have a wedding feast."

Everyone seemed to agree. Everyone except the bride and groom. He ran his hand down her back and molded her against him, hoping she'd pull strength from his touch.

Backing toward the bedroom door, Ford leaned close to Hannah's ear. "It's all right; these are my neighbors. Go get me a shirt and you the robe. I'll block the door and make sure you have a moment alone."

Hannah decided maybe she should think about going back to Fort Worth. At least there the men were only killers. Here they all seemed to be crazy. Three hired killers didn't look so bad compared to fifty insane neighbors. Men were shouting and women were carrying in food as if they'd just come to a social. Several children were playing chase the cat around the huge table.

When Ford pushed her behind him, Hannah ran for the bedroom. As she pulled on her robe and tied her hair back with a piece of string, she thought of locking both doors and leaving Ford and Sneeze to the mob. But she couldn't. Sneeze could take care of himself, but she wasn't sure about Ford. Already his sister was probably yelling for him to cover his nakedness. Gavrila seemed to think the sight of Ford's bare chest was disgusting, but Hannah didn't find it so at all. She'd seen very few men without shirts, and none whose muscles looked like they'd been carved out of oak and tanned by the sun.

Crossing to the bedroom where Ford had slept, Hannah fetched his shirt and noticed the bed. With a few quick jerks, she pulled the covers together. It was time to act like they had a real marriage, she thought, for as soon as she stepped through the door she would surely be in public. Hannah straightened her back and checked to see that her robe was tightly closed.

Ford's gaze was on her from the moment she entered the room. He couldn't help but smile at the sighs as others watched her move directly toward him. She was lovely, even in the dusty-blue wool robe he'd thought was the ugliest thing he'd ever seen when he'd opened it last Christmas. But on Hannah it looked almost elegant, like a ball gown color that should only be worn in candlelight.

Her attention was on him, as if she saw no one else in the room. She marched straight up to him and held the shirt up. When he turned, she slid the shirt over his shoulders and pulled his collar closed around his neck. As he buttoned the front, she smoothed the material. Then to everyone's, including Ford's, surprise, she raised to her tiptoes and kissed him on the cheek.

It was a bold act, Ford realized, but the kiss served its purpose. If there had been any doubt that she was a willing bride, everyone in town knew it for certain by this small action.

Ford could guess what the talk had been on the long predawn ride from town. The men who'd seen the wedding would relate the story to their wives, and they'd spread the word. By dawn, the consensus was probably that they'd save the poor girl from Ford's clutches. After all, if no woman in the territory would be seen with him, it was not fair to make some stranger marry him just because she'd been fool enough to kiss the man.

He could just imagine how all the good wives got together and decided they had to go out and see for themselves. They probably thought the poor schoolteacher would be half-mad by now, after spending the night out on the wild canyon ridge with Sanford Colston, a man whose own father never allowed him under the same roof with his wife and daughter. It was their Christian duty to save the dear child.

But Hannah didn't look like she needed saving. She circled her arm around the back of his waist and held her head high as she took her first look at their visitors. "You didn't tell me you'd invited guests for breakfast, Ford."

Everyone laughed, shattering the tension in the room. Fears for Hannah and invisible crusade banners were tucked away as they crowded around to be introduced to the lovely creature Sanford Colston had somehow captured.

As always, most folks said as little as possible to Ford. But he didn't mind. The words of his stepmother, which had colored the community's feelings toward him, seemed finally buried as he stood close to Hannah. He straightened with pride. In a month, when she left, everyone would remember what a fine husband he'd been. He'd even visit her grave every Sunday, and most folks heading home from church would see him there. They'd think he was mourning, but he'd be kneeling beside the marker and wishing her good luck, wherever she was. He owed her a great debt for what she was doing this morning.

"Ford!" Someone slapped him on the back, pulling him from his planning. "I have to say I'm surprised.

Now I know why you've been taking off for Dallas so often. You've known this lady a long time, haven't you?"

Hannah and Ford exchanged looks, but neither spoke. He didn't want to start a circle of lies that he'd have to keep track of for the rest of his life.

"Stop being nosy, Dave Rickles. The man has a right to privacy in his life," shouted an older woman, who stood six feet tall without her boots, as she pushed her way in front of Hannah.

"My name's Jinx Malone." She pumped Hannah's arm with vigor. "I can drive a full team better than most men and run the mail office in Lewis's place. I've been a friend of your man's since he was jackrabbit size and drivin' bones down to Wichita."

The huge woman took a breath and pulled on the wide belt holding up her slacks. "I buried four husbands and am looking for the fifth. Marriage is a fine fever for anyone to catch."

"Nice to meet you, Mrs. Malone." Hannah smiled for the first time since the company arrived. The gray-haired woman before her was wrinkled by years but full of life.

"Since I'm your husband's friend," she added, as if she didn't give friendship lightly, "I guess that makes me yours also, so call me Jinx. I've had so many missus handles, I forget which one to answer to. My last husband said if he didn't outlive me to start calling myself Jinx, in order to warn number five. So Jinx it is."

"Thank you." Hannah accepted her gift of friendship.

Jinx leaned closer. "He's a good man, that husband of yours, but not too bright." Before Ford or Hannah could argue, Jinx pulled a box from behind her. "'Cause if he had a lick of sense, he'd have stopped by Lewis's store and picked up these things before he left town last night. Smith told me what happened to your luggage. It ain't right, a new bride not having anything to wear."

Hannah looked puzzled as she opened the box. Inside were two dresses, both finer than anything she'd ever had. One blue with a soft white lace collar, the other a dark gray with wine cuffs. She also found undergarments and bath soap and combs and a brush.

"Thank you." She fought down tears as she looked up at Jinx.

"Don't thank me." The large woman laughed. "I charged them to your husband, so he's the one to thank."

Hannah glanced at Ford.

He nodded slowly. "You'd best try them on, darlin'. I'll try to talk these good people into going back home."

"Going home, nothing, big brother," Gavrila shouted so that everyone could hear. "We've come out to celebrate your wedding. I've arranged everything."

Ford stared at his sister, hoping she'd at least look at him while she made plans to ruin his day, but as usual Gavrila paid him no mind and went about her plans.

"If the women will help me, we'll have a wedding breakfast on the table by the time my brother gets shaved and tries to make himself look presentable. Then we'll bring the ragbags in and start piecing a quilt. Since they didn't have rings, we might not want to do the double wedding ring pattern. I've decided on the lone star instead."

Ford slipped his hand around Hannah's and moved

toward the bedroom door. "We'll join you in a little while," he said to no one. They were both running by the time they reached the safety of the bedroom.

Glancing back, Ford saw men moving furniture at Gavrila's command, and several women had disappeared into the kitchen. The quiet of Ford's home was vanishing like a paper castle in the rain.

He closed the door to the bedroom and leaned against it, thankful to be alone. No matter what the occasion, Gavrila always had to be the center of attention. In the past three years, she'd shown no interest in coming out to his canyon house, but now she was acting as if this were truly her home, also.

"I love the dresses."

"What?" Ford had forgotten all about Hannah being in the room.

She'd placed all the things from the box out across the bed. Touching each, she smiled her pleasure. "Thank you. I've never had anything so . . ."

He touched her lips, stopping her confession. "Don't say it," he whispered. "Don't say anything like that to me or anyone else here." He didn't want to think that she'd never been cared for. "You deserve them, and far more. Thank *you* for doing what you did out there in front of everyone. If they didn't think we were happily married before, they do now."

For a moment she looked puzzled. "Oh, helping you with your shirt. It was part of our agreement. I want to make this charade work, for both our sakes."

"So do I," Ford agreed as he moved to the dressing area to shave. How could he explain to her that, though she was not the kind of wife he'd ever have chosen, she was acting like the very kind of woman he'd always dreamed would stand at his side? He knew it was only a performance for the crowd, but she was so attentive and loving out there, he almost believed it was real. "Mind if I clean up in here?"

"No, I don't mind. You might cause quite a stir if you shaved in the kitchen, as we agreed. You're welcome to the space, as long as you keep your back turned. I can't wait to try on at least one of these dresses. Maybe you can tell me about the people while we get ready."

Setting the kettle to heat on the little stove, Ford unbuttoned his shirt and began to lather up for his shave. He squared his shoulders so that there was no way he'd turn slightly and see her dressing.

When he looked in the mirror, he almost cut his own throat with his razor. Hannah's image reflected back. By all that was good and proper in this world, he knew he should step away from the mirror, but Ford remained frozen, unable to do anything but watch.

She stood next to his bed, her back to the dressing area as she slowly unbuttoned the nightshirt. He could measure the progress of each button by the slipping of the shirt from her shoulders. Her gaze was on the new dress when she finally let the shirt tumble to the floor.

The razor slipped from Ford's hand and plopped into the basin water. He hardly noticed.

Hannah stretched her arms above her head, then twisted her mass of hair into one knot. Slowly, as if she wanted him to enjoy the sight of her, she turned as she slipped the silk camisole around her back and began lacing it up from the waist. When her hands neared her breasts, the mounds of creamy white seemed to push up, as if resenting being tied away, even in silk.

Ford felt his throat go dry. To his amazement, she didn't hear his heart pounding and continued dressing.

Next, she leaned forward and slipped into a pair of legging things Ford could never remember seeing, even in the stores. They were silk, with ruffles of lace and bows just above her knee. As she pulled them over her hips, she leaned forward at the waist slightly and seemed to stick out her bottom in a manner that made Ford forget to breathe. The bloomers laced at the knee. As she lifted each leg to reach the ties, the material on the other leg stretched tight, making a clear outline of her form from the waist down.

Her beauty washed over him in scalding waves, warming his blood.

Ford watched as she pulled on white stockings that went all the way to her knees. She leaned sideways to straighten them. A silk shoulder strap fell, causing her camisole to slip and Ford to have to grip the shaving stand to keep from turning to face her.

Hannah seemed unaware of his dilemma, for she continued dressing. She pulled on the high-collared, toe-length navy dress that was very proper, but all Ford could see were the curves beneath the wool. Curves he knew were bound with ivory lace and silk.

He closed his eyes, knowing if he lived to be a hundred he'd always count this view of her as the most beautiful sight he'd ever seen. A few times when he'd traveled he'd gone into saloons where they'd had unclothed women pictured over the bar, but nothing compared with this woman in the flesh.

"The shoes are too big." Hannah startled him.

Ford turned slowly, pulling himself from the dream in the mirror to the reality of her behind him. Impossibly, reality was more beautiful than mirror image. She was brushing her hair in long, steady strokes. "I'm sorry," he said, feeling like a fool. "I didn't hear what you said." He knew she should be able to hear his heart; after all, it was pounding now in his throat.

"I said, the shoes are too big, but everything else is a fit."

Ford caught himself before he yelled, "I know."

"Do you think I could wear my own shoes? The skirt's so long I don't think anyone will notice."

"I think that would be fine." Ford fished for his razor in the now cool water. "But, Hannah, all those things are yours now. Plus anything else you need from the store. Just let Jinx know and she'll send them out with the next load. She was right; I should have thought to stop and pick them up last night."

"We both had a lot on our minds last night. However, thank you for them today." She looked embarrassed by his offer to order more. "You're a good man."

"No, I'm not!" Ford wanted to scream. If she could read his thoughts right now, she would think he was an animal.

Chapter 6 ❖

HANNAH HAD JUST been introduced to a dozen women in the kitchen when Ford entered the room. He'd cut himself in two places shaving and his bandanna was untied around his neck, but she couldn't help but smile at him and take the hand he offered.

His fingers were strong and firm around hers, giving Hannah an anchor in this sea of chattery folks. She'd seen men offer women an arm while walking down the street, but she'd never thought of herself as needing such a crutch.

"I want to have a dinner party in town," Gavrila said, drawing Hannah's attention. "As soon as you two decide to leave this cabin and take your place in the community."

"We're not hiding out here, sister." Ford tried not to think about how long Gavrila would like to see them stay away from town. He knew she saw him as her cross to bear. She'd even told him many times that she'd have a flock of suitors if she hadn't been cursed with him always lurking in the shadows of her life.

"If Hannah feels up to it after the trip from Dallas, I thought we'd ride in tomorrow."

Hannah didn't say a word.

"I assume I'll have to teach the school for a while longer until she gets settled." Gavrila was dragging her burden again. She'd told everyone who would listen how much she hated teaching, but thought she was the only one who could do the job until they hired someone proper.

"No," Hannah found her voice. "I'll take over the teaching on Monday."

She felt Ford's hand tighten slightly around her fingers, but he didn't say a word. "I came here to teach, and teach I will as soon as needed." She knew little about schools. Her mother had allowed her to go for a year once when they'd lived close to a school, but then they'd moved on and Hannah had continued her learning at the kitchen tables where her mother worked. But now in Saints Roost there was nothing to do, and she'd only be in Ford's way if she stayed at the ranch.

"Are you sure?" he asked.

Hannah loved hearing the question in his words, not disapproval. He was allowing her to plan her own moves. "I'm sure," she answered. "Only you'll have to show me the way to the schoolhouse."

"I'll take you there myself. I have to go into town anyway. After that you can ride the bay, if you like, or I'll hitch up the wagon."

A large woman with a hat that looked like several birds had collided atop it pulled at Hannah's free hand. "I must show you something, dear. Step over here."

Hannah glanced at Ford, who nodded but raised an eyebrow.

Hesitating, Hannah opened her mouth to refuse.

Before she could say anything, the lady pulled again, as if in a great hurry.

When Hannah was a few steps away, several men jumped toward Ford at once. He had only enough time to raise his arm to fight before they had him pinned to the wall. Hannah tried to pull her arm free of the woman so she could return to Ford, but a man blocked her way.

"Take her, Justin!" a man yelled as he fought along with several others to hold Ford. "Take her quick. We can't hold him long."

"Yes, sir." A youth grabbed Hannah's free arm and pulled her through the crowd. Suddenly people seemed to close in on her, shoving her along after the boy. All the folks in their Sunday best were suddenly a mob of pushing, shoving madness.

"Cover her head with a blanket!" some woman shouted. "You don't want her catching cold while you're kidnapping her."

Youths, none old enough to shave regularly, framed Hannah on all sides. "Don't worry, ma'am, there ain't been a bride yet that hasn't been found by her groom at least by their twentieth anniversary."

"Get your pans, folks. We want to make so much noise, Ford will never hear her calling. If he's going to find his missus, he'll have to use his heart, because he won't be able to hear a thing telling him which way she's leaving."

Just before panic exploded in her brain, Hannah realized everyone in the room but Ford was laughing. He was struggling wildly against the half a dozen men holding him. His face was twisted with rage. For a moment Hannah saw something savage in him and wondered if his sister might also see the wildness.

Jinx Malone's tall frame blocked the exit suddenly, and the youths stopped pulling Hannah forward. "Don't worry." Jinx smiled at Hannah as though she knew words needed to be said. "Your man will find you. It's all in fun. I've done it several times and always lived."

Hannah wanted to scream that she didn't have a man, but something dark covered her head and the world went black. Hands pulled her forward, shoving her, hurrying her, steadying her. The uproar of the crowd seemed to be farther and farther away as she stumbled across the threshold and outside onto the dirt.

Someone lifted her into the bed of a wagon. "Take her to the cave," said a boy whose voice was just changing. "If her husband can't find her there, he don't deserve to have her."

"He don't deserve her anyway," another answered, as Hannah felt the wagon give to someone else's weight. "What's a man like Ford Colston doing with such a pretty wife? It don't make sense."

"Hush up, you fool! She can hear."

"Well, maybe she's deaf as well as blind."

"Just do your job and take her to the cave. We'll try to lead Ford in as many wrong directions as possible."

"Do I have to stay with her? I'll miss all the fun back here."

"No, tie a rope around the blanket and leave her there. She'll be all right as long as she doesn't move around and fall over a rock or something."

Hannah heard the slap of leather, and the wagon jerked forward. She bounced around in the bed, trying to free her hands, for what seemed like several minutes. Then the wagon stopped suddenly, throwing her against the back gate.

Before she could straighten and fight, a rope encircled her blanket. Though Hannah struggled, her elbows were pinned to her sides with the rope while another loop caught her legs in her skirts. On unsteady feet, the kidnapper carried her down an incline.

"You'll be fine here," the youth said, not sounding at all sure of his statement. He dropped her against a chair-high stone and let out a long breath. "Just sit here on this rock until your husband comes. You're in a cave that's only about ten feet deep. It'll protect you should it start rainin'."

Hannah tried to scream through the thick layer of wool. The sound seemed to travel only as far as her own ears. Minutes ago, she'd thought these were normal people, folks that anyone would be proud to call friends and neighbors. But now she knew they were all crazy. Somehow she'd gotten off the train and traveled to the only town in Texas where every man, woman, and child was mad.

She closed her eyes and forced colors to come into her mind, as she often did at night when there was no light in her little room. "Ford, find me," she whispered over and over as she waited.

When the men stepped away from Ford, they'd expected him to come out swinging and he did. He knocked three of them flat and was about to toss a fourth when Jinx pushed her way into the circle of men.

"Stop!" she yelled.

Ford slowly lowered the fellow he'd been about to throw.

"This is all in fun, my friend." Jinx's voice was a shout on calm days; now it could have bested a train whistle. "They do this at every wedding, Ford. It's called a shivaree. I've had so many I have to kidnap myself now, 'cause there's no longer a man who can lift me."

Ford took a deep breath and tried to force his breathing to slow. Several men moved a step back when he raised his hand and shoved hair from his face. "I know it, but Hannah looked frightened. I didn't have time to warn her. Someone should have explained it to her."

"It's just a game. Folks bring food, they all say how happy they are, and they kidnap the bride. It's not so complicated. You'll find her in no time and everyone will have a good laugh."

Ford glanced around the room. He'd known all these people for years, but in truth he called very few of them friends. He guessed they'd laugh at him about as quickly as they'd laugh with him. But Jinx was right; it was only a prank, and he must play along. He had no choice. He counted this older woman among his few friends, and if she thought everything would be all right, he'd play along.

"Calm down, big brother!" Gavrila moved into the circle of men and Jinx, now that everything seemed safe. Her eyes were wide and her hand was held up toward Ford, as if she feared he might yet turn and strike even her. "No one is going to hurt your bride. Calm yourself. Settle down. Don't go crazy, like some wild animal in the woods."

Ford stiffened. She was using the very words his step-mother used to use to refer to him. His face tightened and he almost growled in anger.

"This is just a game, Sanford." Gavrila's words were loud and spoken slowly. "You can play the game, just like anyone else."

She was doing what she'd always done to him, making him feel like he was an animal she'd found outside its cage and she had to talk in simple language to try and coax him back in.

He saw it in the others' eyes. They were afraid of him. The kind of fear that repulses. And they felt sorry for Gavrila. Poor pretty, tiny Gavrila. He could go to church with them, eat dinner at their homes, even serve on the school board, but he was different. A kind of difference that would never fit into their society. He wondered if he'd ever be accepted by them.

Only Jinx, who herself was an outsider, seemed to never judge him. Ford turned from Gavrila, wishing his sister would grow the wings she thought she deserved and fly away.

Jinx had moved to the corner by the fireplace and was lighting a pipe. Something no respectable woman would have done. But then Jinx wasn't big on accepting any-one's laws but her own. She often said that when her third husband died, she found she missed the smell of his pipe more than she did him, so she took up the habit her-self.

When Ford's eyes met hers, she winked at him. "Better go find that bride, son, before these good people eat you out of winter rations."

No one stopped him as he moved to the door. He grabbed his hat and coat and left. The moment he closed the door, he heard voices start chattering. Ford moved away, into the cloudy morning sun. He didn't want to hear what they were saying; he'd heard it all his life.

Forcing his mind to think, he made a mental list of all the places she could be hiding. The barn was too easy, town was too far. As he walked past the wagons, he ran his hand over the metal of each one's wheels. Sure enough, the last wagon wheel he touched was warm. Someone had traveled fast in this rig only a few minutes ago. And if they'd had time to get somewhere and back while he'd been held inside, Hannah couldn't be far away.

Several youths stood near the barn, as if daring him to try and find her in there. They all held sticks and pans to make noise and set off an alarm. Another group of men was down by the bend in the road. They looked more interested in their own conversation than in playing any games with newlyweds.

Ford walked toward the edge of the canyon. He could go toward town and search every dugout and farmhouse until he found her, or he could head deeper into the canyon. By road it would take several minutes to reach a cave large enough for them to use as a hiding place, but if he climbed the rim, he could be there in half the time.

With a sudden movement, he ran toward the end of the corral, where the land dropped off sharply into the canyon. Before anyone could react and follow, he'd disappeared into the line of trees and brush. As he climbed he could hear them shouting at one another, looking for him, but they had no direction to follow. He was the only man alive who knew this way to the caves from his place. He'd found it one summer when he'd been exploring for colored rocks to use to build his fireplace. A reddish brown streak of rock ran along the rim from just below his corral to the first cave. It was as easy as following street signs in a city, once a man knew the trick.

Within a few minutes, he swung down from the ledge and into the cave. Colder air greeted him as he moved out of the light.

"Hannah?" Ford said, knowing there was no need to yell. The cave wasn't deep, but it twisted into total blackness within a few feet of the opening. "Hannah?"

Just as he'd decided he'd made a mistake, he heard her muffled cry.

"Stay put," Ford ordered as he moved through the blackness. "I'll find you."

The rock was cold and damp as he felt his way slowly. He could stand in most parts, but he remembered the ceiling dipped low in a few places. "Don't worry, Hannah, I'm close."

Sharp edges jutted out, brushing his hair as he moved. The ground was uneven and pebbly. Hannah sounded far away, but he knew she couldn't be more than a few feet from him. Ford fought to keep his hands from forming fists as he thought about how they'd frightened her needlessly. This was a silly custom, probably practiced nowhere else but the plains of Texas.

"Hannah," he whispered as he bumped into something soft.

She stiffened, then relaxed as she recognized his touch. Her muffled cries came in a constant stream.

Ford pulled the rope free, jerking the blanket off her head. While she took a deep breath, he brushed her hair back from her face with both his hands. "Are you all right?"

He felt her nod, but he doubted her answer, for he could feel the warm tears on her cheeks. Slowly, he touched her shoulders and slid his fingers along her sides. "They didn't hurt you, did they?"

"No," Hannah answered. "I was only frightened a little."

Ford laughed. "Well, I was frightened for you—a lot." He pulled her into a hug. "I'm afraid I was so angry I've convinced at least half my neighbors that I'm a wild man."

"Is every day of married life to you going to be like this? I'm not sure I'll last a month."

Ford circled her waist with his hands. "It will calm down. I promise."

He was silent for a long moment, but so close to her, Hannah could feel his heart pounding. "This blackness reminds me of the hotel room where we met." Her voice was so low it could have been a thought.

Pressing his face against her hair, he agreed.

Hannah lifted her cheek to brush his. Something about the darkness made her want to touch this man. In the light there was the reality of who and what he was, but in the blackness there was only the man. A gentle man.

"Our agreement," she whispered, without moving away.

"I know," he answered. "This isn't exactly a public place for touching." He leaned closer, pressing her back against the cool wall of the cave. "But I'm not sure how wide the cave is at this point."

She felt his chest rise and fall against her own. "And we wouldn't want you bumping your head."

"No," he whispered as he lowered his face into the softness of her hair. He leaned closer, protecting her shoulders from the rocks behind her with his arm. She felt so right against him. He didn't want to think about being from Saints Roost, where rules surrounded him. He didn't want to think about her being a robber who'd be gone in a month. All he wanted to do was feel her next to him, close and soft as a woman should feel next to a man.

"Maybe in this blackness you would be only a stranger, as you were back in the hotel," she whispered as her hand cupped the back of his neck.

"I don't even know your name. In fact, this probably isn't happening at all." He played along as his palms pressed against her ribs, just below her breasts. "What are the odds of finding a woman in a cave on my land?"

"And what is the chance that two total strangers will ever pass one another again." She lifted her hands and dug her fingers into his thick hair, pulling his mouth to hers. "But I'll always remember a stranger's kiss," she whispered against his mouth.

He liked the feel of her words. "And I'll always remember the way a stranger felt in my arms."

Their kiss was as wild as the moment. They'd spent the night being proper and abiding by the rules they'd both set, but suddenly there were no rules in the blackness of the cave. His hard body molded her against the rock while his hands moved over her clothes, longing to touch what he'd seen in the mirror earlier, needing to feel the curves he'd only glimpsed and thought too perfect to be real.

Loving the feel of him so close, she found her fingers just as bold in their exploring. She needed to touch him, even though each time she did she felt an increased need for more. Her hands slid beneath his coat and pressed against the muscles of his chest. The cotton of his shirt did little to disguise the feel of him. She could even capture the warmth of his skin through the material.

As her hands grew bolder, her mouth opened to his kiss. His lips were full enough to be tender. She could feel his reaction to her kiss jerk in shock waves through his body.

"Unbutton your shirt," she whispered as his mouth moved to her throat.

Ford laughed against her neck and ripped his shirt open with one mighty tug.

Without hesitation, she moved her fingers across his chest. Her hands slid around his waist and clawed gently across his back.

He growled low in her ear, and Hannah smiled in the darkness and repeated her action.

His kisses were warm and tender as she continued to touch him, first hesitantly, then boldly. It felt good to feel the man she'd seen. The muscles were as tight as

she'd imagined, and his skin seemed afire with a need
for more.

He held her waist as he leaned back slightly, groaning
at the pleasure her touch brought him. When her mouth
brushed his throat, his grip tightened and he almost lifted
her off the ground.

Hannah laughed and leaned back against the rock,
waiting for his kiss. As his mouth covered hers, he slid
his hand up over her breast and pressed lightly against
the material.

The moment shattered like crystal in the wind. She
pulled away suddenly, shoving and fighting for space.

"Hannah, what's wrong?" Ford reached for her, but
she pulled away again.

"Nothing. Just stay away." She moved, feeling her
way along the wall of the cave. "Where's the opening?"

Ford took her hand and pulled her into the shadowy
light halfway to the entrance. "What is it? What happened? Did I do something I shouldn't have?"

"Nothing!" She tried to move past him. "You did
nothing. It's me."

He allowed her to pass. She brushed against him as
she moved into the light, but when he offered his assistance, she pulled away. Anger bubbled over in him and
he didn't even know the reason. "So that's the way it is,
darlin'. You're allowed to break the rules and touch me
in private, but I can't touch you? You're mad because I
touched you. That's it. You can do whatever you like,
but I'm to stay in check."

Hannah straightened her hair and tried to ignore him.
She didn't want to admit that she was wrong to break

their agreement in the blackness. She couldn't tell him that when he'd touched her, the memory of Jude's cruelty had flooded through her. Jude had grabbed her breasts as if they belonged to him and were not part of her body. He'd hurt her with his pawing, and she wasn't about to allow another man to do so. Ford might have seemed gentle, but she was sure he'd turn just as quickly as Jude had and maybe just as cruelly. Her breasts were still bruised, and she didn't need a second lesson to teach her not to allow men too close.

"Answer me," Ford said quietly as he moved beside her into the light. "I need to understand. What happened? One moment you wanted me close, and the next you were pushing me away when I tried to touch your . . ." He couldn't even bring himself to say the word.

"That is the way it is." Hannah's voice was colder than the winter air around them. She didn't look at him as she set the new rule. "I can touch you in the darkness. I can break the rules, but you must never. If you do, I'll leave. I'll turn myself in as a thief. I'd rather be in jail than be pawed by a man."

They moved along the rocks to the easy path toward the road, walking in silence, both thinking the other should speak first. Ford buttoned his coat, not because he was cold but because he wanted to hide the torn shirt, a reminder of how easily he'd been drawn into her little trap. It made no sense.

When Hannah saw a wagon coming toward them, she turned to face Ford. "Agreed? Nothing's changed. You still can't touch me in private. You never can."

Ford felt trapped. He had no doubt that she'd tell everyone in his house how they'd met if he didn't agree. If he did say yes, he'd be promising to never touch her. He could demand that she do the same, but he loved her touching him and couldn't understand why she wouldn't respond in kind. Maybe all women were like her—they liked to touch, but didn't like to be touched. Maybe she was a one-of-a-kind woman, put on earth just to drive him mad. If so, she was doing a great job.

"Agreed," he grumbled as the wagon neared. She slipped her hand in his just as the driver drew close enough to see them clearly.

❖ *Chapter 7*

HANNAH PICKED UP another stack of plates and moved toward the kitchen. She'd already gone through three pans of dishwater, with no end to the work in sight. About the time the children finished breakfast, the adults were starting on dessert. They'd gone through all the china and tin plates Ford had and were using saucers and bowls.

"Dear, you shouldn't be doing that," Widow Rogers whispered in a childlike voice as Hannah passed. "Gavrila told everyone to leave the dishes and help with a signature quilt. She said we can always do them later."

"I know, but since I'm not making a square on the quilt, I might as well do dishes." Hannah leaned toward the tiny woman, who had spent the morning moving from chair to chair, leaning on her cane.

"I wouldn't mind helping you out." Alamo Rogers raised from where he'd been squatting next to his mother. The man had to be near forty, but there was something very boyish about him. Maybe it was his fragile size, or maybe the habit he had of touching his face and hair as if constantly checking to see if he needed grooming.

"No, really." Hannah smiled, trying to be polite. "I can manage."

Alamo glanced at his mother, then took half the plates, as though Hannah's objections had been silently overruled.

Hannah skirted the huge circle of women huddled around the fireplace. They were all talking of things she didn't understand, crops and church needs. Each sewed on a square Gavrila planned to put together for Ford and Hannah's wedding quilt. Hannah didn't want a quilt. By the time it was finished, she'd be gone. She noticed Gavrila made all the decisions of color and size without once asking her brother or his wife for their opinions.

Before disappearing into the kitchen, she searched the sea of faces until she found Ford. Since they'd returned from the cave, he'd made a point of staying half a room away whenever possible. She knew she'd hurt him, but could think of nothing to say, even if they had gotten a few moments alone to talk. He looked as miserable as she. He didn't seem to join in the conversations with the men much more than she did with the women. She'd noticed he went out for more wood every hour and seemed to stay away longer each time. The last time he'd returned there had been a dusting of snow on his hair and shoulders.

The realization that Ford hadn't asked for this situation any more than she had washed over her. Two days ago he'd probably been a happy man living alone out here in his beautiful canyon. Now he had a houseful of people he didn't have three words to say to and a wife who wouldn't let him touch her. To make matters worse, she couldn't seem to keep her hands off him and touched him whenever she pleased. Add the fact that she was a thief. Besides which, they both knew she'd be dead soon to all in the room.

Hannah dropped her armful of dishes into the water and began her chore. Alamo stood silently beside her, waiting for each wet plate she handed him. If only she could wash up the mess she was in as easily as she could clean up the kitchen.

Alamo crossed the room with the first clean load. Hannah was thankful he didn't seem to be a talker. His mother must have taken very seriously the battle cry that had been shouted during the Texas revolution, for she certainly remembered the Alamo when she named her children.

"There you two are!" Gavrila's voice startled Hannah, and Alamo almost dropped the stack of plates he was carrying.

Gavrila hurried into the room as if she needed to stand between the two of them. "Put those plates down, Alamo Rogers. Do you want the other men to see you helping out in the kitchen?"

"I really don't much care one way or the other," he answered in a tone void of all emotion. "Work's work, when it needs doing, and Mrs. Colston looked like she could use the help."

"Well, I need you for something more important, so drop that dish towel."

He did as ordered, but the wrinkling of his thin eyebrows told Hannah he wasn't happy about being dictated to.

Gavrila didn't seem to notice his displeasure. "I need that large basket from the back of my buggy. My brother informs me it is getting colder and we should be starting home. So once more, he's ending my party. I'll have to take the quilt home in a hundred pieces and sew on it myself."

"I thought this was their party?" Alamo nodded toward Hannah.

"Well, of course it is, silly, but someone has to take charge. Now fetch my basket."

Hannah could see Alamo's indecision. He seemed to dislike being ordered around, but he wasn't a man to cause a scene.

"Thanks for helping out." Hannah tried to make it easier on the poor man. "I can handle it from here, and we must do all we can to speed my new sister-in-law on her way."

Alamo's gaze met hers. A smile twitched at the corner of his mouth, telling Hannah he understood her meaning. With a quick wink only she could see, he disappeared out the back door.

Hannah suppressed a giggle. Despite his thinning hair and slim frame, she found the shy Alamo charming.

Gavrila folded her arms and leaned against the counter. "I've been so busy I haven't had time to talk with you. You wouldn't believe all the things I had to do to organize this party."

Hannah noticed her new sister-in-law loved listing all she'd accomplished and all she was about to achieve to anyone who would listen. "You've already told me all you've done this morning," Hannah said, hoping to be spared another listing. But no such luck.

Gavrila saw herself as the busiest person on earth, and everyone else's lives were so dull and slow by comparison, that she must constantly remind them of that fact. Which is what she did while Hannah washed another pan of dishes.

Hannah reasoned her sister-in-law's next favorite activity was planning lists for the rest of the world to follow. When she began giving Hannah several suggestions for improvements that must be made on the place, in order of importance, of course, Hannah stopped listening. She wasn't about to change even the placement of furniture in Ford's house. No matter what Gavrila said, this was not Hannah's home—now or ever.

Gavrila was still talking when Ford placed his hand on Hannah's shoulder. He turned her gently toward him, not seeming to hear his sister only a few feet away. "You've chapped your hands," he whispered to Hannah as he opened her soap-covered fists.

With a damp towel, he dried her hands gently, then ran one finger over the line of calluses at the top of her palm. For a second she noticed his brows pull together in question, but he didn't say a word.

Hannah could still see the anger in his eyes, but he was playing by the marriage rules they'd agreed on. Touching her in public. Being the loving husband.

"It doesn't matter," she answered as his first two fingers continued to circle her palm.

"It does matter, darlin'," he answered and glanced at Gavrila, then back to Hannah. "I didn't plan on you having to clean your first day of marriage. You've done a month's worth of dishes this morning."

Gavrila patted the dish towel as if it would be too much for her to actually pick one up. "We planned to help," she rattled on, "but it wasn't at the top of my list. Other things are more important, brother." She surveyed the kitchen, which still needed an hour's work. "I was just trying to explain to this woman you married that if we had time we'd love to clean, but we must be going. It'll probably be snowing again before we get home."

Ford was stone quiet. If she'd expected him to encourage her to stay, she'd wait forever. He didn't take his attention from Hannah's hands as he continued to hold them in his.

"I should also inform you, dear brother, that I had to practically run Alamo Rogers out of this kitchen."

If Ford heard his sister, he paid no mind to her talk, and Hannah had to admire him for not even blinking when Gavrila was so blatantly trying to cause trouble.

Gavrila backed out of the kitchen, looking as though seeing her brother touching a woman disgusted her beyond words. She whirled to face the crowd. "Well, everyone, we must be going."

To Hannah's surprise, all the women tied off their stitches and the men grabbed coats so they could go ready the horses. They all seemed happy to be leaving, as if each had just been waiting for someone to make the first move. Women gathered up their platters and bowls and children while Gavrila folded the quilt and packed it away in a large basket Alamo had brought in.

"Thanks for coming," Ford managed to say as he left

Hannah's side and opened the door. Hannah had only known him for hours, but she could tell there was no feeling in his voice.

"Don't be a stranger!" Jinx Malone shouted to Hannah over all the others mumbling their best wishes and good-byes. "And if you have any questions about how to handle husbands, just stop by the post office. I'm there most afternoons. I reckon I've fallen in the marriage water enough times to know how to cross the bridge by now."

Hannah couldn't help but smile.

Alamo Rogers didn't say a word as he reached the doorway, but he shook her hand, letting Hannah know that among these strangers she'd found a friend.

Professor Combs cleared his throat so loudly, everyone in the room stopped talking. He was an old man with a white beard he kept trimmed neatly and hair he neglected totally. "Everyone stop!" he yelled. "My watch is missing. Someone must have stolen my watch!"

For only a fraction of a second Hannah's gaze met Ford's, and what she saw in his eyes made her feel like her blood froze solid. Ford accused her. Not with words, but with a look.

"Someone stole my watch!" Professor Combs yelled again, as if everyone hadn't heard him the first time. "I remember putting it back in my pants pocket not half an hour ago."

"Hush up, old man." An elderly lady waddled toward the professor. "You'd lose ever'thing, including your teeth, if I didn't glue them in with a flour-n-water paste ever' morning."

The woman patted at his pockets with her cane until she heard a clank, then pulled the watch from his vest. "There's your watch—not that it matters. The thing hasn't worked in five years. The watch doesn't care what time it is any more than you do, Professor."

Everyone in the room laughed. Everyone except Hannah. She'd seen Ford's eyes. If only for one moment, she'd known that he believed she'd stolen the old man's watch. All she'd ever be to him was a thief.

Ford leaned against the barn wall and watched the snow fall along his canyon. All the folks had left hours ago, but Hannah hadn't spoken a word to him. She'd cleaned the dishes while he moved the furniture back into place. When he could endure the silence no longer, he'd walked into the kitchen and found a plate ready for him. One plate on a table where he always ate alone.

At first he thought she was mad about what had happened in the cave. But she'd been willing to talk, even yell about that to him. Then he thought maybe she was upset about all the company, but she hadn't had a word of complaint when she'd cleaned up, even though she had reason to be angry about what his sister had done to them today.

He watched her from the window as she walked to the road and back. Her arms were wrapped tightly around her waist, and her legs paced in quick, angry steps. She was upset, but he had no idea why. She'd been acting as though she had read his mind when he heard the professor's watch was missing. His first thought was that everyone would suspect her if they knew she was a thief.

Then he thought surely she'd never steal while in Saints Roost. But who could expect a thief to be honest, even for a short time?

Ford couldn't just watch her pace. Yet he didn't have any idea what else to do. Most of the times in his life when he was hurt about something, he'd found it better to just be alone, so he allowed her room.

He worked over by the corral until late afternoon, when the snow started blowing like tiny slivers of ice against his face. Just as the sun was setting, Ford loaded his arms with wood and headed for the house. He had thought Hannah might be ready to explain. He'd even apologize, if necessary. Or maybe she'd yell at him and set down a few more rules. By now he didn't care; he just wanted her to talk to him. Ford had never known until today that having someone around not talking could be lonelier than being alone.

The house was spotlessly clean and silent when he entered. She'd swept the hearth and banked the fire for the night.

"Hannah?" Ford called.

No answer.

"Hannah!"

The living area was silent. He stormed to the kitchen and found a plate of cold meat and bread waiting at his table.

Panic chilled him worse than any winter wind could. She's left, he thought. That's why she was pacing off the distance to the road. While he'd been down at the corral, she'd packed and left, preferring to walk back to town in the snow rather than stay with him. The trip wouldn't be

easy with all the wagon ruts in the muddy road, but at
least she couldn't get lost. With only her bag to carry,
she could probably make it back to town in a little over
an hour.

He'd rushed to his bedroom, knowing he'd find the
old, tattered carpetbag missing. But when his hand
touched the knob, he was surprised to realize the door
was locked and bolted. He checked the other door to the
dressing area from the bedroom he'd slept in last night.
Locked.

When he passed his bed, Ford noticed Sneeze
stretched out like a fur pillow. Hannah was still here;
she'd never leave without the calico.

"Get off my bed," he grumbled at the cat.

Sneeze made no effort to move and Ford didn't push
him off the bed. He just sat down beside the animal and
stroked the fur as he tried to think.

Part of Ford wanted to pound on the door and demand
she come out. Was this the way it was going to be for the
next month? He didn't want her to work like a hired
hand around the place and disappear behind a locked
door as soon as she could each night. He owed her more
than that, but he'd promised to stay out of her way when
they were alone. She seemed to be making sure he kept
that promise.

Ford rambled about the house for a time, then pulled
on his coat and walked outside, strolling to the edge of
the canyon before slowing. Usually he loved the way the
sun turned all the colors of wet rock to diamonds at sunset. But tonight he didn't see the beauty. Part of him
wanted to scream that he didn't want this woman here in

the first place and he'd be glad when she was gone. He wished he could say that he didn't care why she was mad at him this time. What difference did it make? In a month she'd be out of his life and he could live in peace again. All that would remain of her would be a headstone bearing her name.

But another part of him needed to know the reason behind her actions. He'd never thought himself good at understanding people, but he couldn't even get a grip on the problems in this marriage. Be it based on a lie or not, they were bound together—if only for a month.

The sun disappeared, turning the canyon walls into layers of gray and black. The wind died to a low moan, echoing off the walls and whirling the final few wisps of snow through the air. Indians who camped from time to time in the canyon told Ford that twisters build and form along the miles of canyon wall. They'd said the "crying wind" whirls onto flat land about the spot where Saints Roost was built. One old native even said the wind would turn angry and destroy the town someday, but no one believed the tales.

Ford turned and headed back toward the house, deciding he'd never understood women any better than he did the weather in this land. They seemed about as predictable as a tornado.

Just as he reached the edge of the barn, he heard Hannah calling his name.

"Over here, Hannah." The light snow made it hard for him to tell where she was in the darkness.

"Ford!" she called again. "I can't find Sneeze."

"Where are you?" The wind seemed to be whirling her voice around him.

"Here." She moved from the shadows on the far side of the barn. "Do you think Sneeze ran away?"

He could hear the fear in her voice. "No," he said, wishing he believed his own words. "He was in the house a while ago."

"Are you sure? He must have had a terrible day."

Join the crowd, Ford thought. He'd seen the children chasing the huge calico several times that morning, but most cats put an end to any teasing when they got tired of it. "Maybe he's in the barn."

Hannah moved past him, running toward the side door of the barn. "I've looked everywhere inside." She had on the nightshirt and robe he'd given her. The breeze caught her hem.

He thought of ordering her nightclothes tomorrow, but he kind of liked her wearing his. She certainly looked different in them. With the wind pulling at the cotton, he saw the outline of her long, slender body beneath the layers of clothing.

"Did you search the room I slept in?" Ford shouted, trying to clear his mind of the way she looked.

"Yes," she answered as she fought with the heavy door. "Once before I took my bath and again a few minutes ago. He's gone."

They walked every foot of the barn and found nothing but two milk cows, a dozen chickens, four horses, and countless doves along the top rafters. Next they searched the open space between the barn and the house, then the land between the house and the canyon. Nothing.

As they strolled back to the house, Ford tried to sound reassuring. "Don't worry. He'll come home. We'll leave the kitchen window open enough for him to climb in. You know what they say, no one owns a cat. They just decide to live with you." He could tell Hannah was near tears.

"Sneeze is all I have. He's been with me since my mother died when I was twelve. He thinks he has to go everywhere I go."

Ford wished he could reach out and hold her, but she'd set the rules. No touching in private.

He held the door for her as they entered. When he turned, deciding after this morning he'd be wise to lock his house, Hannah let out a cry of joy.

Glancing over his shoulder, Ford saw the cat spread out on a blanket by the rocker. Hannah ran over and knelt in front of the animal, hugging him wildly.

Sneeze looked disinterested in the exchange, but Ford's hand was shaking for the first time in his life as he threw the bolt across the door. He'd lived twenty-five years and no one had ever been so glad to see him.

Hannah left the cat to his nap and smiled as she stood. "Thanks for helping me look."

Ford's knuckles whitened on the doorknob as he fought to keep from moving toward her. "I'm just glad you're finally talking to me."

Hannah looked down at her hands. "I know how you see me, and nothing can change the way you feel. But there's no reason we can't at least speak to one another when we're alone."

Ford had no idea what she was talking about, and de-

cided if he asked he'd only be bringing whatever made
her mad to the surface again. "I wouldn't mind having
someone to sit down to dinner with at night, if that's not
breaking the agreement too much."

"All right."

"And you don't have to work so hard around the
place. Not that I don't appreciate it."

"I don't mind. I'm used to hard work."

He thought of saying that he didn't think thieving
would be all that hard of a job, but he didn't think she'd
take to teasing.

"Well, I'll turn in now," he moved toward his bedroom door. He wasn't the least bit tired, but he couldn't
just stand in the middle of the room staring at her as if
he'd never seen a woman before. "Tomorrow morning
I'll take you up to the school."

"I'm not sure I'll sleep tonight, worrying about what
to teach in the morning. I only went to school for a short
while. We moved around a great deal, and after Mother
died there was no time."

Ford knew he was fishing for something to delay bedtime, but he didn't want to go into his room alone and lie
awake thinking about the way she'd looked in the wind
with her hair blowing around her and the nightshirt and
robe pulled tight against her. "Why don't you start with a
story. I had a teacher who used to read us stories, and I
think that was my favorite time in school."

Hannah opened her palms. "I have no books."

"But I do." Ford smiled. "I've been collecting books
all my life." He crossed to the windows to two long
chests. Lifting the lid on the first one, he smiled. "I've

got everything from Edgar Allan Poe to fairy tales around here somewhere." He shoved several books out of the way. "I'm guessing you don't want Keats or Shelley. Ah, here we are, the brothers Grimm fairy tales. My mother used to read the tales in German, but I ordered this rather questionable translation last year. I also have a rather fine collection of Hans Christian Andersen stories."

"Would you read me one?"

Ford's eyebrows raised in surprise. He'd spent many a winter night reading aloud to himself just to hear the sound of a voice, but to read to someone else? "Which one?"

Hannah didn't want to admit that she'd never heard any of the stories by Andersen, so she said, "Any one. How about your favorite."

Ford thumbed through the book. "Well, I like 'Little Claus and Big Claus,' but the children will probably like 'The Ugly Duckling' the best."

Hannah curled up in a corner of the couch, listening, while Ford folded into his rocker by the fire. His voice was strong and the words he read seemed to tumble out before them, building a story.

When he finished the story, he looked up at Hannah and closed the book.

"Thank you," she whispered. "No one has ever read me a story like that before."

"I'll read you one every night, if you like." Ford shifted in his chair.

"I'd like that very much." Hannah stood and gathered

Sneeze in her arms. She was at her door before she turned. "One more thing."

Ford held the book tightly in his hands as he forced himself not to move from the chair.

"When I'm dead next month, would you mind greatly if I was buried in that quilt your sister is making us?"

Ford's rich laughter filled the space between them. "Of course not. I'll tell Gavrila you loved the quilt so much you couldn't bear to be separated from it. She'll be happy and I'll be rid of the thing."

Hannah disappeared behind her door without another word.

Ford rocked back in his chair, picturing how proud Gavrila would be that her quilt was used to line the casket. She'd never know it would be the only thing in the coffin.

The smile left his face when he heard Hannah push the bolt across her door. She didn't have to lock herself in. He would never bother her. There were a hundred invisible locked doors keeping them apart. The little bolt across her door would do no good if Ford thought she wanted him. But she didn't, just like every other woman he'd ever met in his life. The ugly duckling might turn into a swan, but a hundred years could pass and Ford Colston still wouldn't be handsome.

❖ *Chapter 8*

THE AIR WAS crisp and newborn as Ford and Hannah crossed the distance between Canyon's Rim and town. Except for a few sturdy mesquite bushes and yucca plants, the terrain was so flat and endless Hannah thought she could see the earth curve far in the distance. Low clouds banked to the north, looking like a blue mountain range, with the sky watery gray above and earth almost colorless beneath. There was a loneliness about this land, a loneliness that must seep into the very hearts of the people who lived here.

Ford hadn't said more than a few words to her since dawn, but Hannah didn't mind. Her thoughts were focused on how she could act the part of a schoolteacher for a month. She knew she couldn't read the stories as smoothly as Ford had, and her writing needed work. When Hannah was a child, her mother had always been content to let her draw on any paper they found and never encouraged her to practice reading or writing.

"Don't be nervous." Ford broke the silence as they saw the outline of town. "My guess is, after having Gavrila for a few weeks, the students would love anyone."

"Thanks." She shrugged.

"No," he quickly added, "I didn't mean it like it sounded. You'll do fine. After all, there are only about twelve or thirteen students, best as I remember. How much trouble could a dozen children be?"

Hannah didn't even want to guess. She'd said she was the schoolteacher to get a ride, she'd never thought she'd have to prove the lie true.

"Fellow tried to open a saloon in Saints Roost a while back." Ford seemed to be talking to help her relax. "The whole town got upset and ran him off. We've been using the little building he built behind White and Rosenfield's store for the schoolhouse ever since."

"Wonder if he left a few bottles. I could use a drink about now." Hannah was kidding, but the look on Ford's face told her he believed her request.

Something snapped inside her. If he was going to believe the worst about her, she might as well prove him correct. "Don't tell me you don't drink?"

"No." Ford seemed to be forcing his voice to be conversational. "Do you?"

"I've been known to down a few," she lied. The truth was, she'd cleaned up after so many drunks in the café that even the smell of whiskey made her ill. "Sleeping all day and drinking all night, now that's the life."

"You aren't planning on drinking while you're here, are you?" He glanced from the road to her. His dark blue-gray eyes were troubled but his jaw was rock hard, as though he'd face any problem head-on.

"What!" Hannah acted shocked. "Another rule? First I can't steal and now you're ending my drinking. Is there no fun in this town? Next thing you know, I won't be allowed to gamble."

"I'd think you could stay honest and sober for a month." He relaxed his grip on the reins, guessing that she might be teasing. "As for gambling, you'd have to have a partner in that crime, and there would be none here. So no poker, Mrs. Colston. The gamble we took with this marriage was chance enough."

Hannah raised her chin. "It's a lot to ask, Brother Colston."

He pulled the wagon behind White's store. "I realize that, darlin'."

Several people were milling around, doing their best to act as if they weren't watching the newlyweds.

Ford jumped from the wagon and raised his arms to Hannah. As he lifted her to the ground, he brought her body close to his, so close her dress brushed against his wool jacket. When her feet touched the ground, he didn't immediately release her. The feel of her so near brought an unexpected warmth to the chilly day. He couldn't hide his smile.

"I'll see you tonight, darlin'," he said, loud enough for several people to hear.

Her gloved hand cupped the side of his face. It felt good to touch him, after spending the morning avoiding getting close. She could feel the warmth of him even through the glove. A warmth that was all man and not granite. Hannah knew she was being bold, but she stood on her toes and kissed him on the cheek. She felt his sudden intake of breath as her lips touched his skin.

"Don't be late," she said, louder than needed for his benefit. "I miss you already."

For a moment she looked in his eyes and wished their words were true, but she was not the kind of woman he would choose to marry. He needed a woman who was dainty ribbons and proper lace, and Hannah knew all she'd ever be was unbleached cotton. She stepped away and moved into the one-room schoolhouse, thinking she could still smell the odor of whiskey in the wood.

The room was smaller than Ford's bedroom back at Canyon's Rim. It reminded Hannah of a double-wide railroad car. Wide desks made for two students lined each side, with an aisle in the center and smaller walking spaces beneath the windows on either side. A huge teacher's desk stood in the front, with books piled a foot high on one corner. There was a chalkboard behind the desk, and two pictures were nailed above it—the first of the signing of the Declaration of Independence and the other of Robert E. Lee. A Franklin stove sitting in a square sandbox burned in one corner. It was just enough to take the chill out of the air.

Hannah smiled. The room was perfect—except for one thing. Gavrila was standing behind the teacher's desk with a ruler in one hand and a little boy's palm in the other.

"I'm tired of telling you, Ulysses!" Gavrila screamed. "You can wipe your feet before you come in, or I'll blister you every morning of your life!"

She raised the ruler, and the little boy of about nine who stood before her closed his eyes and tried to stretch as far away from the pain as he could.

"Wait!" Hannah startled everyone in the room with her yell. She forgot all about the impression she must be making and stormed down the center aisle.

Gavrila lowered the ruler and frowned at her sister-in-law, now only a desk-length away.

"Couldn't we just have . . . Ulysses sweep up?" Hannah carefully lowered the book she'd brought and slowly pulled off the huge gloves Ford had loaned her this morning.

Gavrila pointed the ruler at Hannah. "I realize I may not have had the year of higher schooling you did to get this job, and I have no children of my own, but that doesn't mean I don't know what's good for them. I advise half the people in this town how to raise their brats."

"I'm sure you do." Hannah moved to the edge of the desk. "And I really want to thank you for having been willing to cut into your busy schedule and teach this class until Ford could go to Dallas and hire me." She took the outstretched ruler from Gavrila's hand. The woman hesitated as if debating a battle, but when Hannah's grip tightened, she released her weapon.

Hannah turned to the other students who'd been filling the classroom. "I think we should all give Miss Gavrila a big hand for the fine job she did."

Every student except Ulysses clapped, but the applause was pitiful. Gavrila pressed her lips together in a smile and took a little bow.

"Your new teacher is right." She nodded toward Hannah, closing her eyes as if not wanting to even see the woman she was acknowledging. "I do have a million things I must be doing. But don't worry, children. I'll be back every few days to check on things around here. As the sister of one of the school-board members, it is the least I can do. I'll be watching and advising Miss Hannah."

Hannah didn't miss the fact that she'd refused to introduce her by her married name, but Hannah didn't mind. It seemed more natural to be called Miss Hannah.

Ulysses groaned from behind Gavrila. All the other children stood at attention, as if refusing to move until she left. Hannah almost felt sorry for her sister-in-law as she walked down the center aisle without a single student saying good-bye. At the back door she turned and yelled, "You'll have to burn chips for the rest of the year! I used up all the allotment of coal already."

When the door closed behind her, Hannah took a deep breath. "What are chips?"

All the children started giggling at once. The laughter rippled into great waves. For a moment Hannah thought they were going to become ill. Then Ulysses took her hand and tugged her toward the Franklin. "Cow chips, miss." He pointed to the round, dried chips stacked beside the stove. "The cows are kind enough to leave them in the field for us. When they dry, Pa pulls a wagon through the pasture and all us kids run along tossing them in the wagon bed. Course you want to be real careful not to grab and pitch one that's still warm and a-steamin'."

The very walls seemed to be shaking with the sound of the children's laughter now. Hannah tried not to join them. "Thank you, Ulysses."

"And another thing, miss. They burn real good, with a hot blue flame. They don't jump sparks out near as bad as wood and don't smell at all like . . ."

"Thank you, Ulysses." Hannah pointed with her hand for him to sit down.

The boy looked like he wanted to add more, but decided not to push his luck. He took a seat next to another boy about the same age but with light, almost white, hair compared to Ulysses's black curls. The two nine-year-olds immediately began pushing and poking as each claimed his own space on the bench.

Hannah walked in front of her new desk and stared out at all the students. Eighteen. More than Ford had said, and no more than any three of them looked the same age.

"I'm Mrs. Colston." Hannah said her name slowly, letting her mouth adjust to the sound. "But you can call me Miss Hannah if you like. I thought we'd start by letting each one of you tell me your names."

They all talked at once.

She raised her hand. "One at a time, please." She looked at the two boys on her left, who had finally declared a truce. "Since I already know Ulysses, let's begin with him."

Ulysses stood and said his name as he must have been taught, proud and loud.

The boy next to him was a little shy, but rose and told Hannah his name was Rip.

"After the famous Texas Ranger, Rip Ford?" she guessed.

"No," he replied. "My ma seen 'R.I.P.' carved on a stone once and thought it a right pretty name."

Fighting down a smile, she managed to say, "Next."

The Smith children stood as if on silent command, all six of them. They looked very much alike, with reddish hair and button noses. The oldest was dressed in new clothes, but the garments of the others looked progressively more worn. The youngest didn't even have shoes, but wore long wool socks that were folded back over her knees.

Hannah met the Burns brothers, whose every movement seemed to indicate that they'd rather be anywhere else but in school, and the Madison twins behind them looked much the same. A tiny child named Millie sat next to her older sister, Anna. Anna did all the talking for the little one, explaining that Millie didn't like to say much. Her mother had told her when she turned five she could go to school, so last week, when Millie turned five in mid-January, her mother packed her off to be educated.

Lilly and Ruth were in front of Anna. Both were almost full grown and told Hannah that they had been acting as teacher's helpers all year.

Hannah finished the introductions, then gave the fairy-tale book to Lilly. "If you'll read the story, I'll draw on the board." The children quieted as Lilly read. They leaned forward in their desks and watched Hannah draw a sketch of the pond with a line of ducks floating in it. By the time the story was over, she'd won not only their attention, but their hearts as well.

With the older girls' help, the rest of the morning

moved by smoothly. They were happy to explain how the subjects rotated around the room, from easiest lesson to hardest, so that by the time the last was working he'd had a bit of review on every level. While younger ones worked at their desks, they could listen to the lessons of what was to come for them in the future. There seemed to be a circle to the learning that Hannah had never noticed as a child. The final lesson for the brightest was to teach the beginning to the youngest.

When Hannah dismissed them for lunch, they all ran to the back and grabbed tin pails made from syrup cans. Out came colorful napkins covering huge biscuits stuffed with ham and sausage left over from breakfast and fruit stored in cellars since early fall. The Burns brothers both had baked sweet potatoes, which they peeled and ate like apples, and thick slices of bread covered with butter.

Hannah smiled at the sudden chatter that filled the room. Hunger also gripped her, but she could wait until dinner. Two meals a day was enough. After all, that was more than she'd had in total the week she'd been on the run. Those days had been hard, moving from shadow to shadow, trying to find water and food . . . trying to stay warm . . . trying to stay out of sight. After two good nights' sleep at Ford's house, those days seemed far away. He might not be much on conversation, but he'd seen that she had plenty to eat and that her box was full of wood for the fire each night.

Moving to the metal dipper that hung above a pail of water, Hannah drank. She guessed as soon as the biscuits were finished everyone would be fighting over the one dipper.

The children quieted suddenly when the door opened and cold air filtered in from behind the rack of coats. Ford stood in the opening, looking huge among the students.

He cleared his throat and removed his wide-brimmed hat. For a moment he stood silent, taking in the room, the children, the drawing she'd done on the board. "I thought I might be able to have a word with the teacher."

Hannah had to laugh. He was acting so proper.

"Of course," she said, nodding toward Lilly and Ruth, then following Ford outside.

The cold wind twirled her into his arms, and he held her against his side as they moved the short distance around White's store and across the street to the post office.

"What is it?" She knew by the speed at which they were walking that Ford's visit was more than just a noonday call. She suddenly wished she'd taken the time to grab the coat she'd worn this morning. But he had such purpose about him that she simply snuggled closer to him and tried to match his long steps.

He slowed as he reached the plank porch. "When Jinx rode down for the mail this morning, there was a man at the station looking for you. She said he was real worried that he'd lost track of you. Kept describing you to everyone and saying he was worried about his niece Hannah. Until he talked to Smith last night in one of the drinking establishments near where the railroad line ends, he'd about given up hope."

"No one's looking for me," Hannah lied.

"Well, Jinx brought him along with her."

"Are you sure he's looking for *me?*" Hannah froze, almost causing Ford to trip.

He stopped and turned to face her. "Is there anything I should know? This wouldn't be a husband come looking for you, or another customer of your robbery business?"

"No!" She felt as if her world were crumbling again, just as it had the morning in the café when she'd seen Jude shot. Jude's killers had found her; somehow one of the three tracked her all the way to Saints Roost. They must kill her; she was the only one who'd witnessed the murder. "No one knows where I am." She tried hard to believe her words. "There is no one."

"Well, someone sure does." Ford sounded angry. "If he's the law, there's not much I can do."

Ford reached for the doorknob, and Hannah grabbed his hand. "No," she cried. "Don't open the door. It could mean your life."

"What . . ." Before Ford could finish, someone pulled the door from the inside, and Ford and Hannah almost fell into the post office.

"Well, it's about time you two got here!" Jinx bellowed. "I'd think you'd be in more of a hurry to see your uncle, Hannah."

"Uncle?" Hannah turned as an old man shuffled toward her. He was thin, with rugged features and a shaking hand. Though clean shaven and dressed in a suit that must have been cut for another, she knew who he was the moment he stepped from the shadows. Zachery Jess Noble, the drunk who had hung around the bar in Fort

Worth every night since Hannah could remember. Half the time he'd only have enough money to drink, then he'd beg meals from her over on the eating side of Hickory's place. She'd never seen him looking quite as clean or sober before.

"Hello, dear, dear Hannah." He moved toward her as though he were planning to hug her. When she edged closer to Ford, Zachery settled for a pat on her shoulder. "I thought I'd lost you in Dallas, child."

A thousand questions came to mind, but Hannah couldn't ask them with everyone watching. If this old drunk found her, so could three killers. "Welcome to town, Uncle." She almost choked on the words. "I guess you've already met everyone, including my husband, Ford."

Zachery nodded and smiled, first toward Jinx, then at Ford. "Yes, this kind angel brought me here and told me you'd married. I was asking every man, woman, and child if they'd seen you."

Hannah had to get Zachery alone. As a drunk he was usually quiet, but she didn't know what he'd be like sober. "Come, let me show you my schoolhouse, then we'll sit down and visit."

"I'll rewarm the coffee while you're gone," Jinx yelled from somewhere behind the counter. "Ford'll give me a hand."

Zachery tipped his hat toward Ford, who didn't look at all interested in leftover coffee, and followed Hannah outside. She stormed ahead of him until she was across the street and behind the first building, then turned on him like an angry bobcat. "What are you doing here, you old drunk?"

Zachery waved at her to lower her voice. "I came to help."

"Like hell you did!" Hannah could never remember being so angry. "The truth. What's in this for you, and why are you following me?"

Rubbing his chin as though suddenly missing his usually scraggly growth of whiskers, Zachery asked as if he had a right to know, "You love this man you married, Hannah girl?"

"That's none of your business." Hannah wouldn't be put off. He hadn't cared about her all the years he'd been hanging around Fort Worth, so why should he show any interest now? "What are you doing here?"

Zachery opened his mouth as if starting to dodge the question again, then surrendered. "All right. I had to find you. I know you're running because you saw Jude killed."

"How could you know that?" She began to shake with fright. No one had been in the bar that morning. No one but Jude, Hickory, her, and the killers. "Is Hickory alive? Did he live to tell?"

"No," the old man shook his head. "I watched them shoot him several more times in the stomach just to see him jump."

Zachery seemed to be following her logic and answered her unspoken question. "Because I was asleep beneath the bar. You know, along the far wall where the lights never reach? I can store a pillow without worrying about someone stepping in my face while I'm napping."

"Get on with it." She was considering screaming if he didn't answer her questions.

"Well, I saw you run out. Then I heard why they killed Jude, and how they were going to have to kill you, on account of you being the only witness."

"But you . . ." Hannah thought about what she was about to say. Zachery would never be a witness, not even if he saw a man murdered. Even if he did decide to tell the law, no sheriff would believe him. "Why'd you follow me?"

"I didn't have nowhere else to go." Zachery's puffy eyes began to tear. "I was so scared I didn't know what to do. When I crawled out back of the saloon I saw your shadow and decided to follow you, 'cause I knew you'd be running as far away from the murderers as you could get. Whiskey's flooded my brain for too many years. I couldn't think of any plan but following you."

"Why didn't you let me know that you were behind me?" Hannah wasn't sure she believed him. He could somehow be linked with the killers. Maybe they were paying him to move in first and put her off guard.

"I thought if they did catch you, I didn't want to be within blood-spattering distance. I kept up with you until you met up with that husband of yours in Dallas, then I couldn't catch the train fast enough to follow." His hand shook as he waved it over his forehead. "I climbed in a boxcar taking an old man home for burying. While I was in the car, I made use of the box of clothes and shaving stuff traveling with him. It wasn't stealing, Hannah, 'cause he wasn't going to use them again."

"That's fine. I'm glad you cleaned up, but you can't

stay here." The last thing Hannah needed was a drunk visiting her and her temporary husband. Ford, a roomful of kids, and Gavrila were enough to handle.

"I don't have any place else to go. My mind's been floating in whiskey for too long to think. I can't think of what to do. All I know is my best chance will be to stay with you. You're the only person who's been kind to me in years."

Hannah frowned. She felt sorry for him, but she was having enough trouble keeping herself alive; she couldn't adopt an old drunk.

"I won't be any trouble. I won't even drink but a little. I know you don't think much of me, Hannah, but I was from a good family back before the war. I can act real nice if need be. I wasn't always like this." He spread his fingers, trying to hold them still. "I once had a profession and a family."

She wanted to ask what had happened, but she didn't dare. Over the years she'd seen many like Zachery, all with stories that could break your heart in the telling.

"No," Hannah answered. "I can't."

Zachery nodded. "I understand. I'm happy to see you married and settled. No matter what you might think, you matter to me, and I'd like to know that you're loved and happy. I'll just go tell Jinx that I ain't your uncle and she can take me back to the station."

"No!" Hannah reached over and grabbed his arm. "If you tell her that, she'll think we're both mad. A man usually knows his own kin, and a niece should be able to recognize her uncle. If you say anything, they're sure to think something's wrong. And this is one place you can't just walk out of without half the town noticing."

"Then I can stay?"

"Only for a day or two until I can think of something."

"I could get sick and die if it solves the problem." His huge eyebrows wiggled up and down with hope.

No, I'm already planning that exit, Hannah thought. "We'll think of something less final. Maybe you could have to leave on business. Until then . . . no drinking, and don't tell anyone anything about me. This isn't a town like Fort Worth. These people have rules like you wouldn't believe. They don't allow drinking, gambling, or any other sins."

"Well, child, then I won't have to pretend to die; I'm dead already and gone to the pit of hell."

Hannah smiled. "Come along, Uncle Zachery—it's too cold to stand around outside talking. We need to get back to the others. But one warning—if you let me down, I'll boil you in Jinx's leftover coffee."

"I won't," he whispered. "I swear."

Chapter 9

F ORD WALKED OUT onto the porch of his sister's house. The wind had grown colder, whipping around between the few buildings of Saints Roost as though chasing its tail. He hardly noticed. His mood was darker than any storm the pesky wind might be promising.

He'd spent the afternoon listening to Hannah's Uncle Zachery telling war stories, when Ford could think of a hundred things that needed doing back at his ranch. He'd had little experience with what his father loved to refer to as dyed-in-the-wool sinners, but he'd be willing to bet Uncle Zachery got about as close to the truth as he did to a bath in winter.

Jinx Malone was the only one who never seemed to tire of Zachery's stories. The one thing Ford found likable about the man was Gavrila's total hatred of him. From the moment she'd been introduced to him, she'd treated the old man as if he were made of rotting rodents. She alternated between holding her nose and voicing her displeasure. The fact that Uncle Zachery took her open hatred as kind teasing irritated Gavrila into near hysteria and made Ford laugh aloud.

"Hiding out?" A soft voice came from behind him.

Ford swung around and almost collided with Hannah. She jumped back, and once more he saw her hands dart protectively to her face before she could stop the action.

He took a step aside, allowing her plenty of room.

"I'm sorry I startled you," she said as she lowered her arms.

"No." Ford wished he could make her relax around him. He guessed it was his size that frightened her. Something about him had alarmed every woman who came within ten feet of him for as long as he could remember. "I thought I'd go upstairs to a small office I keep in one of the extra rooms, but after being cooped up all evening I needed air." He took a deep breath and switched to the truth. "You're right. I am hiding out."

Hannah moved to the railing. "I don't blame you."

"Is that man really your uncle?" Ford leaned his hip into the railing only a few inches from where her hand gripped the wood.

"Would it matter? Maybe he's as much my uncle as you are my husband." Hannah didn't want to talk about Zachery. If she did, she'd have to tell Ford too much about why she'd left Fort Worth. Knowing Harwell's men had killed Jude and were willing to kill her, Hannah realized they might murder Ford if they thought he knew anything. She didn't want Zachery here any more than Ford did, but she couldn't just turn the poor man out when he thought she was his only hope for survival. After talking with him, she wasn't sure he could survive on his own.

"No." Ford lifted his arms and grabbed the top of the

porch frame. "It doesn't matter who he really is, I guess. He's probably as real as the rest of us in this charade. Just promise not to leave him here when you disappear. With all the grief of your funeral, I don't think I could take Uncle Zachery living with me also."

Hannah laughed softly and poked him in the ribs. "Already critical of my relatives, are you?"

Ford lifted his hands in surrender. "No, darlin', I would be the last person to complain, after what you have to endure with my sister. I tried everything I could think of to talk our way out of having to come to dinner tonight, but she only hears what she wants to. In the end, she informed me that she'd already told several folks we were coming to dinner this evening, so it was settled."

"She's not so bad," Hannah said, trying to be nice.

"Neither was the Civil War," he added. "I'll have to give her one compliment, though. That was the first meal I've eaten at her house, when she didn't have Molly in, that I could finish. It was actually very good."

Hannah wanted to say thank you, because she'd cooked most of it, but Gavrila had taken full credit for the dinner when she'd served the soup.

Ford gently placed his hand over Hannah's on the railing. "Just in case someone's watching from the windows," he explained.

Hannah nodded. She wanted to say that she didn't mind. She'd accidentally touched him every time she could all evening. He might be just holding up appearances, but she found it thrilling to touch him. Her mother told her once that the Gypsies can read people by touching just their hands. The good in a person can be felt with even a slight brush of the palm. Hannah moved her jaw, remembering the last blow Jude had given her. She'd felt the evil that had been in him. She must have been a fool not to have seen it before he asked her to marry him. But before that night, he'd been just one of the hundreds of men who came to Hickory's for a meal and a few drinks. He seemed no worse or better than the others.

"Cold?" Ford asked, moving closer.

"A little," she answered, thinking how Jude's memory always left her feeling cold and empty inside. For a short time she'd believed in a dream. She'd thought that maybe there was more for her than there had been for her mother. But now she knew she'd be lucky to have what her mother had—a place in the shadows to hide until she died. "I've been cold since I stepped off the train. I don't think I've ever been this far north in winter."

"It's getting late. Maybe we'd better say good night to the others and go home." Ford had been wanting to say those words for two hours.

"I'm ready." Hannah didn't want to say anything, but the day had been exhausting, and she felt like she could sleep standing up if she was allowed to be still for three breaths' time. "Let's say farewell to the others and head for Canyon's Rim."

When they were loaded into the wagon ten minutes later, Ford was miserable and no longer cared if he went home tonight or not. Uncle Zachery had decided to go home with them, instead of taking Jinx Malone up on her offer to stay in the extra room off the post office where travelers sometimes spent the night between stages. He said he wanted to make sure his niece was happy, way out on a ranch.

The ride back to Canyon's Rim was silent, except for Zachery's rattling on about how much needed to be done in this part of the country. The only nice thing about Zachery being with them was that Hannah sat close to Ford. She'd probably think him terrible, but Ford enjoyed the feel of her leg against his and the way she brushed against him when the wagon rocked. He put his arm around her and welcomed the nearness as she rested against him. After several minutes, she stopped shivering and relaxed into his warmth. But Uncle Zachery never stopped talking.

Darkness had already claimed the ranch when they reached home. Ford let Zachery and Hannah out at the house and walked the team to the barn. He took his time bedding down the animals, knowing it would be awkward sleeping in the house. He had a feeling if Uncle Zachery even suspected that Hannah and he were sleeping in separate rooms, he'd tell everyone in town.

Ford patted the nose of the bay he'd said was Hannah's while she was here. "We may be bunk mates, old friend," Ford mumbled, "for I may be sleeping in the next stall."

The horse shook his head and breathed out a heavy sound that almost made Ford believe the bay understood.

"I'll have to give up my bed to Uncle Zachery, if he really is an uncle, and he'd be sure to notice if I slept on the couch. So that leaves the barn."

Ford hand-fed the horse more oats. "It'll be cold, but

I've slept in worse places. I remember when you were about all I owned a few years back and we were hauling buffalo bones for ten dollars a wagon load. I used to sleep under the wagon to keep thieves away. The settlers were usually honest enough and collected their own bones, but a few of those old buffalo hunters figured it was their right to steal my load, since they were the ones who slaughtered the herds in the first place."

The side door creaked and Ford turned around. Hannah was standing just inside the door.

"Do you always talk to your horse?"

"Yes," he answered, seeing no point in denying the obvious. "Don't you talk to Sneeze?"

Hannah smiled and took a step closer. "I guess so. I never really thought about it. Sneeze is like one of my family."

"So's the old bay," Ford said. "When I need a horse I have to depend on, I saddle him every time."

"Then why don't you give him a name?"

"A name wouldn't change how I feel about the horse. I've seen men give their mount some grand name, then ride the horse into the ground so bad they have to shoot him. I'd never do that to the bay."

"Didn't you say he was my horse for the time I'm here?" Hannah asked.

"Yes," Ford answered, very much aware that she'd moved within a few feet of him. He liked the way the fresh smell of her blended with the odor of hay.

"Well, then, while I'm here I'm going to give him a name." She touched the horse's nose. "I don't know what, but I'll think of something."

Ford thought of suggesting she think a little longer than she had with Sneeze, for that had to be about the dumbest name for a cat he'd ever heard. "Did you just come out to talk about names?"

"No." Hannah looked nervous. "Since Uncle Zachery arrived, I haven't had time to talk when I knew we were alone. I think it's very important that he think we're happily married."

"I agree." Ford lifted the light from the hook and waited for her to move ahead of him toward the door. "The way he talks, most of Saints Roost would know within hours if he suspected something."

Hannah opened the side door. "He already turned in for the night in your room. I told him if he was planning to have breakfast, he'd better take a bath before he goes to bed. He grumbled, but agreed."

"I guessed he'd take my bed." Ford had already thought their problem out. "I don't mind sleeping in the barn, I'll just follow you in and grab a few blankets."

"No." Hannah took his arm. "I think you should sleep in my room." She pulled him along toward the house. "It's safer. The hands will know something's wrong if they see you bedding down in the barn when they arrive in the morning."

"But where will you sleep if I take your room?"

Hannah's words were a whisper, but Ford heard them like a shout. "In the same room."

"But I thought you wanted a lock between us?"

"I do." Hannah realized she was more afraid of jeopardizing her safety than she was of Ford. "But it's very important that I be able to stay here a little longer.

Maybe even more important than my being safely locked away from you."

Ford hung the light on the outside hanger. The firelight from inside was enough to see the final few feet into the house. "You don't have to be afraid of me, Hannah. I would never hurt you. Even if my sister does think I'm half-wild sometimes. You have my word nothing will happen between us."

"I want more than your word," Hannah whispered. "I want your Colts when we enter the bedroom. Once inside, we'd better be very careful what we say. Uncle Zachery may be listening. If you make one move toward me, a shot is all he'll hear."

Ford couldn't believe she was so frightened of him. Had she really thought the little bolt he put on her door was all that kept him away from her bed last night? "You have my word; I'll not touch you. But if you also want my Colts, you may have them."

Hannah nodded and moved on into the house.

They walked silently across the room until they were almost directly in front of Uncle Zachery's door. "Well, darlin', we'd better call it a night," Ford said. "Tomorrow comes early."

She tried to laugh, but her voice sounded slightly tight to Ford. "Morning comes the same time every day, dear."

They moved to the master bedroom and closed the door. Inside, only the light of the small corner fireplace lit the room. For several seconds they stared at one another, as if not knowing what to do. Then Ford moved over near the armoire. He sat on the ladder-back chair and pulled off his boots.

Hannah tiptoed close and knelt at his side. She leaned over and brushed his ear with her words. "He's still in the dressing area, and the room has no lock except on the door going to the other bedroom."

"I'll correct that tomorrow," Ford promised as he started unbuttoning his shirt. "I can sleep on the floor by the door."

"No." Hannah lifted his Colt from the gun belt hanging on his chair. "I have another idea."

Ford watched as she moved to the other side of the bed and slipped off her dress and stockings. Then she crawled beneath the covers. He removed his clothes, feeling awkward that she was watching. He smiled, realizing she'd watched once before with a Colt in her hand. If she hadn't shot him then, maybe there was some hope for him making it through the night.

When he stepped to the other side of the bed, Hannah turned back just the first quilt. "You sleep between the quilts and I'll sleep a layer deeper. Then we should be safe."

Ford crawled into bed, thinking he was never worried about being safe. Stretching, he felt the gun a layer deeper at his side and decided he should give his safety a little thought. With her finger on the trigger, if she had a nightmare, she might tense and he'd be past tense.

Before he could say anything, Uncle Zachery opened the door of the dressing area. He looked out into their bedroom as if he were a landlord and had every right to nose into other people's bedrooms.

"You already in bed?"

Ford stretched his arm out and Hannah placed her head on his shoulder. To Zachery they must look like they were cuddled up together.

"Good night, Zachery," Ford grumbled, as if the old man had awakened him.

Zachery closed the door without another word, and Ford felt Hannah try to smother her giggles. He kissed her lightly on the forehead. "We pulled it off, darlin'."

She moved back to her own side of the bed.

Ford rolled to his side so he could see her. "You don't need the gun, Hannah," he whispered. "If you don't want me to touch you, I won't." He thought of adding that he might not touch her even if she wanted him to. It seemed to Ford that every time she'd touched him he'd fallen into her trap like some mindless soul. Ford had a will of his own. He decided he wasn't a man to give, or take, affection lightly. She might be heaven to kiss and hold now, but he had to think clearly. In a month she'd be gone, and he wasn't sure he wanted to live with memories. Maybe living with nothing was easier. He was at home with loneliness and could endure it.

She didn't answer or remove the gun. He lay on his back and listened to her breathing slow into sleep. He thought of reaching for the pistol and removing it, but he might startle her. So, even though he knew it was foolish, he lay next to a woman with a Colt in her hand.

Finally, a few hours before dawn, Ford fell asleep. He didn't know when he rolled over with his back to her, or when she'd cuddled against him with only one blanket between them. But he awoke before first light to find her arm around his waist and her cheek on his shoulder.

He slowly rolled over and she cuddled back against his side without waking up. Pulling the covers over her shoulder, he studied her face in the early light. She had high cheekbones and a rounded mouth that pouted slightly in sleep. Her lashes were long and dark against her pale skin. The hand that rested on his chest was well shaped, with long, thin fingers and lines of scratches across the back. The clean, wild smell of her surrounded him, and he thought he could stay in bed forever.

But they both had much to do. Gently, he lifted her hand and pressed her palm to his lips. "Hannah," he whispered. "Wake up."

She moved against him, pressing into his side.

He brushed the hair from her cheek and whispered again as he kissed her sleeping eyes, "Hannah."

When she didn't awaken, he let his lips trail along her face to her mouth. Tenderly, so he wouldn't startle her, he brushed a kiss across her lips.

She moaned again and rolled over, pressing her back to his side and pushing her hips against his thigh.

Ford closed his eyes and tried to decide if he was in heaven or hell.

Chapter 10 ❖

THE FIRST WEEK of Hannah's make-believe marriage passed in a blur of activity. She rose before dawn every morning and dressed while Ford was still asleep. Usually she managed to have breakfast ready about the time he finished shaving. They'd eat together at the little table in the kitchen and watch the sunrise. Sometimes, if she coached him, he'd tell her of his plans for the day. She always talked about the lessons the children would do.

Ford bought Dr. Stocking's old buggy and fixed it up for her to drive to school. It was big and roomy, with a cover to protect her and the smell of old leather to surround her as she rode. Gavrila's hired hand was always waiting for Hannah in town. He'd take care of the rig and the bay while she taught and have the buggy tied by the steps of the school when she finished. On the ride home, Hannah always stopped by one of the dugouts, or soddies, to pay a quick call on a parent. She usually made it home in time to start supper before Ford came in with Uncle Zachery trailing behind him. Ford was always covered with dirt and mud from working, and

Zachery always looked exactly as he had when they'd left that morning.

Zachery took a grand interest in the horses Ford was breeding and spent some days reading books Ford had collected. Then at dinner he'd tell Ford everything he'd learned, as if Ford had never bothered to read the books for himself.

Even though she was tired, she liked cooking for the three of them. While Zachery told her all about what Ford had done on his ranch, Ford washed up at a stand just outside the kitchen door. Ford never said much during dinner, but always complimented her on the meal, even when it was very simple.

The kitchen was better equipped with supplies than the restaurant kitchen had been in Fort Worth. The cellar had potatoes and apples packed in cool sand and shelves of canned peaches and tomatoes. She also found several jars of plum jelly stored with coffee, flour, beans, and sugar in a round tin barrel kept tightly closed. The smokehouse had salted pork, beef, and smoked wild turkey. Hannah found it fun being able to decide on a menu, rather than having to try to make something out of the little that was available.

After supper was Hannah's favorite time. Ford would turn to his books and read to her. She'd draw while she listened, loving the images his words brought to mind. Since the day he'd seen her sketches on the board at school, he'd made sure she had several drawing pads both at home and school.

When the story was over, Ford would look at her drawings and tell her that they were nice. Any disappointment Hannah felt over his comments was more than balanced by Uncle Zachery's ravings about what a great artist she was. Hannah knew the drawings were good, but guessed them far closer to nice than great. But still, Ford's honesty hurt slightly.

Ford asked her one night why all the drawings were so sad, making her realize that as he read she'd always picked the darkest parts of the story to reproduce. Maybe, she decided, the evil was more familiar to her, and the drawings gave her a good feeling that the hero had some-how escaped from the shadowy darkness she sketched.

By Friday night, she was too exhausted to draw as he read, so she sat on the floor beside his rocking chair, her head against his knee, and listened. Uncle Zachery stretched out on the couch and started snoring halfway through the story. Ford's voice lowered so as not to dis-turb the old man.

When Ford closed the book, Hannah smiled up at him. "Thank you," she said, resting her chin on his leg. "I love hearing stories read out loud. It's wonderful."

Ford lightly brushed her hair with his fingers. "You're welcome." Tomorrow they'd be married a week, and Ford was already having trouble remembering what the years of his life had been like alone. Three more weeks and she'd be gone, and he'd go back to reading to no one other than himself. "Are you ready to turn in?"

Hannah stretched as he stood. When he offered his hand, she accepted it, and he pulled her gently to her feet. Her body pressed against his as he steadied her, and neither turned loose the other's hand.

He wished he knew how to make small talk. During

the day he always tried to think of things to say. "How was your day?", "Do you like the children?", "Am I doing something wrong that makes you so afraid of me?" But at night, when he set foot in the house he'd built alone, he'd look at her moving about the kitchen and all words would leave him. He felt like an outsider, unable to play in the world of make-believe she'd built around them.

Now she stood only a breath away, her fingers holding his, and he was speechless. He didn't know women well enough to say what was on his mind. How does a man tell a woman that he likes watching her move? Or that the smell of her hair stays with him all morning? He was sure it wasn't proper to tell her that the first time she touched his shoulder as she served dinner, he'd almost bolted out of the chair.

Hannah looked up at him with her blue eyes and whispered, "I guess we could."

Ford fought to keep from moving. "We could what?"

She smiled, as if guessing his thoughts were heavy tonight, outweighing conversation. "We could turn in early. It seems Uncle Zachery already has."

Forcing himself to look away, Ford tried to shake his mind free. "We could just throw a blanket over him and let him sleep on the couch. That is, if Sneeze doesn't mind us using what has become his blanket."

Hannah thought of saying that Uncle Zachery would be more comfortable in bed, but then she remembered he was used to sleeping beneath the tables and bars with a spittoon for a pillow. "I don't think Sneeze will mind."

Ford lifted the cat while Hannah spread the quilt

Sneeze had claimed as his the night they'd first arrived. As soon as the blanket was in place, Sneeze wiggled from Ford's grip and curled back atop the blanket, beside Zachery.

"He'll sleep soundly in here." Ford tossed another log on the dying fire. "From the clouds I noticed gathering to the north, I wouldn't be surprised if we get another cold front like we did last week."

"The snow wouldn't keep me from going to school, would it?" Hannah moved toward their bedroom.

"It might. I've been snowed in for over a week at this time of year. That's why I keep plenty of supplies on hand." Though he wanted to follow her and keep talking, he couldn't seem to make his feet move. So like he'd done every night since they'd been forced to share a room, he excused himself to check on the barn, allowing her to get ready for bed alone.

"I'll be back," he mumbled as he grabbed his coat.

Hannah turned and watched him go, guessing his reasons for leaving.

She'd just finished combing her hair when he returned. He carried a load of wood in one arm as he entered and closed the door behind him.

When he sat down to remove his boots, she moved to the holster hung behind his chair and pulled the Colt from its cradle.

"You don't need that," Ford said, as he had every night for almost a week.

Hannah hesitated for the first time. "I feel safer knowing I can protect myself."

Ford rested his hand on her wrist, just above the gun.

"From who? Me? Hannah, I won't hurt you." His thumb rubbed lightly across her pounding pulse. He was so weary of telling her, but he'd say the words a thousand more times if she'd just believe them once. "Even if we had no bargain."

She pulled away and he didn't try to hold her. "I need the gun between us." She moved to her side of the bed and crawled beneath the blankets.

Ford twisted out the light and removed his clothes, down to his heavy merino drawers, in the shadows of the firelight. He'd paid a dollar and a quarter for three pairs of the underwear, more than he'd ever spent. He told himself they were worth the price because of the pearl buttons and the ribbing, but in truth, he knew he'd spent the money because Hannah would see them. When he reached his side of the bed he noticed she'd once more pulled back only the quilt for him to sleep under, leaving a blanket between them.

As he rolled his weight onto the bed, he felt the cold steel of the pistol against his side. Frustrated, he refused to move the inch away so he couldn't feel the gun. He crossed his arms above his head and stared at the light from the fireplace as it danced across the thick beamed ceiling. Maybe he'd freeze when the fire died out. Maybe she'd accidentally shoot him in his sleep. After a week of this arrangement, he decided he didn't care.

"You didn't cover up," Hannah whispered.

"What?" They were the first words she'd said to him all week once they were in bed. He'd realized that her not talking was another way of ignoring the fact that they were lying next to one another. "Did you say something?"

"The quilt is still on my side." She shoved it toward him. "You'll catch cold."

"I don't care." He didn't feel any cold at all. In fact, he was warm. Just thinking of her so close to him most nights kept his blood summer-hot. He felt her moving closer, rolling toward him.

"Is something bothering you, Ford?"

Lady, I got a wagon load of bothers and I'm heading downhill, he thought. I'm married to a thief who won't let me touch her, but who'll be dead to all in less than a month. Add her uncle, who spends every day telling me how to ranch when he can't even ride a horse, though he seems to know everything about the animals. Plus, my sister informed me today that she's coming to spend a few days with us to help my wife fix up my house, which I think is perfect already.

"No," he finally lied. "Nothing's bothering me." He was so irritated he didn't know who or what to take out the anger on first. "I didn't think we were allowed to talk while we slept together." His voice was sharper than he'd meant it to be.

Hannah was silent for so long he wasn't sure she was going to answer him.

"I'm trying to make it easier on you," she finally said. "I know you don't want me here."

Ford rolled to his side and tried to see her face in the blackness. If talking was allowed, he was in the mood to talk. "When I was a kid, my first memories of coming home after playing were of having to be quiet because my mother was ill. The neighbors would come in and cook sometimes, but it was usually late, after they'd taken care of their own families. After I got old enough to help out, Dad always had me doing chores until dark, and my food was usually cold by the time I got in. When we moved here and he remarried, I was never invited to eat with the family unless we were having folks over and it would be noticeable if they left me out."

He didn't know why he was telling her all this, but once he started talking it seemed impossible to stop. "After I left home I used to wonder what it was like for a man to work all day and come home to a hot meal that had been fixed just for him." Ford's voice lowered slightly. "This week I've had that and I thank you for it. When you're gone, I'll always remember. It's a good feeling I look forward to every night. So don't think I don't want you here or that your silence will make me forget that you're next to me."

Ford stopped breathing as she reached across and placed her hand on his shoulder. Slowly, with light fingers, she moved her hand across his chest to the place above his heart.

"It'll be a good memory for me, too," she said as she continued to lightly touch his chest. "You really should wear an undershirt or a nightshirt when it's this cold."

"I'm not cold. I learned a long time ago not to let myself feel the weather." He covered her hand with his own. "Before you came, I'd only lit that fireplace in the corner a few times."

She slowly pulled her hand away. "I guess I'm the opposite. I'm always cold. I grew up in the kitchens where my mother cooked. It was always toasty warm, even in the winter. Now, unless I'm standing next to the oven, I'm usually shivering from fall to spring. I've even thought of teaching in my coat."

"The school needs more fuel?" Ford hadn't thought to check. Last month he'd noticed enough coal to last for several months stacked in the bin.

"We're down to burning chips." Hannah felt bad about complaining to him. "But they burn real good."

"I'll see that you have more coal by Monday." He was angry at himself for not having noticed. "And anything else you need, just tell me. We're not a rich school, but we don't want you or the children going without."

"Thank you." Hannah didn't know what else to say. "Good night, Ford."

"Good night, Hannah."

She eased the pistol an inch away.

He hesitated for a moment, then rolled closer to her. "Shoot me if you like," he whispered, "but I'm going to kiss you good night."

He felt the Colt's barrel press into his ribs as he leaned over and lightly brushed her lips with his own. She didn't respond, but she didn't fire, either.

"Good night, Hannah." He rolled away without pulling the cover over him and lay on his back with his arms folded once more above his head.

He couldn't help but smile a few minutes later when Hannah spread the quilt out over his chest and tucked the corners in around his shoulders.

*   *   *

The next morning Hannah was in the kitchen making a late breakfast when she heard someone yelling for help. Drying her hands as she ran, she almost collided with Ford as they both reached the front door at once.

"Help!" came a woman's call again.

Ford groaned as he suddenly recognized the voice and opened the door.

Gavrila was standing beside her buggy, with one hand holding her hat in the wind and the other hand fighting her parasol.

"Did you ever think of knocking instead of yelling, dear sister?" Ford ignored her struggle with the umbrella and hat and moved to the horses.

"I hate this wind!" she yelled back, as if he could do something about it. "All the way from town it's been blowing my hat. I thought I could block it with the parasol."

"Might have been easier just to take the hat off." Ford started leading the horses to the barn. " 'Cause one thing's for sure—the wind never stops in West Texas."

"Sanford, you have no sense of style. It's no wonder you're such a clod. A lady simply never goes out without her head covered. Do you want me to look like a poor farmer's wife, with my head exposed and my face tanned from the sun?"

Hannah helped Gavrila with the parasol as she followed her sister-in-law into the house. The little woman had a way of walking in short, quick steps that Hannah found hard to pace beside.

Ford could hear his sister's cries all the way to the barn when she stepped into his house and saw Zachery was still there. "Hasn't that man left yet?" she screamed. "Did he come for a visit or to board?"

Hannah didn't even try to answer, but Uncle Zachery bowed low and said, "It's good to see you, also, sweet Gavrila. Maybe if you put rocks in your pockets, the wind won't blow you away."

Gavrila huffed and followed her nose to the kitchen. She was halfway through breakfast when Ford returned. He didn't join her and he noticed Hannah also stood watching. Though Gavrila didn't seem to notice that she was eating another's meal, Hannah did, and poured them both a glass of milk. Ford raised his glass in a silent toast to her while Gavrila and Zachery argued in the background.

When she'd downed the last biscuit, Gavrila patted her lips and got to the point. "I've come to help you do something with this horrible house, dear. It's my duty as your sister-in-law. I've talked to half the women in town about some of the improvements you can make so this outpost will look more livable."

Hannah could almost feel the steam coming off Ford as he stood silently beside her. She knew she had to do something fast or Gavrila might be flying in the wind back to town, rocks in her pockets or not. "Thank you for the offer, but shouldn't you rest for tonight?"

"Tonight?" Gavrila looked puzzled.

"For the town social. Someone told me there will be games and lots of food and music. I thought I'd be too tired to attend, but now I think we should go."

Gavrila looked horrified. She prided herself on never forgetting a social function, past or future. Hannah could see her eyes darting, looking for a reason for her memory loss.

"I've been so busy. I'd completely forgotten." She stood suddenly. "I can't help you today. I've got so much to do. Luckily I ordered a new dress last week that I haven't even had time to press." Gavrila almost looked sorry for Hannah. "Oh, you poor child. All I've ever seen you wear are those two drab garments. You'll just have to pick between the less worn and tattered. I'd loan you one of mine, but you're much too tall for anything in style these days. The choices are drab and more drab for you, I'm afraid."

"I'll make do," Hannah answered.

Ford took his sister by the elbow and helped her along. "I'll ride back into town with you. I've a few things to pick up." He glanced back over his shoulder. "Do you need anything, darlin'?"

"No." Hannah took her first deep breath since she'd heard the scream. "Just take your sister home."

Winking, he looked almost boyish for the first time since they'd met. Something about the way he usually stood so still when he was upset had led her to believe that he'd always been grown-up, but now as he hurried Gavrila along he seemed younger.

He didn't return until late afternoon. Hannah had washed all her clothes and hung them to dry in the kitchen, then taken a long bath. She'd washed her hair in the perfumed soap Jinx had brought her and curled it as best she could with rag curls, hoping it would dry before the party. She wasn't sure what to bring to eat, so she baked a pie and a ham, just to make sure. She couldn't believe she was so excited, but she'd never been to a social before.

Ford came in carrying a box about the size shirts come in. He took one look at Hannah sitting at the kitchen table in her nightshirt and robe, with pieces of rags twisted in her hair, and had to laugh. "You about ready for the party?"

She thought of throwing the cold coffeepot at him, but decided she'd only have to clean up the blood and grounds if she hit her mark.

"She's been getting ready all day, son." Uncle Zachery chuckled. "She even made me take another bath, and it hasn't even been a week. Plus I'm not even going to the social. I'll probably die of a fever any minute right here. I'm not interested in any social, so I asked Jinx to come out and keep me company. She told me she hates even watching all the folks get dressed up and parade down the street, so I challenged her to a game of checkers."

Ford held out his free hand to Hannah and she accepted it. He pulled her against him in a hug as he always did in front of Uncle Zachery. "I brought you a surprise."

Hannah took the gift. "You shouldn't have. I don't need anything."

"Now, that's not the way a lady accepts things." Zachery moved closer to see what Hannah was opening. "I'll have to teach you what to say when a gentleman gives you something, Hannah." Zachery was suddenly sounding very much like an uncle.

She pulled a pair of creamy white longhandles out of the box.

Zachery glared at Ford. "And that's not the kind of thing a man's supposed to give a lady, son. You made a big mistake here. A big mistake."

They weren't listening to Zachery. She hugged Ford wildly. "Thank you," she cried with pure joy.

"I figured you could wear them under your dress and no one would notice." Ford grinned. "I wish I could have found some with a few ribbons on them, but at least you'll be warmer."

"You two beat all I ever seen. Don't you know anything? You were supposed to bring her silk and lace and nice things." He pointed at Hannah. "And you should be insulted that your man brings you longhandles, like you were a forty-niner."

Ford pulled her close against him, laughing. "Oh, you mean I should have thought to get her a new dress and maybe new shoes that fit and maybe a coat she could wear besides mine?"

"Yeah," Zachery grumbled. "Stuff like that."

Nodding, Ford looked worried. "I see. I must have not been thinking. You mean gifts like those other boxes I got in the wagon?"

It took a few heartbeats for his words to register on Hannah, then she was out the door running. He'd bought so many things she couldn't carry them in one load. There was even a hatbox.

Ford could never remember laughing so much at one time in his life. He watched her open every box and spread the things out on the bed as if they were fine

Paris originals and not just wool dresses he'd ordered from the mail-order catalog.

He could hear her humming through the door as he bathed and she dressed. By the time they loaded into the wagon, Hannah had tried on everything he'd bought her five times and only made a decision when he'd told her they were going to be late.

As they rode into town, she seemed quiet. Finally, she whispered, "I'll pay you back. I don't know how I'll get the money, but I will."

"You don't have to." He wanted to give her the things. Every time he remembered the rags she'd left in his hotel room, he'd hated thinking of her wearing them. The clothes had put a dent in the cash he kept hidden in his little office at Gavrila's place, but he didn't regret a dime he'd spent.

"But I will," she added. "I swear. I'll pay you back."

❖ Chapter 11

FORD WALKED AHEAD of Hannah into the church where the social was being held, carrying the heavy cast-iron pot filled with the huge ham she'd baked. He could have managed the door and allowed her to walk ahead of him, but she'd pulled back, suddenly nervous. Something in her hesitance made him wonder if she'd ever been to a church social before. In her line of work, he guessed socials were out of place. He tried to imagine her in some dark cave with seedy types arguing over plunder, but somehow he couldn't picture Hannah in their midst, either.

Shoving the dark image from his mind, Ford looked around. This gathering seemed about the same as all the parties he'd been to in his life. Memories of them blurred together in his brain until he couldn't remember a particular social, yet they were all alike. Everyone was spit-n-polish clean, and the furniture in the church hall had been rearranged to make conversations easier. Folks were congregated in small groups, talking, eating, and listening to the piano. Everyone smiled and nodded at whoever stepped through the door, then returned to their conversations about all those not within hearing range.

Ford set the ham down among the endless potato dishes and helped Hannah find room for the pie on the dessert table. Though most folks smiled at them, no one stepped forward to say a word. Ford felt he'd best do something, for Hannah looked as if she might bolt at any moment.

He gently circled her shoulder with his arm, careful not to stand too close in case the widows complained about him behaving improperly in the church building. Leaning near her ear, he whispered, "Frightening, aren't they? And just think, no one leaves until all those sweet potato pies are gone."

Hannah tried to hide her laughter, for he'd guessed her thoughts. There seemed enough food for ten groups this size. "Who are all these people?" she asked.

"Methodists, mostly." He fought the urge to direct her toward his usual corner. Tonight he'd stand in the center of the room. "That's Mrs. Scott playing the piano. My sister seems to be the only young lady in these parts who doesn't take lessons from her. The man leaning on the piano, as if he's afraid it might fly away without his weight, is a Yankee by the name of Taber. He's got a place down by the Salt Fork of the Red River. I learned how to build my adobe from him. He don't talk much, but he can grow anything on that place of his. Has a big enough garden to feed half the town all winter.

"The thin lady next to Taber is named Helen Moore, I think. A marriage agency Taber hired sent her out West to look him over. She's staying with Professor Combs and his wife while she decides if she wants to marry the

Yankee. She's been here so long now, my guess is she will."

Hannah nodded, thinking the couple looked right for one another. The Taber marriage was probably considered far more proper than hers and Ford's. She reached behind her back and laced her fingers with his. She'd taken great care to look very proper tonight and only hoped she wouldn't embarrass him.

He could feel her hand trembling and wished he were brave enough to swing her up into his arms and leave without a word to any of these good folks. She didn't like crowds any more than he did, and he didn't owe these people any explanation. If he'd stayed home tonight, she'd be sitting by the fire listening to him read about now. He'd have his sleeves rolled up and she'd be in the robe he'd loaned her, with her hair tumbling down about her waist. Uncle Zachery would have already turned in for the night, leaving them alone for an hour.

Forcing his voice to be calm, Ford made himself continue. "Then there's the McClellands, and W. A. Allen talking with a few of Colonel Goodnight's men over by the punch bowl."

She was only half listening. Facing the children had been hard enough, but she'd never be able to make all these people believe she was Ford's wife. He belonged here, but she'd never seen this many people in one place—except when the bar was real busy, and then most of them were loud and drunk. These folks were frighteningly quiet. "Is it time to leave yet?" she whispered.

Ford chuckled and tightened his grip on her fingers.

"You're not running out on me, darlin'. If we left a church social suddenly, all the old gray hairs would gossip for days about how you were in a family way."

Hannah blushed.

"Besides . . ." Ford noticed several people watching them, probably wondering what the newlyweds were whispering about. ". . . you're the most beautiful woman here, and I'd like the pleasure of standing next to you a little longer."

"I'm not," Hannah argued. She'd never been called beautiful in her life. She knew she wasn't ugly, but she'd never be beautiful. She was the kind of woman most men don't notice one way or the other. She'd even be willing to bet old Hickory, who she'd worked for for years, wouldn't have been able to describe her even on the day he died.

"Cross my heart." Ford moved his hand over his chest. "Until I saw you in that dress tonight, I thought the prettiest woman I'd ever seen was you in my nightshirt and robe. That image will have to fight with seeing you now. A woman who's pretty and can cook, too, is a rare thing, I think."

"Thank you." Hannah decided it safer to change the subject. Even if Ford thought he was telling the truth, she'd never believe she was any great beauty. "I'm surprised Jinx doesn't come to these."

Ford shrugged. "She usually doesn't. I've seen her at a few picnics. Says they remind her too much of a silent auction, with all the eligible girls parading around all the unattached men, and the girls' mothers following close behind, taking bids. My guess is both she and Uncle Zachery are having more fun playing checkers."

Looking around, Hannah had to agree. "I see what she means about the bidding." As she looked at the many young women strolling from group to group, one caught her attention. A petite blond was watching her openly, as though Ford and she were no more human than portraits.

Before Hannah could ask who the woman was, the blond moved toward them with practiced grace. Everything about her was perfection, from her starched dress to her high-crowned curls.

"Good evening, Ford." Her voice was almost musical. "I'm glad you and your new bride decided to come tonight. I was looking forward to meeting the woman you married."

Ford nodded, suddenly speechless. Hannah couldn't decide whether to offer her hand or bow to the woman who must be the queen of this little society. She was dressed in the prettiest dress Hannah had ever seen, all ribbons and pale cream lace; but on closer inspection, she was older than she seemed—maybe in her mid-twenties.

"Since your husband seems to have lost his tongue, I'll introduce myself. I'm Allison Donley."

Though the woman couldn't have been sweeter, something in the way Ford gripped her hand warned Hannah to be careful. "Nice to meet you, Mrs. Donley."

Allison smiled just enough to show her dimples for a second. "It's Miss, but please call me Allison. After all, I've known your husband for years and years." She turned her attention to Ford. "Do be a dear and get your wife and me some apple cider."

Ford moved away slowly, as if not wanting to leave Hannah's side.

When he was halfway across the room, Allison turned back to Hannah and placed her gloved hand on Hannah's arm. "I'm so sorry for you, dear. Gavrila told me of your forced marriage to her brother. To be hurried into marriage is crime enough, but to a man like Ford?"

It took a few seconds for her words to register. The woman wasn't trying to be friends, she was offering her sympathy. Hannah's pride straightened her back slightly. She felt fiery anger crawl up her throat the way it used to when the good ladies in town would offer her their old dresses, yet refuse to look her in the eye. "There's no need to feel sorry for me, Miss Donley. I married Ford of my own free will and can assure you there is no finer man to be a husband."

Allison looked shocked. "But I thought . . ."

"Whatever you thought couldn't be more wrong, I imagine." Hannah wanted there to be no doubt that the rumor Gavrila was spreading was false. Ford wasn't a rag to be forced on her. He deserved better. "If you've known Ford for years, you must know what a wonderful, gentle man he is."

"Well, no, I . . ." Allison's rosy cheeks were starting to lose some of their color.

"I was attracted to him the moment I saw him." Hannah couldn't help herself. The lie was growing like a mushroom surrounded by manure. "A man so strong and gentle would have to be a fine husband. His every action since we've married has proved me right."

"But, dear, he's . . ." Pretty little Allison couldn't bring herself to use the word. ". . . not handsome."

Hannah fought to keep from laughing. The shallowness of this woman was far uglier than any word Allison could use to describe Ford. "He isn't? I hadn't noticed." In truth, Hannah hadn't given it much thought. Allison, on the other hand, seemed to be getting homelier by the second. If she opened her mouth one more time, she'd be a troll in Hannah's eyes. "What's in the package is far more important than the wrapping, don't you agree? And Ford Colston, the package, is a wonderful man."

Allison looked at her as if Hannah were simpleminded. "Well, yes." She smoothed her dress as if it were her pride. "He's asked me to go walking after church many times and I've always turned him down." The blond lifted her chin, as though proving a point somewhere beyond Hannah's reasoning.

"And you never stepped out with him?"

"No," Allison answered.

"I feel so very sorry for you, *dear*." Hannah used Allison's words.

All the color suddenly left the woman's face and she looked ghost white. Obviously, no one had ever felt sorry for Allison Donley.

When Ford returned and handed her a drink, she downed the entire glass in a most unladylike way.

After she'd walked off without saying a word to Ford, he turned to Hannah. "I wonder what's upsetting Allison?"

"I have no idea." Hannah wasn't about to tell Ford what the woman had said. "She must have a fever; she looks pale."

"I noticed that," Ford answered, but his attention was on Hannah, not Allison.

Hannah slipped her hand around his arm at the elbow. "Do you think she's very beautiful?"

Ford covered her fingers. "I once did," he admitted. "But I was just now thinking that she's too short."

In more ways than one, Hannah thought, remembering her troll comparison earlier.

Slowly, as the evening wore on, folks came by to say a few words to Ford and Hannah. Everyone ate and then listened to Mrs. Scott play several songs. Hannah discovered the only person who really talked to them was Alamo Rogers. Unfortunately, every time he spent more than a few minutes beside Hannah, Gavrila would pull him away. Hannah was starting to wonder if the man didn't have a hook tied to his coattail, the way Gavrila constantly reeled him in.

From time to time, Hannah noticed couples strolling out and returning later. When she asked Ford about them, he said he guessed they were walking up to Eagle Hill.

"Can we go?" she asked, ready for a little fresh air.

"Mostly single couples go," he answered, as if his words made sense.

"Have you ever walked up Eagle Hill with a girl?"

"No," he replied. She could see the pain in his eyes and wondered if it was because he'd never asked a girl, or because none had ever agreed.

"Would you go with me?"

"If you like." His voice sounded tight. "It's only a rise we built up like a fort when we thought we might get attacked by Indians. Things have been so peaceful around here the past few years, the place is starting to go to ruin."

"I'll get my coat." A stroll up Eagle Hill sounded exciting.

She crossed into the back room, where all the wraps were stored, and took a few minutes to enjoy the quiet. Then she dug through the pile of coats until she found the new wool one Ford had given her and ran to join him.

He was waiting at the door, opening and closing his large hands as if forcing calmness through his body. "I thought you were never coming," he whispered. "I figured you'd changed your mind."

"Is there any danger?" she asked.

"No," he answered. "It's only a place for sparking."

"Sparking?"

He took her hand and smiled as though genuinely surprised she didn't know the word. "You know, for courting. For getting close enough to a girl to make a few sparks fly."

They walked out into the cool night air. Hannah hugged close to his side for warmth. "Do you think anyone saw us leave?"

Ford laughed and welcomed her against him as he always did. "I think everyone saw us leave. We're probably the main topic of conversation right about now."

"Then let's stay out a long time and give them something to worry about."

"I love your way of thinking." His arm circled her shoulder.

They walked in the moonlight to a slight rise at the edge of town. Ford took her hand as they headed up the incline to where a stone wall had been built about four feet high.

When they reached the center of the hill, Hannah looked down on the little cluster of buildings. "Not much of a town," she voiced her thought.

Ford moved a few feet away and leaned against the stones. "True, but they had a great dream. They all thought they'd come here and tame the Wild West, bring religion to the plains. Trouble was, when they got here, staying alive and making a living ate away at the dream. They're still holding to their hopes, but the town's not growing like everyone, including my father, thought it would when we settled. The stores do a good business, but most of the cowboys would rather spend their money in Mobeetie or Tascosa. Some think that when the railroad branches off soon, they'll bypass this town completely."

"I like this little place." Hannah moved closer to him, almost touching his shoulder when she joined him in leaning against the wall. "Everywhere I've ever lived has been rough and seemed dirty. It's nice to see people having fun, raising their children, being neighborly, and not needing to wear a gun when they walk the streets."

"You've lived in rough towns?" He wanted to ask so much more, but this was as near a question as he dared.

Sometimes he let himself believe that she was just like the women of Saints Roost, but then she'd say something that would remind him of what she did for a living and how they'd met.

"A few so rough I still have nightmares about them," Hannah answered. "Until I met you, I think I thought most people, even the ones who act nice, were basically bad. I thought that if I turned my back, they'd stab me if they had the chance, and that no matter how nice they looked on Sunday morning, they'd been shooting it up at the saloon on Saturday night."

"And now?"

"You're starting to make me think that there are good men in the world. I never pictured a man reading by his firelight and not drinking himself to sleep every night."

Ford pushed away from the wall. "There are good men, Hannah, but don't look for me to be one."

"But why?"

"Because I'm not. If you could hear my thoughts sometimes, you'd think twice about even speaking to me. Maybe I'm worse than the drunks and gunslingers."

"What kind of thoughts make you so terrible?"

Ford wasn't about to tell her how often he dreamed about the way she kissed him, and how sometimes he'd open his fingers at night and try to remember how soft her breast had been when he'd slid his hand up from her waist in the cave. How could he explain that sometimes in the middle of the night he'd still be awake, thinking about the way she looked in the mirror's reflection while she'd been dressing? He could never tell her of those thoughts or she'd hate him and run as fast as she could back to whatever dark life she'd known before.

"What kind of thoughts?" she asked again, moving closer.

"Thoughts about the way you feel in my arms," he finally answered, wanting to be honest and hating himself at the same time. He couldn't dishonor himself by saying more. Even the few words he'd said probably made it obvious to her how few women he'd held.

"Oh, those thoughts," Hannah whispered in laughter. "I have those also. You're the only man I ever willingly let touch me, or wanted to touch. There's something about you that makes my palms warm, and I want to slide my fingers over you. If you were in a store, they'd have to hang one of those 'do not touch' signs around your neck or I'd be coming in every day."

"I never had a problem until you came along." Ford stared up at the stars, thinking he could almost feel her fingers sliding over the muscles of his back. "I had enough trouble talking to women, never mind thinking about holding one."

She paced in front of him, suddenly needing to change the subject. "What do most couples do on this hill?"

"Hold hands . . . hug. I don't know." He was glad she couldn't see his face. She'd admitted to thinking at least part of what he did as casually as if they were talking about their favorite foods. What surprised him was her admission that he was the first man she'd felt this way about.

"Kiss?" She stopped directly in front of him, startling him from his guessing.

"I suppose." He shoved his hands in his pockets to keep from reaching for her. She had a way of hog-tying his feelings into a knot and declaring him beat before he even knew he was in for a battle.

"Well, then, don't you think I should look like I've been kissed when we go back?" Hannah couldn't help but picture Allison's face when they returned.

"Sounds logical." He stood so still, he didn't even breathe.

"Then you'd better get on with the job." Hannah closed her eyes and waited for him to kiss her. When he didn't, she opened one eye. "Well?"

"Why are you doing this?" Though his face was in shadows, his voice sounded like he was in pain.

"I thought you liked kissing me."

"I do," he admitted. "But every time I kiss you, you either threaten to kill me or I end up married. I'm not some huge toy you can play with, Hannah, then throw aside. I want to know what's going to happen to me this time. Every time I touch you I can't help but listen for the trapdoor to fall open beneath my feet."

"Forget it." Hannah said, then turned and stormed down the hill. She wasn't about to tell him that she wanted him to kiss her because she couldn't stand the fact that Allison felt sorry for her. Or that she wanted to walk back into the social with everyone being able to see that she'd been kissed and enjoyed it.

Before she reached the bottom, Ford grabbed her from behind and twirled her to face him. On instinct, Hannah reacted.

She'd kicked at his legs viciously and slugged his

chest several times before she realized he was no longer holding her or fighting back. Stopping, she lowered her hands slowly.

"Don't ever grab me!" she said, out of breath. "I don't like being grabbed by anyone."

Ford didn't move. "You made your point. I'm sorry. I had no intention of hurting you, only kissing you. I thought that was what you wanted." He was dying to ask her what had happened in the past that made her react so violently to a man's touch, but wasn't sure he wanted to know the answer. This woman was ripping the patchwork of his heart apart one thread at a time.

Widening his stance, Ford locked his arms behind his waist. "You can hit me a few more times if it helps." Her strikes didn't hurt near as much as the knowledge that she was aching deep inside.

Hannah laughed nervously and tried to brush away her blows from his shoulder. "No. You're right again. I may have overreacted a little," she answered. "I don't suppose you still want that kiss?"

Ford chuckled. "And folks think I'm half-wild. More likely I'm half-crazy, because I still do, darlin'."

This time she didn't close her eyes and wait, but stepped closer and pressed her lips hard against his. He didn't pull away, but there was no fire as there had been before. He didn't react at all. She pressed harder, but he remained stone.

She pushed away and turned her back to him. "We'd best be going. We've been out here long enough to have them all wondering. There is no point in standing in the cold."

They'd walked halfway back to the social when he suddenly broke the silence. "Hannah?"

She slowed and looked over her shoulder at him. "Yes?"

"Stop walking," he ordered as he moved closer.

She stopped and waited, trying to make out his expression in the darkness. The lights from the social were stretching out toward them, but she still couldn't see his face.

"I said I wanted to kiss you, but not because of anything folks will say inside." Slowly, hesitantly, he lifted his hands to her shoulders. "I haven't had a lot of practice, but I don't think a kiss should be done just because it's expected."

"All right." She guessed they were near enough to the church that anyone watching could see their outlines. "Kiss me the way you want to, but I won't promise I'll react."

He leaned forward until his cheek touched hers. Then he whispered softly, "Put your arms around my neck. I want to feel you against me when we kiss. I like the feel of you near."

When she did, he pulled her body close. Even through the coats, she could feel his warmth. In case anyone was watching, Ford must be planning to make this kiss look very real.

He slowly moved his mouth across her cheek to her lips, lightly tasting Hannah's skin. As his arms lifted her off the ground, his mouth covered hers. His teeth tugged at her bottom lip until she opened her mouth.

Suddenly all that had gone between them during the

week melted into one moment. She didn't care if the entire town was watching, or if no one was, she just enjoyed his kiss. He made her feel so surrounded with warmth. He wasn't trying to take something from her, or hurt her, he was giving as only Ford knew how to. Giving with such a blend of tenderness and need that she could only answer his silent cries with her own hunger for more.

Ford lowered her slowly to the ground without breaking the kiss. One hand pressed into her back, molding her against him, while the other hand moved into her hair, pulling the ribbon loose.

Huge hands lightly brushed her curls as Hannah moved her fingers into his brown hair. She closed her fist in the soft mass and gently tugged, as though she could pull him even closer.

Ford's arms tightened around her, crushing her breasts against his chest. This was what she wanted from Ford, to be close, to feel him next to her. Hannah needed to believe a good, decent man like Ford Colston could care for her.

A feeling of safety blanketed her as she kissed him in the light from the church. She knew he couldn't go too far, he couldn't make demands on her. He couldn't paw or grab, or hurt her as Jude had. There would be no bruises to remind her of this kiss.

She was left wanting more when he released his grip and pulled slowly away. She could feel his muscles tightening, as if forcing her away took great effort.

"We'd best be going inside." Ford wanted nothing

more than to kiss her again, but not here where someone might watch.

"I wasn't finished," Hannah answered honestly. "Couldn't we do it a few minutes more?"

"If you like, we'll continue once we get home." He could hardly talk for the sudden weight on his chest. Did he really think he could kiss her like he just had when they were in bed without wanting more, far more? "Unless you decide tonight's the night you're going to use that Colt I'm getting used to having jammed in my ribs."

"I never loaded the gun." She suddenly didn't want him to leave her side.

"I know," he answered, letting Hannah know that his word had kept him away, not the fear she'd tried to instill. "I checked it last night."

They moved toward the steps and another couple made more talk impossible. Hannah hurried back into the coatroom without a word. For a long moment she stood alone, thinking of what might happen when they got home. If Uncle Zachery would find another place to sleep, they could stay in their separate rooms and just kiss good night, but Uncle Zachery seemed to have taken root faster than a mesquite tree on a damp prairie. He had even started his own collection of books about horses in one corner of the main room.

She told herself all she wanted was to kiss Ford, for any more might be as ugly as it had been that night with Jude. Though Jude had held her tight, his hands hadn't caressed as Ford's had—they'd pulled and twisted until she'd cried in pain. Then he'd slapped her hard and demanded she be quiet while he felt what he'd own tomorrow. When she'd tried to pull away, he'd jerked a fistful of her hair loose by the roots and pulled her to the dirt, swearing that she'd learn soon enough how a wife should act.

Hannah suddenly ran from the coatroom, not wanting to think of what her life had been like then, or might have been today if Jude hadn't been killed.

Three feet into the main room, Hannah realized everyone was looking at Allison, who stood at the front yelling and crying with echoed shrillness.

Hannah slowly moved toward the crowd, trying to understand what was happening.

"I just got it a week ago! Ordered it all the way from Kansas City," Allison said between crying fits. "The bag can be replaced, but it had the church's building fund in it—forty dollars!"

Someone tried to comfort Allison, but she only cried louder. "It's all my fault. I should have given it to the reverend when I first arrived. But I thought my reticule would be safe in the coatroom."

Hannah looked around. She probably should, but she didn't care that the money was missing. All that mattered was that Ford didn't think she'd taken it. She couldn't bear to see his accusing stare again.

But Ford was nowhere in sight.

Everyone seemed to be talking at once. Several people organized a search of the coatroom, while others agreed to take lanterns and walk the route from Allison's house to the church in case the bag had dropped from her wrist without her noticing. Most folks seemed content to try and comfort Allison and convince her the loss couldn't be her fault. Mrs. Scott even started playing softly on the piano once more, only now her songs were funeral beat.

Hannah paced the floor, not knowing what to do. If anyone in the room knew her past, they'd blame her without even allowing her to defend herself. She should be a suspect simply because she was an outsider, but no one even looked in her direction. Somehow being Ford's wife made her above suspicion. But where was Ford? Didn't anyone notice he was missing? He'd been a step behind her when she'd entered the coatroom, but left her at the door because he didn't have a coat to put up.

Minutes ticked by to the melody of Allison's sobs. The more attention she received, the more hysterical she became.

"I found the money!" Widow Rogers yelled from the coatroom. "Someone stuffed it in the cane holder! The thief must have just wanted your bag, Miss Allison."

Everyone but Hannah and Allison rushed to see the widow count out the four ten-dollar bills.

Hannah stood close enough to Allison to hear her mumble that the money hadn't been in tens, but no one seemed to be listening. They were all shouting praises and jumping around like forty-niners on a good day.

Looking around, Hannah finally spotted Ford, standing over by the door with his hands folded across his chest. She was too far away to see his eyes, but he was the only one in the room not smiling.

She moved toward him, thankful that the money had been found and now she could go home in peace. But when she saw his face, all the blood seemed to leave her body at once.

His stormy gray eyes were accusing her, blaming her for a crime that had already been solved.

The walls closed in around Hannah, and she knew as she'd known as long as she could remember that she'd always be an outsider, with nothing but the darkness to surround her and no man to love her. All her life, like her mother, she'd be nobody's woman, for no one would care for her and believe her . . . even when there was no reason not to.

✤ *Chapter 12*

FORD DIDN'T BOTHER with the lantern. As he walked the distance between the barn and the house, his mood was as black as the inky sky. He hardly noticed the sweet smell of burning piñon wood drifting from the house chimney, or the wind whispering through the canyon in one low, moaning hum.

All he could think about was that Hannah had stolen again, even after he'd asked her not to while she was in Saints Roost. She'd taken too much time in the coatroom before they'd left for Eagle Hill. He should have guessed what she was doing, but he was too nervous about going to the hill with her.

Stopping at the edge of the corral, he stared into the night, wishing he could make sense of the way he felt. Idly, he ripped away a scrap of bark along the fence, baring wood as he bared his thoughts. He'd known she was a thief from the beginning, so maybe he should stop acting like a wounded pup. She was just doing tonight what she did every time she needed money, for no telling how many years. Allison's purse was simply too good to pass up.

The moment Ford heard about the loss, he knew who had taken the money. She'd said earlier that she was going to pay him back for what he'd spent on her new clothes. She probably thought she'd let the theft cool for a few days, then hand him part of money.

When everyone at the social started looking for the church fund, Ford knew what he had to do. He couldn't stand by until someone figured out that his wife was mostly likely the only one who'd spent several minutes in the coatroom alone. No one would want to, of course, but eventually someone would get around to asking one question too many.

He couldn't let Hannah be caught. Ford told himself it would be too embarrassing for her, but honesty gnawed at his gut. A part of him had to tell the truth, if only to himself. Pride wouldn't let them find out about Hannah's past. Not her pride, but his own. He didn't want people saying that now it made sense why a pretty woman would marry such a toad of a man. She had a shady past. If they caught her stealing, it wouldn't be sunrise before everyone in town would also speculate on what else she'd done. They'd say things like, *Of course, no decent man would have her, so she married Ford,* or *A woman like her is lucky to find even one man who'll stay with her for more than a night.*

The cold air froze the moisture around his eyes. He didn't want to be thought of as the leftover man who'd marry her. Ford, at least, wanted the fantasy of believing that she could care for someone like him. He liked remembering how she'd suggested the idea that they go through with the marriage. He liked having people think he was lucky for finding her and that maybe, just maybe, there was more to him than they'd ever seen. After all, a woman like Hannah was willing to stand in public with her hand on his arm.

Someone like him. He wanted to scream the words until he was so hoarse he couldn't say them anymore. All his life he'd heard them whispered, as if everyone was simply enduring his presence.

But Hannah had changed that. Folks looked at him differently tonight. They stayed more than the minimum time to say another sentence or two. Having Hannah at his side had pulled him from the corner. He still couldn't think of much to say, but no one seemed to notice with her standing so close to him, with her hand tucked into the curve of his elbow as though she were proud to be there.

So for purely selfish reasons, Ford did the only thing he could think of to do. He ran the quarter of a mile to his sister's house and took forty dollars from money he'd been saving to increase the herd come spring. He was back at the church before anyone noticed he was gone. They hadn't even really organized a search when Widow Rogers found the money he'd stuffed almost out of sight.

"Ford!" Uncle Zachery bellowed from the doorway. "Are you out here in this blackness? I swear, that blasted wind must have blown away even the stars tonight. This country ain't fit for nothing but coyotes, and even they feel the need to complain now and again."

For a moment Ford thought about dropping Uncle Zachery in the water tank beneath the windmill to see if the old man could swim. A second later he felt guilty about daydreaming of such a thing. After all, the old fellow was Hannah's uncle. He was probably just lonely. When he'd first come out to the ranch, Ford thought it would be for a night, maybe two, but the uncle seemed to be settling in for the remainder of the winter. He'd discovered a long-buried interest in horses and followed Ford around, checking on each animal and advising on each one's care.

"I'm out here!" Ford yelled back. "Just enjoying a few minutes of solitude."

Zachery moved toward him, feeling his way with the points of his boots. "I know what you mean, son. Jinx about talked me out of a listening mood tonight. That woman can come up with a topper story to every one I can think of. I have an idea she does it to keep me off guard when we're playing checkers. I had to wiggle my ears several times just to keep up the rhythm of the conversation."

Ford was glad it was dark and Zachery couldn't see his expression. The thought that maybe he should haul Zachery up the windmill to drop him deeper into the water tank crossed his mind. But he had a feeling even underwater Zachery would still be talking. It was just a guess, but Ford figured Jinx had had to fight for every minute of time to say a few words.

"Hannah told me what happened at the social. It was a lucky thing, finding that money Allison misplaced. She's mighty pretty, son, that Allison Donley. Jinx said you were a little sweet on her once, but I'm glad you didn't get no closer to the honey. A woman who'd just leave forty dollars laying around isn't the kind you'd want to be having your offspring, if you know what I mean. That kind of senselessness might be passed down from mother's milk to child."

Ford had no idea what the old man was talking about. He was only half listening to Zachery. He'd developed the habit within hours of meeting the man.

"Now you take my dear niece, Hannah." Uncle Zachery was moving from side to side as he talked, trying to make sure he was addressing Ford directly, but the blackness made it impossible for him to be sure. "Hannah would never lose money, and she's kind, too." He cleared his throat, forcing his voice to remain steady. "I'll bet my dear Hannah would even give food to a hungry man who had no money. And she can cook, too. A man can smile at about any wife at bedtime if his belly is full of good food. Not that she ain't ever' bit as pretty as that Allison, only in a little quieter way."

Ford didn't answer. He could almost see Hannah feeding hungry folks. But her kindness didn't change the fact that she'd also steal any money lying around or hold a man at gunpoint and take his clothes.

"She's good with the children, too. Everyone tells me so every time I ride to town. She stops almost every day and visits with parents, just to let them know how their little ones are doing. I heard someone say she's a natural-born teacher. Imagine that, Hannah a natural-born teacher, when all I ever thought was that she was a good cook."

"She is that." Ford finally gave Zachery the satisfaction of agreeing with him. In the past week he'd found himself racing the sun every evening to get home for dinner.

"She deserves a good man like you, son," Uncle Zachery said. His eyes had finally adjusted enough to the light that he could see Ford's outline, so he moved closer.

"How do you know I'm a good man?" Ford asked.

" 'Cause Hannah told me you were," Uncle Zachery said simply. "And I ain't never seen you say an unkind word to her, or hit her even once since I've been here."

Ford suddenly felt very uncomfortable. Either this old man knew nothing of what was going on, or Zachery really believed that Hannah was all she claimed to be and he was as good a husband as she told everyone. "I need to check the horses. You'd best get back in the house. This time of night it turns cold."

Zachery didn't argue. His stiff, slow movements told Ford just how tired the old man was. He seemed old in life more than in years, as though he'd aged twice for every day he'd lived. If Zachery had known Hannah long, he surely must know the truth about her. Maybe Uncle Zachery just wanted to believe in the picture Ford and Hannah had so carefully constructed. Maybe he'd seen so much bad he thought he deserved a turn at looking at only the good in people.

Ford crossed back to the barn, knowing he had nothing further to check—he'd already done his evening chores twice. If he kept this up, the horses would be too fat to get saddles on, come morning. But he didn't want to face Hannah just yet.

He straightened the leathering tools as he tried to

place his thoughts in order. Considering what he knew about her, how could he still want to touch her? Nothing made sense anymore. She was everything he'd worked all his life not to be. Finally, when he'd started to be accepted by folks, she had to come into his life. Was he willing to risk what little ground he'd gained because of her? Did the ground matter all that much in the first place?

Ford slammed his hand against the rough wall of the barn. "No," he whispered between clenched teeth. He was willing to risk it all. Questioning his motives all night wouldn't change a thing. He'd put the money back because he couldn't stand the thought of seeing her accused. Part of him might be thinking of himself, but he'd done what he did for her.

Staring up at the starless sky, Ford whispered, "And she wouldn't even quit stealing for a month for me."

When he finally walked into the house, he knew what he must do. She couldn't change just because he wanted her to, and he couldn't stand seeing her practice her trade on people he'd known most of his life. He had to leave.

Ford spread the bedroll out on the long table in the main room and stuffed two books into the bottom of the roll. He grabbed a few basic supplies and added them to the stash.

Hannah was within a few feet of him before he realized she was even in the room. "Mind my asking what you're doing?"

He looked up at her and immediately regretted his glance. She looked so beautiful, dressed for bed in his nightshirt and robe. Gripping his shaving case in both hands, he fought the urge to hold her. How could he still have so strong a need to touch her that his arms felt like they would act on their own if he didn't cooperate?

He stuffed a change of clothes into the bedroll and began rolling it tightly. "I need to ride out to the line shack at the other end of my ranch. Ray says he thinks there might be some fence down, and I need to have it up by spring."

"You're putting up the fence tonight?"

"No." Ford knew his story was flimsy, but he had to get away from her before he accidentally burned every standard he had on the fire she'd started in his gut. "I'll ride over tonight so I can get an early start in the morning. I know the way so well I could make it in my sleep. If I can put in a few full days by not having to come back here, I should be finished before the end of the week."

"You're leaving me here alone." Hannah tried not to make her voice sound disappointed. He had a ranch to run and more important things to think about than her.

"You can keep your uncle."

"Thanks." Hannah's sarcasm made them both smile. "That's another reason you're leaving tonight," she guessed. "You don't want him going with you."

"That's about it," Ford lied. He hadn't even given Zachery a thought. The line shack was rough living, and the old man wouldn't be up to it even if he could ride. The place was little more than a lean-to built with its back to the north wind, but it was better than sleeping out in the open this time of year.

Hannah followed him to the kitchen and watched him pack more supplies. She thought of asking what was bothering him, but she figured he'd tell her if he wanted her to know. She'd tried to guess the answers ever since the end of the social. He'd changed suddenly when they'd all been watching Allison cry. Minutes before, he'd kissed her like she'd never known a man could kiss a woman, then later he'd looked at her as if he'd found her guilty of some horrible crime and was heartlessly waiting for the firing squad to arrive.

As she trailed behind him toward the barn, Hannah decided that what must be responsible for his sudden mood swing was seeing Allison cry. Most likely, he didn't care about the money she'd lost, he'd only been angry that someone had made her so upset.

While she watched him saddle a horse, Hannah's nagging question bubbled out before her common sense had time to act to keep her mouth closed. "You love her very much, don't you?"

"Who?" Ford snapped in a harsher tone than he'd intended. Hannah was driving him mad, following him, watching every move he made. He could almost feel the warmth of her only inches away, and the sweet way she always smelled after her bath was thick in the air around him.

"Allison. You love her, don't you?"

"Why do you say that?" He forced himself not to look at Hannah as he asked. Ford had never thought very much about loving any woman. He'd thought about being married and raising kids, but love was something for the romantic poets, not a struggling rancher. Besides, he couldn't love Allison, not the way Hannah seemed to think. She was like a beautiful painting a man could admire, but never love.

"I know you love her because it upset you so much to see her crying." Hannah's fists were on her hips and she looked at him as though he were the oldest problem child she taught in her one-room school.

"I was upset about the reason for her hysteria." Ford picked his words carefully. "It bothers me that someone would steal the money from a church."

"Oh, but they brought it back."

Ford didn't seem to hear what she was saying as he moved around the horse and stood only inches from her, straightening the saddle. In order to look at him she had to turn directly into the lamplight, while his face remained in shadows.

"Would you have taken the money, Hannah?" His voice was low, but accusing. "If you'd known it was there?"

Hannah straightened. "I might have, if I had to. I'd do whatever I had to do to survive. All I own of value is my mother's bracelets, but I'd even sell them if I had to. I'd do whatever I needed to."

"I guess I'm proof of that, aren't I, wife? You'd even marry me."

She wanted to run, but she could hear the pain in his words. "I married you because I had no choice, but no one forced me to kiss you tonight."

He moved an inch closer. "You don't find that a little odd, Hannah? You said you'd never marry me, but you like kissing me."

"I said I'd never marry anyone." Hannah stepped backward. His anger was starting to frighten her. "And I'll never love any man, especially a man who already loves another."

Ford saw the fear in her eyes and a shock vibrated through him as though he were a well-used lightning rod. "Stop doing that!" he yelled, the anger still flavoring his speech.

"Stop doing what?" She moved another step away.

"Stop cowering down like I might strike you at any moment. And stop telling me I love Allison. I've never loved anyone."

Hannah forced herself not to move. "I wasn't cowering down." Her voice shook slightly. "I'm not afraid of you. I'm not afraid of anyone."

Ford stepped directly in front of her. "Well, that makes one of us, because I'm scared to death of you, darlin'."

He shoved his hair back and crammed his hat low on his forehead. "Don't look for me to be back anytime soon. There's plenty of food for you both. If you need anything, just charge it at the store in town."

Before he could turn away, she stepped between Ford and the horse. "You're running away from me, aren't you?"

Though her words were little more than a whisper, Ford took the accusation like a slap.

"Are you afraid of me or yourself?" Hannah suddenly realized the power she had over this strong man. "You're afraid to be around me. You're afraid of your feelings."

Ford placed his hand on the saddle horn, brushing her

shoulder with his action. "I'm afraid of what I'll do when I'm around you, and I'm worried about what you'll do if I let you out of my sight. To make matters worse, I hate myself, because on top of everything else, all that floods my brain most of the time is how I'd like to hold you." He might as well be honest; lying never had fit his life.

"Well, why don't you?" Hannah answered, her words angry. She wanted desperately to make her feelings fit into what made sense in this world of pretend they were living. "Most husbands at least hug their wives good-bye before they leave for a week."

Ford moved his free arm around her waist and pulled her against him, hard and fully. "Put your arms around my neck, Hannah."

She did as he asked, but their bodies were stiff against one another. He rubbed his rough chin against her cheek and whispered, "Hug me back, darlin', before I leave. Hold me like you don't want me to go."

Hannah heard it then, a need so deep inside him it sliced her heart. How many times had she wished for what he was asking? Someone to hold her. Someone to care. Tightening her grip around his neck, she stood on her tiptoes and melted against him.

Ford closed his eyes and forced back the tears he'd never cried as a boy. She felt so good in his arms. A blending of all the hugs his mother never felt like giving him and all the ones he'd longed for in lonely years of solitude. His other arm lifted her off the ground in an embrace he wasn't sure he'd ever have the strength to break.

Suddenly, he didn't care that she was a thief. He'd cover her crimes as long as he had the money to do so. In the week she'd been with him, he'd grown accustomed to the feel of a woman in his arms, and not just any woman . . . Hannah. That was one thing she'd never be able to take with her when she left in less than a month. The memory of her pressed against him would be with him the rest of his life.

Chapter 13 ❖

Hᴀɴɴᴀʜ ᴄʀᴀᴡʟᴇᴅ ғʀᴏᴍ the bed and tried to remember if she'd slept at all. She didn't want to admit it, but she missed Ford by her side. The warmth of him next to her had helped her sleep. After holding her so tightly in the barn before he left, he'd turned without a word and ridden off into the night, leaving her alone.

She made herself get dressed, but her mood didn't improve. Whatever had upset Ford wounded him so deeply he couldn't stay. Like an injured animal, he wanted time alone to heal. And after the kiss he gave her, Hannah knew somehow she had more to do with the pain he suffered than she thought possible.

For the first time since she'd arrived at Canyon's Rim, the wind bothered her, calling to her through rattling windows, daring her to try and stand against its gusts. Even the inside of Ford's solidly built home gave her no peace. Everything around Hannah reminded her that he was gone and she had no idea why. She knew he liked being with her, yet just when she was ready to allow him closer, he ran. He'd even said he was afraid of her, which she couldn't imagine anyone being. Ford left, saying only that if she needed him, she could follow Carroll Creek north and find the line shack. Though he might distance himself from her, he still wanted her to know that he'd come if she was in trouble.

Hannah shook her head as she cooked breakfast. Ford's actions made no sense. No one had ever been scared of her. For the most part folks didn't even notice her. Before she'd witnessed the killing, she'd gone about her job almost invisibly. She cooked from noon until closing six nights a week. On Sunday, she did her laundry and tried to rest for the next day of work. Once in a while, if the day was nice, she'd walk down by the station and follow the railroad tracks for as long as she dared, wishing she could go all the way to the end.

Somehow, Hannah had the feeling she'd finally found the end . . . right here in the Texas panhandle.

"Breakfast about ready?" Zachery's voice rumbled ahead of him as he strolled into the kitchen, trying to untangle his suspenders as he walked. "I thought you'd be dressed for church by now, girl."

"I'm not going," Hannah answered. "Ford left late last night for the far end of his ranch. I wouldn't want to go to church without him."

"Nonsense, girl. I'll take you. I can hitch up that little buggy of yours and we'll make it just fine. Did I tell you I used to saddle General Lee's horse in the war? I was even quite a doctor of animals then, even went to school once six whole months to learn. But with the war, there was always other things to do—like trying to stay alive."

Zachery laughed, but with no humor in his tone. "By the time the Northern aggression was over, I didn't really care if I was alive or dead. Did I tell you my wife died when they burned Charleston?"

Hannah set the plate of eggs down and shook her head. "No. In truth, you've told me very little about yourself, Zachery. I must have known you for years, but never really said more than a few sentences to you until this week. It's almost like we weren't human, but only things, until we came here. Something about this place breathed life into us, as though we were paper dolls that took shape."

Zachery nodded. The sadness in his eyes always made Hannah wonder if it wasn't easier on him to stay drunk than to face humanity.

"Being sober's what did it for me. It clears my mind so I can think. Unfortunately, I'm also able to remember. I remember some of the hell folks put other folks through back then like it was yesterday. When I was drunk, nobody bothered me. I was just like a chair or a clod of dirt, not worth talking to. Being a thing isn't so bad in this world sometimes."

He took a long drink of his coffee and made a face, as though wishing the brown liquid could be something else.

"But I've good news." Hannah wanted to erase the sorrow in his watery gray eyes. "You can stop pretending to be my uncle. No one's here but the two of us. I'm guessing you have no more wish to go to church this morning than I do, so the acting can stop for a while."

Zachery straightened and squared his shoulders, as if ready for a fight. "I'll have you know I take my role as your uncle very seriously, and I have no intention of dropping the act. Since you were at the party last night, folks will expect you in church this morning, and we're going, young lady."

Hannah was too surprised to respond. She couldn't remember anyone ever talking to her as if she were a child, even when she'd been one. "I don't know . . ."

Zachery waved away her objection. "There's nothing to know about Sunday service. Just stand up when the person in front of you does and pass the plate as fast as you can. When I was young, my family had a pew we filled every Sunday like it was the law in our county. There were so many of us Nobles, someone had to offer to die before anyone could marry, due to lack of seating."

Smiling, Hannah gave in to his request.

An hour later she was riding in the buggy toward town. She'd halfheartedly voiced every objection she could think of, but Zachery stood fast. She'd even reminded him several times that she was not his niece, but the man seemed to have ripped up all the pages of his life and started fresh. The more sober he got, the more fatherly he became. Zachery even drove the buggy with surprising skill, and when they arrived, he took the lead in answering everyone's questions about Ford's whereabouts.

Most of the women shook their heads, disapproving of working on the Lord's day, but most of the men nodded in understanding. Ranch work sometimes couldn't wait for a day of rest.

As they walked into the little church, which had been built in thirds, a fine bell announced the day. Millie slipped her tiny hand into Hannah's. Anna, her sister, was only a step behind. "Mama says we can sit with you since it's your first time here and all. Millie thinks you'll be scared, but I told her Miss Hannah ain't afraid of nothing."

"Thank your mother for me," Hannah whispered as Uncle Zachery motioned them into their places. "And thank you, Anna, for believing in me."

Hannah squeezed Millie's hand. The tiny child still hadn't said a word to anyone but her sister, but her love for her teacher shone in her eyes. Somehow having her near calmed any fears Hannah had about the little church.

Zachery whispered, "Jinx invited me to Sunday dinner and a checker game after church."

Hannah smiled, understanding the reason for Zachery's sudden interest in religion. He and Jinx appeared to be an odd match, but they never seemed to lack for conversation.

"You're welcome to come, too, girl," he said in a self-sacrificing way.

"No," Hannah whispered back. "I've a million things to do at the schoolhouse. You can pick me up there. I ate far too much breakfast to even think about a noonday meal."

Zachery let out a long breath. "If that's what you want. I know Ford expects me to keep an eye on you while he's away, and I don't plan on letting down the husband of my niece, but I would like to play a game or two of checkers. Back in Lee's army I was considered one of the best players, not that we had much time to set up a board. It feels good to get back to playing again."

"Play as many games as you like," Hannah answered. "As long as we get home before dark."

The organ started pumping away and everyone reached for hymnals. Hannah followed, surprised at how well Zachery's advice worked. Church wasn't near as frightening as she'd thought it might be. She noticed everyone had on not only their best clothes, but their finest manners as well. She was almost sorry to see the morning end.

As they walked out, Zachery could hardly keep from passing people in his haste to leave.

He had seemed to enjoy the sermon, but was now thinking only of lunch and Jinx. As he hurried off toward the post office, Gavrila stepped from behind Hannah and locked her arm around her reluctant sister-in-law.

"What, no men today, dear sister? Only one week of marriage and you couldn't keep that brother of mine home! He's wild as the wind, my father used to say. Where has Ford blown off to now?"

"He had work that must be done," Hannah lied. She wasn't sure why Ford had left, but she figured it was to get away from her. Gavrila didn't need to try and guess the real reason.

"It's just as well." Gavrila shrugged. "Ford always goes to church, but it never seemed to knock off any of his rough edges. My father used to say, you can't make a deacon out of a bear no matter how many suits you buy him."

"Ford's a good man." Hannah wasn't sure why she said the words, but whenever she was around Gavrila, she always felt like they needed to be repeated.

"Of course he is, dear." Gavrila glanced toward heaven, as though silently asking forgiveness for the lie. "But just in case he ever is not such a good man, you can always come running to me. I think of you as my sister now. I'll be near when the time comes."

Hannah wanted to escape Gavrila, but somehow she had to see the whole picture; she'd looked at pieces long enough. She had to know why Gavrila had used "when" and not "if." "Have you ever seen him get out of hand? Has he ever hit you or any woman?"

Gavrila shook her head toward the sky once more. "Lord, Lord, I could tell you some stories. And no, he's never hit me, but every once in a while I see that he'd like to, and it frightens me all the way to my toes."

Hannah waited. She found it hard to believe that the man who'd slept beside her all week without ever trying to force himself on her would seem so out of control in his sister's eyes. Also, thinking of slapping Gavrila was not so alien a thought to her mind, either, so she couldn't judge Ford if Gavrila was right and he had thought about such a thing.

Gavrila looked around as if making sure no one listened, but Hannah was certain her new sister-in-law had told what she was about to say many times.

"You should have seen him the year our mother died. She'd been sick for ages—since his birth, really. Thin blood, you know. But when she died, he turned wild. For some time he wouldn't even come into the house, and as far as I know he never entered her room again. His clothes got filthy and his hair matted with dirt, but he didn't want to be around any of us. If Father hadn't left food on the porch every night, he'd have starved to death. I tried and tried to help him, but he wouldn't even talk to me."

"How old was he?" Hannah had seen children who looked completely forgotten and uncared for, but she couldn't imagine Ford as one. Everything he owned, from his thick cotton shirts to his leather boots, seemed the best quality a man could buy in this part of the country. He was no dandy, but there was an order in his house, the barn, even in his life.

"Let me see," Gavrila thought aloud. "I was seven. Yes, that's right, because Father had all the problems of getting me ready for school that year without anyone to help. So Ford must have been six. Father always thought that Mother having Ford less than a year after giving birth to me was what made her ill. Sometimes I swear I can almost remember that first year after he was born, with Mother so sick and Ford crying all the time. It took him months before he finally stopped screaming night and day. Then I never heard him cry again, not even when she died. He just jerked free of the doctor who told us and ran."

"Didn't your father do anything about Ford?" Hannah couldn't believe a parent, even one in grief over the loss of his wife, would worry about one of his children and not the other.

"Of course he did. Once it got too cold for Ford to be outside, Father made him take a bath on the porch before he let him in the house. But Ford was never the same after Mother died. Maybe he wasn't right earlier and we just never noticed. Father wouldn't let him join us at the table because one night Ford growled at me! Imagine that—he growled."

Gavrila leaned closer and Hannah could smell the rosewater perfume she must have bathed in. "I hesitate to tell you this, being that in the future you might have his offspring, but he was the ugliest child ever born. His head and hands were huge and his bones always looked like they might pop right through the skin at any moment. If I were you, I'd give serious thought to being a nonbearing branch of the family."

They had reached the buggy, but Gavrila was still talking. The crowd within hearing made her lower her voice only slightly. "Of course, when Father remarried, his second wife felt the same way I always had about Ford never cooperating with the rest of the family. She wouldn't even allow him in the house, except occasionally. She said he made her think of spiders crawling up and down her spine when she watched him. You know the way he stands so still and stares."

Hannah was surprised Ford had matured to be the gentleman he was. No wonder he told her he was scared to death of her. Every woman in his life had either died or treated him poorly. Gavrila had been only a little older than Ford, so she couldn't be blamed for being frightened of a brother who couldn't share his grief. But the father and stepmother should have helped.

Gavrila waved at several people passing by. "But now I'm not so strict about him being in my house. I even allow him to have an office in one of my upstairs rooms. That way if he ever needed me to take over his affairs for a few days, I could."

"That's kind of you." Hannah said, wanting to add, "since he owns the house," but didn't.

"Well, no matter what he is or how he acts, he is my brother and I'll always love him." Gavrila shouldered her cross again. "He hasn't mistreated you, has he? That is one thing I'd never stand for."

Hannah could see the curiosity in her eyes. She was waiting, hoping, planning. Gavrila was one of those rare people who thought through any possible disaster so completely, she couldn't help but be let down when her strategies were never used.

"No," Hannah answered. "Your brother is the kindest man I've ever known." She watched the disappointment on Gavrila's face.

"Know that I'm on your side if anything ever happens." Her sister-in-law held her chin high. "My stepmother always said that someday I'd have to take charge and that I'd better be ready when the time came. If that includes running his ranch, I suppose I can manage that also. She said he was the sort of man who'd move on when too many people settled around him. He needs his solitude."

Gavrila patted Hannah's arm. "But don't you worry. I'll stay if he goes, I promise. After all, you're family now and I'd think it only right that I look after you and, of course, the ranch."

Hannah wondered if Ford had any idea how Gavrila felt. She was simply waiting in the wings for him to do something wrong so she could step in. What did she think he'd do, go crazy, become wild, or just leave? Hannah could imagine doing all three if she'd had Gavrila for a sister.

But Ford had remained. He'd stayed and built a ranch and seen that his sister was taken care of. He'd turned a deaf ear to everyone's whispers and done what he could to belong in a town that didn't seem to want him.

"I'd ask you to join me for lunch," Gavrila's voice increased in volume, "but I've been invited out. It wouldn't be proper to bring an uninvited guest."

"I understand." Hannah wasn't sure she could eat with Gavrila across from her. "I have some catching up to do at my desk, and then I really need to get back home."

She waved good-bye and walked toward the school. The wind was icy cold but Hannah hardly noticed. Ford, as a little boy, stood before her in her thoughts. She understood the loss of a mother, though she'd been twelve and of an age to take care of herself. Ford hadn't even been old enough to understand. With the death, he lost not only his mother, but his whole family. He'd lost the single person who might have cared about him.

She tried to plan the lessons for Monday, but a little boy with matted hair and dirty clothes stayed in her thoughts. He deserved a loving wife who would fill his home with laughter and children. He deserved someone better than a woman he'd met during a robbery to be the mother of his kids.

She finally gave up trying to plan the lessons and busied herself with cleaning the room. Her contract had very plainly stated that part of her duties included tidying her classroom.

When she swept near the stove, she noticed the coal box was full of coal and knew Ford had placed it there. Hannah knelt beside the box and brushed her fingers lightly over it. He was taking care of her again. No one had ever seen to even her simplest needs. No one but Ford had ever been concerned if she was cold or hungry or frightened.

The sun was almost touching the earth when she realized it was long past the time Zachery had said he'd come for her. Hannah walked out of the school, still thinking of Ford. She made up her mind to convince everyone in town how wonderful he was, so that when she "died," he could find a decent wife who'd love him and make up for all he'd lost. Hannah didn't know how to love like that, but he deserved a chance. If she ever got to heaven, she planned to recommend him for sainthood—if Methodists have saints—just for not having killed Gavrila these past twenty years. Gavrila made Hannah thankful she'd been an only child.

When Hannah reined in the bay in front of Lewis's store and post office, she could see Jinx and Uncle Zachery sitting near the windows, catching the afternoon sun for their game.

Zachery looked up at her and waved, then talked with Jinx for several minutes before joining Hannah.

He climbed into the buggy and took the reins. "Early, aren't you, girl?"

Hannah smiled. "I'm so late we'll be lucky to make it home before dark."

Zachery chuckled. "No need to chastise any further, girl, but I was having me a time." He let out a long whistle. "That Jinx is something else, isn't she? She can tell a story that'll twist moonbeams outa twilight and make me forget how old I am."

Hannah looked at him for signs that he'd been drinking. The woman had to be almost fifty, and not only stood taller by two inches than Zachery, but must outweigh him by thirty pounds. Jinx's hair was salt-and-pepper gray and styled like a tumbleweed. Hannah's smile widened. "Yes, she's something."

"I told her I'd ride in with you tomorrow and make the mail run with her. We'll be back playing checkers by the time you turn the kids loose."

"That'll be nice," Hannah answered, without really listening. She was thinking of getting home and seeing if possibly Ford had made it back yet.

But when she got there, the house was dark. She fixed Zachery and herself a cold plate of fruit and sliced ham with cheese between the slices. Zachery talked as if nothing were wrong, but she noticed he looked at the door several times, as if expecting Ford to walk in at any moment.

While Hannah cleaned the dishes, Zachery excused himself and vanished into his bedroom. She followed his lead and went to bed, but sleep didn't come, and again Hannah spent the night listening to the wind call for her to come battle the night breeze.

When she'd been a little girl she'd believed the wind followed her and whined outside her door, wanting her to play. Her mother had told her once that lost spirits travel in the wind. Right now, Hannah felt very lost and alone. She could almost hear the wind spirits whispering her name.

Ford also lay awake listening to the wind. His line shack didn't provide the protection of adobe walls. Dust seeped through the cracks between the logs. Shadows, made from the single lantern, danced on all four walls and across the empty cot on the other side of the shack from him.

Stretching, he tried to relax on the rough ropes, but he couldn't quit thinking about how much he missed having Hannah at his side.

"Get used to it," he mumbled to the wind. "She'll be gone in three weeks anyway." In no time he'd forget what it was like to lie in the blackness of the night and breathe deep of the smell of her, or listen to the soft sound of her sleeping against his shoulder. "She'll be gone soon," he said again louder, trying to make himself hear.

But his muscles weren't listening and sleep was no closer now than it had been just after sunset.

All his life he'd been alone. Why should now be any worse than the other thousands of nights? As a boy he'd slept outside or on the porch, unless the weather made it impossible. Since he'd been fifteen, he'd spent many a night with only the bay to keep him company.

"I like being alone," Ford told himself, as if saying the words aloud could make them true. Yet if he'd liked being alone so much, why had he built a house with two bedrooms? Why hadn't he stopped Hannah the moment she'd climbed into Smith's wagon a week ago? He could have said a few words and she'd have grabbed her cat and run. He wouldn't have her in his house, her carpet-bag with those bracelets wouldn't be on his shelf, a cat wouldn't trip him every time he got up in the morning, and an uncle wouldn't be living with him.

Ford laughed. His life had certainly changed. To add to his worries, he seemed to have lost his senses if he was sleeping out here in this line shack when he could be home in a warm bed.

Slowly, he realized that it wasn't the loneliness he was hating; he was missing Hannah. He'd tried for years to do everything right. Never lied, never stole, never did anything that would give reason for people to talk . . . always went to church, took care of Gavrila, worked hard. And now a woman had stormed into his life who had different values. If he wasn't careful, she'd upset all he'd built; but for the first time in his life, it didn't matter.

He couldn't stay with her and he couldn't run.

Ford twisted on his side and slammed his fist against the rough wall of the shack. Though dust showered down on him, he slammed again, harder.

"I have to stay away!" he shouted to the wind moaning through the cracks. "I have to stay away from her. . . ." Or what? he thought. Or I'll turn into the animal everyone's always thought I might be.

❧ *Chapter 14*

THE SUN REFUSED to brighten the cloudy sky as Hannah opened her eyes to her second day without Ford. She dressed with only the watery light from the window and hurried to the kitchen to cook breakfast.

Zachery was already sitting at the little table she and Ford usually shared. He had the coffee boiling and was stuffing the last of an apple pie into a huge basket. "I thought I'd take lunch for Jinx and me today. She said yesterday that the meal she fixed me was the first one she'd cooked in a month of Sundays." He laughed. "I guess cooking isn't one of her finer qualities."

Hannah couldn't help but wink. "You might check into how some of those husbands died before you eat too much of her cooking."

Zachery crammed a loaf of Hannah's best bread into the basket. "She already told me. Two of them died in the War Between the States. One Yank, one reb. I guess that kind of evened the score for her in the war widow department. Then she married and moved out here with number three. He was killed herding cattle into Kansas. The last one died in bed."

"Of natural causes?"

Zachery laughed. "What he was doing was as natural as breathing." He closed the lid on his picnic basket and moved toward the kitchen door. "I'll get the buggy ready. I sure wouldn't want to keep Jinx waiting." He giggled to himself as he opened the door. "I plan on taking me a long breath today."

Hannah had no idea what the man was talking about, but she was glad one of them looked like he'd had a good night's sleep. She'd have trouble staying awake in school today after all the tossing she'd done before dawn.

Hurrying, she grabbed her things and joined Zachery. All the way into town, he talked about how much he liked this country. Sometimes Hannah would have to take a close look at him to remember the man she'd known two weeks before. His speech was clear now and he stood straighter than she'd ever seen him stand. Though the puffiness was still under his eyes and deep wrinkles crisscrossed his cheeks, he looked younger by ten years than he had the day Jude was shot. With Jude's death, it seemed, Zachery was reborn.

When he left her at the school, he promised he'd be back by midafternoon to see her home and not keep her waiting again. Hannah waved him away and walked inside to a waiting class. The Burns brothers and the Madison twins still grumbled about getting started, yet everyone else looked excited, causing Hannah to abandon her weariness and take joy in teaching.

As all days seemed to with the children, the hours passed by so quickly she couldn't believe it was time to

go. Even after she dismissed her pupils, she stayed to do
a few of the things that must be done to get ready for tomorrow's lesson.

An hour after school was out, no one waited beside
the buggy. Hannah finally climbed in and drove around
to Lewis's store and post office. She expected to see Jinx
and Uncle Zachery playing checkers by the front windows of the post office, but they weren't there. Lewis's
store, which shared the same building, had a sign that
read GONE FOR SUPPLIES barring the main entrance. Hannah walked to the middle of the dusty street and stared
up. The second floor was dark.

A prickly feeling that something was wrong crawled
up her spine. Jinx lived above the store and spent most
of her time there, when she wasn't making a run for the
mail or rewarming the coffee for anyone who dropped
by. Zachery had told Hannah that Jinx always finished
the run by early afternoon, sometimes even before noon.

Hannah walked around the building, trying every
door.

Nothing.

What if Harwell's men had ridden into town? They
couldn't have missed seeing Zachery sitting in front of
the window at the post office. Maybe they didn't know
he'd witnessed the murder, but they might have guessed
he'd know where to find Hannah. What if Jinx and
Zachery had encountered the three killers on the road
and now the two were both dead in the ditch. Even if
they'd been younger, three against two couldn't have
been much of a fight.

Zachery had told her more than once that he'd heard

enough after the shooting to know that the three killers would never give up until they'd cleaned up after the job. As far as they were concerned, Hannah was that messy part they'd left behind.

Hannah forced herself not to panic. At this point she was only speculating. Perhaps nothing was wrong. Zachery and Jinx might have gotten bored playing checkers and decided to go for a ride. Maybe the mail had taken far longer today. What if they'd broken a wheel and had to walk miles to a farm? A hundred explanations besides Harwell's man catching up with them were possible.

Yet the three men in yellow slickers with guns drawn seemed to wait in the corner of her mind.

She looked at the sun. Zachery knew she always wanted to be home before dark; they'd talked about it yesterday. If she didn't leave now she wouldn't make it home before sunset, and the last thing she wanted to do was to be on the road, unarmed, after dark. Climbing back in the buggy, she drove down the road toward Tascosa until she reached Professor Combs's house, then she turned and backtracked through town. No sign of Zachery or the wagon Jinx hauled mail in. All the businesses were closed for the night, and everyone except Hannah had vanished to their supper tables.

Looking at the sun, Hannah tried to think logically. If she stayed in town and waited for him, the only two places where she could spend the night were the school and Gavrila's house. Though there were no curtains on the schoolhouse windows and no place to sleep, it still seemed more inviting than Gavrila's.

Her only other choice was to leave for home alone

and hope Zachery could find a place for the night . . . assuming he hadn't been kidnapped or killed by Harwell's men. If she were home, she could protect herself, but here she was an open target.

Hannah reached in her purse and pulled out paper and a pencil. She scribbled a note to Zachery and stuck it in the crack of the door frame of Lewis's store. "Gone home," was all she wrote, knowing Zachery would understand. If the trouble was only a broken wheel or something, he could always sleep in the little room at the post office folks sometimes rented while waiting for the stage. If he was fine, he could take care of himself, if there was trouble, Hannah wasn't sure she'd be of any help without even a gun at her side.

The bay navigated his way to the ranch with no guidance from Hannah. She spent the thirty minutes watching for danger alongside the road. The endless plains stretched for miles in all directions, soothing her worries that someone might sneak up on her. A winter sun turned the sky brilliant with color, then disappeared, leaving the land cold.

By the time the horse turned into the gate and started the short distance down the road along the canyon rim, he was in full gallop. He seemed as ready to get home as Hannah.

"We made it," she whispered as she jumped from the buggy and opened the barn door.

She'd seen Ford pull the rigging from the horse several times, but she'd never realized how difficult it might be. The old bay appeared in no hurry now that he was home and stood patiently waiting as she worked the tight leather straps.

"I should call you Patience." Hannah fought her nervousness by talking to the horse. She told the bay all about how unafraid she was as she rubbed him down with a handful of dry straw and filled his trough with feed.

Once she was finished, she had to face the house alone. Walking slowly across the moonlit yard, she forced herself not to run for the lantern. If someone was watching, she'd spot him more easily if she wasn't carrying a light. Ford's house wouldn't be an easy place for strangers to find, but the people in these parts were so friendly they'd probably lead Harwell's men right to her . . . if the killers knew enough to ask for Ford's place.

The kitchen doorknob turned easily in her grip and the door opened soundlessly. She tiptoed inside, listening for any sound, looking for anything out of place, trying to sense if even the air had been disturbed lately. Silence met her. Only silence.

Feeling her way through the kitchen, she then crossed the wide living space to her room. Sneeze jumped from a blanket on the rocker and followed her, stretching his limbs as he moved.

Hannah let out a long breath. If anyone had been in the house, Sneeze wouldn't have slept through it. Ever since half the town had showed up the morning after their marriage, Sneeze made a habit of disappearing under the table whenever a stranger came into the room.

Once inside the bedroom, Hannah lit both lamps and

retrieved Ford's Winchester from above the wardrobe.
She locked both doors leading from her room and collapsed on the bed, relaxing for the first time in over an
hour. Finally she was safe. If Harwell's men had Zachery, they wouldn't get her—not tonight anyway.

But when she crawled into bed, she could hear the
wind whining through the canyon. Locked in the corral,
the horses' whinnies grew louder, then faded again,
making Hannah realize they were pacing back and forth
like worried souls at hell's gate. The night held the chill
of promised rain, but none fell to muffle the sound of the
wind and horses. Within an hour Hannah also paced her
confinement.

She finally abandoned the safety of her bedroom and
followed Sneeze into the living area. The huge drawing
pad Ford had bought her was leaning against the corner
of the rock fireplace. Blank paper seemed to wait patiently for her to give shadow to her thoughts with charcoal, as she always did when she couldn't sleep. There
was more than enough paper and firelight to draw by.

Hannah curled her feet beneath her and opened the
tablet. Tonight no fairy tales came to mind, only the
memory of the men in Hickory's place. Though no one
might want to see the pictures, she drew all the ugliness
of the moment Jude had been shot. In charcoal the
sketches took form as she remembered; they were dark,
ugly, haunting. The room seemed as it always had to
Hannah, without warmth or color. She drew Jude falling
into a river of his own blood . . . and a man with twisted
features firing as his mouth opened to yell something

lost beneath the noise of the gun. . . . She drew herself curling up as small as she could in a darkened corner.

Finally, when the sketches were petaled out from her like the leaves of a flower, Hannah felt the exhaustion she needed to sleep. With her head against the cushion of the couch, she finally rested.

Hours later Ford entered through the kitchen door. He'd thought the night air had chilled him beyond feeling until he stepped into the living area and saw her curled on the floor, surrounded by drawings. A warmth spread through him that had nothing to do with the dying fire in the fireplace or the solid feeling he always had when he walked through the threshold of the house he'd built by himself. He took in the scene before him as a man takes in a work of art, whole and all at once . . . Hannah, the Winchester by her side, her hair caping her shoulders, the drawings.

Ford slowly removed his hat and coat without taking his gaze from her. He placed a boot on the bench by the door and unbuckled his spurs. The rowel jingled lightly as he set the spur on the bench, but Hannah didn't move. Slowly, he carefully unbuckled the other spur, closing his hand over the back wheel to keep it from making another sound.

She slept on as he pulled his muddy boots off, set them next to the door, then unbuckled his gunbelt and lay it beside the spurs. On stocking feet, he finally approached her.

One by one Ford picked up the sketches, holding each to the light. The pictures were dark and haunting and of a scene he only hoped she hadn't seen in real life. One man, tall, with only slits for eyes, held a gun out that left no doubt it pointed the finger of death toward someone. Another man, old and weak-eyed, stared from the paper as if he were looking at his own coffin. A cowhand gripped his gut as he tumbled forward.

The last drawing he lifted was of a woman, huddled among broken chairs in a corner. She was curled in a human ball with only her hands clearly showing, but Ford could feel the fear she must be experiencing from the death grip she had on her knees. Though her face was completely hidden, she wore five thin gold bracelets on her wrist.

Closing his eyes, Ford took a deep breath, hating the sketches and knowing at the same time that they were the best she'd ever done. He hated the knowledge they brought with them. She'd seen what she drew. Hannah had been there. The bracelets had to be the same ones he'd seen her remove the night she met him.

He didn't want to think about what she'd witnessed. There had been enough ugliness in his life. Part of him wanted to believe her life had been better. She was too lovely not to have been surrounded by beauty. But the pictures told her story. No wonder she continued to steal! She was fighting the only way she could to break free of the charcoal world she'd come from.

Ford knelt beside her and gently brushed her hair off her cheek, wishing he could somehow brush away her past as easily.

He'd made himself a promise in the two days he'd been gone. He would follow the rules she set, even if it clawed him up inside. For the next three weeks he'd do whatever he must do to protect her. Then when she was gone, he'd do what he'd always done—he'd endure the loneliness in silence.

Chapter 15

HANNAH CAME AWAKE all at once as someone touched her cheek. In sudden panic, she stared up at a huge shadow of a man leaning over her.

With instinct liquefying into fear, Hannah sprang at the intruder with all the force she could muster, shoving hard against his chest with both her hands. He fell back, almost hitting his head against the fireplace stones. She jumped atop him, kicking and fighting like a mountain lion.

I'll survive! she screamed inwardly. *I'll fight until the last breath leaves my lungs. I won't let them kill me easily.*

"Stop!" Ford shouted. "Hannah, it's me!" He tried to grab her wrists, but her fists were moving too fast in continuous blows against his chest.

For a moment he wondered if she might know who he was, yet still be fighting him. The worry made him cease trying to defend himself. If he'd made her so afraid of him, he deserved her blows. He turned his head to the light as she bloodied his lip with her fist. The cut didn't hurt nearly as much as the knowledge that she felt the need to fight him.

Hannah froze above Ford when she saw his face. She'd heard her attacker shouting, but she was far too frightened to listen to what he was saying. Now when she saw Ford's eyes staring back at her, she realized what she was doing. He hadn't been threatening to kill her, he'd been yelling her name.

Sitting up atop his chest, she screamed, "Oh, my Lord, Ford, you're hurt. You're bleeding!"

He wiped the blood away with the palm of his hand and raised one eyebrow. "Don't act so surprised, darlin', since you were the one throwing the punches. The way you were hitting, it's a wonder all you did was bust my lip."

She wanted to help, but she had nothing with which to wipe the blood trickling toward his chin. "I thought you were Harwell's men come to kill me," she said, more to herself than him. "I thought I'd be shot at any moment, so I was trying to fight as long as I could."

Ford propped up on his elbow, ignoring the crimson dripping into the two-day growth of whiskers below his lip. "Who are Harwell's men?"

Hannah wasn't prepared to explain. Not now, not ever. Knowing Ford as she did, she imagined he'd want her to do something foolish like go back to Fort Worth and testify. He'd never understand that the sheriff might be in on the killing, and even if he wasn't, he'd never believe her. Zachery may have been right when he told her Jude had swindled Harwell and the gunmen were just evening the score. In a town like Fort Worth, cattle swindling would have been considered good reason for killing a man, and Jude's murderers would probably walk free even if she did risk her life to testify.

"No one." She shook her head, making her hair fly around her shoulders. "I must have been dreaming. I don't even know anyone named Harwell."

"You were doing some powerful dreaming if you drew these pictures in your sleep. These drawings look like a killing in some seedy saloon."

Hannah stared at him. His hair was damp with rain, his clothes dirty, and his lip now covered with blood, but at the moment, all his attention was focused on her. She'd need to keep her wits if she planned to make him believe her. Ford wasn't some drunk she could talk into swallowing something foolish.

"Forget my dream." She changed the subject. "We've got to do something about that lip."

Ford leaned his head back. "I'd get a rag, but I'm being used as a chair at the present time."

Hannah jumped off him, realizing she was the reason he stayed on the floor. "I'll get the towel. You lie still or you'll drip blood all over the rug."

She ran to the kitchen and got one of the good towels from the rack, not one of the flour-sack rags from the bottom drawer. Pumping a pan of water, she dipped the cloth into the cold water and ran back to the fireplace. Ford was still spread out on the floor. At first she thought she might have really hurt him, but then she realized he was smiling.

As she knelt and lifted his head onto her lap, he whispered without opening his eyes, "It's good to be home, even if that wasn't the reception I'd expected."

Hannah wiped his face with the timidity of an old maid changing a baby's diaper. "I'm glad you're back and I'm sorry I attacked you. But I was so worried that someone might break in."

Ford opened his eyes and studied her. "What's happened?" Before she could start another lie, her added, "And tell me the truth, Hannah. The Winchester wouldn't be at your side if you'd just stayed up late to draw."

Nodding slowly, she silently agreed to at least part of his request. "When I got out of school today, I went over to the post office. Zachery had said he'd be playing checkers all afternoon with Jinx, but the place was locked up. I couldn't find anyone who knew where they'd gone. It's as if someone rode into town and snatched them away. I looked for them as long as I could, but I had to make it home by dark."

He lifted the Winchester. "You're afraid to be alone here at Canyon's Rim? I thought you felt safe in the house, if not with me."

Hannah wanted to say, no, she wasn't afraid, she'd been alone most of her life, but she could never remember a time when she'd felt safe, even alone. After her mother died, she used to pile all she owned against the door at night, hoping for security, yet still she'd jump at every sound, and the flimsy walls could never keep out the whine of the wind.

Dabbing at the blood at the corner of his mouth, she admitted, "Most of the time I'm more scared of being with people than I am of being alone. But Zachery and Jinx's disappearance makes me nervous. I can't help but think something bad might have happened to them. And that maybe whoever got them might come after me."

Ford didn't miss the terror in her eyes, as though she'd opened the door to something horrible once and was never sure it completely closed behind her. "I wouldn't worry about them, Hannah. I don't know about Zachery, but Jinx can take care of herself. I'd bet the bay that no one could pull that woman out of the post office against her will without half the town hearing the ruckus. And when she makes her rounds, she's armed better than most stage guards."

He covered Hannah's hand with his and pulled the towel away from his chin. "I know what you mean about being alone sometimes. I've spent weeks out at the line shack, but tonight the walls seemed to be closing in on me. I didn't care that it would take me most of the night, I couldn't bear to spend another hour out there. We left too much unsaid between us when I rode out." He rubbed his thumb across the back of her palm. "I'd have come back sooner if I'd known you were afraid."

Hannah didn't want to talk anymore. He might ask too many questions she couldn't answer. She pulled her hand from his grip. "I think your lip has stopped bleeding."

Ford didn't move. "Thanks."

Rolling the towel around her hand, she didn't look at him as she whispered, "Maybe we'd be better off if we left some things unsaid between us. Sometimes it's easier to be polite strangers than for two people as different as we are to become friends."

"If that's the way you want it. Just promise me you'll

stop acting like I'm some animal you're afraid of half the time. I'm growing hoarse from telling you I won't hurt you."

"I'll try." Hesitantly, Hannah combed her fingers into his hair. She liked the warm brown of it, the color of the earth. "I'm glad you're home."

He closed his eyes and rolled his head slightly into the folds of her robe. The little boy in him surfaced when he wasn't staring at her with eyes the color of winter storms. Something had touched her deep inside when she'd heard Gavrila talk of him running wild, without anyone to care for him. Reflections of the boy inside the powerful man somehow made her less afraid.

Still stroking his hair, she asked, "Why'd you leave Saturday night?"

"It doesn't matter," he answered in a voice that sounded tired. "My reasons may be one of those things we're better off leaving unsaid. I couldn't stay gone, even when I knew I should. Being with you is like riding into a stormy wind you know could become a twister at any moment, but you keep on riding. Reasons don't matter anymore."

"You matter, Ford," she said her thoughts. "I wish I was the kind of woman who could love you for a lifetime and grow old with you."

He stared up at her and she could see her words echo in his gaze. They both knew she wasn't the right woman for him. They both wished she were.

"I'll settle for the kind of woman you are, Hannah, and maybe three weeks will have to do for a lifetime." He raised up slightly. "I decided out there alone that for the next few weeks nothing matters but being here. Most days I feel like I'm battling the world, but I can't fight myself as well. Something told me it was time for me to come home, and here I'll stay."

Ford's hand circled around her neck and pulled her down gently until she could feel his words brush against her lips. "I want to spend time with you and hold you and live by whatever rules you set." His kiss was sad and tender, telling far more of the way he felt than words ever could.

Deep inside, Hannah cried from a longing for what would never be. He was a good man living by a strong code. She was and always would be on the run, always looking behind her for a shadow with a gun pointed at her heart.

His kiss tasted bittersweet but she didn't try to stop him. When his tongue brushed across her upper lip, she opened her mouth slightly, welcoming him.

Gently, he placed his free arm around her waist and pulled her into his lap without breaking their kiss. She moved willingly, needing to be in the safety of his arms.

The kiss deepened, drawing needs to the surface in them both. He allowed his fingers to move over the folds of her robe, but he wasn't embracing her, only touching. Holding her was all he'd thought about last night while alone in the line shack. He had to come back. When she was gone, he had to have at least one memory to keep him sane. In his long, lonely life, Sanford Colston would have one memory of a woman in his arms.

His mouth moved along her cheek and down her

throat. "I missed you," he mumbled, without thinking that he was saying the words aloud.

Tears trickled from the corners of her eyes as she snuggled against his chest. She didn't want to admit it, but she'd missed him as well.

His long fingers moved over the wool robe once more. He wanted to tell her that he longed to end the marriage terms of touching in public. He wanted the rules reversed so he could make love to her now. But he knew she'd bolt if he even tried. Burying his face in her hair, he realized he wasn't even sure what to do if she asked him to make love to her. A boy can imagine, a man can guess, but Ford had never asked anyone. He didn't know for sure all the rules between a man and woman when they became lovers. What if he did something wrong? What if she knew how the game of love was played and laughed at his efforts? He was too old to be naive and too young not to care what she thought.

But kissing her wasn't wrong. He was sure nothing that felt so right could be wrong. When she came to him all soft like she was now, he wanted to pull her against him and never let go. Yet he'd stepped too far before and frightened her. He'd made himself a promise at the cave that he wouldn't be that impulsive again.

Hannah felt his hesitation, first in his kiss, then in his hands. Something was holding him back, keeping him from doing more. His kiss warmed her body and made her breasts feel full, but there was no promise of more to come. Maybe he'd had enough rejection in his life, and then again, maybe he wasn't as attracted to her as she'd thought.

Ford slid his hands along her arms and pushed her

gently away from him. When his mouth left hers, he drew in breath as though he were drowning.

"You'd best get dressed. It will be daylight soon," he managed to say.

Hannah nodded, but she couldn't seem to relax her fingers enough to let go of the fistful of shirt she held.

He covered her hand with his own. "We can't do anything about Zachery until sunup. Then I'll ride into town with you. I wouldn't worry too much until we know there's been trouble. Jinx has a reputation for doing impulsive things without answering to anyone, and Zachery strikes me as the type who'd follow along."

"Do you think that's all it might be?" She didn't want to think about there being more. In truth, she wanted to ask Ford to kiss her again, but thought he'd think her bold.

He stood and pulled her up beside him. "I think that's all it is. I'm sorry you were so worried." He brushed her hair back off her shoulders. "Why don't I cook breakfast and you get ready for school, Mrs. Colston? It wouldn't do to have the teacher show up late. . . . Maybe we can have a talk about these drawings on the way to town."

Hannah placed her fists on her hips and leaned an inch toward him. "I have a better idea. Why don't you take a bath, Mr. Colston? You're filthy. I'll cook breakfast and then we will *not* talk about these drawings on the drive in."

"I didn't hear you complaining about me being dirty a minute ago." He couldn't resist moving his hand along her arm.

"I was busy thinking of other things." Hannah smiled.

There was something irresistible about him now, with his scratchy whiskers and mud-smudged clothes. She'd heard someone say once that animals mate by scent. Without any logic at all, she realized she loved the way the air smelled when Ford was around, mud covered or not.

"Like the way I kiss?" Ford asked, a newfound pride twisting the corner of his mouth into a grin.

Hannah moved toward the kitchen. "Yes, I like the way you kiss." She giggled as she disappeared. "And that subject I would like to talk a little more about one day."

She'd half expected him to follow her into the kitchen. When he didn't, she was surprised to find herself a little disappointed. Hannah couldn't remember ever feeling so young. He made her think there was good in the world and men worth flirting with . . . men who made safety seem like a right and not a luxury.

As she lit the lantern and the stove, Hannah felt her body relax. Maybe Ford was right about Zachery; she might be panicking over nothing. Even the wind didn't bother her when Ford was home.

She reached into the cool box and retrieved a handful of eggs and a small pitcher of milk. Ford kept few chickens and no milk cows, but he had supplies delivered twice a week from a farm a mile west of them.

Cutting thick slices of bacon from a salted slab, Hannah dropped them, one at a time, into a wide cast-iron skillet. She pulled the biscuit bowl down from a top shelf and lifted the cloth cover from it. Her mother had taught her years ago to always make biscuits in the same bowl and rarely wash it. The sides soon became caked with flour, making the mixing of each new batch easier than in a clean bowl. Also, after a few tries, the measuring became more exact and the biscuits tasted perfect every time.

She'd just set the hot bread on the little table when she heard footsteps crossing the living area. Turning, she was surprised at the change in Ford. His hair was wet from washing but combed back and his face was clean shaven. He leaned against the kitchen door with his arms folded across a shirt he hadn't finished buttoning. The smile on his face left no doubt he was enjoying the view.

Hannah moved toward him. Without hesitation, she reached for the bandanna in his hand and began tying it around his neck. He smelled of soap and shaving tonic. She liked the way he stood motionless and allowed her to touch him. She was doing a task wives must do all the time for their husbands. The small intimacy made her fingers tremble. Her hands slid over the clean cotton of his shirt and began buttoning.

"You didn't finish dressing," she whispered as she watched his eyes darken.

"I was afraid I'd be late for breakfast." He showed no sign of caring that there was food on the table.

"How's your lip?" Hannah moved her fingers over the corner of his mouth. "All healed?" She couldn't resist trailing her fingers across it as she asked.

"I'm not sure," he whispered, closing his eyes as he enjoyed her touch. "Maybe you'd better test it."

He didn't move as she stood on her toes and lightly tasted the corner of his mouth. Her breasts pressed against his folded arms, making every muscle in his arms tighten.

"I truly do enjoy kissing you," she whispered as she lightly repeated her actions.

"Is this an attraction you've had with many men?" he teased.

"No," she answered. "I've only developed the weakness lately. I think I must have caught the illness in a hotel room in Dallas."

"What happened there?" he mumbled as she continued to tease his mouth with her light kisses.

"I met a man who kissed as if it weren't a game or a war, but a gift." She leaned closer, pushing him against the door frame with gentle force.

All his restraint shattered. Ford unfolded his arms and lifted her off the floor. With all thought of breakfast forgotten, he carried her to the couch and dropped her among the cushions. A moment later he spread out beside her.

"I'm through pretending I don't want this as much as you do. If you want to kiss me, then I'll kiss you until you've had your fill of it. And if you like feeling me next to you, then I plan on getting as close as I can." He shoved back her hair and placed his hands on either side of her face. "I don't want to frighten you, Hannah, I only want to drink a little deeper of this pleasure we've both found."

"I'm not frightened," she answered. "And I've been thirsty for more since that first night."

Ford wrapped his arms around her and pressed against her, letting his weight cover her like a warm blanket. He kissed her deeply and fully as he'd dreamed of doing all night.

"Had enough?" he asked as he shifted and moved her atop him.

"No," she answered as she wiggled above him, driving him slowly mad. "I never had a man offer to just kiss me and hold me."

"Never?" He found it hard to believe that she hadn't been kissed a great deal.

Hannah laughed. "Oh, I had offers, but they were always for more, much more. I just need to be held, because for me there can be nothing else. If I allowed something between us, I'd only end up hurting us both when I leave. This way all we'll have is a few kisses to remember . . . or regret." She tasted the corner of his mouth again. "A few wonderful kisses."

"Quite a few, I hope." Ford pulled the collar of her nightshirt down and kissed her throat.

"Aren't you hungry?" Hannah asked, laughing against his shoulder.

"No," he whispered as he rubbed his cheek against her hair.

"Well, I am!" came a voice from behind the couch.

"Yeah, when are we gonna get to eat that breakfast we passed in the kitchen?"

Ford bolted up so fast he almost tumbled Hannah to the floor. They both leaned over the back of the cushions and discovered three children staring back at them from the shadows.

Hannah looked at Ford. "Smith children." She nodded her head once.

"Oh? That explains everything." Ford forced down a few comments he'd like to add. He knew they were Smith children; anyone could spot the red hair a mile away. The question was, what were they doing in his house? And how long did they plan to stay?

❖ *Chapter 16*

"So PA SENT us over to go to school with you," Travis Smith mumbled between bites of biscuits. "Pa said he already has a passel of kids, and if there's gonna be room for one more to ~~come into this~~ world, we've all got to scoot over."

"Is your mother doing all right?" Hannah put her uneaten biscuit back on the empty platter and passed it to Sarah Smith.

"She was yelling when we left," Sarah whispered as she hesitantly took the last piece of bread.

"In pain!" Hannah had never been around a woman who was with child, but she'd heard stories and knew birthing killed more women than anything else.

"No," Travis answered. "She was yelling for us to mind you while we stayed here and keep out of Mr. Colston's way."

"Stayed here!" Ford frowned. "You can't . . ."

"Of course they can, Ford. Their mother's having a baby."

Hannah stared at him with hundred-proof challenge in her eyes. Though he knew the children would be staying, he didn't want to give in too easily. Ford tried to think of something clever to say, but all he could think about was that she'd called him by his first name. "I don't know," he mumbled. "Maybe I'll stop by the Smiths' after I drop you all at school and make sure it's all right. It doesn't make sense that Smith would send the kids out this far to board when his cabin is on the other side of town. There must have been ten families you could have stayed with on the road to here."

"Oh, it weren't far," Sarah said. "Jinx brought us here in the mail wagon. Miss Hannah's uncle Zachery said it would be just fine with you for us to stay. He said his niece's husband has got plenty of food to feed a few more."

"Jinx!" both Hannah and Ford said at once. "Zachery?"

Travis's head bobbed. "Sure. She's been at our house all night. Her and Dr. Zach."

Ford and Hannah exchanged glances with one another, then he leaned closer to the child and slowly asked, "Who is Dr. Zach?"

Travis shrugged. "I know he ain't a human doctor, but he was all Pa could find when Ma sent him to town yesterday. Dr. Stocking was over at the JA Ranch sewing up a cowhand who danced with one too many longhorns."

Sarah giggled. "You ain't supposed to dance with them longhorns."

Travis straightened, trying to look taller in the chair. "I know that," he said to his sister, then turned back to Hannah. "Your uncle told Pa birthing a horse and birthing a human couldn't be all that different so he'd try to help. But when he came out of Ma's room after a few hours, he sure looked like he was going through something different."

Ford stood. "Get dressed, Hannah. I'll have the buggy ready in ten minutes. We need to find a few answers."

Hannah lifted a plate, but Sarah's tiny hand touched her arm. "You go ahead, Miss Hannah. Me and Travis can clean up. We do it ever' morning."

Smiling her thank-you, Hannah rushed to dress. Within half an hour the five of them were snuggled into the buggy. She wanted to go with Ford to the Smiths' cabin, but children were already arriving at the school when they pulled into the yard.

As he helped her down, she whispered, "Tell Uncle Zachery I plan to kill him when this is over."

Ford chuckled. "I figured that. But you'll have to stand in line. I can't believe the man volunteered my house." Ford laughed, taking away any threat he was issuing. "Zachery had you worried when he disappeared, didn't he, darlin'?"

"Panicky is more like it. I kept picturing him and Jinx dead on the road somewhere. Now that I know he's safe, I plan to murder him for worrying me." Putting her hand against Ford's cheek, she added, "I don't know why you left Saturday night, but I'm glad you're back."

"So am I," he said without offering any reason for his leaving. "I'll pick you up as soon as school is done. Then maybe we can have a talk."

There was nothing more to say. She wanted to kiss him good-bye, but she knew there were probably a dozen faces pressed against the window watching. The expression in his eyes told her he was thinking the same thing.

Awkwardly, as if he'd never tried such a foolhardy gesture, he lifted her hand to his lips. He turned her glove over, palm up, and pulled down the leather far enough to press his mouth against her wrist where her pulse beat strongest.

Hannah's heart moved all the way to her throat and pounded so wildly she was sure he could not only feel it in his kiss, but hear every beat. His lips were velvet against her skin, his breath warm. When his tongue slid lightly across her wrist, Hannah felt all the air leave her lungs at once. She looked up in his eyes and saw something she'd never seen before. *Passion.*

His grip on her hand was tight, steadying her as he slowly replaced the leather over the skin he'd tasted.

"I have to go," she managed to mumble. The kiss had been polite to anyone watching, but Hannah could still feel the tickle of his tongue against her wrist. In a moment's time, he'd sliced through all the pretenses they played and told her of a need deep within him. A need only she could fill.

"Until tonight, darlin'."

His eyes seemed to be telling her so much more than his words. For an instant, she thought he was going to pull her into his arms and kiss her again. If he did, even with everyone watching, she wouldn't try to stop him. The touch of his tongue had stirred a hunger for more deep within her.

"Until tonight." She slowly pulled her hand from his,

brushing her fingers along his palm, silently telling him she didn't want to let go.

He cupped his hand as if not wanting to end the touching. Then without another word he turned and climbed back into the buggy.

Hannah stood on the steps of the porch and watched him disappear around the corner of White and Rosenfield's store. He sat so straight, so strong, his shoulders wide, his powerful legs propped against the side frame of the buggy. She wasn't sure what she'd silently promised for tonight, but she'd made up her mind to allow him closer, if only to prove to herself that all men's advances weren't harsh and cruel.

As she approached the school, she realized she'd been right earlier. All the students' faces were flattened against the windows, watching.

She ignored their smiles and jabs at one another as she started the second day of her second week of school. Within minutes the whirl of activity made her completely forget everything except trying to stay ahead of the race learning and its distractions waged.

At lunchtime she walked over to White's and charged another box of soft charcoal pencils, knowing that Ford wouldn't mind the only expense she'd ever indulged in for herself. If he said anything about it, she'd offer to pay him out of her wages. When she stopped by the students' homes after school, the children would always tell their parents about her drawings, and sometimes she'd leave them a sketch to keep. So she was always in need of more pencils.

Several people came into the store while she took a

little time to look around. They were talking of the weather and complaining about the lack of mail service while they looked over the new merchandise. Their general consensus was that anyone who went out to the Smith cabin never returned. Mrs. Smith must be keeping everyone busy out there.

The Burns brothers came in to buy candy sticks. They both nodded toward Hannah as they passed her. The Burnses were one of only a few families who sometimes sent extra money with their children to school. The brothers giggled and shoved one another in some childhood secret as they stood before the counter and waited for White to have time to wait on them.

Hannah thought of correcting them, but remembered that she was no longer in the classroom.

Turning to leave, she almost ran into Gavrila, who was rushing in. As always, she was overdressed in her layers of wool. A heavy wool dress, a coat, and a full-length cape seemed too much protection for a day that had warmed enough so that the children had elected to eat their lunches outside.

"Hannah!" Gavrila looked truly surprised to see her sister-in-law. "I thought you'd be at the school. Is something wrong? Do you need me to go over and take charge?"

"No," Hannah answered calmly. "I just walked over to get some charcoal pencils." She resented Gavrila's constant need to check up on the school's progress.

"Oh," Gavrila answered. "Well, I probably wouldn't have time anyway. You wouldn't believe my day." She passed Hannah and directed her words to everyone within ten feet. "I've just run in to pick up a few things. Talk at the sewing circle today was that we're in for our first spring storm. Nothing's worse than early thunderstorms when it's still winter weather." She glanced around to ensure that everyone in the store had stopped his or her conversation and was listening to her. "I hate this weather. A lady can never plan even her clothing. One minute it's sunny and an hour later a norther blows in all the way from Canada, with nothing to stop it but a few rows of barbed wire."

No one said anything, so Gavrila continued. "It's as unpredictable as that brother of mine."

"The Ford I know has always been a kind gentleman," Hannah said, stanching her desire to ask Gavrila if she really thought of herself as taller because she cut Ford down. Her lines were too polished not to have been practiced since childhood. Hannah could almost see a brother and sister fighting over too little love and attention. Gavrila had turned outward, needing everyone's attention and approval, whereas Ford had turned into himself.

Gavrila leaned close and whispered in a voice still loud enough for everyone to hear, "Well, I hope you never find anything different."

Hannah moved out of the store before she said anything in answer. She couldn't change Gavrila's mind about Ford, but she didn't have to listen. She hurried back to the school and rang the bell for lunch to end. Most of the students were still chewing as they ran back in, but none complained, because right after lunch was everyone's favorite hour. Story time. One of the older girls would read and Hannah would open her sketch pad and draw.

Today's story was Andersen's "The Princess and the Pea." Several of the children commented that Hannah drew the princess to look like Gavrila. Then they all laughed at how such a silly prince in the story would want a woman who turned black-and-blue from sleeping on a pea tucked beneath twenty mattresses. Since most of them slept on corn cob bedding or in bedrolls brought out by the fire after supper, they couldn't imagine any-one, except maybe Gavrila, complaining about a pea.

Hannah hung the drawing up with pride among the others. If she stayed the full month, the walls would be covered with her drawings and she'd have a wealth of stories dancing in her head.

When she dismissed school, cleaned all the boards, and banked the fire, she was starting to feel the exhaus-tion of two nights with little sleep. Two more of the Smith children had made it to school, and all of them seemed to have plans of going home with her.

"Is everyone ready?" she asked as she moved toward the door.

They all fell into line like ducklings as she walked out. She could see Ford's buggy parked beside White's store, but he wasn't in sight. Glancing across the street, she noticed Lewis's store and post office was still closed. Trying not to let her disappointment show, she walked into White's.

Ford almost collided with her. He was loaded to chin level with supplies.

"Evening," she bowed as she held the door for him.

He didn't speak as he passed her.

Hannah motioned for the children to follow. "Is something wrong?" she asked as she helped the children into the buggy while he loaded the back.

"No," he answered, but his words were almost a snap.

Watching him closely, she commented, "I didn't think we needed any more supplies." Even with the extra children to feed, Ford already had enough stocked to last several months.

"I just wanted to make certain. I thought I'd get everything so you wouldn't have to worry about going into White's again."

"I don't mind going in." Hannah couldn't make the pieces fit together, no matter how she turned his words. "I went in at lunch today."

Ford climbed in beside her and sat Sammy Smith on his knee to make a little extra room. "I know; Gavrila told me."

Another piece, but no sense what the puzzle was, Hannah thought. Why should Ford be angry that she'd used her lunchtime to buy pencils? Or was he mad that she'd talked to his sister? Or had his sister told him something? Hannah was too tired to try and make sense of any of it. She leaned back against the side of the wagon and tried not to think about how tired she was. With the children, there was still much to do before bedtime.

"Did you see Zachery?" she finally gathered the energy to ask.

"Yes," Ford answered, his voice still laced with a formal flavor. "He said to tell you he's real sorry to have worried you. It seems he and Jinx were in the middle of a checker

game when Smith ran up asking for help. Zachery didn't
want to go, since he's only delivered cows and horses, but
Jinx pulled him along."

"How is Mrs. Smith?" Hannah couldn't help but think
that Zachery would probably be the last person she'd
want around if she was in labor. She suspected most of
his personal stories were picked up from another in a bar
and were not true-life experiences.

"The woman's having a hard time, but Smith told me
none of her young ones pop out in less than two days.
He wouldn't consider them worth raising if they didn't
take a while to deliver."

"Should I go help?"

"Have you ever played midwife?"

"No."

"Then maybe Jinx and Zachery should handle it. I
know I was no help while I was there this morning. We
can do our share by taking care of these children. Smith
kept the oldest one at home to help with the chores and
cooking."

Hannah didn't say anything else and Ford directed the
rest of his conversation to the children. Once they were
home, it took both of them to get all five fed, bathed, and
bedded down in the living room by the fire.

Ford carried the empty hot cocoa cups into the kitchen
and set them down beside the sink where Hannah was
standing. "I thought I'd sleep in Zachery's room tonight."

She'd felt the tension all evening. He was distant, formal, almost a stranger. "What's wrong?"

"Nothing," he answered for the third time since they'd
been home.

Only now they were alone, and she wasn't going to let it pass as she had earlier. "Soemthing is. You've been acting like a different man than the one who dropped me off this morning."

"Not different," he whispered, "only wiser."

"Don't you want to kiss me anymore?" Hannah bit her lip. That wasn't the question she'd wanted to ask, even though it had been on her mind all evening.

"Whether I do or don't doesn't matter!" he snapped. "The fact is, I'm not going to. The way I figure it, we've got two and a half more weeks. It would be best if we stayed as far away from one another as possible until you leave."

"Until I die, you mean."

"Until you die," he repeated. "And until then, stay out of the store or anywhere else but school and here."

"But why?"

"I don't have to give you any reasons. So far I've let you set all the rules. Well, now I'm setting one of my own. I'm telling you to stay away from everything and everyone but the school and here."

"And if I refuse?" Hannah couldn't imagine why he'd make such a request.

"Then I'll . . ." Ford gripped the counter and tried to hide his frustration. He'd made up his mind he wouldn't discuss the theft White had reported this afternoon. A stationary box with paper, ink, and silver-tipped pens had vanished sometime around noon. He'd tried to tell himself that Hannah hadn't taken it, but who else would? They'd never had a theft in Saints Roost before she came. She'd been in the store; she'd told him so her-

self. He hated himself for suspecting her and hated her
even more for not being what he wished she were.

"You'll what?" Hannah faced him squarely. "You'll
hit me?"

Her challenge shook him from his thought. "No." He
forced his voice to stay low so as not to wake the children. "How many times do I have to tell you I'll never
hurt you?"

"You say that, but your mood changes for no reason."

"I don't have to explain." He knew he couldn't tell her
what he suspected without hurting her more than with
his silence.

"Your sister told me you might turn wild," Hannah
snapped. "But she was wrong. You only turn cold."

"Maybe you'd better be thankful I don't turn wild.
Maybe there is something in me not quite civilized after
all. Maybe you shouldn't push me too far, Hannah."

"Is that a threat?"

"Take it any way you like, but stay away from everything but the school and this house." Here she could take
anything she wanted and he wouldn't care.

"And if I refuse?" She had to push him. She had to
know the limits of this man. If he was the kind to beat
her, Hannah wanted to know now so she could draw her
battle lines and prepare a defense.

Standing directly in front of him, she leaned closer,
putting herself in harm's way. She'd cowered before,
when Jude had first hurt her, and something had snapped
inside her. She'd not back away again. Her fear had
given Jude power, and the blows had only grown harder
the second time.

Ford bumped her with his shoulder as he turned his back to her. "Just stay away from the folks of Saints Roost and from me." His voice was bitter.

Hannah raised her hand to touch his shoulder and demand to know why he'd changed so suddenly, but he was gone. He almost ran from the kitchen.

He didn't stop running until he reached the safety of the loft. He walked to the opening and grabbed the beam above his head. Leaning out into the night, he took a deep breath and tried to force his body to unknot.

He had to stay away from her. She was everything he'd fought all his life not to be. Her eyes made his very insides melt, yet she pushed him to the limit, both with a longing to hold her and with her thefts.

Maybe the rumors about him were true. For the thoughts he had of what he'd like to do with Hannah were wild and untamed.

If it were a time before civilization and rules, he'd run back into the house and sweep her into his arms. With her heart pounding against his, he'd run to the caves where the ground was soft and the world was silent. He'd kiss her fully as his hands tore her clothes away and his body pressed hers into the earth. He'd fill his hands with her full breasts and listen only to her soft cries of pleasure.

"Stop it!" Ford yelled. He grabbed his head, trying to force the thoughts of her beneath him from his mind. This wasn't the time before civilization and he wasn't some caveman who took a mate violently. Regular folks don't have such thoughts, he reminded himself.

"Normal!" He laughed. "Civilized!" He only had to

make it two and a half more weeks, then maybe the wild streak within him would die away and he could bury it along with his make-believe wife in a coffin lined with a wedding quilt . . . and stolen dreams.

✤ *Chapter 17*

HANNAH PASSED THROUGH the week in a daze of endless chores. When she wasn't at school teaching, she was working at the house, trying to keep five children clean and fed. Uncle Zachery was welcomed home as a hero to all the children for helping Mrs. Smith bring another redhead into the world. The Smiths couldn't bear to name the girl Zachery after him, so they settled on Janie Noble Smith, using his last name as her middle name. He walked a little taller and didn't seem to feel the need to talk all the time. Of late he much preferred folks talking about him, and was willing to allow them all the time they needed to express what a wonderful job he'd done with the birthing.

When Zachery returned, Ford took up residence in the barn, saying only that all the people bothered him after spending so many years living alone. Hannah knew that wasn't the reason, but she refused to press him anymore for an answer. He was a man who spoke what was on his mind only when he wanted to.

He sat across from her each night, listening to the children talk, but never said anything directly to her. She found herself feeling lonelier than if there had been no one in the house with her at all.

Saturday arrived and with it a ton of laundry. Hannah enlisted all the children's help. By midmorning a full assault had been launched against the piles of clothes and bedding. She rolled her dress sleeves to the elbow and held the lye soap in her hand until her fingers cramped. Piece after piece moved through the boiling pot and onto the scrub board. The wind was cold, chapping her hands, while the hot water stung, but this was the first sunny day she could do her chore and Hannah wasn't going to waste time complaining.

Between loads drying, she baked and watched Ford moving about the yard, mostly working, but sometimes stopping to see if he could lend a hand.

Finally, Ford and Zachery loaded the children, along with all their clean clothing, into the wagon for their journey home. Hannah packed the boot full of food, including a roast with potatoes and three apple pies. She kissed them each good-bye and said she'd see them on Monday. They waved at her until the wagon turned out of sight.

When she went back inside, the house seemed too quiet. She could hear the wind promising a storm and the crackling sound of wood in the stove, sounds she hadn't noticed with all the children about. Hannah walked around picking up things that had been moved during their stay. All week she'd thought about how much work came with five young ones around, but she also thought about the fun. They'd laughed and teased one another. The older ones had been afraid of Ford, but Sammy seemed to believe his seat was on Ford's knee. Whenever they were eating or riding in the buggy, he took up that position without hesitation.

Though Ford hadn't tried to be overly friendly, he'd constantly helped out. Without a word he'd assumed the job of putting out the beds in the big room every night and making sure there was plenty of wood to last until morning. She also knew he'd tripled his order for milk and eggs. He'd even hung a swing in the old cottonwood a hundred yards up the road.

An hour after the children had gone, Hannah was so absorbed in daydreaming about what having a real family might be like that she didn't hear Ford returning until he was already at the back door.

When she glanced up, his abrupt appearance frightened her and she let out a half cry as he turned the knob on the kitchen door and entered.

Ford's face darkened when he saw her expression.

Hannah closed her mouth and tried to smile, but the effort was wasted for he didn't look at her again. "You startled me," she said as he turned his back and removed his coat.

"I seem to have that effect on a great many people, according to Gavrila."

Hannah could see the tightness in his muscles. She didn't want him to be uncomfortable. Though he'd been nothing but kind to her, the wall he'd built between himself and the rest of the world wouldn't allow him to accept anyone else's kindness.

For a few hours, earlier in the week, she'd seen him relaxed and happy. When he'd come back from the line shack he couldn't seem to get enough of her touch, her kisses. They'd parted that morning with an unspoken promise of what would come the first time they had a few moments alone. But when he'd picked her up from school everything had changed. Hannah had been over the day a hundred times in her mind. She could think of nothing that would turn him against her. She'd taught school; she'd bought pencils; she'd spoken to Gavrila.

He sat down at the table now almost a stranger, nothing like the man she'd held before the Smiths came. Hannah placed a plate in front of him, feeling as she had for years when she'd served food to men who didn't even bother to look at her. They'd usually treated her as though she were invisible, someone to serve them, nothing more. For years she'd cooked and cleaned without anyone even noticing her, unless a customer needed more food or drink.

Hannah's pride wouldn't allow Ford to do the same. He'd at least talk to her while they shared a meal. "Where's Uncle Zachery?"

Ford stared at her hands as he spoke. "He decided to stay in town for a few hours and have a meal with Jinx. He said not to wait up for him, because he might be in late."

"Oh." Hannah didn't know what else to say. They were alone for the first time in days and she wasn't sure how to act. Zachery was constantly talking about nothing, but at least he kept the silence from consuming them.

Ford stood, almost knocking the chair over. "I'll be back in a minute."

He didn't look at her as he disappeared out the kitchen door. Hannah watched him go, wondering how she'd ever survive another two weeks with his coldness. She knew she should be planning. He'd promised her a train ticket and whatever she wanted to take with her. She wouldn't be safe here forever. It would be better to think about where to stop next, but Hannah couldn't seem to get her mind to reason.

When he returned, she was leaning to feed Sneeze a scrap of meat. The cat purred his thanks as Ford set a leather pouch, beaded on the front, on the table and waited for her to stand. When he pulled the strings open, she noticed it was fur-lined and she moved closer in interest.

Ford sat down and turned toward her. "Come here," he ordered, even though she was only a few feet away from him.

Hannah watched as he opened layers of oilcloth. Moving beside his knee, she leaned close with curiosity.

"Hold out your hands," he said more gently. "This doesn't hurt."

She leaned against the inside of his knee and lifted her hands.

Gently, Ford rubbed the oily lotion into her chapped fingers and palms. "A woman in Tascosa makes this oil from a plant. She swears it will fix anything but a broken heart."

Hannah was having trouble listening to what he was saying. His fingers were firm and strong as he rubbed the oil into her chapped hands. She moved closer, leaning her leg against the inside of his leg.

Ford stiffened and tried not to notice. He hadn't thought about how close they'd have to be when he'd gone after the medicine. After the last theft, he'd promised himself he'd stick to their original bargain until she left. The plan was to give her all the extra cash he had, both in town at his office and here in his desk, so that she could live for several weeks while he told everyone she was visiting family. At some point she'd telegram that his wife had been killed in an accident and sign it by another name. He'd board the train in grief and return a few days later with a coffin.

He had it all figured out, even down to what he'd say to everyone at the funeral. What he hadn't counted on was how hard it would be to stay away from her until she left, or how impossible it was to sleep knowing that she was only a few feet away and more than willing to allow him to sleep beside her.

"I think all the oil is rubbed in," she whispered as she moved an inch closer.

He could feel the warmth of her, even through both layers of clothes, as she leaned against his leg. She was making it so hard to stick to his plan. All he had to do was move his arm around her waist and with one tug she'd be in his lap. Then he could lean into her, feeling the softness of her against him.

Pulling away suddenly, he toppled his chair backward as he tried to keep from touching her. "I think we'd better eat before the food gets cold," he mumbled as he picked up the chair and tried to sit as far away from her as possible at the tiny table.

Hannah sat across from him, wondering at the strange feelings she was having. She'd always wanted to touch this man, even from the beginning, and now that he seemed to be pulling away, the need was even stronger.

"Are we going to church tomorrow?"

"Yes," he answered between bites. "Gavrila has invited us to Sunday dinner, along with a few others. I think she's planning on giving us the wedding quilt then."

"You mean the burial quilt," Hannah teased, but he didn't smile at her attempt to lighten the mood.

He still wasn't smiling the next morning as they rode to church. Hannah had no idea where he'd slept, but it hadn't been in her room. From the dark marks beneath his eyes, he wasn't sleeping anywhere at all.

She studied him closely. From the looks of him, she was having a bad effect on Ford. If she didn't leave soon, he'd be a walking dead man. He appeared to have lost weight, and most days he'd seemed to be pushing himself to the limit. This morning, even before sunup, she'd heard him working in the barn.

Uncle Zachery, on the other hand, had never looked better to Hannah, despite the late hours he was keeping. He talked about his evenings with Jinx, but Hannah was as silent as Ford. She had to figure out what was eating away at him before whatever it was drove them both crazy.

Accidentally, she rocked her leg against his when they hit a bump in the road, and she felt his muscles tighten.

An idea took hold in her mind. If he was going to build walls between them, she might as well test their strength.

Slowly, almost accidentally, her leg brushed his once more. He didn't move, but she knew he was aware of her. She could see it in the way his fingers whitened around the reins and hear it in the sudden change in his breathing.

While Uncle Zachery kept talking, she slid her hand behind Ford's back and lightly brushed the hair at his collar. The act was a little thing any wife might have done, but she noticed Ford's jaw tightened to granite.

The game gave her far more pleasure than she'd guessed it might, and judging by Ford's face, it awarded him far more pain. If she continued, maybe he'd snap and tell her what was eating away at him.

While they rode toward town, she played with the hair just behind his ear, catching the thick strands between her fingers and tugging. When he didn't respond, she tugged harder.

Ford moved away slightly, but there was nowhere to go—unless he jumped. He had no choice but to endure her advances until they reached town.

But town was no refuge. When he helped her from the buggy, Hannah leaned into him, moving her body along his slowly.

She heard him bite back a moan, but he didn't say a word to her. For a breath, she pressed so hard against him she felt his heart pounding. He stiffened, but refused to even look in her direction.

In church, she laced her arm around his and leaned her breast against his shoulder as they shared a hymnal. He didn't move, but she smiled when he seemed to have forgotten the words.

Once when a man near the back dropped the offering plate, Hannah twisted around to look, shoving her hip against his side and sliding her hand along his arm while no one was looking. Ford appeared to have turned to stone, but his breathing seemed to speed up until she moved back into place beside him.

"Are you all right?" she whispered as she leaned against him, her mouth so close to his ear no one could have heard her words.

He didn't answer.

As they walked out of church, Hannah took every opportunity to touch him. He gave her a quick, angry glare, but didn't have time to say anything before others joined them and they all walked the short distance to Gavrila's house. Hannah talked to everyone about the sermon and how much she'd enjoyed the Smith children, but her fingers never let go of his hand. When he tried to pull away, she dug her nails into his skin and scratched.

Once, when talking of how happy the children were, she lifted his hand in hers and held it to her chest.

Ford almost lost his footing.

Of course she helped him, even dusting him off with gentle strokes as though he'd actually fallen.

He didn't respond, but followed the Burns family into Gavrila's house, marveling at how no one had noticed her advances but him.

Harold Burns and his wife, Amy, were standard guests when Gavrila had a dinner. She detested their two boys, but considered Burns one of the richest men in town, and therefore his family was the most qualified to be guests. She suffered their sons by always putting the two boys at a small table out of her line of vision by the kitchen door.

As the adults took their places, Gavrila gave her standard threat to the children not to touch anything or she'd know.

When Ford pulled Hannah's chair out, he leaned close to her ear and whispered, "What the hell do you think you're doing?"

Hannah smiled up at him as if he'd said an endearment. "I'm keeping up my end of our bargain—the one you're so set on keeping. Touching in public, remember?"

He leaned close again. "Well, stop overdoing it! You were outright attacking me in church."

"Tell me what's eating at you and I'll stop."

"Nothing is bothering me but you, darlin'." If church had lasted another hour he'd have gone stark raving mad from her movements next to him. She'd managed to rub almost every part of her body against his, while looking like an angel in church every time he glared at her.

Hannah smoothed the hair off his collar and leaned her breast against his arm. "I don't plan on stopping until you start talking. Unless, of course, you tell me you hate my touch and that's the reason you've been avoiding me since Tuesday."

Ford stared at her with angry eyes. Though he couldn't take much more of her flirting, he couldn't lie and tell her he hated it. She must have a pretty good idea what her touch was doing to him. He'd sworn to be a gentleman and ride this marriage out. If he ever grabbed her and showed her how he really felt about her pressing against him, he'd probably frighten her to death—or she'd go running to Gavrila, swearing the rumors about him were true.

The others filed around the table and took their seats: the Burnses, the Combses, and of course Widow Rogers and her son, Alamo, who had the choice seat next to Gavrila. No one seemed to notice that Ford was silent. They were all too busy telling Gavrila what a wonderful meal she'd prepared. Ford knew she had two women in the kitchen doing all the work, but as always he didn't say anything as he watched his sister rattle on about all her many responsibilities.

Every now and then, Gavrila would reach over and swat at Alamo's arm or shoulder. To Ford it seemed more an ownership pat than an endearment, and it was nothing like the pats Hannah kept giving his knee under the table.

As he lifted his first bite of soup, Hannah's hand slid up his leg as boldly as Sherman's advance into the South. Ford almost dropped the spoon.

"Ford!" Gavrila shouted from the other end of the table. "Watch what you're doing."

He bit back a comment and stared at Hannah, who had the nerve to smile as innocently as a cherub.

From then on, he watched his wife closely. She was so calm as she talked with the Combses on her right while her left hand slid up the muscle of his thigh. When she turned her attention to him, it was even harder trying to remain proper. She always managed to brush his arm or reach out to touch him in some little way that looked endearing to everyone at the table but was driving him mad.

Ford focused his attention on the other end of the table, where Gavrila seemed to be courting Alamo. Until his marriage, Ford had never seen her give Alamo more than a passing glance, but today she was definitely sighting in for the kill.

Hannah made him forget all about anyone at the table as she accidentally dropped her napkin and leaned low, brushing his side, to retrieve it. He felt the softness of her breast and shoved the image of her dressing in the mirror's reflection from his mind.

He barely made it through dessert without strangling Hannah. When everyone left the table, he grabbed her hand and pulled her toward the stairs.

"I'd like to show you something, darlin'."

"But the guests . . ." She tried to pull away.

"We'll only be a moment." He tugged harder. At this point, he was willing to drag her up the stairs. She'd played with his leg until the muscle felt like it was on fire. She'd leaned so close he'd never forget the way she smelled or the feel of her words against his throat. She'd driven him completely mad by brushing against him and then looking to all the world as if she hadn't noticed the effect she had on him.

Hannah managed a smile at the watching guests. "I'm coming, dear," she said unnecessarily, for they were already a third of the way up the stairs.

Ford didn't slow down until he was inside his office and had slammed the door. He pushed her against the wall, planted powerful arms on either side of her, imprisoning her effectively without touching her. "What in the *hell* do you think you're doing?"

Hannah stared out the curtainless window into a cloudy sky that seemed colorless compared to the thunderstorm in Ford's eyes. "Nothing. I haven't been doing anything except keeping to our agreement."

He swore beneath his breath and turned his back to her. Lord, if she only knew how dearly he wanted to hold her. But a thief wasn't what he wanted in a wife, and she couldn't seem to give up the profession. She'd proved that in White's store. Ford wasn't the kind of man who could play games at loving. He'd replaced the writing kit she'd stolen by making an all-day ride into Mobeetie, where he'd guessed another store had probably received the same shipment as White's store. Mr. White had been surprised Friday when he found it beneath a sack of flour. Told half the town what a fool he'd been to think someone stole it in Saints Roost. He even convinced himself that he probably accidentally laid the flour on top of the kit.

"I don't remember you swearing until lately." Hannah moved behind him, looking at the plain room he called his office. It had none of the color or warmth of his home, and she guessed he spent as little time here as he must. "Swearing's a bad habit for a godly man like yourself, don't you think?"

"I may take up drinking next, if you don't stop." He braced his hands on either side of the window frame. It was so hard not to turn around and pull her into his arms.

Maybe he'd died that night in Dallas and this was some level of hell. If so he didn't want to see the next level.

Hannah slid her hand down the center of his back, making him arch his neck. "I told you from the first I liked touching you." She wanted to scream "talk to me!" but she'd tried one too many times already to break the shell around this man. The only way she seemed to reach him was with her caress.

"But do you have to . . ." He couldn't finish. How could he ask her not to make him feel? How could he explain that after a lifetime of not being touched, her nearness was driving him mad.

"Turn around," Hannah ordered. "Face me, Ford."

"No," he answered. "I can't and stay a gentleman."

She played with the muscles along his back as she pressed her cheek near his ear. "I don't want to argue with you. Is it so painful to feel my touch or to look at me? You're the only man I've ever wanted to be near. I see nothing wrong with touching you or letting you hold me."

Ford closed his eyes, thinking she'd never know just how painful it was to deny her request. "Why are you doing this? And don't tell me it's because of our bargain. What you've done today goes far beyond any agreement."

Hannah rested her chin against the back of his shoulder and wrapped her arms around his waist. "I've never felt safe with a man before. I guess I just want you to notice me." Shame for the forward way she'd acted whispered through her desire to touch him again. He was the only man who'd ever treated her like a lady and he was trying to keep his distance. They both knew the closer they got the harder it would be to say good-bye. She had to be able to walk away in only two weeks. "I'm sorry I'm pushing you."

His muscles relaxed across his shoulders and he turned around. "Don't, Hannah. I'm only a man. We both know there can be nothing between us, and to pretend otherwise is only a fool's dream."

"Don't close me out like I'm nobody." Tears threatened to tumble. "Don't walk around me as if I'm not there. Don't sit across from me at a meal and pretend you're alone, even if you wish you were."

"That is not it at all, darlin'," he whispered, turning slightly. He felt like a snake for making her so sad, even though he knew his actions were right. "I'm very much aware you're here."

"Couldn't we find someplace in the middle where we could both be comfortable?" She didn't want him being cold to her. In a way his cold politeness was worse than outright anger.

He offered his hand. He hadn't thought that his actions were hurting her; he'd only meant to protect himself. "I have a great deal to learn about women. For the time that's left, is it possible we could be friends?"

"That's a start." She accepted his hand.

Ford closed his fingers around hers. "I have no wish to hurt you." He only guessed, but all the signs were there—someone had hurt her, maybe even hit her before. He could never add more bruises to her heart. "There can never be more between us. We made a bargain to help one other out, nothing more." Each word seemed to knife its way past his throat, hurting Ford as much as Hannah.

"Nothing more," she echoed without looking at him. "You're sure?"

"I wouldn't allow there to be," he answered, wishing he could believe his words.

She nodded, knowing there was no use arguing. Ford didn't want her; what else was there to say? She'd complete the bargain and leave without pestering him anymore.

They walked hand in hand down the stairs and into the parlor, where they'd been married only two weeks before. A hush fell over the room when they entered, leaving no doubt that they'd been the topic of conversation only moments before.

"There are the newlyweds!" Gavrila's voice was loud enough to wake the barn owl. "I was just telling everyone that from the way you two acted on your wedding day, you must have known one another for a long time."

Ford wasn't about to be drawn into one of his sister's conversations. He'd learned after years of embarrassment that he couldn't win. She was far quicker at crisscrossing meanings of what was said than he'd ever be.

Gavrila stared at him, then let out a long-suffering sigh as she turned to the others. "My brother never seems to want to talk about anything but the weather."

Hannah watched, wishing Ford would say something, not understanding why he didn't.

Turning her attention to Hannah, Gavrila counterattacked Ford's silence. "Perhaps you'll enlighten us, sister-in-law. Just how did you and my brother meet?"

Hannah's hesitation was so slight, no one but Ford noticed it.

"We met one night when Ford helped me catch a train. In fact, if he hadn't been so kind and generous I never would have made it. From that night on, he was my knight in shining armor. Men so good are rare indeed."

Everyone, including Gavrila, looked interested, so Hannah continued. "When I heard he was searching for a schoolteacher, I knew I was right for the job before he even thought to ask me." She smiled at the Burnses. "I knew any town that had a fine resident like Sanford Colston couldn't be anything but an upright, God-fearing place."

Gavrila looked disappointed. She obviously hadn't intended the conversation to turn into a tribute to her brother.

Mr. Burns started talking about school improvements and Hannah smiled, realizing Gavrila had lost all control of the room. Mrs. Burns and the widow laughed over the past two almost-thefts in town. Hannah had heard the children talking about how White thought someone stole from him.

She stood close to Ford, touching him whenever she could, but no longer playing the game she had before. He never returned her light pats and caring little caresses, but he didn't pull away from her either. They'd reached a truce that seemed to allow both to breathe.

When they finally stood to leave, Hannah thought

Ford seemed more relaxed than she'd seen him in days. He enjoyed talking about improvements in the town, and his ideas were solid. Burns pumped his hand, showing a new respect for Gavrila's brother that he hadn't displayed before.

Gavrila missed the conversation, for she had caught the Burns brothers playing with her tea service, which always sat in waiting by the windows. She scolded them so harshly that Mrs. Burns apologized for her sons as she ushered them out the door. The boys only glared at Gavrila and tried to collect their marbles before she noticed them rolling around the serving tray.

Alamo and his mother hurried behind the Burnses as if escaping the plague. Widow Rogers said a thanks and waved, but Alamo didn't even look back as he helped his mother out the door.

Gavrila stomped her foot as she turned back to Hannah and Ford. "Children are such a bother," she whispered so the departing guests couldn't hear. "I'm never having any, and I hope you'll follow my example, Hannah."

Ford pulled Hannah toward the door, knowing it would be wise to follow now that all the guests were out of hearing distance. "Thanks for the meal, Gavrila. But if you don't mind, we'll plan our own life. As for children, we plan to have one for every year we're married. And don't worry, we'll visit you often."

Hannah couldn't help but laugh at the expression on Gavrila's face.

Ford swung his wife into the buggy and slapped the reins before Gavrila had a chance to reply. They had almost arrived to pick up Uncle Zachery before he stopped laughing, then glanced at Hannah and had the wild thought that he wished it were true about the children.

But then he realized half of their children would be unlucky enough to look like him and the other half would be thieves.

Chapter 18 ❖

UNCLE ZACHERY TOOK fifteen minutes to tell Ford and Hannah that he couldn't go home with them. It seemed Jinx had talked him into riding out to the Smith place just to double-check on the baby, then she'd invited him to supper again. For a woman who claimed she cooked little, Jinx was certainly keeping the oven warm lately.

Ford offered to come back for him or let Zachery borrow one of the horses he kept in Gavrila's barn, but Uncle Zachery insisted that he'd take care of himself and they shouldn't bother to wait up for him.

Though Ford waved, calling back that they'd see him later, Hannah knew Zachery wouldn't be returning tonight. She'd seen him glance toward the door of the extra room off the post office. She wasn't sure why her new uncle wanted to stay, but she guessed it had more to do with Jinx than checkers.

Hannah and Ford pulled out of town alone for the night for the first time in a week. She tried to think of something to say, but it was hopeless. Hannah thought of apologizing again for the way she'd acted in church, but she didn't really regret what she'd done. In truth, she'd never dreamed church could be so exciting.

Glancing over at Ford, she wondered for the hundredth time what there was about the man that made him so touchable. He seemed to try hard to be proper, as though nothing in this world could bother him.

Hannah couldn't hide her smile. *I bother him,* she thought. *I cannot only disturb that proper air, I can make him feel things deep down where he doesn't want to admit he has emotions.* His sister might have known him all his life, but Gavrila was wrong about Ford. Deep within him wasn't an animal, but a wealth of untapped senses. Feelings so deeply rooted in control, Hannah might never pull them to the surface.

"What's so funny?" Ford interrupted her thoughts.

"Nothing," Hannah replied hastily, trying to tuck her thoughts into proper order. "I was just thinking."

Ford waited. He didn't question her again or attempt to pry, he just waited for her to continue. His silence made her nervous.

"I was thinking what a pretty day it is." Hannah mentally slapped herself for not coming up with something more interesting to say. When she got out of this mess, she planned to spend her days following strangers around, eavesdropping on their conversations so that she'd know what things normal, everyday folks talked about. Ford sure wasn't giving her any practice.

He seemed to be battling the same problem she was, for he started twice before he finally said, "Yes, it is."

This time it was Hannah's turn to wait for more. Of

course if it took him three tries to think of those three words, she might be in for a long wait.

Ford opened his mouth once but changed his mind. Finally, he smiled and added, "Looks like we may be in for that storm tonight that's been promising to drop by for a visit." He glanced at her as if giving her a chance to talk, then added, "See those clouds along the horizon?"

Hannah loved the sunsets on cloudy days out here on the plains. The sun seemed to spread for miles and turn the bottom half of all the clouds to gold, then orange, and finally violet. She wondered if the sun felt sorry for these people living out here in this treeless, colorless land and decided to paint the sky brilliant every evening just to give them something to look at besides tumbleweeds and brown buffalo grass.

She smiled again, thinking that she was starting to sound like her mother. To her mother everything, even the moon, sun, and wind were beings in their own right. The moon could dance, the sun could kiss your cheeks, the wind could call you. Hannah only believed such folly in the night when reality was covered in shadow and walked between the real world and dreams.

Hannah fought to keep from laughing; she *was* starting to think like her mother.

"You're smiling again." Ford's low voice interrupted her thoughts once more. "You like watching the clouds?"

"I was thinking the sunset is beautiful." She realized they were talking, but neither seemed to be following the other's conversation very well.

"Yes, it is," Ford added, but he was looking at her and not the sun. "Very beautiful."

"My mother used to say that when the sun goes home each evening, it pulls a blanket of fire behind it."

"That's what it looks like," Ford agreed. He wanted to ask about her mother, but he didn't believe in prying. However, he couldn't help but wonder what it would have been like to have had a mother to tell him such things as a child. His father had always been very practical, never wasting words. In fact, he never talked to Ford unless he had to, and then only in short sentences or orders mostly.

They rode the rest of the way in silence. When they were back on the ranch, Ford worked in the barn until it was dark, and Hannah cooked supper.

They were halfway through dinner when he said, "One of my mares is fixing to foal any time now and I thought I'd sleep in the barn tonight. She can probably handle everything without me, but if there's trouble, I don't want to lose her or the foal."

Hannah wanted to argue that he could take Zachery's room. At least then he wouldn't seem so far away. But she knew he was trying to make it easier for her. Something was still bothering him, holding him at a distance, and she'd given up trying to speculate as to what it could be.

"I'll get you extra blankets. I can smell rain."

Ford didn't look at her. "Me, too. We need it. Seems like spring comes earlier when we get rain."

They needed to talk, but Hannah didn't know where

to begin. After taking a long drink of milk, she asked, "Are you going to read a story tonight?"

Ford shook his head. He downed another quick bite and stood. "I'd better be getting back to the barn."

Before Hannah could speak, he was gone, as though he couldn't wait to be out of her sight. She tried to understand his strange behavior as she did the dishes and prepared for bed. He should be more relaxed when they were alone and didn't have to pretend anymore, but he'd been like a man forced at gunpoint to be near her.

When she turned out the lights, Hannah curled on the couch and watched the fire. The wind was blowing again, whipping around the house, rattling the windows. Why was it she always heard the wind when she was alone?

Closing her eyes, she tried to remember how her mother used to hold her on nights like this and tell her not to be afraid.

Someday you'll dance with the wind, child, her mother would say. *Until you do, you'll always be afraid.*

Hannah stared into the light of the fire. That was it, she decided, she was afraid. Like her mother, she'd held on to what she had no matter how hard and dreary it was because she was afraid to step out and look around. Tonight she'd still be working for old Hickory, scrubbing floors, cooking, doing dishes, if she hadn't seen the murder and been forced to run.

She was a person who not only never welcomed change, but hid when it came knocking. She'd never done anything in her life but what she had to do to sur-

vive. Never in her life had she tried something wild.
Never had she tried to dance with the wind.

She'd never been brave enough to dance with the
wind, even once. She'd run, she'd hidden, she'd tried to
make herself invisible, but she'd never stood and fought
for anything . . . because nothing in her life had ever had
color before she came here.

Ford checked on the mare. She was still hours, maybe
even a day or two, away from foaling, but he had to have
some reason to leave the house. Hannah's touching this
morning had shattered his reserve. He needed time to
pull his emotions together.

The barn had always been his refuge as a boy. The
lowing of the animals and the smell of hay were welcoming to his senses. When he'd been small the barn
was the one place Gavrila never ventured. It was his
alone. As an adult he realized she'd resented him for in-
truding in the world she liked to create as a child, and
like their father, blamed him for their mother's death.
He'd thought only animals were allowed in the barn
when he was small. He could be there because he was
more animal than boy.

Climbing the ladder to the loft, he fought back the
childhood memories. He'd been his own man for years
now. He'd worked day and night hauling buffalo bones
to get enough money for the land, then he hadn't stopped
until his house was built and his herd big enough to matter. There were years Ford didn't really remember passing as days, only in weeks of endless work.

He leaned against the opening and looked out on the

grassland between his place and the edge of the canyon. The land was so flat a man could be almost to the edge of the drop into the canyon before he realized it was there. Supposedly, Coronado had almost fallen off the rim when he stumbled across it in the middle of a hailstorm. The conquistador led his men down the rock walls, and when the weather cleared held a thanksgiving service for the blessing of the canyon.

Ford could hear a storm coming in. Moisture was thick in his lungs. The rain was always needed, but he dreaded losing the work time. He'd been piling up little chores he could do in the barn if he should be forced inside for a day. From the look of the clouds, tomorrow might be that day.

Turning out his light, he stared across the buffalo grass to the dark shadow outline of his canyon. It looked almost like a black river tonight, cutting his land only a hundred yards from his home. Some folks didn't want to live this close to the drop. They said it was dangerous. But Ford loved the beauty of it. He didn't even mind the stories he'd heard of how on windy nights like this a man could hear the ghosts of Quanah Parker's fourteen hundred horses riding the rim. Colonel Mackenzie had ordered his men to run the animals off the walls of the canyon to end the war with the Apache. The strategy had worked, saving hundreds of both Apache and soldiers' lives, but some said the cries of the horses falling into the canyon still carried on the wind.

Ford didn't believe in ghosts, but tonight he could almost believe he saw one dancing in the tall grass.

She twirled in the wind, her hair flying around her like a midnight cape. Ford watched her dance, letting the wind direct her in first one path, then another. Her long, dark robe circled around her legs, almost like an old-fashioned hooped skirt, and the snow of her nightshirt glistened in the smoky moonlight.

He watched as she lifted her arms and circled, not caring that the wind whipped her hair into her face. She twirled like a beautiful top, without direction, without purpose, dancing to a melody only she and the wind seemed to share.

"Hannah!" The realization that his vision was real shook Ford like a blow. Hannah was circling below him with her eyes closed, dancing as if she had no idea that the edge of the canyon rim zigzagged into the land only yards from her feet.

He bolted from the opening and slid down the ladder without wasting time on footholds. Running across the barn, Ford almost pulled the door from its hinges in his haste.

Running in long, powerful strides across the field, he closed the distance between them in seconds. He stopped suddenly, his back to the canyon and his feet firmly planted in the buffalo grass. He waited as she twirled toward him, looking far more like a dream dancing with the wind than a real woman.

She danced with her eyes tightly closed. Feeling a freedom unlike she'd ever felt, she twirled, letting the wind direct her. She hit his chest suddenly, without warning. The wind had drowned out all sound but its own music. Finally she'd answered the wind's call and danced, loving the freedom she felt. But her folly ended abruptly when she bumped into Ford. For a moment, she hugged him tightly as her mind pulled back to the world around her.

"Hannah!" he yelled above the storm as she clung to him. "Are you all right?"

Suddenly resenting his interference and embarrassed that he must have been watching her, Hannah shoved away from Ford with all her strength.

"Go away!" she screamed, the wind pulling at her hair and clothes as if wanting to draw her back into its own private waltz. Ford had turned down her advances one too many times for her to believe that he could care for her.

"Hannah!" Ford yelled, grabbing her arms and forcing her against him.

"No!" she cried, struggling to run. She'd made enough of a fool of herself earlier with this man that she didn't want him to see her now. "If you can't care for me, let go of me!"

The first drops of rain blended with her tears, but she fought on. "You don't want to touch me!" she screamed, too far beyond reason to care what she was saying. "If you don't care enough about me to look at me, let go of me now!"

Ford forgot all about the edge of the cliff only steps away or the rain starting to pound his shoulders. Control anchored deep within him snapped, shaking his body to the core. "How could you think I don't want to touch you?" he shouted. "How can you believe I don't enjoy looking at you?"

He turned loose one of her arms and felt the sting of her slap before he could grab a handful of her hair and pull her mouth to his. Wildly, without any thought that she was unwilling, he kissed her, tasting deeply and long of a passion he'd spent a lifetime denying.

He'd wanted to kiss her like this from the beginning, from that first night in the hotel. He didn't care that he was bruising her lips, or holding her so tight she probably couldn't breathe. He wanted to taste her until he'd never forget. The hunger for her was too great to be hidden any longer.

With one sudden twist, he dropped to his knee, pulling her down against the inside of his leg. She struggled against him, fighting both him and the rain-covered ground. Without lessening his hold, he lowered her in the tall, wet grass and spread himself over her.

Releasing her hair, he placed his hands at her waist and moved up along the sides of her slender body, allowing his thumbs to move boldly over the fullness of her breasts as he shoved her arms above her head. As he pulled her wrists high above her, she arched her back, pushing against him with her upper body as her hips moved to be free of his weight against her abdomen.

She was twisting, struggling beneath him, but his mouth swallowed her protest. He could feel her moving all along him, pressing her body into his, pushing softness against muscle. With only slightly more pressure, he flattened her breasts against his wet shirt and his knee forced her legs apart as thunder rattled the earth and lightning blinked in the sky.

She tried to move her arms, but he pushed them high, pressing them into the grass as his hands moved from her shoulder to her wrists over and over, stroking her until she was finally still to his touch. He wanted to satisfy himself with the feel of her body in his hands, so he moved over her from arm to waist with bold hands and strong fingers, loving the feel of her moving beneath him as he explored.

He broke the kiss for a short time, raising up enough to jerk the belt of her robe open and shove his hand beneath the heavy material.

She didn't cry out but gulped for air as he spread the robe wide on either side of her. Her hands lay lifeless above her hair and she fought to breathe as rain soaked her body, making every curve visible through her clothes in the lightning flashes.

He felt the rise and fall of her chest as he slid his large hands over the cotton of her nightshirt. He could feel the peak of each breast and the rounded softness fit the cup of his hand. With a low growl, he lowered his mouth to taste the cotton covering her breast and pull at the peak beneath that was warm and hard and waiting.

She moved, trying to sit up, but he stroked her gently once more, his hand branding a path over her body, until she was still and allowed him to feast on the tip of the other breast.

Rolling to one side, he pulled her hip against him just below his waist as he moved his hand boldly over her body. Now he could touch her more freely and she could feel his need for her pressing against her hips. She lay still beside him, stretching her arms above her as he examined every curve. Her eyes were closed and her soft sounds blended together in the storm. The rain seemed to melt away the cotton until he could feel the warmth of her skin beneath his touch. Demandingly, he slid his hand lower and watched as she arched her back when he pressed against the warm place between her legs.

He leaned over her, feeling one breast press into his side as his free hand caressed the other. His fingers twisted into her long, flowing hair and pulled slightly. When she leaned her head back as he'd silently commanded, his mouth closed over the pulse of her throat. She moved from side to side as he licked the rain from her throat and tasted her silky skin. Instinctively, his hand tightened around her breast, kneading gently until she was still once more and he could continue.

Without a word, he rolled her over on her stomach and pulled the robe away. She curled on her side in the grass as he moved his hands over her back, pushing her hair away so that he could taste her neck as his fingers cupped her hip. He twisted, pulling her leg over him so that he could slide his fingers up from her knee and bare her thigh to his touch.

He heard her cry out softly as he bit gently into the warm skin below her ear. He moved lower, ripping the nightshirt from her shoulder in his hunger. When she called his name, he reached around her and pulled her against him. Now her hips rested against the center of his need and his hands were free to close over her breasts and catch the points between his fingers.

There was no hesitation in the way his fingers circled her breasts, tugging, feeling, exploring. When she struggled, he stroked and held tightly until she stilled in his arms so that he could continue. The thunder shattered the land, but he couldn't hear a thing over the pounding of his heart.

She shouted again, but he barely heard her above the storm. This was what he'd wanted from the start, he'd wanted her in his arms. When she pushed at his chest and tried to sit up, he moved her atop him until he could cover her lips with his own once more. Now the kiss was deep and hungry, demanding all she had. He loved feeling her soft body twisting above him, torturing him with her softness as he parted her lips again and again, trying to drink his fill of the taste of her mouth. Her breasts were pointed and full and her mouth honey.

She stopped moving and her body relaxed, becoming softer and more exciting to feel. Now she offered no resistance to his advances. He lessened his hold so his hands could explore, but he didn't allow her mouth to move away, for he'd captured it and didn't plan to let go until he no longer felt the need throbbing inside him.

Suddenly, her fist gripped a handful of his hair and yanked hard, pushing his cheek into the mud. Before his passion-flooded brain could react, she rose above him and straddled his waist. He offered no protest as she shoved his wrists into the dirt above his head with more force than he'd thought her capable of.

"Wait! Slow down!" she shouted above the storm. "Are you attacking me or loving me, Ford, because by heaven, I can't tell."

A pound of the tension and an ounce of the passion left him as he laughed, really laughed, for the first time in his life. "I was saving you," he managed to say as he made a slight effort to shove her away and was rewarded

by her leaning lower atop him. The nightshirt hung so
loosely off her shoulder, he could see the rise and fall of
the tops of her breasts.

"Saving me?" She pushed his hands into the mud and
straightened her back, affording him a full view of her
transparent nightshirt. "Saving me from what?"

Ford didn't move as he yelled, "The canyon!"

Hannah looked puzzled for a moment, then glanced at
the dark line marking the canyon rim only a few feet
away.

The rain made it impossible for him to see her face,
but he knew what she must be feeling. The sudden realization that she'd almost danced off the edge, where the
fall might be a hundred feet before jagged rocks slowed
her progress and another fifty feet before she'd tumble to
a stop.

He'd expected her to show fear with the knowledge
that she'd almost died, or gratitude to him for saving her,
or even a crying fit from uncontrolled hysteria . . . but he
never expected anger.

Hannah turned on him with an anger that wilted the
storm around them. Before he could anticipate it, she
slugged him—hard.

He'd seen this side of her before and decided he'd
better react before she bloodied more than his lip this
time.

"Wait!"

"How dare you!" she yelled.

He grabbed one fist in midflight to his nose. "How
dare I what? Kiss you like you've been begging to be
kissed?"

Thunder rattled across the land, competing with them.

"How dare I touch you all over, completely, the way you've been begging me to touch you with every inch of that perfect body of yours?"

She tried to pull free of his grip, but he wouldn't let go. "How dare I taste . . ."

"Let go of me! I don't need anyone saving me by throwing me into the mud!"

Ford opened his hands. Suddenly all his anger was directed inward. He *had* kissed her against her will. He'd held her down while he'd touched her in places he'd never touched a woman before. He'd ignored her struggles while he'd enjoyed the way her body pushed against him.

Hannah staggered to her feet, shivering with cold. Her hair was wet and twisted around her shoulders in a mass of mud, her nightshirt soaked and covered with dirt and grass.

He stood to follow, but she raised her hand. "No! No more! Don't touch me. Don't follow me. I'll bolt my door tonight, and if that doesn't stop you, I swear the Colt will be fully loaded. I'll need no more saving tonight."

With a sudden cry of frustration, she turned and ran, disappearing into the storm like the dream he'd first seen dancing.

Ford raised his fist to the wind and yelled a cry from so deep inside him it sounded inhuman. It didn't matter that the rain cut into his cheeks with icy bites, or the wind froze his shirt to his sides. He didn't care if lightning struck him dead at this very moment, or if the wind blew him off the rim.

All his life he'd been fighting against people thinking something was wild and different about him. But until tonight he'd never believed it.

Now, after the way he'd acted, he knew it was true. He'd attacked Hannah with the instincts of an animal. He'd held her down, he'd tasted her flesh, he'd even branded her with his touch.

He cried again and dropped to his knees, knowing what he must do for Hannah's sake. Somehow, he'd find a way to kill the animal within him before the wildness destroyed him as a man and her completely.

Chapter 19 ✤

FORD STOOD IN the center of the kitchen, feeling like the fool he was. He'd washed his face and hands in the cold water on the porch, but mud was still caked on his clothes. He stayed in the barn until realizing that he'd have pneumonia by morning if he didn't get into dry clothes. Now that Ford was in the house, he didn't know how he could possibly knock on Hannah's bedroom door without her shooting him on sight with his own Colt.

The memory of what he'd done out in the grass made him feel even dirtier. If ever there was a man who could write a book on how not to make love to a woman, he must be the one. Kissing her lightly was one thing. He'd mastered that. But the next step was a hundred-foot drop. What kind of gentleman grabbed a woman and pulled her into the mud in the middle of a rainstorm? If his sister knew about what he'd done, Gavrila would have him caged like a mad dog.

He hadn't meant to hurt Hannah, yet he must have with his rough treatment. Ford closed his eyes tightly, as if he could make the picture in his mind disappear. He hadn't even meant to kiss her. When he'd run from the barn, his only thought had been to stop her from plunging off into the canyon. But when she'd slammed into him, then hugged him as if he were her only rock, she'd shattered all his reserve into a million pieces. Like the storm that raged around them, the fury of his longing could no longer be bridled. The wildness of her dance had shattered what little control he'd held on to all day. Before he realized what was happening, he was kissing her, and that kiss started a hunger that made him feel like he'd starve if he didn't try to sate it.

He hadn't noticed the icy storm or the mud. All he'd seen was Hannah beneath him. All he'd felt was her moving against him, driving him wild with the feel of her.

Then she'd gotten angry, not over him attacking her, or trying to make love to her, but because he'd saved her from certain death. He'd acted a fool and she was completely mad; they were a perfect match for one another, it seemed.

Ford wondered how he'd ever face her again when he wasn't sure he could face himself, come daylight. He was certain no gentleman ever boldly ran his hands up and down a woman the way he had. And he hadn't just kissed her, he'd devoured her. Just the memory now made his cheeks warm with embarrassment and other parts of his body afire with need.

"What are you doing here?" Hannah's sharp voice sounded from behind him.

Ford turned slowly, steeling his body for what he might have to face. She stood in the doorway, the light from the fireplace shining in a glow around her form.

Her hair was clean and she'd found another one of his nightshirts to wear. Since the robe she'd borrowed was probably lying in some puddle, she'd pulled on one of his flannel work shirts. Wool socks covered her legs where the nightshirt didn't reach. Though she looked warm, clean, and inviting, he imagined he was the last person she wanted to welcome nearer.

He looked but saw no gun in her hand.

"I said, what are you doing here?" she repeated as she took a step into the kitchen.

He could say the obvious, that he needed to change his wet clothes before he died of a fever, or that there was nowhere else out of the rain to wash up but in the house, or that the rain had turned to sleet, leaving the barn freezing. But all Ford could say in answer to her question was, "It's my house."

Hannah heard the longing in his words. Words that asked where else would he be welcome if not here in his own home. She could see that he had to change clothes. In truth, except for his face, the man looked like a huge mud-pie man. The places on his clothing that weren't covered with mud appeared to be frozen stiff. Just the sight of him made her shiver, though Ford didn't seem overly bothered by his appearance.

"I could get some water and wash up out on the porch." He lifted the wash pan and moved it below the pump. "I'll be out of your way in a few minutes."

Suddenly the dirty little boy Gavrila had described tracked across Hannah's mind. "You'll do nothing of the sort." She didn't meet his gaze lest he guess her thoughts. "I'll heat the water for you for a proper bath, and put coffee on. From the looks of you, it'll take a pot of coffee and a tub of water just for starters."

Ford watched in amazement as she moved around him and began filling the extra kettles with water. He figured if anyone on this planet had a reason to hate him right now, it was Hannah, yet she was helping him. He must have driven her completely crazy, or else there was so much mud on him she didn't even know who she was talking to.

"But—"

"Go get out of those clothes and put on another kettle in the dressing area. I'm afraid I used most of the extra water with my bath, but there's still a fire in the stove. The water should be ready by the time you peel a few pounds of that mud off you. I'll bring you fresh clothes."

Ford moved slowly to the door. He wasn't in the habit of having someone order him around in a tone that seemed to indicate she was doing it for his own good.

"And pull off those boots right here in the kitchen before you track more mud in!"

He followed orders. "Yes, ma'am." Even if he'd disagreed, he was far too tired and cold to argue. Ford walked to the dressing room between the two bedrooms and slowly removed his clothes. His body felt stiff and even the warmth of the dressing room didn't help his muscles relax.

Hannah's torn nightshirt lay in a puddle of mud in one corner, reminding Ford of what he'd done. He'd never be able to explain his actions to her; he didn't even understand them himself.

When she tapped on the door, he wrapped a towel around his waist and opened the door for her.

Standing with a kettle of boiling water in each hand, Hannah still froze at the sight of him. His body was carved of lean muscle from shoulder to calf, just as she'd imagined it would be. She'd seen a few men without shirts before, but none who looked like Ford. What puzzled her greatly was that he seemed embarrassed by showing such perfection.

Hannah poured two steaming kettles of water into the tub and then added what looked to Ford to be about a cupful of cold water. "Climb in," she said, pointing at the tub.

He stared at the hip tub he'd thought was quite a luxury when he'd bought it. Soup didn't steam as much as this bath, but she didn't seem to have any patience for the water to cool.

"I'll bring more in a minute." Hannah waited with one hand on her hip. "But first get in so I'll know how much more to heat."

"Are you planning on watching me boil?"

"I might," Hannah answered, showing no sign of retreat.

Ford tried staring her down, but she didn't move. The look he'd used to frighten away anyone he didn't want around had no effect on her. Since he couldn't stand before her in a towel forever, slowly he stepped into the tub.

Biting back a yelp of pain, he carefully held the towel in front of him as he lowered himself into the water. His icy bones felt like they were shattering an inch at a time as they moved into the steam.

"Just as I thought," she said. "We'll need at least two more of these kettles for you to take a decent bath."

Ford was fighting to keep from screaming. "Do you think you could get the next pot of water a little hotter?" he whispered sarcastically.

"I can try," Hannah answered, deadly serious.

Ford had about reached the point that he no longer had to bite down on his lip to stay in the tub when she brought in another kettle.

She mixed the same degree of cold water with the hot and poured it over his back. Ford forced himself not to say a word. He closed his eyes and kept reminding himself that the bath would cool in a minute but her anger might outlast him.

Hannah knelt at his side and plopped a bar of soap into the water by his arm. Before he realized what she was doing, she'd lathered his shoulder.

He caught her hand with his own. "What do you think you're doing?"

He could never remember a time in his life when anyone helped him bathe, yet she seemed to be doing so as though it were a routine they'd set.

"I'm helping you." Her gaze was fixed on the washcloth in her hand as she answered.

"I don't need any help bathing," Ford said slowly, thinking maybe she planned to kill him later, and if he were clean it would make the laying out for the funeral easier.

"Suit yourself." She plopped the rag into the water

and stood. "But you're not sleeping in the same bed with me if there's an inch of mud left on you."

Before her words had time to register, she crossed to the door and disappeared into his bedroom.

For a long moment, Ford stared at the wall, not believing what she'd said. Then he dropped his head into the water and shook it, hoping the heat would thaw his brain.

When he raised his head, he slung his hair in a wide circle, streaking the walls as he climbed from the tub and reached for his pants.

Hannah heard him through the door and realized what he was doing. She walked across his bedroom and crawled into her side of the bed. Tucking her knees beneath her chin, she sat with her back against the hand-carved headboard and waited.

As she'd expected, the wait wasn't long. Ford opened the door as he pulled on the shirt she'd left out for him. His hair was still dripping and he'd only taken the time to button a few necessary buttons on his jeans. His clothes clung to his hurriedly dried body, revealing finely carved muscles.

For a long time they just looked at one another across the endless space between where he stood at the door and she sat on the bed. The frown on his face would have been frightening if she hadn't known him so well. Inside this powerful man was a gentleman who'd spent a week being kind to someone else's children and who'd offered her refuge even when she'd robbed him. Tonight she'd learned he was also a creature of passion . . . deep, wild, untamed passion.

"I figure you got a right to hate me." His low voice whispered across the room, almost in a caress. "I had no right doing what I did out there in the storm. I don't suppose you'll believe me, but I never meant to hurt you. I'm not even sure how it all started."

"You didn't hurt me," she answered. How could he have thought he'd hurt her? His advances had been demanding, strong, passionate, but never hurtful.

He leaned his head against the door frame and closed his eyes. "When you asked if I was loving you or attacking you, I realized I must be doing a terrible job if you couldn't tell the difference. I've wanted to touch you all day. I thought I could control the need, but tonight, when you danced in the wind, all the longing seemed to explode out of me."

She didn't answer. She couldn't. His pain seemed to warm the air between them. Hannah couldn't tell him that she'd known what he was doing and her words had been an effort to get him to slow down a little, not stop.

Until tonight, she'd thought she could play with the attraction between them and never have to carry it any further. But tonight, when she'd looked up into his stormy face and felt his hands boldly move over her, she'd known better. Ford wasn't a man to be toyed with and forgotten. His emotions ran far too deep, so deep she was afraid of falling into them as she almost had the canyon and never surviving the tumble.

But she wanted the wild man in him more than she'd ever dreamed she could want a man.

The hesitant rancher before her wasn't the same man she'd known before tonight. She'd learned his secret in the storm and was drawn to it. Her mother had once told her to find a man with great passion if she ever married, for even if it cooled over the years, the embers would warm her all her life. Ford's passion had shocked her with its fire and need.

"When I saw you dancing so close to the edge, I panicked. All I could think about was losing you." Ford didn't open his eyes as he continued. "Funny, isn't it. I'll lose you in less than two weeks, anyway, but I had to kiss you. Just once before I lost you."

He couldn't bring himself to look at her. "I guess I can't lose what I never really had, but in the rain and the storm all I could think about was holding you in my arms the way I've longed to hold you since the day we married."

When she didn't answer, he finally looked at her, but the shadowy light hid her face. "I don't blame you for being mad at me and I swear I'll keep a room away until you leave, but don't tease me like you did just now. Don't say things as if we were really married and planning to share a bed."

"I wasn't teasing, but you are right . . . you'd better stay a room away while we talk some before you come closer."

He folded his arms and waited, still leaning against the door frame.

"I won't be handled like a sack of potatoes to be tossed first one direction then another. And there'll be no more pulling me into the mud and ruining my robe. I've grown used to having everything clean around me these past few weeks. I'd like to see how hot this fire we have for one another burns, for I've never felt like this before and may never again."

Ford turned slowly to face her, his feet spread wide apart as if waiting for her blow to strike. "If we're going to talk, then you'd best talk plainer, Hannah, because I'm not sure I understand."

She laughed suddenly, a nervous little laugh that lightened the tension slightly. "I'm saying I'd like to share a bed with you, Ford, but not the ground. I haven't enough clothes to go rolling in the mud again."

"To sleep?" Ford couldn't believe what he was hearing. Flirting had been one thing, but to go to bed with her after feeling her in the rain would only lead to one result. Even just talking about it, he could feel his control slipping.

"That, too," she answered as she spread the cover on his side. "I'd like to sleep with you between the same layers of sheets."

"But I never . . ."

"That's obvious from your courting tactics." Hannah laughed again. "I don't hate you, Ford, and I didn't mean it when I asked if you were attacking me. I've never been loved, but I've been attacked, and it hurts far more than your kisses or touch. Just start a little slower and try not to reach full gallop a yard from the gate."

Ford moved to the foot of the bed and gripped the railing so tightly his knuckles whitened. "Are you sure you want this? I'll not touch you if you have any doubts, because if I ever touch you again I'm not sure where I could stop."

"Are you certain you want me?"

"No," he answered. "Yes." He didn't want to ask all the questions that were between them. He only wanted to answer from his heart, and he wanted her more than he wanted his heart to continue to beat.

Hannah knew exactly how he felt. One minute she wished she were as far away from here as possible, and the next minute she couldn't get enough of touching him. But they'd started something, maybe from their first kiss, that needed to be completed, or they'd both spend the rest of their lives wondering about what might have been.

Slowly, she reached out a hand and covered his fingers. "My mother always told me that someday I'd dance with the wind and run wild in paradise. I didn't know until you kissed me out there that she was talking about you. Part of you is gentle and kind. You're the first man I've ever felt like I could look up to. But another part, the side I saw tonight, is wild and untamed. A man with a hunger so deep it sets me on fire just remembering the way you kissed me and touched me, as if I'd been born for that one night in time, and all the ones before and after didn't matter."

Hannah crawled closer to the foot of the bed, where he stood. She knelt and drew up even with him, only a breath away. "I want both parts of you beside me tonight. I want all of the man."

Her fingers slowly climbed from his waist to his shoulders, pushing his shirt away in their journey. Lightly she moved her touch over him, feeling his skin as he had hers.

"You don't hate me?" he whispered as he fought for control while she moved her lips up his throat.

"I want you to love me," she whispered against his skin. "I want to dance with the wind while in your arms and feel wild and free. I need to believe that a man needs me, just me for a time."

Ford could take no more; he closed his arms around her and pulled her to him. The hunger he'd felt in the rain was a driving, maddening river of fire, but it was nothing compared to what he felt now with her so warm and willing in his arms.

He dug his hands into her hair and tilted her head back so that he could kiss her.

She gave him what he wanted, but after one long kiss, pulled away, shoving at his chest.

"Slow down," she laughed. "We have all night."

She turned to remove his flannel shirt, but Ford couldn't control his haste. Before she could hang the shirt, he swung her into his embrace and moved around the bed.

He dropped her onto the cover and heard her giggle a moment before his body and his mouth claimed her.

If she'd had any hope that he'd love her slowly and easily, it evaporated in the heat of both their passions. While she tried to unbutton his jeans, he ripped her nightshirt open with one mighty jerk. She arched her back in pleasure as his mouth found her breast with a hunger that brought her pure joy.

He couldn't seem to get enough of her body. The more he tasted, the more he wanted. His hands moved over her, almost bruising her flesh with his intensity.

They rolled across the covers, feeling one another, kissing, holding, loving.

When they were both burning with need, he rose above her and for the first time since the dance began, he hesitated. Her need was too great to allow him to stop. She circled her arms and legs around him and drew him to her, feeling a light pain before pleasure consumed her.

They moved in perfect rhythm with one another as though they were a matched set, each balanced to the other's needs. Finally, Hannah's mind exploded into paradise and she heard a cry of pure pleasure, but she wasn't sure if it was from her or Ford.

For a long while they lay wrapped in one another as they settled back to earth. Ford's hand gently caressed her breasts while her fingers stroked his back in slow, lazy movements.

He pulled the cover over their bodies, and Hannah curled against him in sleep. He listened to the steady sound of her breathing against his chest. Smiling as his thumb brushed the peak of her breast, he felt it harden in welcome even as she slept. He slowly moved his hand down to her hip and pulled, drawing her tightly against him, loving the way her skin felt against his.

Moaning as she dreamed, she nestled closer to his warmth. He smiled, knowing that soon he'd wake her again with this need he had for her. If she wanted a man to need her, she'd found someone, and he was near starvation. He also knew this passion wasn't just because he wanted a woman, he wanted only Hannah.

Maybe he'd try to go slowly, as she suggested, tasting each part of her body, feeling her move beneath him, making her scream his name in passion. He thought of a hundred things he wanted to do, and all of them involved making love to her.

She was a wonder, this woman beside him. All his life he'd fought to keep the wildness at bay, and tonight it had been that very wild animal that she'd wanted. She hadn't hated his loss of control, she'd loved it, even driven him to more.

He played with her breast, remembering the way she'd moaned when he'd tugged at her and kissed her in places he'd never dreamed a woman would want to be kissed. He felt a longing stirring deep inside and kissed her cheek.

When she didn't move, he tugged at her bottom lip with his teeth.

She wiggled, searching for more warmth, but not turning her mouth from his.

He kissed her again, feeling the hunger in himself growing.

"Wake up," he whispered as he planted light kisses over her closed eyes. "It's time to dance with the wind again, darlin'."

She moaned and stretched, sliding her body against his in a manner that inflamed his desire.

"Wake up, darlin'." His lips touched her ear. "I'm in great need of only you."

"Ford," she whispered as she pressed her breasts against his chest. "Will you love me again . . . even if it's in my dreams. Please, love me again."

He tasted her mouth lightly, wishing he had words to tell her how he felt. If hearts could explode with happiness, his was about to burst at any moment. Ford never dreamed being with a woman could be like this, all warm and comfortable and passionate.

"Hold me," she moaned against his mouth in a voice blanketed in sleep as she lay back, offering her unclothed body to his view.

"All night, if you want," he answered between light kisses.

She sighed and smiled as he stroked her with fingers already familiar with giving her pleasure. "Love me again," she whispered.

He didn't have time to reply, for his body and heart were already answering her request.

❖ *Chapter 20*

FORD LOWERED THE tray of coffee down on the stand. The room was still in shadows, with only the fireplace and gray windows offering any light. He carefully circled the bed and sat down next to Hannah, leaning his back against the headboard and closing his eyes as he let out a long sigh. The night had been wild and wonderful, but now he wasn't sure he had the energy left to hold his coffee mug.

Remembering, he gently brushed a curl from Hannah's sleeping face and leaned to kiss her mouth. She tasted so good he'd decided sometime during the night that he'd never get his fill.

"Wake up, darlin'," Ford whispered against her bottom lip as he trailed kisses down her chin.

She moved in her sleep, letting the cover fall dangerously low over her shoulder. "Is it dawn yet?" she mumbled, rolling over and shoving her backside against his leg. "I don't have to get up until almost dawn."

Ford laughed. "It's noon. The rain just makes the room stay dark."

"Noon!" Hannah sat up suddenly, completely forgetting she was nude. "I've missed school. The children will be worried."

Ford didn't look the least upset, in fact he smiled as he took in the view. "Don't panic. I told Roy to ride in and ask Gavrila to take your place for the day. My sister's been trying to get back in that school since the day you arrived."

Hannah rubbed her eyes and scooted closer to the coffee. "How could I have slept until noon? I never did that even when I had to work until after midnight."

She blushed suddenly and reached for the sheet to cover herself. "It's your fault." Her bottom lip came out like that of a child's. "You woke me up twice last night."

Ford smiled. "I seem to remember you waking me once, also, sometime before dawn."

Hannah laughed as she let the covers fall away in an effort to reach the extra coffee mug.

Her immodesty had the effect she'd hoped for. Ford's breathing suddenly stopped and his grip tightened on his cup. He didn't move as she wiggled back to him with her coffee in hand.

She drank long, then stretched again, reaching to set the mug back in place.

He almost spilled the coffee as he slammed the cup down on the stand nearest him and moved toward her.

Jumping out of his grasp, Hannah laughed. "Oh, no, you don't! I haven't even finished my coffee. Plus, people don't do the kind of thing you're thinking about doing until long past sundown."

Ford moved slowly toward her. "How do you know what I'm thinking?"

"Maybe I don't." She shrugged, allowing the cover to fall completely away from one breast.

His sharp intake of breath made her giggle.

"Then again, maybe I do."

He sprang then. Before she could protest, he'd pulled her beneath the covers and kissed her wildly. His hands moved across her as if starved for the feel of her. She squealed and wiggled and protested while she giggled, but he had just one goal—to hear her cry his name again while lost in desire.

Their loving was the way it had been the first time, without barriers, with a haste that comes only with swimming in deep waters of passion.

When they'd finished, Ford's clothes were scattered across the floor and Hannah was curled atop him, too exhausted to move even if she'd wanted to.

He lifted a handful of her hair and took in its fragrance as if he were committing her scent forever to memory. "When your heart slows, darlin', I plan to carry you out into the dressing area and bathe you. I'd even like to brush a few tangles out of this hair. Then I'll wrap a towel around you and we'll eat something before retiring for the evening. There'll be no need for you to bother getting dressed today if you don't wish to."

"But what will people think?"

"They'll think you've taken to your bed." He laughed. "Which is exactly right."

Hannah raised up on one elbow. "I never thought it would be like this. Not half so wonderful."

"Me either," Ford answered honestly as he gently lifted her elbow off the dent she was making in his chest.

"I guess I never thought a woman would take to me the way you seem to have."

"You make me feel beautiful," she whispered as she moved up slightly so her lips could reach his. "Beautiful and wanted. I love the way you never have enough. You come after loving as if you've been starved. I guess we both do."

"You are beautiful," he answered, "and wanted. I seem to frighten most folks, but I don't ever want to frighten you." He kissed her gently then, as if proving how much she was cherished.

She'd expected him to make love to her again, but he was true to his word. He lifted her and carried her to the tub.

He must have started the fire when he was up making coffee, for the little room was warm and the water already hot. While she tied her hair atop her head, he poured warm water over her as she stood in the tub.

Hannah didn't sit down, but allowed him full view of her as he soaped her body and washed each part. His hands, covered with soap, slid easily over her curves as she turned slowly around.

When he finished, he wrapped her in a towel he'd put across the back of a chair by the stove. The material was warm against her skin and Hannah sighed as he covered her with not only the towel, but his arms.

"There's something I need to say," he whispered against his ear. "But I don't know the words. I wish I knew how to tell you half of what is churning inside of me."

Hannah leaned against him and answered, "I know

how you feel. I want to love you again fast because we have so little time, and I need to love you slow so I can remember everything. Last night was the most wonderful of my life, and I wish our time together would never end."

His arms tightened around her. "Wish it would never end," he repeated against her hair.

Wrapping her arms around his neck, she kissed him slowly and tenderly, realizing her heart belonged to this man and would for the rest of her life. Every beat would remind her of the time they'd had together . . . of the feelings he pulled so strongly to the surface.

The rain still pattered against the windows, but Hannah hardly noticed as she lay wrapped in Ford's arms while he slept. It had to be close to three in the afternoon. She'd slipped into one of his shirts after her bath and planned on wearing it to cook supper, but he'd talked her into cuddling beside him until he fell asleep and now she didn't want to leave.

Even in his sleep, Ford caressed her. Each time she moved he'd pull the covers closer, or slide his hand along her leg, or cup her breast gently before settling back into his slow breathing.

She looked at him closely. To be honest, he was not what most would call handsome. But at this moment he looked perfect. For Hannah he was the finest-looking man who'd ever walked on this earth.

She lay her cheek against his shoulder and closed her eyes, knowing that she'd need rest if the night to come was to be a repeat of the last one—which she hoped it would be.

Wind whirled outside and rain tapped against the window as Hannah drifted from a perfect day into sleep.

An hour later horses' hooves thundered, blending with the rain for a moment, not pulling Hannah from dreams. But when she felt Ford's body stiffen beside her, she knew something was wrong.

He climbed from the bed in one fluid movement and pulled on his jeans. "Get dressed, darlin'. Several riders are coming fast, and I'm thinking it's trouble driving them through this rain."

By the time she slipped from the bed and lifted her dress, he was already out the door, buttoning his shirt as he moved. She hurried, feeling his worry as the horses drew closer.

Hannah pulled on her stockings as a pounding sounded at their front door. She grabbed her shoes and ran to see what was happening.

As she stepped from the bedroom, men in wet-blackened dusters poured through the front door. Fear ran through her veins, blending with the memories of the morning Jude had been killed. Their dusters might not be like the new yellow ones the killers wore, but she could smell blood in the air now as she had then. These men had the same hurried look about them that Harwell's men had, only Ford was holding the door for them to come in, and none carried guns in their hands.

"Take him over by the fire!" Ford shouted.

"He's hurt bad," Roy, Ford's hand, yelled above the racket. "We wanted to take him to Doc's place, but he insisted on being brought back here to Hannah. I had to ride double with him because he's in no shape to even set a saddle."

Hannah shoved her way through the crowd as Roy continued. "Most of the men in town rode north after the gang that took Miss Gavrila, but a few of us wanted to come get you."

"Gavrila?" Hannah heard Ford ask in a voice that was much calmer than hers would have been. "Someone's abducted my sister?" His last words were filled with disbelief. Kidnapping Gavrila would make about as much sense as stealing dirt.

Hannah tried to push past the last man between her and the person lying on the floor, but the short fellow stopped her. She looked angrily into the face of Alamo Rogers.

"Don't look, Miss Hannah." He shook his head. "He's hurt bad and bleeding in several places. It's not something a lady should see."

She pushed again. She could fight her way around the little man if she had to, but he'd been kind to her and she didn't want to hurt him.

"Let her pass," Ford's voice sounded from just behind Alamo, where he was kneeling. "My wife is no weak flower and I'll not have her treated so, even in the name of protecting her."

Alamo opened his grip on her arms and stepped to the side. His whole body seemed to silently apologize for what she was about to see.

She moved around him and knelt beside Ford. A scream caught in her throat as she saw the bloodied face of Zachery sticking out from beneath a muddy coat.

"Zachery!" Hannah held his face in her hands and turned him toward the light. She didn't notice the blood dripping through her fingers, or her own tears as she glanced over each cut and bruise. All she saw was the fear shining in his eyes. "What happened to you?" The last she'd seen him, he'd said he would be playing checkers with Jinx and might not be home.

Zachery blinked. "I had to get to you, girl. I had to warn you," he whispered. "Harwell's men found me. There's no telling how long they hung around outside the post office waiting for me to come out. They beat me, thinking I'd tell them where you were, but I never told." He closed his eyes as new pain seemed to course through him. "I never told, Hannah. They said the sheriff had a letter from here inquiring about a woman and man who met our descriptions. Whoever wrote the letter even had my name right, but I still wouldn't tell them anything."

"What's he saying?" Ford asked as he placed a comforting hand on her shoulder. "I couldn't hear all of it. Someone wrote a letter?"

"It doesn't make sense," she lied. "Who would write a letter asking about me?"

Hannah's gaze met Ford's and in an instant they both whispered the same word, "Gavrila." Organized, planning Gavrila.

"Because I wouldn't talk," Ford said, taking all the guilt, "she must have decided to write. I remember her even asking someone at the dance if they knew a Fort Worth lawman's name. The sheriff would be a logical person to know a few facts. She's always been like that, having to know every detail."

"It doesn't matter," Hannah whispered. "They'd have found us eventually anyway. The men who did this never stop until they find who they are looking for. It was just a matter of time."

"But I didn't tell them where you were," Zachery mumbled. "I let them keep hitting me, and I wouldn't say a word."

Hannah squeezed the old man's hand as she looked at Ford. "Help me get him to bed and I'll doctor these wounds." She didn't want to see the question in her husband's eyes so she quickly moved her attention to Zachery. "Don't worry, Uncle, I'll patch you up just fine."

Zachery's eyes didn't open, but his grip on her fingers was strong.

Several men stepped forward to help. "We'll get him stripped and washed up, ma'am, while you collect the bandages," Roy offered with the respect any hand would pay the boss's wife.

"All right." She glanced at Ford, but he was already directing men to ready his horse and make enough coffee to fill everyone's cup.

Hannah ran to the kitchen and collected all the things she might need to doctor. The only thought on her mind was that Harwell's men had found them. She had given them the slip in Dallas. Gavrila's letter must have seemed like a great stroke of luck for the killers. She'd only guessed before that the sheriff might be involved, but if he turned over a letter, he must be mixed up with the killings.

Hannah gripped the medicine box until her fingers whitened. Though they might have only beat up Zachery, they would kill her. There was no doubt in her mind she'd be dead, and anyone else as well who tried to stand in their way. If they'd killed Jude so quickly, they wouldn't hesitate to slit her throat.

Ford crossed the kitchen, buckling his gun belt as he moved. "I don't know when I'll be back, but you should be safe enough here. I left the Winchester and a box of rounds in our bedroom. I wish I could stay, but I've got to help look for Gavrila. She's my sister and I'm one of only a few men who know this country well enough to travel at night in the rain without getting lost."

"The men who beat Zachery really kidnapped her?" The idea sounded too far-fetched to even be repeated. "Are you sure?"

Ford stopped and looked directly into her eyes, as though hating to tell her, but knowing it had to be done. "After the men beat up Zachery out back of the post office, they were seen talking to one of the Burns boys, who skipped school today. The boy thought you were at the schoolhouse and pointed them in the right direction when they asked about anyone new in town."

Ford leaned down and strapped on his spurs. "When they asked Gavrila if she was the new teacher, she told them yes. The children said the men threw a blanket over her head before she could get a good scream out and rode off with her doubled over a saddle like a sack of cornmeal."

"Poor Gavrila!" Hannah cried. "If she'd only told Harwell's men the truth, they'd have let her go."

"Because they were looking for you, right?" Ford finished her sentence.

Hannah closed her eyes and nodded. "If Gavrila wrote a letter, she told them where to find me."

"And they beat Zachery trying to get to you, didn't they, Hannah?"

She nodded again, knowing that she'd have to tell Ford the whole story. He'd probably think her a coward for running, but it had seemed her only way to survive.

Ford pulled her roughly against him. "Well, they can't have you. I don't care what's happened in the past. I don't care what you've done. I don't care if you rob half the people in Saints Roost blind. I'm not letting you go, darlin', and that is final."

"But I didn't do anything. I didn't steal . . ." She returned his hug, wondering what he was talking about. How could he think that Harwell's men were chasing her because of something *she'd* done? How could he hint that she'd taken anything from the people in town? He wasn't waiting for her to explain, he was telling her it didn't matter. Then the realization shook her . . . it did matter. She thought back to the night of the party and his sudden mood change. The way he acted after he knew she'd been in White's place the day someone was thought to have stolen. "But I never . . ."

He kissed her hard on the lips, then let go abruptly. "We'll talk later. Right now I've got to find Gavrila. If we're lucky we'll have two hours of daylight before we'll be searching in the dark." Lightly, he touched her cheek with the knuckle of his first finger. "Don't worry, darlin', everything is going to work out between us. I learned something last night. I learned something matters more than what folks think. You matter more to me than all the folks in town."

"But Ford—"

"Forget what they think, forget the agreement we made. I don't care what you've done. You belong with me, and any man who plans to take you will have to kill me first." He grabbed his hat and was gone before she could speak.

Hannah gathered up the supplies and walked toward the bedroom door. "But you didn't learn to trust me, Ford," she whispered as tears bubbled from her eyelids. She'd learned to love last night, but she couldn't live with him as long as he believed her a thief. For the first time she understood why he'd acted so angry at her. He'd thought she took Allison's money and the kit from White's store. He thought, as he always had, that she was a thief.

For all their safety and her own sanity, Hannah knew she had to leave, and soon. With Ford not believing in her, there was no reason to stay and fight Harwell's men, even if the odds were with the townspeople—Ford's mistrust had turned the odds against her.

Chapter 21

HANNAH MOVED THROUGH the activity in the living area. A few men warmed themselves by the fire while others prepared weapons for a fight. Most days these men seemed like farmers and rangers, but today she was reminded that they'd settled this land and had fought before. Alamo Rogers was leaning over the great table studying Ford's maps.

"If they're headed north," Alamo's voice was almost a whine of panic, "I see only one way to catch them in time. We'll have to go through the canyon."

Roy shook his head. "Ford's the only man who knows that crack in the earth well enough to take a horse across it, and I doubt even he could do that in this rain."

"We've got some daylight left; we can cross by then and come back the long way after we find Gavrila. Ford's saddling the bay now and my guess is we best be ready to ride down into the canyon within minutes." Alamo tried to stand tall. "Because if he goes that way, I'm right behind him."

Several men agreed.

Hannah smiled at Alamo's bravery and opened the

door to the bedroom, where they'd taken Uncle Zachery. She knew without asking that what they were attempting was dangerous, but Ford had to at least try to find Gavrila, even in this storm. If Harwell's men had her, they'd likely murder her at any moment. The fact that they hadn't shot her on the spot at the schoolhouse surprised Hannah.

As she entered Zachery's room, several men stepped back from the bed. "We did the best we could," one mumbled by way of apology.

Hannah set her pan down by the bed and looked at the old man. The other men had wiped the blood off his face, but several places where the skin had been rubbed raw were still seeping, and an inch-long cut just over his left eye looked like it would need a few stitches to heal. She could see knuckle marks where a fist had bruised his cheek.

"You look terrible!" she scolded Zachery, as if he could have helped his appearance.

"Thanks," he mumbled between swollen lips. "I doubt even Jinx will be able to stand the sight of me for a while."

He laid his hand over hers as she doctored the cuts. "I didn't tell, Hannah. I told you I'd keep your secret and I did. They kept telling me that someone mentioned I was missing after the killings, so Harwell figured I was with you. They didn't even remember your name, but when the sheriff got a letter from Saints Roost asking about me and you, Harwell's men had the missing pieces. They could have beat me to death and I wouldn't have given you away."

"I'm proud to have you as an uncle," she answered. "I'll get you patched up in no time."

"I'm not hurt as bad as these townsfolk let on. I've been banged up worse than this and left in the alley to heal."

Hannah suspected his words were true. She'd seen drunks fall and bloody themselves without even spilling the bottle they carried. But the "no time" to fix him up tonight took her over an hour. She stitched up two cuts, one on his face and the other on his arm. Then she wrapped what she guessed to be a few broken ribs. Luckily he wasn't spitting up blood, so they'd heal in time. Though other injuries looked bad, the wounds would scab and heal in a few days.

While she worked, Zachery talked of bits of conversation he'd heard between Jude and Hickory. The bar owner had tried to convince Jude how bad Harwell's men were. They had money in every illegal game in the state, from cattle rustling to land fraud. But Jude wouldn't listen. He'd not only joined them, he'd stolen from Harwell's men.

"I didn't know," Hannah whispered.

"I guessed that." Zachery knotted the sheet in his fist and fought to continue despite the pain. "I'd hoped he'd marry you and settle down and you'd never know. But he'd had too much to drink the night before the shooting and bragged not only of teaching his new wife who was boss, but of cheating his partners."

Hannah didn't try to stop the tears that rolled over her cheeks as she continued doctoring.

They were both exhausted by the time she turned down the light and told him to sleep a while.

As she moved away, he grabbed her hand once more and pulled her back. "They'll find out Gavrila isn't you and come back. You know that, don't you, girl? It's only a matter of time before they come riding for you."

"I know that," she answered, for she'd been thinking the same thing. "I just hope they don't hurt Gavrila."

Zachery chuckled, then cried out at the pain it caused him. "Unless they kill her fast, she'll give them far more hell than they'll ever give her. My thinking is they'll let her go to stop the entire town from coming after them. But it's hard to outguess a nest of rattlers like the kind of men Harwell hires to do his dirty work."

"If she dies, it will be my fault." Hannah fought down a sob.

"No, girl. You didn't cause this situation. You're only trying to outrun it." His voice lowered. "Which we have to do as soon as possible. I don't plan on being here when they ride back through. I don't think I've got another beating left in me to survive."

"You'll go with me, then?" Though she knew she'd make much better time going alone, Harwell's men might kill Zachery the next time they found him. "I've been thinking I'll have to start soon and travel fast."

"I'll be ready to at least sit in a buggy come morning. If we can get to the station, we should have no problem taking a train—if this storm lets up."

"I'll be ready."

Zachery didn't let go of her hand. "What about Ford?"

"If I stay it could mean his death."

"If you go you'll break his heart. Which to some men is a kind of death. The man loves you dearly."

Hannah shook her head. He'd never spoken of love. He desired her, that was all. In a few months the fire he had for her would cool and he'd find another. Any woman who had any sense could tell what a great lover he was and would be happy to share his bed and his life.

"Get some sleep." Hannah turned down the light and backed away. The old man closed his eyes and appeared to be asleep even before she reached the door.

She couldn't bear to go back into the room she and Ford had made love in, so Hannah bolted the doors and curled up on the couch in front of the fire. Sneeze walked across her legs and curled into the vee of her knee.

As she watched the flames dance off the shadowy walls of Ford's house, she planned what she knew she must do. If she left a little after daylight, Hannah could be in town by the time folks started stirring about. She'd say that she was worried about Uncle Zachery's health and was taking him home to Fort Worth. Everyone would protest, but she'd insist that the old man trusted no one but their family doctor and they had to hurry to catch the train.

Then, when she got to Wichita Falls, they'd change trains and head east. By nightfall, if she was lucky, they'd be safely out of Texas. She drifted into a fitful sleep, waking to every sound the wind made, as if it were intruders at the door. Finally, she gave up even making an effort to get a night's rest before their escape.

Hannah drank coffee until almost dawn, then dressed

in the plainest of the dresses Ford had bought her. She pulled her carpetbag down from the shelf and reached in it for her five gold bracelets. They slid easily onto her wrist.

She moved her arm, welcoming the sound of their jingling. Her mother was right—Gypsy blood did run in her veins. She was born to stay on the move, and folks would always point a finger toward her if something was missing. Only this time it had been Ford who accused her. And this time he accused her of something she hadn't done.

Hannah took off one gold bracelet and placed it in the drawer where Ford kept extra money. She knew the bracelet was worth far more than the few dollars she took, but it was the only thing she had to barter with, and she didn't want him thinking she'd stolen from him again.

Pulling on her coat, Hannah wished she could leave everything behind, but she'd come to him with nothing, not even clothes. Maybe the few weeks' work she'd done at the school would equal the garments she took.

Remembering their bargain, she looked around the room. She'd said that she would take one thing of value when she left and that he'd promise never to follow her or try to get it back. But how could she take the very rooms that made her feel welcome with their colors, or the warm air that smelled of home, or the way he made her feel safe and secure in his arms?

When she stepped outside and into the predawn air, rain hung thick with promise, like a damp cloth. She ran to the barn and started getting the buggy ready. The horse didn't cooperate like the bay had and it took Hannah several tries to pull on the rigging and buckle everything in place.

Rain splattered around her as she ran back to the house. Zachery was up and waiting for her. His face looked worse than it had the night before, but determination set his eyes.

"Are you sure you're able to travel?" Hannah reconsidered their plan for the first time. He didn't look like he'd make many miles without collapsing.

"We have to get you out of here, girl," he answered soberly as he pulled on his coat with one hand and picked up the rifle. "I don't think I can drive the buggy, but I can hold on to this. There was a day I could shoot."

Hannah kissed him on the cheek. "Thanks, Uncle."

He nodded and slowly made his way outside, embarrassed and pleased by her affection.

"Come on, Sneeze." Hannah held the carpetbag open.

The cat backed away.

"Sneeze. We have to leave." The cat had always come to her when she called.

Sneeze turned around and hurried to his blanket by the fire.

"Please, come one," Hannah whispered, knowing it was useless. Sneeze had found his home.

Hannah closed the door, wishing she didn't feel like she was losing hers.

Ford spent two hours crossing the canyon with his band of men. Alamo was the least skilled with a horse, but he'd also been the only one not to complain. His determination matched Ford's, and for that he gained respect among the others.

By midnight they'd ridden out on the other side of the ridge and headed west to a place where the land rose slightly. The rain having slowed, they'd be able to see for miles come daybreak and hopefully would find Harwell's men. Now there was nothing to do but wait until dawn and try not to freeze without a fire.

Ford wrapped his arms around his chest and tried to keep his hands warm while he paced several yards away from where the others huddled to complain. He'd turned what he knew over and over in his mind. These men who were chasing Hannah were far too mean to be the law, even if Zachery was right and a letter to the sheriff had brought them here. Though Hannah hadn't said so, he knew they planned to kill her if they found her. They'd almost accomplished the job with Zachery, and he didn't even want to guess what they'd done to Gavrila.

His sister had been pampered and spoiled all her life, until she was now more fragile than people guessed. If he didn't find her soon, the men might not have to kill her—she'd die of fright. Gavrila needed to be in control, so being kidnapped must have been top on her list of nightmares. Who'd ever believe that it would actually happen?

He saddled up, deciding that riding in the dark was better than freezing to death on the damp ground. The men agreed and followed. Instinct drove him more than anything. The ground was too muddy for tracks and the air too thick to let sound carry, but still Ford moved on.

When he spotted a flicker of a campfire, Ford was

more surprised than any of the men behind him. He motioned for silence and they all swung from their saddles, pulling their rifles as they dismounted.

Ford leaned close to Alamo. "You go around behind them, in case there's trouble. I'll walk in from this direction. If shooting starts, try to get close enough to Gavrila to help her. Don't worry about me."

Alamo nodded and moved away.

Ford allowed him time to get into position before heading toward the camp. He knew he was walking into the pale morning sun and wouldn't see them until long after they'd spotted him. The men behind him kept their guns ready as they silently crossed the grass, cutting the distance to the camp with each step.

As he walked, Ford braced himself for a bullet. He was an open target, but on this flat land it was the only way he would have a chance at saving his sister. With luck, whoever was around the fire would be watching him and not Alamo. The little man might have a chance to slip in and get Gavrila out before the shooting started.

When he was within twenty yards of the fire, he heard his sister scream. Instinct fueled his actions as he broke into a full run into the sunlight with his guns drawn. He'd have to wait for a round fired at him to even know where to shoot.

No shots came!

Ford slowed his pace as the outline of Gavrila and Alamo came into view. They were standing side by side while he untied her hands. No one else was in sight.

"Well, it's about time you got here, Sanford!"

To his relief, she wasn't hurt, but angry. To his surprise, her anger was directed at him.

"I've been sitting out here in the rain half the night, waiting for you to find me. If you'd taken much longer the fire would have been out and I'd have been dead for sure. What took you so long? Were you home in bed with that wife who's fool enough to think you're a knight?"

Ford opened his mouth to defend himself, but she'd guessed exactly what he'd been doing when she'd been kidnapped.

Gavrila stormed toward him. "If it hadn't been for Alamo finding me, I'd be dinner for the coyotes tonight. Thank the Lord *he* saved me."

Alamo tried to explain that it had been Ford who'd led them here, but she wasn't listening. She screamed and stomped and yelled as she told of being kidnapped and dragged out here to the middle of nowhere.

"And when they pulled that smelly blanket off me, they all started swearing because I wasn't her . . . whoever 'her' was. My hair was the wrong color, one yelled, while another had the nerve to say I was too short." Gavrila turned toward Alamo. "You should have heard the words they were using. Every last one of them needed his mouth scrubbed with soap, and I told them so."

Alamo's eyes widened. "Did they hurt you?"

"They threatened me something terrible." She leaned against Alamo's shoulder. "One offered to cut out my tongue."

Ford added, "I'm surprised they didn't kill you, after what they did to Zachery."

Gavrila's voice lowered slightly as Alamo patted her shoulder. "I think one would have . . . the one I kept screaming at to take me home. But the leader told him that they weren't getting paid to kill me and he 'didn't do no dirty work for free.'

"When I corrected his grammar, he reconsidered, but decided it would be better to leave me out here to die on my own. They ate supper without offering me a bite and rode out."

To Ford's shock, she began to cry, and Alamo pulled her against him.

"Did they say anything about continuing to look for someone else?"

Gavrila stopped her sobbing long enough to mumble, "I heard one say that they'd find the little Gypsy if they had to search all of Texas, and when they did they'd make her pay before she died for all the trouble she'd caused them."

Ford moved to his horse. "Alamo, take my sister the safe way back to town and stay with her until she calms down."

Alamo nodded.

"I'm riding back across the canyon. I can get home faster that way."

"But there's no need to take such a chance," Alamo answered. "It's a miracle we made it before. One fall and you'll break you neck."

"I have to get back to Hannah!" Ford shouted as he mounted and rode off. He didn't have time for explanations. He knew the men would be headed right for his wife.

He rode to the edge of the canyon and gave the bay his head as they started down. The animal had made the trip many times and knew the treacherous path as well as Ford.

The ground was wet and gave easily beneath the tired horse and exhausted rider.

Ford pressed on, knowing the chances he took, but also fearing what the men might do to Hannah if they found her with only the already injured Zachery to protect her at the ranch. He knew from what Gavrila had said that they were hired killers and were very determined if they'd crossed half of Texas to find one girl. He also assumed they weren't familiar with using her name if they called her the Gypsy girl. She hadn't been part of a gang of thieves as he'd thought, but she must have witnessed something terrible if they felt they had to kill her to keep her quiet.

Her charcoal sketches came to mind. She'd drawn what she'd seen, Ford was sure of it now. Somehow she'd witnessed a murder and would pay with her own life. He'd thought she was running from the law. It had never crossed his mind that she might be running because the law couldn't protect her. If Gavrila's letter had been mailed to a sheriff and ended up in the hands of these men, maybe Hannah was running because she didn't feel she had anywhere else to turn.

Ford leaned lower, encouraging the bay to move faster. He must get back to her. Whatever the problem, they could face it together. If he had to, he'd sell his land

and relocate with her somewhere safe. They could start anew in a place where she didn't have to live in fear.

The bay stumbled and panicked as his back legs slid out from under him.

"Whoa," Ford tried to calm the horse. "Easy, boy."

But the bay jerked wildly, trying to climb to higher ground. The rocky edge of the canyon gave way and the horse and rider tumbled.

Chapter 22 ❖

FORD LAY VERY still, knowing he was in too much pain to be dead. The bay and he had rolled like tumbleweeds down the rocky slope of the canyon until finally they'd hit hard on a ledge. He could feel the weight of the horse on his leg and hear the animal's heavy, painful breathing.

"You're hurt bad," Ford whispered between clenched teeth, "aren't you, boy?"

The bay jerked his head toward the sound of Ford's voice. He struggled to get up, but the effort was too much for the old horse.

Ford knew that the animal's legs were broken and he knew what must be done.

"It's all right." Ford put a hand on the horse's mane as he pulled his Colt from its holster. "We've been together a long time; I'm not going to let you suffer now. Easy boy . . . it's only going to hurt a moment longer."

Tears blended with the rain on his face as Ford lifted the gun to the horse's head.

Before he could force himself to pull the trigger, a mighty shake ran through the bay, as if death jerked life from the powerful beast in one great pull. The animal stilled, no longer hurting. The weight of the bay seemed to double against Ford's leg as he lay the gun aside and let pain wash his mind into blackness.

Just as White was opening his store, Hannah and Uncle Zachery reached town. Hannah pulled up beside the porch and leaned out of the buggy. She tried to keep dry, but the effort was useless. She only hoped Zachery was nestled far enough back in the buggy to have been spared the icy rain. "Any word from Gavrila, Mr. White?"

The store owner leaned out as far as he dared without getting wet. "Alamo Rogers brought her in half an hour ago, safe and sound and yelling to high heaven. I figured Ford and the others would be home by now. Can't believe this storm hasn't let up. If it gets any colder, we'll have snow."

She didn't want to talk about the weather, but politeness demanded she agree. Hannah was thankful Gavrila was safe . . . and that she'd missed Ford's homecoming. Hannah wasn't sure she could face him and tell him she had to leave. He'd probably want to stand and fight and she had no desire to put his life in any more danger because of her. "Did they catch the three men?"

"No," White answered. "Appears those men were looking for someone else and picked up Gavrila by mistake. When they realized it, they just left her out on the plains. She told me she would have died for sure if Alamo hadn't saved her." White laughed. "She was hugging the poor man like he was last Christmas's favorite toy."

Hannah didn't know if she felt happy for Gavrila or sorry for Alamo Rogers. "Post a notice at the school for me, will you, Mr. White? Say that we're not having classes for the next few days."

"Sure thing," the storekeeper agreed. "After the scare the kiddies went through yesterday, they need a few days off. This weather will keep all but the town pupils at home, anyway."

Hannah fought down a sob. "And would you mind telling Ford I'm taking my uncle by train to Fort Worth and that I'll be back as soon as I can?"

White shook his head. "Ain't nobody leaving by train today, so you'd be wasting your time riding all the way over to the station. A rider was by about sunup and told Jinx that a section of the track got washed out a hundred miles south of here. The rider said he heard no one was killed, but five carloads of barbed wire marked for the JA Ranch are down in a wash so far they'll never be retrieved. I'd suggest you take the stage, but it won't be by until tomorrow morning—if it comes then, what with the roads all muddy."

Hannah only half listened. Her mind was searching for a way out of town and out of Ford's life. She couldn't go back to the ranch and she didn't have enough money for a hotel room near the station. The rain was so bad she wasn't sure how long a buggy could negotiate the roads up ahead. There had been several times even between the ranch and here that she hadn't been sure the wheels would stay on the muddy road. If White was right and the rain started freezing, she'd be fighting mud in places and ice in others.

Looking to Zachery for an answer, Hannah felt panic deal her another blow. He was slumped in the corner with a thin line of blood trickling from the corner of his mouth. Except for the places on his face that were bruised and cut, his skin was pale white.

"Are you all right?" she asked, finally able to control her voice. "Uncle Zachery?"

Slowly he opened his eyes and whispered, "I'll make it, girl. We got to get you to safety."

But she knew he wouldn't survive. The rocking of the buggy would kill him even before they made it to the train—if there was even a train to catch in the next several days. Hannah fought down a scream. Her world was turning even colder than the weather, and she had no place to run for shelter. She couldn't go on and she couldn't go back. She'd spent all these weeks running, only to be trapped now by a storm. Harwell's men would have an easy time locating her. They would ride in and shoot her before anyone had time to react.

"You all right, ma'am?" White leaned farther into the rain.

"I'm fine," Hannah lied. "Thank you." She had to think of something. If she was trapped by the storm, the riders might be also, at least for a few hours. "Do you know if Jinx is over in the post office?"

White pulled back into the shelter of the porch. "I think she's down at Gavrila's place helping out. I heard her say she'd check on the woman, then she planned to ride out to your place if the weather lightened up a bit.

She's fit to be tied ever since she heard Zachery was beaten. Says she only let him out of her sight for an hour yesterday and look what happened to him."

"Thank you, Mr. White. We'll find her. You stay dry." Hannah didn't wait for him to say anything more. She knew he wanted to be in out of the rain, even if he was a talker most days. She drove the buggy through town and turned into the final gate. The last place she wanted to go was Gavrila's house, but it seemed the only refuge.

Ford woke with a stream running beneath his arm and rain pounding on his face. Several yards up the canyon, water cascaded off the prairie flatland in a long, thin waterfall. Pebbles and pieces of grass danced in the silver sheen as they tumbled along with the water toward the canyon floor.

Grabbing hold of a root, Ford pulled himself inch by inch from beneath the dead horse. When he was free of the weight, he rolled onto his side, pulled his hat over his face, and tried to get air into his lungs without taking in too much rain. Part of him wanted to curl up beside the bay and wait out the storm, but he knew he must keep moving if he was going to be any help to Hannah.

Suddenly the memory of her washed over him, warming him from deep inside. It had only been hours since he left her and already the ache to hold her again was strong. He just wanted to be in the same room with her so he could smell her presence. Ford longed to stretch out beside her and tell her about how he felt finding Gavrila and having the bay die. He needed Hannah in every part of his life, in every part of his being, until there was no point where he stopped and Hannah began. He wanted to do the little things that made him smile deep inside, like telling her to put her arms around his neck and then feeling her grant his request.

Ford didn't feel the icy rain or the pain from several bruises and scrapes. All he felt was his longing for Hannah and a consuming sadness that she would never be his wife for every day left in his life, even though he knew they were married until death in his heart. She'd made it plain from the beginning that she'd be leaving him when the month was out. Though he knew she enjoyed their lovemaking, he couldn't ask her to honor a marriage she'd been forced into. She might like being in his bed, but there was much more to marriage than mating, and he couldn't sentence her to having to look across the table at him for three meals a day until one of them died.

Ford rolled to his feet and began to move slowly. What had taken him a few hours to cross on horseback would take him three times as long on foot. The rain washed away direction and time. Ford's head throbbed. He touched his forehead once and felt blood, but nothing mattered except fighting his way back to Hannah.

Moving endlessly, he forgot the rain-covered familiar landmarks. He stumbled more times than he could count, sliding along the canyon walls sometimes for several feet. Slowly, he began to climb. His survival depended on him reaching the top.

The sky turned from gray to black by the time Ford finally reached the rim of Palo Duro Canyon. His head was still bleeding and he'd scraped most of the hide off one arm. His leg throbbed in pain and he could no longer move the fingers of one hand. But he'd climbed the endless walls of the canyon and made it out.

For some time he stumbled in the blackness, hoping he was heading in the right direction. Normally, he could walk four, maybe even five miles an hour, but now he had no sense of time, and he knew he was moving slower than usual.

Finally, Ford saw the twinkling of several lights in the distance and headed toward them. He thought for a moment that he'd reached Saints Roost, but as he drew closer he realized his mistake. This was not even a town, but a collection of tents built in a circle.

Ford forced himself to move forward, even when he recognized the place. It was a tiny town constructed of canvas so the residents could pack up and move rapidly. The men in Saints Roost who had heard about this place spoke of it only in whispers when no ladies were within hearing distance. Folks called it Feather Hill because of the mattresses used by the women to practice their trade.

Though he'd known of its existence, Ford had never even ridden by. A town of gambling and drinking and other sins . . . as evil as Saints Roost was good. His father would have called it a Sodom in modern times.

Ford wanted to turn from the evil place, but he knew he had to get help if he was ever going to make it back to Hannah. Maybe he could borrow a horse. Maybe someone would help him if they didn't rob and kill him first. He had no idea what kind of wicked people must fester in a place like this one.

Tripping over one of the ropes holding a pole to the

first tent, Ford fell face first into the flap marking the front entrance. His head hit something hard and he rolled in pain as women screamed and light blinked for a second. Then everything went black for the second time in hours.

Hannah sat beside Zachery's bed and tried not to think about her need to get out of town. Her needs had to wait. The doctor had checked Zachery carefully and told Hannah she had done a fine job of nursing, but the old fellow shouldn't be moved for several days. Her drive in the rain had cost him dearly, and another outing in this weather might kill him. He needed rest and a warm bed to heal.

Hannah fought back her tears with her last bit of energy. She was so worried about Zachery and terrified that at any moment Harwell's men might arrive that she couldn't get her heart to stop pounding. If the buggy ride didn't kill him, Harwell's men surely would. How could she have ever thought she'd get away from them? They were paid killers and she hadn't even fired a gun more than a few times in her life.

Zachery touched her hand. "It's all right, girl. You go on without me. I'll be fine here. Jinx'll watch my back if trouble comes."

She shook her head. Even without the killers chasing them, she wouldn't leave Zachery here in the house with Gavrila. That'd be a fate worse than a bullet.

Jinx had met her on the porch and helped carry Zachery to the extra bedroom upstairs. While they dried him and waited for the doctor, Hannah could hear Gavrila crying through the wall. She'd gotten more upset by the hour, it seemed, and now wouldn't allow anyone but Alamo near her. His mother came over and tried to help, but Gavrila had screamed until she'd left the room.

Hannah knew she should go to her sister-in-law and comfort her, but couldn't bring herself to. Each time a friend tried to enter the room, Gavrila would scream with fright and order them out, then she'd demand Alamo stay beside her. He was her hero, it seemed, and the only person she trusted.

Jinx saw the doctor out, then walked Hannah across the hall to Ford's office.

"We need to talk," Jinx began.

Too tired to think of a story that made sense, she might as well tell everyone that she was the one the kidnappers were looking for. Then they could sacrifice her and they'd all be safe again. When Harwell's men came, she'd go with them. They didn't know Zachery had seen the murders; they must have thought he was simply traveling with her. Maybe if they killed her, they'd go back to Fort Worth.

"You're the one those riders in the yellow slickers were looking for," Jinx announced before Hannah could state her thoughts.

"Yes."

Jinx put her arm around Hannah's shoulder. "Don't look like the first Christian volunteering for the lion's cage. Ford's not going to let anyone hurt you, and I'm guessing everyone in town feels the same. It'll take more than three snakes to kill this nest of doves."

"But I'm not what everyone thinks I am. I'm . . ."

Jinx smiled. "None of us is, child."

"But I lied to get here. I lied to get the job." Hannah suddenly wanted all the truth out. "Ford met me when I was robbing him in Dallas. I took the man's clothes, and he didn't turn me in even when he had the chance. He's been so good to me—all of you have—and all I do is bring these men here to upset the entire town and almost get Zachery and Gavrila killed. And the poor children must have been frightened out of their minds! Then every man had to ride out in the middle of a storm to look for Gavrila."

"Hush now." Jinx patted Hannah's shoulder. "I won't hear anymore. You didn't hurt Zachery, those low-down varmints did that. And I don't reckon Ford minded being robbed, or he would have complained a little louder instead of looking at you like he was about to bust at the seams from loving you."

Hannah opened her mouth to deny the words, but Jinx held up her hand and continued, "As for the kids, from what I hear, half of them were cheering when Gavrila was abducted. Gavrila's in there wailing like she's afraid her shadow's going to slit her throat. Well, she may just be getting out of this day the very thing she'd been wanting all her life: a real live hero to take care of her."

Hannah brushed a tear from her cheek. Jinx had a way of clearing the air. "But I lied. I lied to everyone."

The older woman laughed. "Hell, I reckon we've all done our share of that. I convinced my first three husbands I was a virgin, and that ain't no easy lie."

Hannah smiled. This woman was so honest even her

confessions made you feel like you could tell her anything.

"All we got to do is keep you safe until Ford gets here."

"He won't come. I told him when I left not to follow. It was part of the bargain we made when we married."

Jinx winked. "I got a feeling he'll come. Until then, you keep a gun close by and sleep with one eye open. I'll sit up with Zachery. I didn't survive the War Between the States, Indian attacks, and four husbands to be killed before I marry number five. You can count on me backing you up if there's trouble."

"I'll make a bed downstairs so I can see both doors." Hannah didn't feel so alone now. Jinx was making it plain that she planned to stay and help, and somehow the impossible suddenly seemed possible.

"But he's one of those saints," Ford heard a woman whine.

"I don't care!" yelled another. "Pour some more of that whiskey down him before he freezes his . . . his wings off."

Ford felt fire dribble down his throat and came full awake. He spit and coughed while he fought off the thin arms that tried to hold him down on a feather bed.

"Get the man some water!" shouted a woman standing at the foot of the bed with a thin cigar in her mouth.

Ford glared at her and nodded his thanks. Several women were in the room, in total wearing what would make up one outfit, he figured. The leader drew his attention. She wasn't old, but there was a hardness about her that made her eyes seem ancient. She was wearing a robe Ford could almost see through. And if women were valued by the pound, this one would have been priceless, for her width almost equaled that of the bed.

"You alive, cowboy?" She pulled the cigar from her mouth and turned her blood red lips into a smile. "We patched you up as best we could."

"I'm alive," he answered.

"From that bump on your head, we thought you must have taken a tumble in this storm and accidentally landed in our fair Feather Hill. Since I'm the unelected mayor of this here place, I guess I'll be the one to welcome you. Name's Felicity. That's Latin for happiness, don't you know."

Ford's head hurt too much to remember any Latin, but he had no doubt the woman lived up to her name in many a cowboy's dreams. "I'm Ford," he mumbled. "My horse lost his footing and fell in the canyon." Ford closed his eyes. "I have to get back to my wife."

Several of the women laughed.

The leader grumbled at them and they all fell silent. "Normally, we have men stumble in here and stumble out a little happier and poorer than before. But you're different. I can tell by your eyes you're one of those men who only sees one woman. Unfortunately for my business, it's probably this wife you're wanting to get back to."

Ford cut his gaze toward her, wondering what the lady-of-the-line, as he'd heard them called by the railroad workers, was up to. He couldn't tell if she was playing him or not.

"You see, ladies," the woman began, "what we got

here is a gentleman, and you all got to treat him different."

The girls laughed, but she quieted them with a wave of her cigar.

"You don't understand." Ford ran his fingers through his still damp hair. "My wife is in danger and I have to help her."

"Oh, but the Lord helps those who help themselves, and we plan on encouraging you to help yourself. Would you like another drink?" She motioned for someone at the door to get another bottle. "In a few hours, you're going to forget you even have a wife. Most of the men who come in here do."

As the door opened, Ford could see what looked to be a smoky bar just beyond. Several men and women were laughing and talking. He knew he could stand and walk out of the room. None of the women would, or could, stop him, but he needed a horse. If this woman was the leader, she was the one he'd be wise to talk with.

"Can I buy a horse?" He stood and fished in his pocket, hoping he had enough money with him.

"How about we just take you for a ride?" one woman asked, and the other women laughed.

While all the girls joined in with suggestions, the door opened again and a little boy entered, carrying a tray with several glasses and a bottle. The boy looked up at Ford and almost dropped his load.

Ford wished he had time to explain to the child what he was doing here. "Do you have a horse or don't you? That's all I want."

The huge woman looked frustrated, but the boy set the

tray down and walked over to Ford. "Hello, sir," he whispered as he extended his hand in a formal handshake. "I'm Rip. I know who you are."

Ford knelt on one knee to the first friendly face he'd seen in what seemed like years.

"Is Miss Hannah feeling better?" Rip asked with a worried look. "We sure do miss her. Miss Gavrila went riding with some men today and we didn't have anyone to tell us a story. I sure do like those stories your wife tells."

"You're Miss Hannah's husband!" the leader shouted as she gently pushed Rip aside. "Well, why didn't you say so?"

Ford raised an eyebrow. He'd known a few of the children from Feather Hill had been coming over to the school, but he never thought of the adults in the tent city as parents. "Hannah is my wife," he said slowly.

The leader tossed her cigar in the washbasin and slapped him on the back. "She's a fine lady, she is. A fine lady. One day she even stopped by here and brought Rip home. Come right in the bar like she'd been in one all her life and sat to visiting with me about my boy as proper as if I'd married his father."

Ford thought the fall into the canyon had been a long drop. Until now. All the air left his lungs and he swore his heart stopped at the idea that his wife had done such a thing. When she'd said she was visiting some of the parents, he never dreamed she'd walk into such a place.

"My wife!" He tried to breathe normally.

"Sure," the leader smiled proudly. "Gave me a picture, too, and told us all a story about a knight. She even said you was her knight, 'cause you'd kill any dragon for her."

Felicity turned to the others as if they couldn't follow the conversation. "This here's Miss Hannah's man."

All the women were talking at once as the leader produced the picture and they all admired it.

"She's a fine lady and a great artist," Felicity proclaimed. "This is the finest thing anyone's ever given me. I'm gonna have it framed someday when I get a place with real walls and a wood floor."

Ford looked at the sketch. It was Hannah's, all right. No better than the ones he'd seen her draw at night. Only he'd hardly taken the time to look at them, and these folks seemed to think they were of great value.

Ford looked again. The work was fair at best. What made the picture so special was the honor she paid the prostitutes by offering it to them. Her small gesture had given them value and maybe allowed Rip to walk a little taller.

"She is a great artist," Ford agreed. Look what she'd done for them and for him. "I'm very lucky to have her for a wife."

All the women nodded.

"Will you help me? If I could just borrow a horse, I'll return it as soon as I can."

The leader waved Rip toward the door. "Get him one of our best. The black we took in trade last week should be fast." Felicity giggled. "His owner sure was." She turned to Ford. "Come to the bar and I'll get you some coffee to keep your insides warm."

He followed her out of the room and to the bar area.

While she poured the coffee, they talked of Gavrila's kidnapping. He was amazed at all she knew of the town. People who didn't even suspect she lived out here in these tents were people she seemed to know. While he downed his second cup, he told her how Hannah was afraid sometimes and of the drawings he'd seen one night when she'd stayed up waiting for him.

"She's seen a killing." The woman nodded with an air of one who'd seen all there was to see in life a few times herself. "And those men looking for her aim to silence our Hannah."

Ford wasn't sure he liked the prostitute claiming Hannah, but it felt good to talk with someone about his worries.

"I wish I could find them first," he said as he drained his cup.

The woman pulled him toward the back of the tent. "We had three strangers come in here a few hours ago. I think they're playing cards in there." She held a flap an inch open. "I know it's a long shot, but do you think those could be the ones planning to kill her?"

Blinking in the smoky light, he looked closely, then stared once more through the opening. Hannah's horrible sketch of a man smiling while he fired his guns at waist level had come to life before him. The man stood at a table, threatening the dealer with the same evil smile, which cut ripples across his face.

"That's him!" Ford mumbled and reached for his Colt.

The holster was empty.

Chapter 23 ✦

"I WANT'A SEE your hands, dealer!" the gunman growled as he waved the firearm above the gambling table.

The dealer raised his hands as his eyes widened to poker chip size.

Ford glanced behind him. He saw nothing to use as a weapon. No gun in sight, not even a stick. If he didn't do something quickly, the killers Hannah had drawn in charcoal would spring to life and destroy again. With walls of canvas, others could be hit if anyone fired.

Felicity did what she did best. She read his mind and stepped past him into the gaming room, making a great show as she moved forward.

Ford followed seconds later, hidden in her shadow. He moved toward the back unnoticed while everyone, including the gunman, watched Felicity. The air was so thick with smoke, Ford almost tripped over a broken chair in one corner as he moved directly behind the gunman. He could easily jump the killer from behind, but two partners sat on either side of him, laughing at the dealer's fear.

"What's going on in here, boys?" Felicity sashayed over as if she wanted to join in on the fun. "You three newcomers having a little fun?"

"I'm thinking you might want to get a new dealer," the gunman said. "I could help rid the earth of this one."

Felicity laughed and looked at her employee. The slight nod between the two was barely noticed by Ford. "If you're going to kill my dealer, best do it *now*."

With her last word, everyone jumped at once, taking the three hired killers by surprise. Felicity fell against the one nearest her, knocking him on the floor flatter than a water-batter pancake. The dealer dove toward the other seated gunman, shoving him out of his chair as a bullet split the canvas behind where the dealer had been sitting. Ford raised a chair and shattered it across the standing gunman's head an instant after the outlaw had pulled the trigger.

Before Ford could move, the room seemed to fill with people. A few of the girls helped the dealer tie up his captive, but the one Ford had hit was out cold, as was the man Felicity had toppled.

The huge woman stood and straightened her robe. "Lordy, lordy, that was fun!" She slapped her hands against Ford's cheeks. "I know you got to get home to that wife of yours, but you come back anytime for a visit. I ain't had so much fun since I was arrested by a group of Texas Rangers down near Big Bend."

Ford moved toward the exit. "You'll keep these men tied up until I return with the law?"

She followed him to the flap that served as her front door. "You bet." Grabbing one of their slickers, she handed it to Ford. "Since it's still raining, you'd best take one of these newfangled yellow things they're wearing as dusters. These three ain't going to be needing them till you get back. This material looks like it's coated with oil to keep the rain out."

Ford slipped into the slicker and disappeared out of the tent.

Rip was waiting with an able horse. With a nod to the boy, Ford stepped into the stirrup and kicked the animal into action. He knew that now that the killers were tied up, Hannah was safe, but he couldn't wait to get back to her. He wanted to tell her all that had happened to him, suddenly realizing he'd never had anyone to share things with before. He also had to tell her he understood why she'd been running. If three men like those he'd just seen had been chasing him, Ford decided he'd have done whatever he had to to escape them.

He covered the distance in record time, despite the rain. When he reached his barn he'd decided he would offer Felicity a good price for the horse, if she was interested. There would never be another like the bay for him, but this one was a powerful animal. When the ground dried a little, he'd maneuver back down into the canyon and bury the bay on the side where he died.

The house was dark as he walked toward it. Hannah must have turned in early. Every bone in his body hurt with exhaustion, but his steps were quick. He'd spent the night hunting Gavrila and a day fighting his way back. Now all he wanted to do was hold Hannah in his arms and tell her he understood.

Sneeze met him at the door, purring loudly. Ford

scratched the cat's head and wondered why Sneeze's milk bowl was empty.

He refilled the bowl, pulled off the slicker, and was two steps into the living area before he remembered his boots. Hannah wouldn't have to remind him again. If she wanted no mud on the floor, he'd try to remember. Ford backtracked to the kitchen and pulled off the wet leather.

Almost running across the main room to his bedroom, he half expected her to be asleep on the couch, but he was glad she'd already turned in. Sliding in beside her beneath the covers would be a wonderful way to end the day. He'd hold her tightly and tell her she had nothing else to fear.

As he entered the bedroom, the first thing he noticed was how cold the room seemed. Hannah always lit the fire. But there was no firelight. Only the shadowy light from the window crossing an empty bed.

Ford let out a deep breath and walked to the other room. Of course, he thought, she was sitting up with Zachery.

The other room was empty as well.

Alarm crept up his spine. He walked back to his room and struck the light. There must be a dozen explanations why she wasn't here.

Hannah had taken Zachery into town to the doctor after all, and they'd been trapped by the storm. She'd ridden in to check on Gavrila. His sister must have gotten home hours before he ever reached Feather Hill. But why hadn't Hannah returned here? She must know that he'd come here first looking for her.

Slowly, hesitantly, Ford forced himself to turn toward the wardrobe. Her clothes were still hanging beside his.

Cold dread forced him to look up. To check the one thing he knew she would take with her if she was truly gone.

The carpetbag was missing!

She's done it, he thought. She's left me.

Like a wild man, he rummaged through the house, not wanting to believe his own fears. She'd taken her comb and brush, her coat and gloves, her carpetbag. "Dear Lord," he swore aloud, "she's taken the bag." There would be no reason for her to take the bag unless she was leaving for good.

Finally, when he pulled the bottom drawer of his desk open, Ford admitted the truth to himself. All his money was gone. She'd left one gold bracelet behind. As if one gold band could keep his heart from shattering.

Ford stormed out of the house, grabbing the slicker and his hat as he moved. He had no idea where to look, but he wasn't going to let her disappear out of his life without facing him. If the whole world thought him a little wild, he was about to prove them right, for he'd either find Hannah or go mad trying.

Hannah couldn't sleep. She'd piled layer after layer of Gavrila's handmade quilts on the floor in front of the fireplace, but her bed still wasn't comfortable. She could see both the front and back doors, but she didn't feel safe. The Winchester lay by her side. She curled in a ball, her knees to her chin, and wondered if she'd ever be able to sleep soundly again.

The rain finally slowed, but the wind kept whining outside, whispering between the buildings of a danger she couldn't see. It didn't call her to dance tonight, but warned her to be alert. Whenever she tried to sleep the wind seemed to moan louder, pleading for her to be ready.

From time to time she could hear Jinx moving about Uncle Zachery's room and Gavrila calling for Alamo, who had spread a bedroll in the hall beside her door.

Hannah knew it was after midnight, but she couldn't relax. Harwell's men were out there looking for her, and she was trapped here by the storm.

Wind whipped up and she thought she heard a horse. Then it quieted outside and the room seemed to grow darker. Hannah felt someone coming even before she heard the footsteps on the porch. Hard, fast steps of someone storming toward the back door with great fury.

She raised her rifle and waited for the trouble she knew would come.

The knob rattled, then gave. The glass in the door sounded almost like a hurried chime as a man in a yellow slicker stepped through the back entrance.

Shaking badly, Hannah could barely bring the gun to her cheek and sight.

The moment she saw the yellow slicker, she pulled the trigger, shattering the silence of the house.

The shadow ducked but kept coming as the sound of the gunshot rattled through the hallways. Hannah cocked the weapon, pushing another round into place. She raised the Winchester once more and aimed, dead center, at the slicker moving toward her.

"Hannah!" Alamo screamed from the stairs, just before she pulled the trigger.

A slight jerk caused by the distraction made the bullet miss her mark.

Hannah's fingers trembled as she lifted the weapon once more.

Before she could recock the Winchester, the stranger reached her and ripped the barrel of the gun from her.

"Hannah!" Ford shouted with a mixture of anger and fear in his voice. "Stop trying to make yourself a widow!"

"Ford!" Hannah cried as she realized who she was shooting at. He pulled her up into his arms and held her so tightly she couldn't even shake.

"I'm sorry," she whispered when tears allowed her to talk. "I thought you were . . ."

"I know," he answered. "I was a fool to wear the slicker. In your drawings there was no color. When I heard the first shot, I realized my mistake. But I'm happy to know my wife is the worst shot in the state."

Alamo advanced only halfway down the stairs. "Ford. I wasn't sure it was you on that black horse, but no man walks with the stride you do when you're in a hurry."

Ford didn't loosen his hold on Hannah as he looked up. "How's my sister?"

"She's still really delicate."

Alamo wasn't telling Ford anything new. "Maybe she'll feel better knowing we caught the three men. They're tied up over at Feather Hill."

"Feather Hill?" Hannah leaned back to look at Ford.

He laughed. "I met a friend of yours over there. Quite a lady."

Jinx stormed down the stairs with a lantern in one hand and her gun in the other. She took one look at Ford and swore. "You look like something even a cat wouldn't drag home. It's about time you showed up to protect this wife of yours. I've been pulling double duty as both nurse and guard."

"Protect her? I was worried about her killing me a few minutes ago," Ford answered. "As to where I've been, it's a long story I'll tell everyone over breakfast. Right now, I haven't had any sleep in two days."

"Well, then, let's get to bed." Jinx started back up the stairs. "Ain't many a story worth ruining a good night's sleep over."

When Alamo and Jinx disappeared upstairs, Ford pulled Hannah into his arms and kissed her. "We've got some talking to do, darlin'," he whispered between kisses, "but it'll wait till morning."

When she was light-headed from being kissed, Ford pulled away and removed his coat and gun belt. Silently, he pulled the bandanna from his pocket and circled her wrist with the material. Then, using his teeth to pull the knot, he bound his own wrist to hers.

"We'll talk in the morning," he whispered as he eased her down on the quilts. "Right now I have to get some rest, and I don't want you running out on me while I'm asleep. You've got some explaining to do, and I've got—for the first time in my life—some things I have to say."

"But—" Hannah started to protest, knowing if she

chose to leave, the knotted bandanna couldn't hold her. He was asking her to wait, but still not trusting her word.

"Tomorrow," he whispered as he closed his eyes, already beyond her hearing.

Hannah covered them both with the wedding quilt and kissed her sleeping husband. "Tonight, darling," she whispered softly. "I'll hold you in my arms one more time, but tomorrow I'll leave my heart forever in Texas . . . forever with you. No bandanna or words will keep me."

❖ *Chapter 24*

"Oh, my goodness!" Gavrila crowed like the dawn rooster. "He's tied her to him!"

Hannah blinked away the morning light and tried to figure out where the screeching was coming from.

"Look, Alamo!" Gavrila yelled. "My brother's tied his wife to him for the night. Isn't that the cruelest thing you've ever seen? He should be whipped. I always said I loved my brother, but I won't stand for any man mistreating a woman."

Ford rolled his face into the covers. He'd done something wrong again. His intention wasn't to tie up Hannah, only to keep her near until they could talk. He'd been so tired last night he couldn't think straight, much less tell her how he felt about her. Now Gavrila would tell everyone in town he'd tied Hannah up, and the next thing people would think is that he beat her regularly. It would only be a matter of time before everyone hated him and tried to save her from the beast she'd married.

Hannah tugged at their bound arms as she sat up and stretched.

"You poor, poor child!" Gavrila shouted. "I know

what it's like to be tied up and forced to stay some place against your will. I'm so sorry." She reached to untie the bandanna around Hannah and Ford's wrists, but Hannah pulled away.

"No!" she snapped. "You have it all wrong. Ford didn't tie me; I tied him."

Everyone, including Ford, stared at her.

Hannah hesitated, then reached to pull the knot free. "You see, dear sister, your brother is a wild, loving man. Sometimes in our bed, during the loving, he . . ."

Gavrila screeched. "I can't hear such things!" She stormed toward the stairs. "Alamo, did you hear what she said—and in the house my good father built? I've never heard such talk in my life. To think they spent the night on all my good quilts!" She screamed again just to shatter the air. "And then to try and tell me things no lady should ever have to hear. I can't stand such thoughts, much less have to hear the words said right out loud."

Alamo leaned a knee on the pallet. "Do you think I might borrow that bandanna for a while? Wild and loving might just run in their blood, and I'd like to be prepared."

Hannah smiled and handed him the handkerchief.

"We probably won't be down for breakfast!" he shouted as he took the stairs in a charge.

Ford burst out laughing. "If he's alive by lunch, I'll give them this house as a wedding present." He glanced at Hannah. "Tell me, darlin', what is it I do 'during the loving'?"

A pounding on the door sobered their laughter and

saved Hannah from having to answer. How could she ever begin to tell him how alive he made her feel and how loved "during the loving"?

Ford stood and tucked his shirt into his mud-splattered pants as Hannah tried to push the wrinkles out of her dress, but it still looked hopelessly slept in. The floor that had been so uncomfortable in evening had turned warm and relaxing with Ford by her side.

"Morning, Reverend," Ford said as he opened the door.

"I've come to see if your sister is all right." Reverend Carhart removed his hat and glanced at the blankets by the fireplace. "You two are still cuddling by the hearth, I see."

Hannah looked embarrassed, but Ford only nodded as he closed the door.

"My sister is recovering nicely, but unable to see guests at the moment."

The reverend seemed relieved. He'd done his duty and it hadn't proven as painful as he'd thought. "I'd best be going, then. Smith's outside waiting for you. He said when you stopped by his place last night, you told him you needed his wagon to haul three rats to jail first thing this morning. You'd best take them over to Tascosa, because there isn't a man in town who'd not want to string them up after learning they were planning to kill Miss Hannah," he said. He hesitated a moment before adding, "And of course after they kidnapped Miss Gavrila."

"I'd almost forgotten about the men," Ford reached for his gun belt. "I left them over at Feather Hill, so I won't ask you to ride with me."

Carhart nodded and didn't ask any more about the men, for he had other things on his mind. "Thank the Lord the storm's over. It left a wide sweep of destruction in our little community. Several homes were damaged in town, and I plan to ride out and check on all the farms later today."

He moved toward the door, a man with a mission to complete. "Funny thing, too. You might be interested in this, ma'am. The back porch at White's blew off and underneath we found a stash of things you wouldn't believe. Allison Donley's purse, with forty dollars still in it. A writing kit just like the one White thought was stolen, and a number of other things folks around here have been missing." He pulled something silver from his pocket. "I even noticed the creamer from Miss Gavrila's tea service and brought it back to her."

Hannah and Ford were silent. She couldn't bring herself to look at him. The words he'd said before he'd left her at the ranch echoed in her mind. If he'd thought she was stealing from the folks in town and some of the things had been replaced, Ford must have been the one replacing things reported stolen.

Carhart set the creamer back in place. "I guess Gavrila hadn't even missed it yet." The reverend laughed. "Two of your students, the Burns boys, claimed it was just a joke, but their father sure didn't see the humor in it as he dragged them across the street. My guess is you won't be asking either boy to sit down for a while in school."

He nodded and let himself out, leaving the room silent.

Ford took a long breath. I've done it again, he

thought, as he guessed what Hannah must be thinking. He'd told her it didn't matter how much she stole from the town, but suddenly he knew it mattered a great deal that he'd thought of her as a thief. If there was a manual somewhere on how to do the wrong thing in a relationship, he must be the bad example in every chapter.

"You replaced the money?" Hannah whispered.

"Yes." He could feel the noose knot around his neck.

"And you bought another kit and put it in White's store because you thought I'd taken one that day I told you I was in White's buying charcoal?"

"I did." He couldn't look at her and he couldn't lie.

"You believed I was stealing from these people? That's why you said it didn't matter?"

Ford could only nod as the noose tightened, but it was his heart that clenched in response. He was losing her, not by what someone else did, or because of the bargain, but because he hadn't believed in her.

"Ford!" Smith yelled from the front of the house. "Daylight's burning."

Forcing himself to look at her, Ford saw what he feared. The pain in her eyes was too deep for tears to wash away. "I have to go," he mumbled, wishing the right words would come to him just once. "We can talk about this when I get back."

She didn't answer.

Ford moved toward the door. He needed to be alone. He wished he could run into the prairie like he had as a child. But he'd given up running long ago. How could he ever find the words to tell her how he felt? When he'd thought she was a thief and he'd loved her anyway it had been one thing. But the tables had turned. She was genuinely innocent and he had judged her falsely. Now she was the one who would have to forgive. Though he'd been strong enough to forgive her when he'd thought she was a thief, he wasn't sure he had a right to ask the same of her now.

Ford knew there was something he needed to say, but words wouldn't come. He couldn't look at her and see the pain in her eyes again. He'd shattered his only chance at happiness and needed time to think of how to repair the damage.

Walking out without another word, fear kept him from even glancing back. Fear that whispered there was no hope.

"Be here when I get back," he ordered when he'd meant to request. "We'll talk." Somehow in the time it would take to haul the men to jail, he'd think of a way to make her believe he'd only done what he thought was right. Somehow he'd find the words to tell her he loved her.

Hannah closed the door to the little room furnished for travelers, noticing there was no lock. She'd talked Jinx into letting her spend the night at the post office so that she'd be ready for the next stage at first light. If Ford had to take Harwell's men all the way to Tascosa, he wouldn't be back until tomorrow. She couldn't bear to stay in Gavrila's house any longer, so the tiny space suited her needs.

When she learned Ford thought her a thief, she realized he'd always see her as such. Even if for a short time she'd believed they could be married like normal people, his lack of trust had shattered her hopes. She'd made sure Zachery was recovering, then left the house. She needed time to think as desperately as Ford seemed to. Only Hannah had to decide where to go next. There was no use waiting for Ford to return. They had nothing more to say to one another. The month was almost over and their bargain would be up in a few days.

Curling up in the middle of the bed, she thought about how her life had changed in the weeks since meeting Ford. He'd added color to her world. She'd met folks who were kind and good, not because they were afraid of the law, but just because it was the right way to be. She'd learned to love.

Hannah closed her eyes and slept the kind of sleep that even erases dreams. She'd be on the stage at dawn and this part of her life would forever be over.

Late into the night, she heard the door creak and she jerked fully awake.

"Who's there?" she whispered, hoping there would be no answer.

"Don't be afraid," Ford whispered back.

Lightning bolted through her nerves. She reached for the lamp.

"Don't strike a match, Hannah." He moved to the side of the bed. "I'm not sure I can say what I have to say in the light."

"We have nothing else to talk about." She pulled the covers around her as though they offered protection. "What are you doing here?"

"I could ask you the same question . . . but I know the answer. Jinx told me a few minutes ago that you're planning to leave on the first stage out."

"It's time for me to go. Our bargain is up." She was glad he'd asked for the darkness, for she wasn't sure she could leave him if she saw his face.

"The bargain was you'd take something of value when you left."

She held her hands in her lap to keep them from shaking. His voice sounded angry, but she refused to let him frighten her. "I took nothing but my clothes and enough for the stage."

"No. You took something I can't part with and I want it back." Ford moved around the bed in the blackness, keeping her guessing as to his location.

"I took nothing!" Hannah couldn't believe he was accusing her of stealing again. She'd realized finally that he'd replaced the items and money in an effort to protect her, but his not believing her still hurt deeply. Now he was accusing her once more.

"Your *uncle* told me where to find you." The way he said the word "uncle" made Hannah bite down on her bottom lip. He must have found out the truth about Zachery. How could she convince him that she took nothing from his house, when he was telling her he'd discover another lie.

"What else could I do?" She tried to guess where Ford was in the room. "I couldn't turn Zachery away. He was running from the same killers I was, only they didn't know he was a witness."

"Don't change the subject," Ford stormed. "I don't

care if he's your uncle or not. I've come because of what you've taken."

"I told you! I took nothing. The only time I ever stole or robbed anyone was the night I took your clothes. I know you'll always see me as a thief, but I'm not."

She felt a shift in the bed and knew he'd sat down beside her. "You can't take from me this time!" His voice was hard, but she could feel the warmth of his body only inches away. "Give it back or I won't let you go, Hannah."

Anger twisted inside her. "I took nothing! I tell you! Nothing!"

He grabbed her shoulders and held her tightly at arm's length. "Yes, you did!" he whispered between clenched teeth. "You took my heart, and I can't live without it."

Hannah could feel his pain in every word. He didn't know how to tell her he loved her. She guessed he'd never heard the words and couldn't say them now, though they were the only words that would heal the wound between them.

She shoved his hands away from her shoulders and moved out of his grip. She guessed he loved her since he'd replaced all the missing things, but she needed to know he trusted her. Without the trust she couldn't stay.

Ford forced out the words he'd been repeating in his mind all day. "I never meant to hurt you. I cared for you so much it didn't matter to me if you robbed me blind. I'm sorry I never figured out that inside such a wonderful woman couldn't live a thief. You did what you did when we met to stay alive and I had no right to judge you. All my life I've been trying to *do* right and you've taught me what it means to *be* right."

He reached for her, but she moved away. "Folks might say you did the wrong thing, taking my clothes, or going to Feather Hill, or lying about an uncle. But you did it for the right reasons. I seem to have done the right thing for the wrong reason. I should have believed in you. But leaving me and taking my heart is too great a price for me to pay for my crime, so give it back. You're not taking any stage while you've got my heart packed away in that Gypsy bag of yours."

She darted from the bed into the darkness. "Well, I'm not returning anything!" she shouted with all the anger he'd expressed, but feeling like she was melting inside from his few words. "I love you, and I figure it belongs to me now."

Ford sprang toward her, but she darted away. "Then you're not leaving me, darlin'. I'll swear I'll always trust you, but it'll take me a lifetime to prove it to you."

He stood so still he might have been made of stone. He'd laid his offer on the table, and now he had to wait to see if it was good enough.

"I might stay for a while if we can strike another bargain." She smiled at the shadow of the man she loved as he raised his head.

"Name your price." The words stumbled from him. He didn't dare breathe. Of all the struggles he'd fought in his life, this was the only one that mattered. Words had never been important to him, but now words were the only way to make her see how much he needed her in his life. "I'll pay it."

"Do you love me?"

"Yes," he answered, knowing that he had from the moment she'd touched him.

"Then say it." She moved closer. "Say it every day and just maybe I'll stay."

"I love you," he whispered as she moved gently into his arms. "I love you, Hannah, darlin'."

"Then let's start over from the beginning." She circled her arms about his neck and pressed her heart to his. "Take off your clothes."

Epilogue ❧

HANNAH STOOD AS still as she could beside Ford while the preacher rambled on about couples finding one another in the twilight years.

She could feel the warm spring air drifting through the open windows and smell the wonderful aroma of prairie flowers that now covered the altar with bluebonnet blues and fiery Indian paintbrush reds. Everyone in the church seemed almost giggly with excitement over the wedding—everyone except maybe Zachery. He appeared nervous standing beside his bride. Jinx looked younger in her new store-bought chambray shirt and brushed leather riding skirt. Her boots were polished and her hair combed, making Hannah realize what a beautiful woman she could be when she chose to spend the time. She'd refused a wedding dress or veil, saying at Zachery's age he deserved to see exactly what he was getting in marriage.

Hannah didn't miss Jinx's wink at Zachery as the minister pronounced them man and wife. While the couple kissed, she sidled closer to her own husband. The warmth of his strong body drew her as it had months ago. He welcomed her against his side, placing his arm around her shoulder.

When all stood and the piano began to play, Hannah slid her hand along Ford's thigh as though by accident.

"Stop that," he whispered while everyone else watched the newlyweds stroll down the aisle.

Hannah pressed her fingers against the soft cotton of his shirt. "Stop what?" She clawed lightly against the material.

Folks began to crowd toward the door. She gently pushed her breast against his arm as she followed. His muscle tightened and Hannah couldn't stop her laughter. She loved the reaction she had on this man and never planned to give him any truce.

When he held the door for her, she moved slowly past him, pressing her body against his until she could feel the heat from his skin increasing.

He remained stone. If she hadn't known him so well, she'd have thought he had no reaction to her touch, but she played his emotions perfectly.

They walked, hand in hand, to Gavrila's house. Hannah's sister-in-law had insisted on giving Jinx and Zachery a reception, and she'd only wanted help in the planning from one person—Alamo.

Hannah ran her thumb in circles along Ford's palm as they walked. Occasionally, she stepped closer, brushing her side against his. He didn't react.

"It was a lovely wedding, Jinx," Hannah said as they all eased into the shade of the porch.

"Best one I ever had." Jinx grinned and slapped Zachery on the back. "I knew if I could get him all patched and healed he'd make a handsome groom."

Hannah looked at Zachery, who still appeared to be a little pale, even though it had been two months since he'd been beaten by Harwell's men. The realization that he was married seemed to be settling in around him. He'd insisted on remaining her "uncle" despite Ford's knowing the truth. Now even Gavrila had warmed to the idea that he was a member of the family.

"Some men get better looking every day." Hannah couldn't resist running her fingers slowly down Ford's spine. He straightened slightly, but didn't look at her.

Shifting, Hannah pressed against him, loving the way his breath suddenly stopped. All the other guests were talking and laughing. They didn't see her hand lightly brush his thigh.

"Everyone in the dining room!" Gavrila yelled. "I'm ready for the couple to cut the cake."

As Hannah joined the others, she felt Ford's fingers close around her arm and pull suddenly. Before she could react, he was moving up the stairs, almost in a run. "We'll be there in a minute," he mumbled in a low tone she might have mistaken for anger if she hadn't known him so well.

She was out of breath by the time he pulled her into the first room and slammed the door behind them.

"Ford!" she smiled as she tried to scold. "The others are waiting. We can't just run off from the wedding."

He pressed her body against the back of the door with his own and lifted her head.

His mouth came down on hers with a wild hunger he

could never seem to satisfy. She didn't have to touch him to make him want her. Just the smell of her, or how she moved, or knowing she was looking at him, was all the spark he needed. But when she touched him—all control snapped.

Hannah pushed him away. "We have to go downstairs," she said between kisses.

Strong hands burned across her body, carrying warmth through the clothes. "Not yet," he whispered in her ear.

Hannah pushed against his chest. "We can't be doing this now. We'll have to wait until later, when we get home."

"I am home," Ford mumbled as he pulled at the buttons of her collar. Home would always be Hannah. When she playfully slapped him away, he slid his hand behind her back and pressed her hard against him. "Tell me you don't want me, my darlin'," he whispered against her hair.

"No." She kissed his jaw. "I'll never say that."

He stepped suddenly away and crossed to the window. Their wedding quilt lay neatly folded on the window seat. Ford tossed it over his shoulder.

With a sudden haste, he swung her up into his arms and headed toward the back stairs. "We're going home," he said as he took the stairs two at a time. "Jinx and Zachery will understand."

"But . . ." She could think of no reason to stop him, or of another place she wanted to be. "But why the quilt?"

"In case we don't make it all the way home." He winked.

Hannah laughed as she glanced over Ford's shoulder to see Gavrila staring openmouthed at them crossing the yard to the barn.

"Wild!" Gavrila shouted. "Both of you are wild as this blasted Texas wind."

Hannah snuggled closer against Ford's chest and felt the rumble of his laughter.

"Want'a dance with the wind?" He kissed her neck.

"Forever," she answered. "Forever."